Legacy of Dragons: Resurgence

T.D. Raufson

Printed in the United States of America
First Printing, 2015
ISBN 0988863588
ISBN-13: 978-0-9888635-8-3

Twin Cedars Enterprises
twincedarsenterprises@gmail.com
www.twincedarsenterprises.com

To Ann

Contents

i

CHAPTER 1 - RESURGENCE

September 6, 2012 – 0730 EDT - Washington D.C.

The surreptitious troop carrier labored down Pennsylvania Avenue toward the White House in the brightening dawn. Its assault went unanswered by any of the security posts lining the roadway because it was exactly what the guards expected to see, a beat-up old school bus loaded with children.

The grim, focused faces of the troops, thirty teenage boys clustered into squads, looked ever forward to the point where the doors would open and disgorge them onto the field of battle. In sets of two, they sat staring forward at the target, alone with the thoughts all warriors carried over the wall and into the breach.

Any outside observer would see well-disciplined children on a field trip to the nation's capital, not an invasion force set on insurrection. If they gave it any further thought or were very observant, they might become concerned. They might even puzzle about teenage boys and how they are never that well behaved; but, by that time, the carrier would be past them and one step closer to its target.

Adrian sat, grim faced, among the four other members of his squad. Soldiers like him who had trained over the past weeks to confront whatever resistance they met within the halls of the White House with decisive violence. They were more than his friends now. They were brothers, and he worried about what was really going to happen when they reached their target.

1

A few weeks before, standing on the misty grass of St. George's Orphanage and School, wondering if his cousin had lost her mind, Adrian could not have imagined being their squad leader.

They had all shared similar stories of the emergence with him. Each had their own tales about struggling against the madness, the hunger and confusion that had immediately driven Adrian's father to attempt suicide. They each had found a way to overcome, escape, and finally find their way to the school. Most of his squad had overcome far more difficult struggles than he had, and yet they had no problem following him. Adrian didn't feel like a leader. He wasn't the same kid who had watched his father try to kill himself, training had taken care of that, but he questioned if he had really earned the two chevrons sewn onto his uniform hanging in his locker at Saint George's. That symbol and the duty associated with it weighed heavily on him as they rode toward their destiny.

Still, beneath the surface, Adrian struggled with which parent would ultimately win. Would he surrender to his father's catatonic mental prison at the critical moment, or would he freak, like his mother, when the time came and run from the conflict? Either choice would mean abandoning his troops in combat. He inhaled a deep breath and looked out the front window to let the struggle between his parents calm down.

His hand found the small, leather bag in his pocket that held the trinkets he had collected over the weeks at St. George's. He counted each item off in his mind; the discarded grenade pin that almost killed Juan; the earring that had cost them all extra push-ups. He paused on the pentacle pendant and released the small bag to settle into his pocket. The relaxing surge of satisfaction at still having it calmed his fears a little, and his thoughts shifted to the day he had earned his new chevrons and the pendant. That day was their last break before loading these buses, and the day he had finally met Mikhala.

Mikhala, fallen1-87, had followed him to Virginia after he had posted the link to the PLA site on her forum. Through his cousin, she had found him, but had not been able to talk to him until training had paused that one day. He would not soon forget that meeting.

"You're thinking about her, aren't you?" the boy sitting next to him asked in a conspiratorial whisper.

"No."

"Liar."

Adrian shook his head and looked at Chip. His real name was Chan Lu, and he was Adrian's closest friend.

"You know me too well," Adrian admitted.

"You've been surrounded by a cloud since we boarded this bucket. Now, as we get closer, you're smiling. Yeah, you're hard to read. Spill it."

"I don't know where she is."

"Yeah, and she doesn't know where you are, either."

"I may never see her again."

"Nope, and we all know that. She knows that. There's no reason you should be struggling with this. We all said our goodbyes last week."

Adrian nodded and looked at his boots.

"But, you didn't say goodbye—Okay, there's more to this story, then. What did I miss?"

"Our goodbye was—more of a—hello, and I can't stop thinking about her."

Chip grinned in the low light and shook his head.

"You should know better than to start a relationship before a mission like this."

"How exactly am I supposed to know better? Did you go to a class that I missed? Where was it held? What was it, Relationships and the Partial Soldier? Like the old VD movies?"

Chip elbowed him in his upper arm, and they both shifted in opposite directions. Their playful movement stood out against the focused background of soldiers who stoically reviewed the mission ahead of them. The sudden disturbance caught the attention of the first sergeant. Adrian felt his gut tighten.

The first sergeant stared at them, and the air around Adrian seemed to chill. He could see him chewing on the problem. Adrian straightened up in the seat and they both looked back out the front window. The first sergeant stopped ruminating before he leaned forward to share his conclusion with their lieutenant, who was driving the bus.

"Busted," Walt whispered from the seat behind them.

Garrett giggled quietly beside his brother.

"Nothing I can do about it now," Adrian whispered.

"Nope, that's for sure," Chip agreed.

Adrian forced his thoughts back to the mission and tried to forget about Mikhala and the silliness that had most certainly drawn the wrath of their first sergeant. Any concentration was difficult as he watched First Sergeant Rodriguez contemplate his future with the lieutenant.

After a few more moments of whispered discussion, Rodriguez stood up at the front of the bus. Adrian shrank into his seat and thought about the one chevron he would be sewing back onto his uniform when they returned to base—if they returned to base.

"Listen up!"

No one had been talking.

"We're getting closer to our insertion point. In a few minutes we'll be executing one of the most critical missions in today's operation. Looking back here just now, I noted a problem." He paused and let his meaning settle onto each soldier. As hard as it seemed for those soldiers to be grimmer, they suddenly became even more subdued.

Adrian didn't look around. He knew who had screwed up. He knew exactly what the sergeant had seen.

"Relax." The word struck them all like a foreign command, and they paused waiting for the command of execution.

"This is supposed to be a bus full of teenage boys, not an assault force delivering an ultimatum and judgment to the leader of the free world. I need for you to be boys again for a little while. You've not acted your age for a long time. I know this will be difficult for you, but I need for you to try. Our lives could depend on it. Corporal Fieldman here—in his undisciplined fit—showed me what was missing. If it hadn't been for the corporal, I never would have realized what was bothering me."

Adrian realized slowly that the first sergeant was not chastising him. He was complimenting him. He wanted them to stop being soldiers. Adrian stared at Rodriguez for clarification, unsure what he really meant.

"I'm proud of you as partials and soldiers. You proved your abilities or you wouldn't be here. No doubt, we'll accomplish our objective—unless we get caught before we get through the doors."

He waved his hand to emphasize the point that they should not worry about the mission.

"After today, the world will never forget the Partial Liberation Army. This is the end of hiding and being hunted; but, for just a little while, I need all of you to relax."

His piercing black eyes paused on Adrian.

"You boys are scary. Nothing like a bus full of school boys should look. This is exactly what I want to see when we're facing the enemy, but we don't want to draw attention to ourselves at the wrong time, and stepping off this bus like an invading army will draw attention. I know what's ahead of us is exciting, maybe a little terrifying, and you want to do your best; but, getting caught as we walk in would ruin the plan. For the next little while, I need you to act like boys on a field trip."

"So you want us to be rowdy. Cluster with our friends. Be completely non-military?" Jay, the fifth member of Adrian's squad stood and asked from his seat behind and to the right of the rest of the team.

Adrian's head snapped to look at his most difficult and most intelligent squad member. If he wasn't busy hacking something with his phone, he was making an inappropriate comment to a female soldier or the first sergeant. He could have been squad leader, but he had struggled to get to private first class. Adrian was about to reprimand him.

"Exactly," the first sergeant said. "Don't worry about the details. Buddy up with friends. Break squads if you have to. When the action comes down, you'll do what you've been trained to do. You'll be in the right place."

For a moment longer, everyone looked at Rodriguez expecting, this was a test. The squad leaders didn't know how to react. Adrian could see confusion on their faces. He let his mind crunch through what the first sergeant was saying again, and he finally started to understand.

He had to think back to days beyond the push-ups, calisthenics, drill, mud, and blood. He had to go back to the boy he had been before the emergence. He reached up to loosen his tie just as Rodriguez was making it an order.

"Move, gentlemen!"

The bus erupted.

While other squads were breaking up to find friends, Adrian and Chip held their seats, as did Jay. Adrian looked back over his shoulder at the last two members of his squad.

"Don't look at me. I'm not going anywhere," Garrett said as he high fived Walt, who was already sitting next to him.

"Yeah, and don't ruin it by saying something profound, Adrian. That would be completely against orders," Walt said as he was pulling the tail of his shirt out.

"Way to go, suck up," Jay said from his now private seat which he enjoyed by stretching out across it.

Garrett yanked at the knot of his tie and left it askew around his neck while he laughed at Adrian's discomfort.

"That's right. You may get another commendation for that, Fieldman, and just remember, you owe it all to me," Chip added.

Adrian laughed and ignored their fake jealousy.

"Hey, want to see something wicked cool?" Jay asked as he thumbed through something on his phone. He had turned his back to the window with his legs in the seat.

"No," they all answered in unison and laughed. It was not always safe to share what Jay found on his phone. Single combat with the first sergeant was safer.

"Your loss," Jay said as he shrugged and turned toward the seat behind him.

"What have you done, Jay? Hacked some local surveillance system so you can watch someone brush their teeth?"

Jay simply grinned mischievously and leaned over the back of his seat. The two young privates in the seat behind him stared at the screen without speaking as Jay accelerated some rite of passage.

Adrian gave him a severe look. Jay shrugged and nodded toward Rodriguez. "What, boss man? They're about to go into combat. They could die in a few minutes. They should at least know what they've missed."

Adrian shook his head and looked forward again as Rodriguez was walking toward the back of the bus.

"That's right, relax the dress code some, too. You're high school aged," Rodriguez coached as he monitored the chaos he had unleashed. He looked at the two young boys transfixed on Jay's phone and laughed. "As always, Howard, you push my orders right to the edge."

Jay shrugged again and swiped his phone to find something else for the two boys, who were now his best friends.

Adrian felt some of the stress slip from his shoulders. He slumped a little in his seat and made eye contact with the bus driver, who was watching him and his squad.

Their lieutenant, a full dragon named Galiarat, nodded with approval. When their eyes met, Adrian thought he could see relief. He was turning the bus into a parking area and approaching a line of buses that were disgorging children into scatter diagrams that were supposed to be lines. Lack of order was the rule on the field ahead of them, and Adrian suddenly understood how close they had come to failing the mission because of not looking the part. He nodded his understanding as he filed that lesson away for the future.

"So, what do you think?" Walt's voice broke into Adrian's thoughts as he realized he was not listening to their conversation.

"I don't think he's interested in whether you look up your ex-girlfriend when this is all over," Garrett said, laughing.

Adrian grinned at how his squad kept him involved but understood why he was outside of their jocularity. He allowed the conversation to remind him of the kiss he had shared with Mikhala as he had stroked her satin black hair a week before. They had tried to say goodbye, but they had promised they would find each other on the other side of what was to come.

"I'll be keeping my eye on you, Corporal," she had said as they had been forced to return to their rooms.

The bus came to a stop, and the lieutenant turned to look back at them all. Adrian sat up in his seat, pressing his feet into the metal floor and instinctively rolling onto his toes. The mission rushed back to the front of his mind, saving him from further thoughts of Mikhala.

The conversation continued around them like an afterthought. His squad was preparing to move. Gear was being collected. Jay had shut off the phone and was sitting on the edge of his seat even as he laughed with Garrett at an inappropriate joke about Walt's high-school sweetheart.

The first sergeant's head was suddenly next to Adrian's. He whispered, "A good leader worries about details, Corporal, like when it's time to turn on the heat. Your squad is strong. They know their job. You'll know when it's time. Trust yourself. Trust your squad. I do. Keep your eyes open. Stay loose while we walk in. Get them up front somewhere. The rest will take care of itself. Never doubt your mission."

The first sergeant's strong hand on his shoulder as he walked past reassured Adrian as much as the words. Adrian stood to lead his squad playfully off the bus.

As each group stood up behind them he could feel the pressure to exit grow. They were taking the order to relax seriously. A couple of boys behind them started pushing. Someone else was snapping people ahead of him with his tie as if he was driving cattle. As the excitement built Adrian watched for the lieutenant to drop the ramp and let them off the landing craft. When the hand moved and the doors opened, Adrian shifted his weight forward and led his men out into the cool morning air.

He felt his feet touch the ground, and more tension drained. They were here. The mission was moving. All of his worries vanished as he focused on what was next. Their disorganized approach was part of the mission now, so he embraced it and laughed with another of Garrett's jokes.

There was a fog holding on, and there was a threat of rain. Adrian couldn't help but hope, as he led his troops toward their target, that it did rain. Perhaps when it did, after they had made their stand, it would wash away the human's stranglehold on this world. He would do his best to achieve that mission. For the dragon that had saved him from the horrible life he had lived since the night he had emerged and for other partials like him, he would fight today. Soon, partials would complete what should have happened as soon as they emerged.

September 6 - About the same time – Around Andrews Air Force Base, Joint Base Andrews, MD.

The platoon of partials stalked forward through the low brush and trees as they reached the edge of their cover. They were all fully armored for combat, only with subdued colors. It had taken several days of training to teach the troops to control their pigments so that they could better blend into their surroundings. The yellow and blues of some of the Asian blends were still a challenge. It was good that most of them tended to be in logistical or support units.

Lights from the active runways and nearby hangars of one of the largest military bases in the country punched through the foliage that was just beginning to show signs of changing colors. Second Lieutenant Lewis Carvell signaled the rest of his troops to stop with a simple hand signal and dropped to a knee to scan his surroundings.

Smelling the air and scanning the no-man's-land beyond their tree cover with his enhanced vision, the platoon leader looked for any sign that their approach to their assault position had been observed. He could not sense cameras or passive sensors, but he knew they were out here, and thanks to a partial former employee he knew where. Not far behind where they were waiting there was an active gate monitoring everyone who entered the base. Satisfied that they were still concealed, he focused on the next obstacle. The fence blocking their approach was visible in the low morning light. When the signal came, they had to clear the fence and cross the open field to the area between the two runways where their target was quietly spinning.

With another hand signal, the platoon dispersed into the cover. Squad leaders took control of their men and silently moved them into supporting lines. Without a sound, each squad vanished as their leader shifted them from visible to invisible with a thought. When they moved again, they would phase back in to avoid friendly fire. The secret of magical camouflage, invisibility, had been discovered during combined exercises about a week before. They had also discovered, at some cost, that a squad could work as a team while invisible, but a platoon could not. There were too many tell-tales that would draw unintentional fire during the excitement, but in small squad maneuvers it was invaluable.

The 11th Wing of the Air Force District of Washington along with the 113th Wing of the D.C. Air National Guard were only a part of the threat from this base. Along with their rotary wing emergency response, they could easily fill the air with fixed wing fighters from both Air Force and Navy units operating on the field.

It had been two months since Nethliast, the king of the dragons and their leader in this resistance to human supremacy, had taken to the air to demonstrate the superiority of dragons to the German Air Force and the world. Since then, all military bases were on some level of alert. That meant ready air support like this had to be cut off if the dragons had any hope of securing their targets. This base was crucial to their plans for other reasons. The air defenses stored on this base were needed to keep this and other airspace safe for dragons. No one intended to wait out a siege of Washington, D.C., by the massive military units surrounding the capital. This strike would lead to submission to the new leadership. While the governments were becoming accustomed to that fact, dragons had to be safe to fly.

Carvell was glad he didn't have to worry about the anti-aircraft systems. His target was to take out the local radar. Once he had accomplished that mission, he was to fall back and wait for further instructions.

He needed current intelligence on the airbase beyond the wire. What was waiting for them in that no-man's-land?

He focused a little on his form. Small leathery wings grew out of his scale-covered back. He looked up at the trees and lunged, flapping a little to help his powerful legs propel him to his target. Catching the trunk of the tree with his left hand and wrapping his arm around it, he dug the claws on his feet into the soft wood. Focusing his vision on key points around the airbase, he zoomed in and out checking movement and expected aircraft positions.

Military airbases were never static. Planes were always landing or departing, and logistical movement never stopped. Soldiers, both on and off duty, were always moving around. A C-17 was loading next to a hangar halfway down the runway. A flight of marine reserve helicopters was refueling on the ramp. A deviation from what he expected appeared in the form of two A-10s idling in the alert run-up position on the base. The pilots were in the cockpit waiting for the call on the opposite side of the parallel runways.

The A-10 was an interesting choice for an alert fighter. It was a ground strike fighter, not an air support and superiority fighter, so it didn't normally make sense in the alert role. But to Carvell it made perfect sense. It was a conscious decision. Whoever had made it understood their enemy.

Dragons were heavily armored slow-moving beasts. It was why Nethliast had been able to take out the two fighters over Germany. They were at a disadvantage at the speeds required to keep pace with him.

The A-10 could linger over the base at slow airspeeds. It was armored and slow like dragons, but it was also very maneuverable. It could turn better than any of the faster planes and dogfight the dragons. But what worried Carvell the most was the devastating 30mm gun on its nose. It was a dragon killer. A good pilot could hang out over the airfield challenging dragons who came to help the ground troops and then turn in on his platoon and wipe them out with the gun. Their assault could be over in seconds if that plane made it into the air. He logged the threat and shared it with his Guardian Angel, the name that had stuck for their scrying battlefield observers. She took the message and assured him she had shared it up for analysis.

Carvell scanned the tower. Like the anti-aircraft, it was not his target, but it worried him. If the team assigned to take it out failed, the men within could easily direct support, including the A-10, to any location on the base. He and his platoon had a long run, in the open, to the radar installation at the center of the field.

He knew the commander of the platoon assigned to the VORTAC just beyond his target and was confident he could get the mission done, but he had never met the platoon leader assigned to assault the tower. There was nothing he could do about it now, however. Pushing other males' missions out of his head, he focused on the spinning antenna of the radar that formed the long-range eyes of this airbase. That was his target. As soon as they hit it, the systems in the tower would fail over to other systems from the national coverage net, but ILS, takeoff, and landing at this airbase would be out. If everyone else did their jobs, this base would be ineffective for a little while. Then all they had to do was escape back into the world they were part of as thousands of defenders crawled out of the houses and barracks all around them. He looked up at the cloudy sky that shrouded them and relaxed a little. The cover would help, some. Rain would be a welcome, helpful ally.

He dropped from the tree, fluttering his small wings to reduce his impact. When he touched down he signaled the unseen squads to move up and began the slow, quiet crawl to the fence. In a few more minutes, Rodriguez and his storm-troopers would give the signal that they were in place and Carvell's team would light up this gray, September morning with a scene no human in this lifetime had ever seen.

Carvell reached out to his Guardian Angel again. The comforting mind that awaited his update responded immediately, and he reported his platoon was in place. With his update he sent a complete report of the field, including visuals. The calm response reassured him all was proceeding as planned.

September 6 – 0745 EDT – Falls Church, Virginia

"All units at Andrews are in position and holding for the go order. They still need a threat analysis from the change in alert aircraft," Mikhala reported over her shoulder to the priestess who stood in the apex of the communications and logistics center for this coordinated mission. Other similar reports were coming in from all around the world as similar units moved into place.

The reports went unanswered, but Mikhala knew they were not ignored. The priestess knew what was going on around her while she maintained a higher view of each operation at her center console. Set into the Mission Control style pedestal in front of the priestess was a collection of large crystal spheres she used as a focus to remain connected to the critical parts of the mission and the command structure above her. Fluid made an easier medium to scry through, but crystal was a reasonable second choice because of its stability. Ariela could switch to any of the views her subordinate observers were managing in their own crystals with a call to hand off, and that was where they all had focused much of their training.

Mikhala and the twenty partials around her on the top tier kept the priestess aware of the situation in the field in case she needed to observe and report a change. They were all expected to be as capable as the priestess and able to take over whenever she was out of the center or as a task force observer if a campaign needed to expand.

Each station on either side of Mikhala was monitoring a key strike force deployed around the world. Mikhala was assigned Andrews because of its critical importance and her demonstrated skill. Skill that she maintained by monitoring another continuous view of a different mission area in her mother's never far off antique compact. Something about the old mirror made it as good as any crystal. It enabled her to juggle views at will and gave her an advantage when handing off information immediately.

Mikhala scanned the entire theater around Andrews, checking each unit to make sure she was still in contact while they waited for the execute command. Keeping the connection with a rapidly moving and emotionally charged force was difficult. The emotion made it easy to keep track of them, but it also overwhelmed the messages coming in. They had only experienced it in training, so this live execution was challenging at a much higher level.

"Ready?" Kara, the controller next to her, asked.

"Stand by."

Kara nodded and checked a few things on her own view while Mikhala adjusted.

"Ready."

With little or no waver in the image in her sphere, her focus shifted to a mountain top installation with a large white sphere sitting on top of a square, metal tower. She quickly identified the primary forward observer for the task force. He was a nervous lieutenant. They were all fresh from boot camp technically, so she could excuse some nervousness, but he was unfocused. She could nearly taste the sweat on him. Calming him down, while she could, might save the mission, but she doubted it would stick when she transitioned back. Part of his problem was his observer. Kara had done nothing to relax the team on the mountain side. She would have to talk to her about that in their after action review.

Just in case, Mikhala scanned the grounds around the dome for others who could act as backup forward observers and found a few options.

"No wonder you wanted to switch for a few minutes. This guy shouldn't even be out there. Can't you calm him down?"

"What? No—I had that under control. I just wanted to practice on a larger theater. This is hard to handle. Too much going on."

"It's a big mission. Andrews is no joke. It has to go well."

"Well, you can have it back."

"No arguments here. See if you can't calm him down. If not, I've tagged some options for backup. You'll need them."

"There's no calming him down. I think it's genetic. Thanks, the backups might help. Ready when you are."

Mikhala made sure her view was strong and then answered, "Go."

The comforting feel of her groomed observers settled back into her mind as the image of Andrews filled her crystal again. She had shifted the mountain top radar facility to her mirror to make sure it wasn't lost by the less trained observer.

"Salenko," a voice from around the pedestal called. "Advise all Andrews teams of the alert fighter change. Direct Foxtrot Company of their new objective. They need to stop those fighters early or we risk losing the ground force. Tell them we're adjusting air cover, but it will not get there in time."

Mikhala shared the change of orders with the Foxtrot commander individually, then advised the other leaders of the change. With the intelligence disseminated, she relaxed her presence to keep from spooking them and just watched the area for any indication of trouble. She sighed into the wait, glad that they had spent so much time rehearsing this back at Saint George's.

"You really want Pam's station for a few minutes, don't you?" Kara joked as they waited.

"Part of me would like it for about a minute, but I'm not sure I would be able to passively watch. I would probably just have to switch right back."

"Why? Don't you think he can handle himself?"

"I know he can handle himself." She scowled over her shoulder making sure to shield her emotions from the field observers, "But, he's in the White House. His company is delivering the ultimatum to the president. Too much stress for me to watch."

"No one better if you ask me," Kara said.

Mikhala felt a little surge of jealousy, but she let her pride in Adrian replace any concern she had over her neighbor's attention to him. Jealousy was impractical.

"I'm not supposed to even know where he's at. Pam should not have shared that information with me or anyone else," Mikhala said as she scanned her field again.

"Pay attention to your section leader, everyone." The booming voice of command fell around them all. "She's just made a critical statement about OPSEC, and you should all listen. Now, let's keep it quiet as we approach execute." Everyone focused back on their own observers. Their commander, Captain Appleton, walked behind each of them to reinforce their focus.

Her ability to monitor more than one location at a time allowed her some flexibility in where she was focused. Even though she knew it was inappropriate, she reached out for just a moment to look in on Adrian in her mirror.

She watched as his team entered the White House and followed the guidance to the briefing room. She hesitated a few seconds on his location and just watched him. She could feel the coiled readiness. They knew it would not be much longer. She took a moment to send him a bit of her confidence. He would never really know it was out there or where it came from, but it might help. Without a hiccup in her connection to the observers at Andrews, she released Adrian to what was to come and checked her primaries and backups again.

She scanned all of the positions and verified everything was still in place. Satisfied everything was set, she allowed herself a few moments of private thought about Adrian. She reminded herself of their commitment, made over an MRE cracker spread with peanut butter in the grass outside Saint George's. On the other side of all of this they would be together. The world would be different, but their commitment to one another would stand.

September 6 – 0750 EDT - The White House, Washington D.C.

Adrian and his fire team were through the security checkpoints and inside the room where the president would unveil her election year plan for education. There was a big stir about getting this last minute change in before the election and how it would affect voters. She was introducing a new Secretary of Education who would implement her plan with only months left to get it done. Little did the humans know that all of this would be meaningless in a few minutes.

Adrian didn't care. The president had taken no action to save any of the partials or even to stop the hunting since they had emerged. She was not demanding that the hunt squads stop. She was not declaring partials equals and giving them fair representation. As his father would have said, none of this political manipulation really mattered. What mattered was what the president did when things were bad.

Before the end of this press conference, she would become a part of the PLA's solution. She would get one chance to prove where she stood. As much as he hated the politics of this publicity ploy, he realized it was what had allowed them to reach her.

He deftly negotiated his way toward the front of the room where the organizers had lined off an area for a select group of students. They wanted the presentation to feel like a cozy meeting with the president who was uniquely positioned to help the children.

Several of the boys in his group had the attention of the Secret Service. Not because they were terrorists planning to force the hand of the President of The United States, but because they were still playing around as they headed for the barrier. Thousands of young men and women were descending on Washington to observe their government at work. Teachers were salivating at the wonderful opportunity this was to teach, but to the Secret Service, this was one of the most difficult types of events to secure. In this case, they had to protect the president without looking like jackbooted thugs while doing it.

The room they had selected for the press conference was one of the large open rooms used for public relations in the White House. The walls were covered with miscellaneous paintings that Adrian didn't recognize or care about. Rows of seats were spread out across the room like an indoor amphitheater. A small dais occupied the front tenth of the room with its own door in the back of the small stage. Adrian could not suppress a feeling of relaxed familiarity, since they had trained in a room exactly like it as they prepared for this mission. Whoever had planned this mission had been in this room. They had stood where Adrian stood. In a moment of amazement, he could not believe how insecure this was. How could they expose the president to such a threat. Then he remembered that school children, until today, were not considered a terrorist threat.

Never stopping as the students flooded into the room, Adrian guided his team to the front of the line. Chip and Jay were beside him. A young intern greeted them by adjusting the too short hem of her skirt down over slightly thick thighs and trying to stretch unyielding material in her blouse over her suddenly overexposed ample chest. The grin on Jay's face told the complete story. In an uncomfortable few seconds, he had succeeded in distracting her from her real job, and all it had taken was a bad outfit choice.

A silent statue of an ebony skinned, black suited man observed over her shoulder as she greeted them.

"I need to see your seating passes for this section," she mumbled while blushing uncomfortably at Jay, who refused to look anywhere above or below her chest.

Adrian showed his pass. Each member of his team held up a plastic card that indicated they were part of the honor student section.

She nodded and adjusted another part of her wardrobe in hope that it would reinforce parts that were failing her. The statue didn't move, but he watched as they walked past the last barrier that would keep them away from the President.

Once through the rope, Adrian moved to the front row. His target was five seats on the left side of the small dais. Their focused efforts and blocking by other teams behind them had guaranteed their access. Now they had to take advantage of that and reach what their training had identified as the sweet spot for this exercise.

Several dislocated reporters who were accustomed to holding the front seats were glaring at them as they sat down. Adrian relaxed a little as other students from other schools started filling in open seats. Without being too obvious, he scanned the crowd and noted that several other teams were also holding their goal.

The crowd was starting to settle into the room, and Adrian ticked off the milestones in their battle plan.

Other students and teachers were beginning to line the walls as the seats became scarce. All of the reserved seats were full. Volunteers were filling in seats with individuals. Some of those, unidentified to the volunteers and the crowd, would be security plants.

With her job done, the young staff member who had seated them closed off the rope barrier and moved to a place at the front of the stage with her shadow. Adrian focused his draconic hearing so he could make out what she was whispering to the guard.

"It's amazing how popular this has turned out. Don't you think it's great? I mean, I've not seen this many high school kids here, ever. It just…"

She was talking to calm her nerves until she saw Jay staring at her again. She fidgeted with her clothes.

The disinterested bulk next to her grunted and listened to his earwig telling him there was a disturbance between two boys in the hall. Adrian knew, according to the plan, that the disturbance would not be one of Saint George's students.

"I don't think they'll all fit, though," she continued. "Look at them all." The nervous girl laughed. "You guys sure are agitated over the mix-up." She rolled her eyes, and the shadow frowned a very small frown. "I don't know who overscheduled the schools, but they're all coming. Who would have ever guessed they would care about the Secretary of Education? It's not like she'll serve long if the president doesn't win. We're setting up overflow in another room. Latecomers will just have to watch on monitors. I wish you guys would relax a bit. They're just kids." The girl seemed to have no way of controlling the flow of speech.

The secret service agent opened his mouth to say something and changed his mind as if he decided his comment would not matter.

"I can't believe someone allowed that orphanage to bring all of their senior boys. But, most of them are well behaved. Most of them." She looked at Adrian. Her eyes asked him to help her with Jay. Adrian repaid her confidence by staring a little too long at her chest and thighs and grinning. Her face exploded with color as she blushed and turned away. She tried again to pull too little fabric over too much skin. She finally surrendered and retreated out of the room with an exasperated sigh.

"Just kids, right?" The agent parroted with a smile as she brushed past him.

Adrian elbowed Chip. *They don't have a clue, but the Secret Service guys are on their toes. Be ready.*

Chip nodded. No matter what his face showed, Adrian knew the message had been passed to the others of his team. They had all momentarily scanned the men in the black suits that were obviously Secret Service. Adrian continued to tick off the checklist.

Fire Team One, in position, he reported to Rodriguez.

A clipped acknowledgment came back to him. The romantic in him was disappointed there was no static in the message or no squelch break at the beginning and end.

Next step, identify the quiet men so others behind them could mark them.

Adrian nodded, and Jay pulled out his phone. With an over-loud click, he expanded the keyboard and started typing with both thumbs. A short man behind them in the press area suddenly became interested in them. A black suit separated from the wall to approach Jay.

"Son, you're going to have to give that to me."

"I'm sorry." Jay looked up from the device at the agent. "Why?"

"You were told when you came in here that no cell phone use was allowed. You'll have to hand it over."

"You can't confiscate my personal property like that. I've done nothing wrong."

Jay was pushing it a bit, but it was getting results. Several men and a few women in seats behind them were watching the petulant boy arguing with the Secret Service agent too closely even though their conversation could not be heard two seats away.

Notices back and forth between the fire teams behind him told Adrian the task was successful.

"Good enough. Now give in," he sent to Jay.

"Son, you're either going to have to hand it over or turn it off."

"Oh, you didn't say that I had a choice." In a most convincing reversal, Jay dramatically pushed the button to power off the phone and put it back in his pocket.

The black suit nodded and returned to his place at the wall mumbling about having resolved the situation, and how he hated kindergarten days. Adrian almost laughed but caught himself. Movement at the stage indicated they were getting ready to start. The crowd settled more as teachers who were paying attention took charge of their students. A very attractive and confident woman took the stage, and everyone became silent.

"Good morning," the woman said in her tour guide voice, "Thank you all for coming. Before we get this started, I wanted to come out here and talk to all of the students who have come so far to visit us, and thank the press corps for understanding the unusual seating arrangements." She smiled an apologetic smile to the people sitting in the rows behind Adrian and then continued. "So, students, I'm sure most of you have never been at a function like this..."

Adrian let her voice trail off in his mind as he continued his checklist. The crowd relaxed into apathy, which was why they had selected the young woman to soften them up. He looked around the crowd as if he was looking for one of his friends and secured the position of each team in his mind. He could feel the time for action approaching as the items fell off of his checklist.

When his gaze returned to the stage he felt a sudden pang of pity for the ten or so black suited agents and the equal number of shills in the crowd who probably wouldn't walk out of the room in a few minutes. But his pity was short-lived as he reminded himself that they would kill him without remorse if they knew what he was. He was not human anymore, and they would never feel pity for him. That was the whole reason he was there.

September 6 – 0805 EDT - Andrews Air Force Base, Joint Base Andrews, MD.

"Go, alpha wing."

The voice started a countdown in Carvell's mind. The same message had triggered dragons and partials all over Washington, Maryland, and Virginia to start the infrastructure attacks. The same command had been given all over the world.

His countdown had almost run down when the silent wings crossed the fences ahead of him. Acid rained down on the barrier that was only a dragon's length away. The metal smoked and buckled under the assault. With a hand motion, his squads were up and through the breaches before the dragons had crossed the field and well before any human eyes could figure out what they had just seen. The first noise of their assault was the nearly simultaneous down-strokes of the dragons as they pushed for altitude.

The discordant silence of their attack struck Carvell as he watched streams of fire fall from the sky to consume equipment and men. The sound of their approach in leapfrogging jumps was eerily quiet and unopposed. Several flights of dragons crisscrossed over the field, raining fire onto the parked airplanes and soldiers in a soundless assault.

Finally, an alarm klaxon shattered the harsh silence. The clamor of war rushed back at them as soldiers fired at the retreating dragons in ragged resistance, but none of their return fire was directed at his platoon. They were covering the ground in thirty foot leaps, landing, watching for movement, and jumping again, always keeping the target in front of them.

They crossed the first runway in a leap and landed in the grass without any resistance. Carvell risked a glance at the alert fighters. They were not in the air yet, but they also were not neutralized. Where was Foxtrot? He started to call for an update but didn't. He had to finish his own mission.

Fuel tanks were starting to cook off and explode all over the airstrip. Gunfire was cracking into the morning air, but still none of it threatened his platoon.

"All squads, converge," he signaled.

The outer arms of his approaching wall swung around to engulf the target. As the ends met, the support teams dropped into pairs behind the assault teams that proceeded to the target.

One soldier in each pair extended his hands and projected an invisible shield out in front of him. The second soldier watched for assaulting troops and held a powerful blast of magic for anyone who approached too closely.

Carvell concentrated on the magic they had been trained to use in the last couple of months. He focused on drawing the power to him from all

18

around. As the tingle and burn of the energy filled him, he aimed it at the block wall of the building supporting the spinning radar dish. At the distance he had practiced hundreds of times, he released the energy he now felt boiling beneath the surface.

The blast of mana rushed from his hands and manifested as the conjured magical force he wanted. It ripped into the block wall and detonated inside, spewing chunks of concrete and metal out into the morning sky. He felt a trembling in the ground. As planned, another member of his platoon had thrust his hand into the earth to disrupt the soil around the building. Another explosion ripped the building into small chunks and threw debris further out around him. The ground beneath the building turned to mud and what had not been destroyed in the blast sank into the ground. The dish, still spinning from inertia and connected to its now unstable supports, dipped as its foundation fell into the hole. The orange-red structure dug into the ground, throwing dirt and clods of turf at its attackers in a feeble attempt at defense.

Carvell looked around. The flanking squads still had their hands out shielding their partner from attack. Several soldiers scanned for targets for direct fire but found none. Gunfire was still nowhere near them.

The tower was in flames. A blast of lightning energy ripped through the metal and concrete at the center of it. Another orange blast of concentrated magical fire followed it, and the interior staircase erupted in a flash of orange and blue. The tower separated in the middle and crumbled in on itself. He knew the fight there would continue as the foot soldiers of the PLA found their way in and executed the men trapped below in their control rooms. The gunfire was concentrated in that area.

With his primary mission accomplished, Carvell reported in and asked for permission to move to their secondary target and secure the aircraft.

"*Stand by,*" his guardian angel called back.

The mind he touched was calm even though the world had erupted in violence.

"*Foxtrot has been delayed. One of the alert fighters is still operational. You're the closest to the target. Stop it, and then move to your secondary.*"

Carvell raised a hand to get his platoon's attention, but knew he would have to give verbal directions for this.

"*First and Second squad on me. We're stopping the warthog. Everyone else rally with Sergeant Callaway at the secondary objective. Secure the perimeter like we practiced.*"

With no more words his platoon split and charged off toward the A-10. The plane was designed to take off in under two-thousand feet on an unimproved runway, and it looked like that was the pilot's plan.

"*Take him out if you can hit him. Put some pressure on him. Don't give him a straight run.*"

Red and blue bolts blasted away from the charging partials as they landed from their last jump and released energy they had held during the assault. Carvell was proud of the control they were showing. Several of the initial rounds were close. They passed just in front of or just behind the aircraft and exploded into buildings beyond it. There was no way he could get one of his squad members in front of the aircraft to destroy its runway in time.

"We're too far out for that. First squad, close on him. Second squad, lay down cover and keep him from accelerating to takeoff speed. Thompson, can you create a trench long enough from here?"

A soldier to his left dropped to one knee and thrust a hand out to touch the ground. A rounded, meter wide trench formed in the ground racing out from his hand at the aircraft. It was on target and far enough ahead that it would cross in front of the racing aircraft. The pilot was watching the trench race across his path. Carvell could sense him urging his plane to greater speed with no hope of beating it.

Ten meters from the target the trench deviated as it struck rock and passed far behind the aircraft. Thompson shook his head at the failure and fell over from the aggressive release of mana. A medic rushed to his aid as the others continued to pursue the accelerating aircraft.

Aware now that he was a target, he had survived, and that his runway was far shorter than before, the pilot committed to the takeoff. The scream of the turbines told Carvell they were not going to stop the plane on the ground.

"First squad, get down there and put some fire on him. He's going for it."

A blue bolt slammed into the left tail fin and exploded. As the debris showered down around the accelerating plane, the pilot adapted to the damage and the plane rotated and climbed slowly into the air. Out of habit the pilot dropped flares as he banked to the left to avoid the low trees. A fireball exploded in front of the right wing but still failed to stop the climbing plane.

In a few seconds the plane had pulled up and away from the ground troops where it could loiter and harass. Carvell thought about the situation and how dangerous the one plane they let get off the ground was.

"He's coming back around. Hold fire until he is lined up on his target. Get your shields ready. When he's most vulnerable, we'll take him out,"

He watched the pilot line up on the end of the runway. First squad was the target and there was nothing he could do to help them. He needed them to hold his attention.

"Simpson, with me."

Carvell leaped off toward the position first squad was holding. He wanted to be close but not with them. After four good jumps they were about a football field closer.

"Can you see him?" he asked.

The soldier beside him nodded while staring at a spot in the sky.

"Can you put one in that cockpit?"

"He's too erratic. I can't focus it fast enough."

"When he rolls in to fire you'll have around five seconds while he holds the target. I'm going to force him to dive while you focus. You need to take him out. You've got one shot, soldier, or we're next."

Simpson nodded and focused out in the morning sky. Carvell watched the plane for any sign that he was ready to fire. He was zoomed in on the nose of the aircraft. Simpson was right. He was rolling and yawing to keep the ground forces from getting any solid hits, even though the sky was full of exploding blue and red bolts of fire and lightning.

Suddenly the bouncing stopped. The nose dipped. The pilot was on target and engaging. The nose of the plane flashed. Without waiting Carvell released his own fireball at a place directly in front of the plane. If it hit, great. If not, it would force the pilot to react. In the same instant that the red bolt flashed away from him, he turned his attention to the soldiers down range.

"Now, Simpson."

The crackling sound of seventy rounds per second penetrating the ground and his own soldiers sickened him as sparks flashed and smoke exploded from the ground around first squad. Part of him wanted the crackling sound to stop, but the longer it went on, the longer Simpson had. As he switched his view back to the nose of the plane, he hoped first squad's shields held but doubted there was any way they had survived. Simpson's fireball was glowing in the cockpit in an expanding blast of released energy. It consumed the front of the plane and then set off secondaries as the ammo drum under the cockpit was compromised. By the time the grunting sound of the huge cannon reached the ground, first squad was likely dead and pieces of the A-10 were showering down on the D.C. suburbs.

"Any survivors of first squad, form up at the secondary objective. Second squad, fall back to the secondary objective."

Switching his focus to his Guardian Angel, he calmed his thoughts before he flooded her with what he was feeling and then sent his message. *"Aerial threat neutralized. Moving to secure secondary objective. Back door is open."*

"Roger, message delivered. By the way, first squad was wiped out. No survivors."

Carvell nodded and grunted his response as he jumped across the open land toward the only cluster of aircraft not burning on the airfield. He took some satisfaction in knowing that their sacrifice was worth something.

September 6 – 0815 EDT - The White House, Washington D.C.

Adrian's announcement that the president was on the stage had launched the first wave of the assault. As soon as their success was verified, he would be cleared to move. He had heard the "back door" report and knew it was enough to start, but they needed the warehouses and the ordnance. Once the trucks were rolling, the next phase could begin.

The president had been going on about her new education plan for five minutes, and she had only now started to explain how the new secretary was going to bring about a new era in education. Adrian didn't care. All that mattered was that she talked long enough. If she ended too soon, they would have to move even if the other teams were not clear. They could not afford to lose this opportunity. There was a message to deliver. They had to hold the room, and she had to be in it. As soon as the news of the attacks reached the Secret Service agents, the president would be whisked away to safety in the basement where no partial could ever reach her.

"All fire-teams, I have control. Stand by," a voice in his head told them all to get ready.

The big agent on the wall suddenly reached for his ear. His eyes expanded and the muscles along his neck twitched.

Movement in the crowd started to draw attention from the president. She glanced at her security detail but never missed a cue. Adrian casually tightened his muscles and prepared. He could feel the rest of his team tensing as the room started to fall apart. They were running out of time. Adrian shifted forward onto the balls of his feet and prepared to make the call when the voice filled his head again.

"Execute, Execute, Execute."

Adrian looked directly at the president and cast his spell. She stopped in mid-sentence with her hand pointing out at the crowd. The confused look on her face told him she had realized in that final moment that something was going on.

The four closest guards tumbled to the ground as bolts of magical energy drilled precise holes through their vests. The remaining six were staring at the president and holding their ears.

None of the partial assault teams had moved enough to give away their actions, and the six agents had no targets. They started to move to protect the president, and several more bolts flashed away from supporting fire teams in the audience. The not so silent coup was underway.

Behind Adrian, the quiet men that had been identified in the crowd stood and drew pistols searching for targets. Partials near them knocked their weapons away. Loud crunching snaps announced the end of the resistance.

Mere seconds had passed. The crowd was starting to react. The first scream filled the air as someone behind the press corps realized something bad was happening.

Adrian rolled out of his seat in a single smooth movement and sensed rather than saw his squad as they followed him in a rush for the stage. Chip followed on his left while Garret and Walt moved to the right. Jay came out of his seat and anchored the middle. Adrian vaulted the low dais and landed next to the podium. Each boy reached his assigned point and formed a tight circle around the frozen form of the president. With their backs to her body, they waited to see what the next response would be. Adrian doubted it would be anything like the devastating onslaught of partials that they had trained to defend against.

Adrian was facing the open doorway behind the stage as a line of Secret Service agents charged at him with their pistols drawn. At the same time, any of the people who remained on the stage were rushed down the hallway in a tidal wave of human fear.

The lead agent's face broke through the crowd, and Adrian registered a brief look of appreciation when he saw the teenage boys guarding the president. He nodded at Adrian and motioned for his own team to take their place.

"Move aside," he growled as he approached. "We have this."

Adrian transformed. Green and glistening blue scales covered his body beneath his school uniform. His face expanded into the dragon's head he had woke with that long ago night.

The agent registered the transformation but could not process what it meant before Adrian grabbed him and tossed him from the stage into the crowd. He catapulted into the middle of the press corps that was caught in indecision about whether to run or stay and collect the story. His body slammed into three chairs and the floor with a clatter and a meaty thunk. The agent didn't move, and Adrian's team subdued the other agents on the stage.

"Secure the president and hold this location."

Adrian kept his eyes down the hall, waiting for any more resistance.

A stream of partial dragons in pairs flooded past him and down the hall.

With their position secured, their dragon leader strode to the front of the room and stood in front of the podium. The president was still held where she stood, able to witness it all.

Galariat transformed. Red, yellow, and black scales flashed across his body, replacing the suburban teacher disguise with thick muscles and threatening black spikes. His partial form emphasized his Native American roots. Large, feathered wings expanded from his back to fill the room and sent reporters retreating from him. Several stumbled away in a panic, but a couple stood their ground and continued filming. Galariat placed his powerful arms on his hips and stared into the frozen eyes of the president.

"I have a message from the Partial Liberation Army. On behalf of my brothers and sisters, we demand equality in this government. You are to submit to our authority as we establish a government better suited to dragon and partial dragon kind. When we release you from the hold we have on you, your response will decide the fate of everyone in this building. Madame President, do you surrender or do we make an example of you and everyone here?"

Adrian, who had cast the spell to hold the president, released her so that she could respond. She took a moment to stabilize herself from the spell. The pause caused Adrian to turn around to look at her as she was straightening her white business suit.

She cleared her throat before beginning in a very authoritative voice. "I am the president of the United States. We have a policy that you may be aware of. We do not negotiate with terrorists."

The members of the crowd who understood the depth of her statement gasped.

Her answer, which Adrian actually expected, meant the government of the United States would be sacrificed as an example and replaced with a Governor once full control was finally surrendered. But, as some in the crowd understood, she had signed a death warrant for everyone in the White House. Adrian stepped away from the president.

She had to sense how serious they were. He could see her physically tense her shoulders in reaction to her impending death. She tried to look casual as she looked up as if something had drawn her attention away from Galariat. He was impressed at how she kept herself together in the face of death.

The sounds of sobs from the audience filled the silence as Galariat drew power from the earth and air around him. He would not waste effort or risk taking too long. She would die like her security detail, from a simple bolt of magic that would take her life.

The dragon's hand began to move up to release the force. Her eyes rolled back as if she was talking with someone in her mind. Adrian recognized it from the numerous times they had made them resend messages when they failed to resist the automatic physical response. Before he could react to her obvious contact, he felt the sudden rush of magical power. It thrummed past him like a stiff breeze. He was moving when she raised her hands across her face and shouted, "No!"

A force struck Adrian and threw him back against the wall. Blue flame like Saint Elmo's fire engulfed him and exploded away from his body as he struck the sheet rock.

The same wave slammed into the rest of Adrian's squad and Galariat, pushing them and the first three rows of chairs away from her, breaking the concentration required to marshal the mana. It blasted a hole in the floor instead.

A wall of thin, blue smoke rose from the final edge of the blast zone.

Adrian lifted himself from the floor and rushed her physically, wrapping her in his arms. He overpowered her as she continued to tremble from the release of magic. He didn't have time to think about what other power she might manifest. She had the same shocked look that had frozen on his father's face when he had emerged, but she was starting to recover.

Galariat stood up and flapped his wings in agitation at the surprise but made a quick decision. He saw how Adrian had captured her and nodded.

"Take her out of here. Her own kind will see what she is. Now she will be just like us. Nethliast will have to decide her fate. Move."

Adrian cast his hold spell on her again and lifted her from the ground.

"Let's move, team," he said. They all turned to collect the frozen form.

With the four members of his team holding some part of the president, they turned and walked through the crowd of reporters and panicked students. None of them knew how to react to the violent and strange events that had occurred around them.

Other partials used their imposing figures to move the crowd aside and make a path for his team to carry the figure through.

Rodriguez and two squads of spiked and angry looking partials followed them out of the building and toward the waiting van.

"Get her to the van and then to the airport," Rodriguez sent as he passed the doorway.

"Good job, Fieldman." The first sergeant singled him out for a message as they were clear and climbing into the van. *"Everyone else, release the press, torch the structure."*

CHAPTER 2 - REALIZATION

September 6 – 0730 EDT – Signal Mountain, Tennessee

Elaine's body knifed through the surface of the cool water. As she broke through again, half way down the pool, she felt invigorated by the chill. The mist rising into the cooler morning air scattered away from her with each vigorous stroke.

Since leaving her mother's house over two months before, Elaine had spent most of her time reading what seemed like every book in the three story library of the manor house overlooking what locals called Tennessee's Grand Canyon. She could never have imagined or even written the tale that had unfolded from the simple letter and lost manuscript her idol, Helena Schwendeman, had sent her after her death. Elaine turned at the end of the pool and kicked off for another lap.

It was that same day when Elaine had returned the manuscript and Helena's request for help that she had met Melissa, Charles, and the most difficult challenge of her life. Melissa was the new matron of the estate. With that inheritance she had also accepted the legacy of dragons that Helena had protected for centuries in the appointed role of ambassador of the dragons. She was also Meliastrid, a full blood copper dragon. As far as Elaine could tell, she was the only dragon with a metallic color. Charles was her butler, body guard, and the most beautiful man she had ever seen. He was the definition of the word paladin, and, whether he knew it or not, he lived by a code of honor no man could hope to keep. That made him irritatingly chaste in her mind, but her perspective was decidedly skewed.

Elaine felt mana bubble out all over her at the thought of Charles as she turned again. Instead of thinking of him, she pressed the magical essence back and focused on the work she still had to do. The challenge unleashed on them when Melissa failed to complete an ancient spell designed to keep dragons trapped in human form was, as far as they knew initially, to avert the inevitable conflict growing around them between humans and dragons. Many dragons believed humans had trapped them, particularly Nethliast, Meliastrid's spurned mate and a powerful black dragon.

Then Elaine had discovered Melissa's role as ambassador of the dragons. She had admitted that she, as Meliastrid, had cast the spell that trapped the dragons, not the humans. It became clear to them all that Helena had a plan that went beyond the spell. They needed to figure out what it was before Nethliast agitated the dragons to war. The problem with figuring out what really happened was that the spell had mangled dragon memory. It caused debilitating headaches any time they tried to remember critical details. Whether Helena knew that would happen or not, that was one way Elaine had been able to help. She had found Helena's older publications and compared them to her newest novels. With the frustrating and exciting help of Charles, she had discovered Renard and his plot which had led dragons to sacrifice themselves to trap him.

She turned for another lap. As she stroked at the water she thought about what it meant for the spell that had trapped Renard to be broken. It meant that a human wizard—which was an oddity at that time—was now free in this time, and it was possible that he was the last person who possessed the Heart of the Dragon, the talisman of the dragon species that had powers that no one could remember, but apparently provided some sort of stability to dragon kind. Both Melissa and Kaliastrid believed it was the key to fixing the their memory problem and even clarifying Melissa's role as the ambassador.

Elaine's new exercise routine felt like a vacation compared to the challenge and the risk resting on her small shoulders. She loved what she was learning, but it was a tedious exercise that seemed unending and must be broken up by some physical exercise or she would go mad. It gave her an outlet for the mana built up throughout the day, caused by two emotional vexations she could not deal with directly. In addition to all of the other challenges she had not expected as she prepared to take on her mother's dream of becoming an engineer, Elaine had learned she was an enchantress and that magic was very hard to control.

The history she had been taught in high school was nothing like what Helena's journals said, and she struggled with which one to believe. The evidence of the research told her that the real story was locked up in fiction because humans actively tried to make dragons vanish in history like they had in the present. Had she not experienced the reality of dragons in her real world, and the magic that flowed through her even as she swam, Elaine never would have accepted that the history she had been taught might be false. But she could not deny the fact that magic was all around her and dragons existed.

She stopped at the wall and paused to catch her breath before she turned to start her next lap. The pool was small, but it was more than she had ever had access to. The first day she had felt relaxed enough in the manor to even try to swim, it had forced long forgotten memories of her father into her mind which blended with the reality that was Kaliastrid, Melissa's mother and an adoptive mother figure to Elaine. Her father had taught her to swim. It was one of the best memories she had of him, but the years of school and fighting with her mother over her future had buried that memory until the day she had finally decided to take a break and a swim. He had been happy when he could connect with her and the earth. But gradually those times had been replaced with life in Atlanta. He had tried to stay. He had tried to be what her mother wanted. But, Elaine knew that he had to leave. He had to go be part of the land and be close to nature. Neither her mother nor Atlanta gave him what he needed. Elaine knew he had stayed as long as he had for her. He had sacrificed so much, delaying his dreams, just so she would remember him and embrace what he believed was the right way to approach life. His only purpose over those years had been to make sure she understood how important it was to chase her dreams and that life was about more than one's body image. He, more than anyone else, was the reason she had walked out that door to see what Helena wanted her to do. His free spirit and desire to know what else was out there had poisoned her against staying and waiting for her corporate jumpsuit, but it was also the reason she was able to help with this worldwide challenge that most humans didn't even know was going on around them.

Elaine felt the thrill of the magic fill her as she thrummed the chord of irritation and love that came together in her mother, her father, Kaliastrid, and Charles. It quickly rushed through her body and started to bubble around her and the hunter green spandex one-piece she was wearing. She forced herself to swim on. The bubbling energy enveloped her and heated the water as she cut through it. She focused on her strokes instead of her parents or her somewhat dissatisfying figure to keep the magic at bay. Some day she would really control it. Some day she would know everything there was to know about it. Some day she would master this ability that wanted to explode from her soul and was only mastered by intense concentration or absolute emotionless distraction.

She swam the rest of her laps thinking of nothing but the strokes to avoid boiling or freezing herself. When she finally dragged herself out of the pool, she was appropriately tired. Her arms ached from the physical exercise, and she could feel the natural heat still making her sweat. The cool air around her sucked the warmth from her body. Goose pimples raced across her arms and up her legs, and she shivered with elation at the feelings. This was one of the positives of her new magical abilities. She was hypersensitive to her body and every weird sensation that came with it. Because every emotion could blossom into a raging fire or bolt of uncontrolled lightning, the micro-focus on her feelings was required to broaden her understanding of sensations she had previously paid no attention to. She toweled off in the cool air and looked at the brightening sky. The soft terry-cloth fingers tingled across her skin. Red streaks ran through the clouds, and she suddenly felt the ancient mariners' warning brace her for the day. As Bradbury had so aptly put it, she thought, something wicked this way comes.

Shivers wracked her, but she refused to give in to the elements. She had to complete her morning ritual which she could thank her other parent for. Her mother's strict adherence to a morning yoga and T'ai chi practice had actually helped define her own meditation and exercise. With it, she had slowly gained control of her powers.

Standing at the end of the pool on her towel, she began the ceremony that had become more powerful each morning. First she called the never far off fire into her palm and played with it like Aldrich had taught her. Once the flames covered her hand, she let the magical warmth race across her body like a second skin. It consumed her, warming the chilled skin and evaporating the water that still covered her. Micro-control of the element kept it from burning her or her bathing suit. In her hand, she made the ball grow larger.

Focusing on the ball, she pushed it out away from her hand onto the surface of the pool. With intense concentration that required physical tension in her muscles, she allowed it to grow into a bonfire that reached to the sides of the pool. The heat from the flames still warmed her even though the fire had left her when she pushed the ball away. With it enlarged but still under control, she focused on the conflagration, adding excitement and emotion to the manifestation. It became energetic, consuming the air in leaping gulps. She laughed at the emotional discharge. Her magic had always been connected to her emotions. Learning how to use them made her stronger. With each change, she remembered the feeling in her body that had caused the transformation. Finally, with intense muscular contraction and mental effort, she squeezed the fire back until it was a ball of flame no larger than her hand on the surface of the pool. Then, with a thought and a clasping of her hand she extinguished the flame.

She repeated this same exercise with each element she had read about in the book Kaliastrid had given her. The small manual seemed fantastic in its existence, and, although it was geared toward raising dragons, it was helping her discover her own abilities. Blending it with her mother's training, Elaine was able to explore her own body and emotions within the magical envelope.

Standing with her feet spread a shoulder's width apart on her towel, Elaine inhaled the sharp air into her lungs and relaxed her mind. She waved her right hand across her body, causing a wave of force to extend away from her. When it struck the surface of the water, it created a small wave that rushed toward the end of the pool. With her left hand she repeated the move with more power. A larger wave pushed across the surface. Focused on the pattern of increasing techniques, Elaine escalated her power until each punch of her fists struck the water ten feet away, drilling into the surface as if a rock had been thrown into it.

Sweat dripped off of her shoulders as she finished the magical kata. With her physical and magical energy at a low ebb, she settled into a cross legged seat on her towel. Because she had been attuned to her magical aura for the entire exercise, when she settled onto the ground she was able to levitate herself slightly above the towel. With a hand on each knee, she reached her magic aura out around her, searching for other magic as she breathed in the charged air.

The first entity she felt near her was Aldrich, who was standing in the library watching her through the window that looked out onto the pool. She grinned at the idea of the priest watching her exercise her magic. She liked to think that he was proud of her for learning so fast and being so powerful.

Next she felt the brilliant glow of the talisman that Melissa wore around her neck and the weaker glow of her dragon form sleeping in her room. In the room next to hers was the similar aura of her mother. She was awake, and a different magical presence surrounded her. Something or someone else was with her. Elaine could not identify which. She had learned how to sense magic but identifying each new one required her to see the specific person or item it was attached to. Once she could tie it to a person or thing, it became a regular fixture in her magical environment. She had not expected it, but even Charles had a magical aura. His was much weaker then everyone else's in the manor, but she could not deny that he had one.

Elaine had no idea how far she could reach with her magical sense. Each morning she tried to push it out further to find her true limits, but she had never been able to sense specific magic beyond the boundaries of the manor house and gardens. At its furthest reach she trembled from the exertion of the exercise. That morning, just at the edge of her perceptions, something new connected with her magical grasp. It was a sharp stab into her brain that she had not expected. Someone else's emotions were flooding the magical ether.

The surface of the pool reacted to her thoughts, and she inhaled sharply from the surprise. At first the pool trembled and became agitated as if storm winds were blowing across it. As she focused on the emotions, the surface calmed, and images flitted across it. Images of fire and flames filled the pool. Dragons flew across the sky, burning buildings and men running before them.

The images on the water's surface, similar to a modern combat action movie, surprised her. At first she wondered what ancient memory she was sharing with someone, but then the modern elements rushed to the forefront of the vision. Unable to maintain the focus, she released it and dropped the two inches to the ground. Elaine huffed out her breath as she bounced against the hard surface. The images in the pool vanished, and the surface became agitated again.

Struggling to remember what she had seen, she focused on the modern buildings to try to identify landmarks. She shook her head at the confusion. The vision had been recent. It actually felt like it was happening as she was watching.

The strange feeling of goose-flesh and fire told her to get control. Two quick breaths and then a long slow one settled her as the emotions of the actual observer threatened to get out of balance. With control engaged, she reached out again. Quicker than before, she found the flow she had been part of, and the pool water smoothed into a flat screen. More powerful and different emotions spiked into her mind, and her focus was drawn to a new place. A scene took shape in the pool.

The president of the United States was surrounded. She was terrified. The young men surrounding her dropped back behind her as the dragon standing in front of her pointed at her. She was going to die. Elaine could feel the fear, but that was not all. Deep within the terrified leader Elaine could feel mana building. Elaine had never been so connected to anyone else's emotions. She could feel the terror build. Elaine's hand trembled. The emotion fueled the magical furnace at her core. Fire rippled out across Elaine's arms as the terrified woman clutched at anything to save her life. Magical energy leached across their connection until Elaine was dragged into the president's consciousness. Elaine was now standing in the room facing the dragon who was about to kill her. Her magical energy was flowing into the president. For that moment, they were one.

"No!" the president and Elaine shouted simultaneously. Their emotions flowed away from her creating a wave of force that disturbed the surface of the pool. The release broke her connection. She collapsed onto her side next to the pool, trembling. She could still feel the fear in her own mind. She was very weak from the effort exerted by the resistance. Her heart raced. Ribbons of smoke rose from the scorched towel she had been sitting on.

Suddenly Aldrich was standing over her. His brows were furrowed. He mumbled to himself until he noticed she was looking at him. "What was that?"

"I don't know. Was it real? I'm not sure where it came from."

"You saw a real event. I saw it with you. You or she drew me in."

"Where was it?" Elaine asked.

"I expect it was in Washington. Maybe it will be on the news."

"That could not be real. How did a dragon get into the White House? Who were those other boys? This had to be a dream."

Elaine moved to stand but could not sit up without Aldrich's offered hand.

"No, child. Trust me. You witnessed a real event. You contributed to that magical blast."

Elaine felt the chill of her own fear fill her. What had she done?

"So, someone tried to kill the president. A dragon tried to kill the president, and I... We prevented it."

"No, she prevented it, we just provided the magical power to do it. I know. I saw it. Wodin hasn't warned me, so whatever is happening is outside of my ability to change or outside of his desire to change."

Elaine stared at him with a curious look.

"That's just how it works sometimes." He grinned as he helped her up and provided what support he could as they walked toward the house.

As a pair, they walked beside the black wrought iron fence surrounding the pool. Aldrich handed her the lightweight robe she had hung next to the gate as they walked through it, and she tossed it over her shoulders. Charles was standing in the door to the library dressed to take on an assault, as always. His hand rested on a pistol on his hip. Without a thought he helped her slip her arms into the robe.

"What's going on? Who screamed? Is she all right?" he asked. A first aid kit sat open on the table.

"I did... I think," Elaine answered as she kept them moving toward the theater on the bottom floor of the manor. "I'll be fine in a few minutes. I'm just a little drained."

Aldrich nodded.

"Something's happening in Washington. Someone's tried to kill the president. I don't know what happened, though." She felt like she was babbling.

Concern crossed Charles' normally placid, if morose, face. "And you know this how?"

Aldrich looked back and motioned for Charles to follow as Elaine pressed on.

In the library she found the remote to the projector and television receiver. Concealed rollers pulled back curtains that hid a professional projection screen. The lights dimmed as the projector cast the international news onto the screen.

A crawler at the bottom of the screen announced that several world governments had been attacked by an unknown force that resembled the lizard people who had appeared a few months back.

The somewhat frazzled reporter who was used to delivering financial news to early morning office workers was explaining the difficulties they were having verifying the news coming in: *"...and it seems the only real verification we have is from Washington, D.C., where a live telecast of the president's announcement of the new Secretary of Education was interrupted by lizard men and what some are referring to as a demon. These assailants, who referred to themselves as the Partial Liberation Army, made demands before openly attacking the president."*

The image on the screen changed to a high quality video of five half-dragons surrounding the president of the United States while what Elaine could only guess was a partially transformed dragon pointed his hand at her. She slumped into a cushioned chair as the moment she had experienced replayed on the large screen.

"That's what I saw," she cried, drowning out what else the reporter had to say. "They threatened to kill her. We released a magical blast that knocked them down and knocked me out for a moment. That's when Aldrich was standing over me."

"Wait," Charles asked, "You witnessed this? How?"

"I don't know how, but I more than saw this. I experienced it," she answered quickly and a little defensively.

The scene played again.

"It doesn't matter how." Aldrich reminded him and looked at Elaine. "What matters is what it means."

"I don't know that either. It seems to mean that half-dragons and possibly dragons attacked the president."

When the recorded scene ended again, she stared at the screen as the image changed to various still images from around Washington.

"It was more than an attack on the president," Charles said as he pointed to the screen where new images were coming up.

They watched as an early morning image of Washington appeared on the screen.

"These images have just arrived from one of our reporters who was at the announcement this morning. He was able to escape the destruction and fire that followed and is live from his computer. Mike, you're live with us here, how did you escape this carnage?"

An image of the Capitol building with flames pouring out of every window and black smoke billowing around the trademark dome filled the screen as a distant, distorted voice reported, *"For some reason, Heidi, we were released. I expect it was to get this report out. They seemed to want the world to know what this was about."*

The scene changed and was replaced with video from inside the briefing room of the White House and a stock image of the reporter who was speaking.

"Who are they, Mike?"

"They called themselves the Partial Liberation Army. They demanded the president surrender the government to them. She refused. As they were preparing to kill her, some force exploded from around her, knocking them back."

"They were going to kill her, Mike?"

"Yes, I'm sure that was their plan, but once the blast or force was set off... whatever it was that knocked them down, they changed their minds. They grabbed her instead of killing her and took her. I'm not sure where they went, but a small group took her out of the briefing room. The others then systematically killed whoever was left as they set fires throughout the building. We heard gunfights throughout the building before we were escorted out. As they walked us out, the building was fully engulfed in flames."

The anchor could not control the shock and terror in her voice. She fought for something comforting to say. *"If you are just joining us, we are on the air live with Mike Russ, Washington Correspondent, who has just escaped the assault on the White House. So, Mike. Are you telling me that the President of The United States is a prisoner of this army, the Partial Liberation Army, which attacked us this morning?"*

"Yes, Heidi. That is exactly what I'm saying. We are not sure where they took her or why. It was a small group that exited with her before the massacre started. The chaos of this situation has made it difficult to track the story. I tried to follow them when they took her, but a wall of partials blocked my way."

Several more images followed his report as they discussed his use of the term partial. Images and video showed dragons in flight burning long paths of ground leaving behind burning structures and vehicles in the streets. The still photographs had been taken by a professional who had the eye to capture the moment of terror that everyone was experiencing. Elaine felt the fear that had filled her as the president resisted the attack bubble up inside of her again.

"They shouldn't be showing these images," Charles said. A flare of an emotion she had never felt from Charles filled the room for an instant. She stared at him wondering how he could sound so calm but be filled with such anger. "There's no verification of the source. This is all too sensational. It could endanger soldiers on the scene." His last comment reminded her that he *had* seen worse. He was trying to protect people who had not seen war before, but there was still something else burning in his mind.

"But, it happened. I saw it," she said.

Charles nodded, sadly accepting what she said. The rage she had felt extinguished. The burning anger that had been in his eyes, vanished. A shiver of fear ran up her back as she thought about the self-control required to dial back that rage. She touched his hand, and he looked into her eyes. Whatever had been there was gone. She no longer felt the heat that had flowed off of him a moment before. He was back to his even and balanced feelings. He turned his hand over and held her hand in his briefly before releasing it. She clutched the warm hand as it fell away and seized the momentary contact. His warmth filled her, and she wished he would hold her and protect her from whatever seemed to be suddenly devouring the world.

Charles recognized the change in her eyes and moved again to release her hand. She decided she had to let him know how she felt. As his hand fell away, she reached out and wrapped her arms around his neck. She felt his comforting arms around her waist. He supported her as she squeezed him as if she was going to break him, but he did not return her fervor. She suddenly realized he was comforting her, like a father.

"I'm okay. Thanks," she said as she disengaged from the troubling show of affection.

"Are you sure?" he asked.

"Yes."

Hiding the embarrassment she felt by turning to watch the screen, she wondered if there was any way through his armor, and who really possessed his heart. Aldrich politely ignored the emotional moment and continued to watch the screen.

The images changed as the two reporters talked about the destruction of the US capital. Their talk shifted with the slide show of pictures to midday London captured by official cameras. These safety cameras showed similar scenes around the House of Parliament. A sharp image from a dash camera showed the same destruction in the Red Square. The images seemed to be coming in from all over the world. Elaine suddenly felt the depth of the attack. This was not just national. This was a coordinated attack around the world.

"*This scene is repeated all over the world,*" the anchor confirmed as Elaine thought it. "*We have verified what we are showing you has actually happened. This is not a hoax. The capital of every major country in the world is currently in flames, and we have no idea if the national leaders have survived.*"

"Eir, help us all," Aldrich mumbled as he watched the screen change with more images. "Maybe you should wake Melissa."

"I'm awake," a voice said from the doorway. Elaine felt something other than anger from her. If she could believe her own senses, it was fear. Charles immediately turned to face Melissa standing in the doorway to the darkened theater.

"What's going on?" she asked. She didn't enter but maintained a distance.

Charles, as always, tensed when he knew she was there. No matter how much Melissa pretended he was her friend, he could not relax his vigilance around her. It was like she was a china doll. Elaine knew, from her own research, what dragons were like, and she was no delicate specimen. She wished Charles could see that. She wished he could sense the fear that was filling her at that moment, but she knew she was destined to always pale in Melissa's presence. She had tried to break through his barriers but something kept him from accepting how Elaine felt about him.

"I'm sorry if we disturbed you," Charles began. She waved his apology away like smoke. Some of his rage actually re-emerged at her passive dismissal of his apology.

"You didn't. Something else woke me. The amulet was glowing with agitation, and I couldn't sleep anymore," she commented as she walked toward them and watched the screen change to another disturbing picture of an official building Elaine did not recognize, "I came down to see what was going on and if anyone else had sensed it. What's on the news?"

"Rome—Berlin—Washington," Aldrich answered for each image as it changed, shaking his head. "The whole world has been attacked."

"By the half-dragons?" she asked.

"And dragons," Charles answered sharply. Elaine stared at him in amazement. The unspoken had come from him, laced with anger.

Melissa stood and watched without answering. She didn't react to Charles' barb.

"Capitals around the world appear to be ringed with anti-aircraft that is keeping any air traffic out, military or civilian. At the moment, they are sieged cities, and we can only pray for those trapped behind the lines drawn by those rings of fire."

The screen filled with a new image of Washington encircled by a ring of fire half-way between the beltway and the core of the capital.

Kaliastrid walked into the theater at that moment. Elaine noted that she didn't seem to pay any attention to the screen and the news that played on it.

"I see you've all heard the news," she said with no emotion.

"What do you know of this, mother?" Melissa asked with acid on her tongue.

"Nethliast's alive."

Melissa spun on her mother as she continued.

"He's begun his move. It's much bigger than we ever thought. He and his core supporters have moved against nearly every government."

"I thought you killed him," Elaine said.

"We were never really sure," Melissa answered with a dismissive wave of her hand.

"We are now," Kaliastrid shared. "I've had verification that he was seen this morning overseeing the attacks. Him and a nearly mirror image of himself that's overseeing the assaults in South Africa, Russia, and the Middle East."

"From whom? Who sent you this new information?" Charles asked accusingly.

"A young male in Berlin contacted me just as the attacks started," Kaliastrid answered his question without letting his angry mood agitate her. "When I asked him where, so we could try to help, he told me it was no use. It was happening all over the world."

"How did he contact you?" Melissa asked.

Charles nodded to the question. He was looking at them both like he had looked at the agent, Loxley, who had surprised them the day she had fought Nethliast.

"He contacted me on your father's crystals."

The shock of that news traveled through each of them. They had all talked, more than once, about the ominous disappearance of the dragon King, but to have a strange male dragon use the crystals, verified what Kaliastrid had long feared. Nethliast, or someone, had captured Valdiest.

Charles' mood grew even darker. Elaine tried to get his attention to provide some solace and to get some idea of what was suddenly bothering him, but he was staring at Melissa. The hint of anger she had seen in his eyes before was now a smoldering agitation. She had seen hints of it over the past month since they had come back from Washington, but had not pushed for an explanation. Her first impression had been that she had rejected him, but that was her own fantasy overlaying reality. This anger came from a deeper place. He was blaming her for what was happening. How could he? He knew how hard Melissa had worked to stop Nethliast. She had fought him in the air over their heads. Without the talisman and with their memories a mess, they were fighting from a disadvantage.

"You may as well speak your mind, Charles," Melissa added dryly.

"I'm just disappointed." His word choice showed he was still being diplomatic in his speech even though Elaine knew the emotions ran much deeper. "You had the opportunity to stop this."

"Charles, I tried." There was no mistaking the hurt she felt at his accusations.

"You had the chance to tell them. You held back the one fact that might have saved lives today. I told you that day. More than one of my missions in Iraq failed because of bad intelligence or lack of intelligence. Good men die when someone holds back information." He waved his hand at the screen where more images from the scenes were playing, all diplomacy lost as his agitation won out over self-control. "You've put thousands of lives at risk to protect your precious secret."

In his last statements, Elaine could feel his anger pouring from him. He was thinking of men he had stood beside while watching the destruction that dragons unleashed upon his brothers. That was where his anger was rooted. He was at odds with his passions. On one side was his care and obvious love for Melissa and on the other was his devotion to the soldiers, sailors, airmen, and marines who were faced with fighting dragons.

"How would my telling them that have stopped any of this?" Melissa asked in a sharp tone Elaine had never heard her use before. It was imperious and had an immediate effect on Charles. Like a gate slamming down on a castle entrance, he drew up inside of himself. He stood up straight as if the master of the house or his commanding officer had called him up short. Elaine could see the pain Melissa was inflicting on him, but Melissa could not.

"If I had told them that dragons can take human form, I would be in a lab somewhere. You know I would do my best to protect them, but I ultimately would have to hurt someone to get away, because I would have to get away. So, I would be trapped in a catch-22. But worse, so much worse than that, would be the witch hunt of other humans who are not dragons, but were seen as different. And tell me, logically, what good would that scenario do? The same dragons and half-dragons that did this would have succeeded just as well because they would be no closer to being able to discover who is and who is not a dragon. There is no dragon detector that would have stopped this."

Melissa was not being completely honest. Elaine could see magical creatures when she tried. Melissa and Kaliastrid had both been able to tell she was enchanted when she first arrived. She assumed they hadn't thought about that ability rather than believing they were lying. She kept it to herself.

"With respect, you could have helped them. You can tell when there are dragons near. You can sense them," Charles answered with a more controlled and professional air than he had used previously, and it caused Melissa to step back. She had seen the barrier fall around her friend and realized, too late, that she had shut him down.

"Yes," her tone softened as she adjusted to the situation. Elaine could see the struggle on her face. A very sorrowful look clouded it as she tried to reverse the crushing effect of her position and the awkwardness and confusion she had created by allowing him to feel like her friend while she still maintained the control over him. "Charles, you are correct. We could have detected them."

"To no avail. The two of us could have stood guard over the president," Kaliastrid answered in defense of her daughter, "but there is more to this than one person. This happened around the world. We are the only dragons who are not under Nethliast's control. There is no way we could have protected them all."

"Of course, you're correct, ma'am." Charles answered, closing the door on his emotions again.

The sudden change in tenor had taken Melissa by surprise. She had expected the fight to escalate. She didn't seem to know how to react.

"Excuse me," Charles continued. "I'm sure I have somewhere else I need to be."

With an air of dignity Elaine had not witnessed in her life before arriving at this manor, Charles exited the room.

"Well done, Melissa," Kaliastrid said as Melissa exhaled her frustration into the room.

"I know. I screwed up."

"Yes, you did." Elaine could not hold back. "You ignored his reasons for disagreeing with you. You belittled his concerns, and then, when he still held to his beliefs, you treated him like your servant. You've not done that since I came here. You drew him out like he was your friend and then, when he acted like a friend and told you the truth, you smashed him with your royal fist."

Melissa stood stunned in front of her. Elaine had never been so forward, but she had never witnessed Melissa be so imperious.

Aldrich, who had been watching the whole exchange and the news, responded. "The search for the talisman is the only way to stop this from getting worse. We can't be distracted by this, no matter how bad it is. You can't fight all of dragon kind. As much as Charles feels that you've broken some moral rule, he will understand the tactical disadvantage you're in. I'll speak to him and fix this once he has calmed down. We can't lose focus now. We must redouble our efforts and not let this get out of control."

"You may convince him that I had no choice, but you cannot fix what I did. That injury will cost me, I'm afraid." Melissa's answer showed that she realized her mistake, but it was too late to really fix it. All she could do now was admit it and apologize.

"Excuse me, I need to get back to my work," Elaine said in an unconvincing excuse to get out of the theater. She needed to see if Charles was all right and she suddenly didn't care if Melissa knew she was angry. Without worrying about how her excuse was received, she slipped out between Melissa and Aldrich to follow Charles to the place she knew she would find him. She didn't understand why the kitchen was where he went when he needed to be alone, but she knew that was where he would be.

Running down the hall once she was away from the theater, she pushed the swinging door open and slipped into the stainless steel and wood of his sanctuary.

"Charles?" she called meekly.

"Yes, Miss? Is there something you need?" He stepped out of the wood and metal to appear before her as formal as he had ever been.

Elaine wanted, again, to hug him, to fix the hurt she knew he felt, but couldn't bring herself to feel the wall of his professionalism rebuff her again.

"I am so sorry that she did that to you. She never should have cut you off like that."

She could sense that threatening professional wall hovering over her and backed up a step. She had to take a risk before he closed her out and forced her out of his fortress entirely.

"Yes, I need something. I need something from you. I need Charles, the guy who helped me dig through all of those books and crates over the past few months. I want the one who embarrassingly uncovered my favorite peasant blouse and collection of corsets in the attic. Not this stiff and formal Jarvis fellow. Have you seen him? Have you seen Charles?"

She could see him relax a little, but the pain of what was going on was still clear in his eyes. "What can I help you with?"

"Better, but I was, obviously, hoping for an honest talk."

"Okay. I'll try." The barrier retreated a little but she could still feel the delicate fear of being smacked again.

"I know you're upset, but I don't think it's really about what she didn't tell them."

He stiffened and started to walk back into the kitchen. She should have softened that a bit. He was a delicate, strong man.

"Wait, don't run from me, please. You've lost friends. You expect the rules to keep that from happening, but it doesn't always work that way. This is going to hurt, but you have to hear it. No one would have won anything from her sharing that secret. She's right, she probably would be captured, and you would have been pushing down the pillars of the temple on the heads of the Philistines to find her." Elaine could not believe she was being so honest with him and possibly destroying what little chance she had with him.

"You must think I'm pretty simple," he said sharply, but he didn't retreat from her words.

"No, just the opposite. You're beautiful and regal in the way you see right and wrong. You are an amazing pillar of light in this world of gray, but the world doesn't always work the way you see it. You're like a knight in Helena's novels that is fighting a dark evil..." She stopped herself before she said, *and I love you for it.*

"That's pretty deep for someone your age. I know, trust me. The world is not black and white, but I can hope that good will remain pure. I'm not as simple as that. But, as long as I can, I will stand for that good to win. I just can't believe that she doesn't see that she has any responsibility in this. That's what bothers me. I've followed leaders who never once struggled with decisions to send men to their deaths. I've meet men, like that agent, who make plans without once thinking of the toll in lives. I've seen what it does to a man, and I don't want her to be that. If that is the ancient soul inside of her, my Mel is lost forever. I swore before I left my squad that I would be a better officer than that."

Elaine could sense that they were finally getting to the core of his anger. She pushed him to keep talking. "Why didn't you?"

"Become an officer?"

"Yeah?"

"That's another long story of arrogance." He waved at the air as if to say it was not a conversation for this time.

"Except for the fact that the governments of the world were just wiped out, I have the time."

She backed up to a nearby stainless counter and jumped up to sit on the edge. It was a mistake. She could not avoid the cringe as the cold countertop bit at her uncovered thighs. Committed to the action, she crossed her legs and placed both of her hands into her lap like a young student listening to the teachings of a master.

"I'm not going to go into it. I'm still trying to figure out how much of Helena's actions were really altruistic like she said. There's so much deception in all of this, but, according to her, for the right reasons. I guess that's why I want Melissa to be honest about things. Helena deceived me to get me back here, and I'm not sure why. She never told me, but whenever I tried to get to the reason she would just tell me I was meant for more than dying in the desert."

"Sounds like my mother."

"Really? You've never talked about her."

"Not much to tell. She wants me to become her mini-me. I don't want to."

"Being yourself does not seem to be a problem for you."

Elaine grinned at him and realized this was the most relaxed he had been since she arrived. She was on the other side of his armor. He had let her inside the fortress, and, with unimaginable clarity, she realized she had to tread very carefully.

"Maybe, but this is your tale, not mine."

"I see. Well, to keep it to the short story that it should be, let's just say that I love my father. I left him here when I thought everything was okay and joined the Marines. He even gave me his blessing to go the way I thought I should. But, after a few years and a war, his health suddenly turned bad, and he asked me to come home to help him. I couldn't refuse my father's wishes, so I left the service. At the time, I was on my way to Officer Candidate School. I requested hardship leave to take care of him. I completed my third year with the local reserve unit. I technically could have just left because my year was over, but I had re-enlisted to go to OCS. Over that year—after it was too late to really change my mind—I would never get another shot at OCS—I figured out he wasn't as bad off as he had indicated. Helena had convinced him, somehow, that I had some higher purpose, and if I stayed in the Marines, I would die. Even to his deathbed, he never changed his mind about what he did. He died before I could reconcile this, and I will carry his deception at the orders of the head of the manor with me forever. He believed his deceit saved my life."

"But, you don't think so?"

"Does it matter? I don't know, maybe it did. But that was not his decision to make. This is not what I trained for. It was not Helena's place to decide my future. Maybe my death then would have stopped this. How do I know someone else wouldn't have helped Melissa more than I did? Maybe they would have been able to get her to complete her task and stop the emergence?"

"Oh, Charles. That is not your fault. Helena knew the forces raging for and against that spell had reached their balance point. She knew, because she was so sick, that the deck was stacked against it. She thought Melissa stood a better chance of succeeding than she did. You can't take the responsibility for today because of not knowing the true meaning of your mission."

"Perhaps I shouldn't, but I can't deny the way I feel. I was taught by my father and the Marines to take responsibility for my actions. But, that doesn't matter right now anyway. The unthinkable outcome of all of this has happened. Melissa was right when we met the president. This was inevitable."

"Nothing is fixed. Everything can be changed," Elaine countered.

"Really? I tried to get out of this life once, and the dragon ambassador drug me back for some reason. Now, I've failed at that very mission she brought me back to accomplish. We haven't countered this. We haven't even slowed it down."

"How can you be sure? First, how can you be sure this is the mission you were meant to accomplish? Maybe there's more. You can't believe that this is all your fault, but, if it is, what are you going to do to fix it?"

"Nethliast seems to have all of the advantages. All we have is theory. We need to stop this before more people are hurt."

"So, this whole agitation today is about more than one secret she didn't tell."

"I guess. Today solidified it for me. I should have been there, not here. If I had..."

"You'd be dead," Elaine finished his thought with unwavering finality.

"You can't be sure of that."

"Sure I can. So can you. The partials didn't take prisoners today. You saw the same images I did."

Her forceful conviction made him pause and think. She watched him fall back through the images they had seen. He was partly focused on his thoughts and a sliver of Charles was with her. He mindlessly reached over and stroked a strand of her longer hair, the lock that Kaliastrid usually wrangled, over her ear. It was a gentle show of affection that she had longed for. She smiled at his soft touch and leaned into his hand. His eyes returned from his thoughts and he suddenly realized what he had done. As his fingers fell behind her ear and her cheek settled into his palm, he withdrew his hand as if he had touched a hot stove. Elaine could feel the expulsion from within his fortress as he stood straight up. Panic filled his eyes, and the pain of rejection filled her chest. She reached out and captured his hand in hers and pulled it to her. He started to speak.

"Stop," she said before he could say anything. "It's okay." She smiled at him, trying to calm his agitation. She rubbed his hand between hers. He resisted, but not so much as he could have.

"No. I shouldn't have touched you. I'm sorry. I was thinking about one of the images we saw and the brutality the partials had shown and—I...I didn't mean to be forward."

"You didn't hurt me. You were being nice. My hair is always in my face. I don't mind." She pulled his hand up to her chest and squeezed it as if she could calm the panic in his mind with a hug.

He seemed to relax some, but she could still see him chastising himself for breaking some unspoken rule.

"Tell me about the image you were thinking about," she said to break him out of the spiral.

His eyes cleared a little. "I'm not sure about it. I need to see the footage again. There's something wrong about it, considering what you said. I wonder if they're still playing it in the theater."

"It doesn't matter," she said as she jumped off of the counter maintaining control of his hand.

"It might be important. I think I saw something that might be a clue."

"I don't mean what you're saying doesn't matter. I'm saying that it doesn't matter if they're still showing them. We can look at the images on my tablet. I'm sure they're online by now. I'll go upstairs, change, and bring it back down to the library where we can research this together."

Hoping she could use the research they had worked so well on to pull him back from the panic, she yanked his arm and pulled him out of the kitchen, toward her sanctuary. They had spent so much time together in the library that she might be able to keep him relaxed there. Maybe she could save him, like her father had saved her. He needed to get back to his soul.

September 6 – 0850 EDT – Washington D.C.

Silas was reviewing the completed partials report for the fourth time since coming in to his new Washington office. Colonel Holloway was, at that moment, at the White House awaiting his meeting with the president, to review it. Silas could not squelch the nagging feeling that something was wrong, no matter how many times he read the report. It was a career killer for him and her, but it was on target with the threat level warnings. This was not the first time he had recommended that she raise the threat level, but she had not agreed. She didn't believe he had proved there was a real threat. Holloway's official support in her office might make the difference, if it wasn't too late. Silas looked up into the gray dawn that agreed with his nagging apprehension. He could not shake the impending feeling of doom.

Since that first day months ago, Silas had worked through several different government credentials to gather the data in the report. He had even captured a dragon, for what it had been worth. She had come to him in human form to warn him of the threat of the partials and the dragons. Her ability to take that human form was a surprise he had included in the report to support his conclusion. She had never fully transformed into her dragon form. Her simple demonstration had convinced him. Xue White had risked her life to warn him, and he had paid her patriotism back by sedating her and locking her away where she could not run away with her family.

Silas knew better than to base his recommendations on one source. Xue had not been the only one to come to him. In the report, he had argued for a more aggressive approach to the partials problem based on Xue White's admonition. But it was the recommendation of Helena Melissa Schwendemann, the self-appointed dragon ambassador and probable dragon herself, that had pushed it over the edge. Xue had said there had to be a leader. Miss Schwendemann had named him.

Each day that he walked through the doors downstairs and the alert level had not changed he was nervous. He had initially recommended they change the threat level to orange. Tara just didn't feel that they had enough to take to Congress and the American people. She said they could only push so far until someone had an actual conversation with the partials' leader, a dragon named Nethliast. But, since the day in Washington when Melissa had warned them, Nethliast had conveniently vanished.

Before he could verify any of the things Xue had said or even the things he had witnessed, the partials had vanished. The initial encounters had become the fantastic news of yesterday as they dropped back into the human panoply they blended into. People of the world, resilient in their belief that nothing like that could be real, convinced by ages of science that proved magic was not real, returned to their normal lives and stopped looking for lizard people. They conveniently let those stories become like Roswell. At least most of them did. There were still reports coming in about hunt squads that were tracking and killing partials in human form. The problem with those groups was that they were getting the same reputation as witch hunters through the lens of time. Their problem was the same as his. If they killed the partial in human form, which was the only way they could, it stayed in that form. No kill squad since that first day had ever actually killed a verified partial. Silas still had no idea how to verify someone was a partial even if he had one lying in front of him.

It had been two months since a major sighting. Silas didn't like it. He didn't believe they had appeared simply to disappear. They were still out there, and his gut, along with warnings from two dragons, said they were up to no good.

The report included all of the information he had already shared with Tara about their abilities, the most critical of which was the ability to take human form. They didn't just look like humans. There was no way to tell the difference. He had included a section in the report on the probable threat of a dragon uprising, independent of the partials. Holloway had warned him not to stir the pot by including that part, but he had left it in. If he was right, he had more to worry about than his career. If he was wrong, having his name on a report describing a potential uprising of partials and dragons would kill his career independent of the detail.

Since the ride around D.C. with Miss Schwendeman, he had struggled with where dragons really fit. She presented a puzzle he didn't like, and he liked most puzzles. Her stories matched crazy tales his great-grandfather liked to tell of an alternate world in a long-lost time when dragons and magic existed. Every time the old man had told one, it was in the same hushed tones as if he was sharing a secret that could not get out.

He would have to be satisfied with what he had until Miss Schwendeman was in a place where he could interrogate her properly. Until she left the castle of a manor where she was hiding, there was nothing he could do. But she would not stay there forever. Someday she would leave, and then his plan to get some answers would begin.

Thinking about how he would treat her differently, Silas flipped open the manila folder on his desk in the FBI headquarters that described what the scientists down the hall were finding out about dragons, specifically one Xue White. If nothing had changed, the folder contained nothing. He had planned on completing his research in a base he had secured outside of Knoxville. There he might be able to put his captive at ease, but Tara and Holloway had insisted that they keep everything close. She had, instead, set up the laboratory in the FBI headquarters, and basically imprisoned him with his one specimen. She had argued that it was best, in case the partials did return. Well, what she didn't know wouldn't hurt her. When Melissa did move, she was not coming to Washington where he could not secure her. She was going to the base he had set up in Oak Ridge.

Silas closed the empty folder. For a moment he let the nagging worry about the absence of partials fill his mind. They were up to something. He looked at his watch even though he had no appointments. He felt late. The hackles on his neck suggested he move. He ignored them. Maybe he should move the dragon to the facility in Tennessee. Tara was wrong. He would deal with the consequences later.

He made up his mind.

He wasn't going to sit and wait.

He was moving her.

He grabbed his never far away roll of tools, paused to look at the reports, and left them on the desk. They were useless. He didn't have time to worry about them. He had to go.

As if they were married to his own paranoia, the fire alarms in the hallway suddenly blared. His hackles said 'I told you so,' and he nodded. The alarms were confirmation. He didn't pause for an explanation.

No one else seemed to share his prescient thought. As was common whenever the alarms were tested, everyone looked around for some reason to believe it was nothing, just another drill to waste their time.

Silas' gut disagreed with them. Something was wrong. He was down the hall and in the stairwell before the first office worker was out of his chair.

When he reached the laboratory, the doctors were ambling out into the hallway to exit the building. They looked at him, and his quick movement into the lab, like he was overreacting. Silas let his gut lead him.

In quick steps, he reached the containment area where the last two nurses were heading toward the exits while talking about the reality show they had watched the night before. He had not started with a plan, but now he had one.

"You, come with me." He pointed at one of the nurses he had worked with before. She stopped where she was and stared at him as if he had just called her something offensive.

"Can't," the second one said defensively. "We have to get out. Fire drill. The safety team will be coming around making sure the building's empty."

"Then, get out," he replied flatly. "She's coming with me."

Not waiting for her acceptance, Silas grabbed her by the arm and pulled her back toward the locked room where the dragon was chained to a bed. Her friend, now just ready to get away, turned in frustration.

"What are you doing? We have to get out..." His captive's initially playful protests cut off abruptly when she stiffened and stopped moving.

Silas turned to figure out what was stopping her. The hallway beyond the open laboratory was filled by a roiling column of fire. The defensive nurse, rushing to get out of the building, threw her hands up as if she was going to block the unstoppable death that engulfed her, but the intense heat and flame ended her resistance and reduced her to ash and dust in a bright flash like a sliver of wood inserted into the flame of a cutting torch. The glass walls lining the hall exploded inward in a shower of safety glass. Silas ducked instinctively even though the debris could not reach them. He could feel the panic suddenly building in his captive's body as she pulled against his hold. He had to get her to refocus and keep her from thinking about her dead friend until he had what he needed.

"We may be safer in here," he said pulling on her arm as she continued to stare at the hallway where her friend had died. "Come on, we don't have time to think about it."

She trembled and resisted as he drug her into the small medical treatment room outside of the locked suite. Getting her away from the evidence of death helped her a little, but she was still in shock.

"I need to wake her up. Draw the stimulant." He pointed toward the locked room. The nurse slowly surrendered to his charge and moved toward the cabinets along the opposite wall.

With shaking hands, she fumbled in a drawer that held nothing but tongue depressors before she found the drawer of sharps she was looking for.

"Take a deep breath and calm down. I don't need for you to make a mistake. Think about what you're doing."

"I..." her response was lost in numb confusion. She chose to just nod quickly as she tried twice to seat the needle onto the tube. With the needle finally in place, she inhaled and paused before she removed the safety cover. Having found some stability, she walked to one of the over shelf cabinets where the medicines were held. She pushed a few aside and picked twice before she found what she was looking for.

Inside the small room, they had no idea what was happening in the lab or the building. The blaring of the alarms continued to assault them, and as she was shoving the needle into the bottle, the sprinklers opened up. Water rushed out like rain and soaked them both in seconds.

"Let's go. Ignore the water and get her awake."

"Are you sure you want to wake her up?"

"I don't want her to die in here while we escape," he said, changing his plan as the situation required.

The nurse nodded and then exhaled a nervous breath. She laid the needle down on the prep tray. It seemed she was reconciling herself to the task when she turned sharply toward the door and ran out into the laboratory. Silas made a grab for her arm. Her wet skin slipped between his fingers. He took two steps after her and then relinquished her to the lost. It was a waste of time to chase her. With a moist curse he snatched the needle and hoped for a moment that he could find a vein. He hadn't tried an intravenous injection since his field first aid course in Turkey, and he had been hungover then.

He stepped through the door just as a second flash fire filled the hall as if someone was waiting at one end with a flamethrower. Any hope that she had escaped died in a tortured scream. Silas refocused on his task.

The medical suite had two rooms connected by a small hallway. The common entrance to the laboratory was in the center of that hallway. Silas turned his back on escape and worked the locks to open the door to the secured room. Inside, the young Asian woman he had sedated so long ago was resting in a normal hospital bed. There were no sprinklers in the isolation room, so the room was dry. It was hard for him to believe she was really a dragon as she lay sleeping. He had never seen her take the complete form and every test said she was human. She was connected to an IV. Silas relaxed. He could easily administer the drugs through that.

He had already wasted too much time. Keeping his own panic under control, he found the injection port, inserted the needle, and pressed the plunger home. He had no idea how long it was going to take to wake her up, and he wasn't sure he wanted to wait. In the seconds he considered leaving her after giving her the stimulant, her vitals changed on the monitor. Her eyes were fluttering open. She was groggily looking around the room when a flash of yellow scales crossed her face. Her eyes suddenly cleared of any drug haze. When she recognized him something happened he was not prepared for. Yellow and blue scales exploded across her body. She jumped from the bed, ripping restraints free as she did. Her left hand grabbed him around the neck. He could feel the cold of her talons teasing his skin as she thrust him against the wall and held him there. For a moment she paused as she listened to the alarms and something farther off. His feet dangled as she held him up by the neck, and he struggled with the sudden lack of air.

She snarled at him, "I warned you. Now look what you've caused. You brought this on yourself. If you had acted sooner, this could have been avoided. Arrogant human fool. You never learn."

When the last words cleared her lips, she vanished. He dropped a foot to the floor and stared at the empty room, sucking air into his lungs. Now he was standing, dripping on the tile floor—alone.

"Well, that's gratitude," he said to the empty room before he walked out into the sprinkler-soaked laboratory.

The shattered glass walls that had opened onto the hallway were now gaping holes surrounded by metal frames. From where he was standing he could see the charred remains of both nurses, but only because he knew where they had died. The water flowing down the hallway was mingling what little remained of both of them. It was not coincidental that the fire had caught both of them. Silas' hackles reminded him that they existed. Someone was waiting, watching this hallway for anyone who had not escaped earlier. No one was supposed to escape this building alive.

Instinctively, he checked the roll of tools in his waistband, and reached for his service automatic. It was, as always, loaded and ready. He assumed, based on the evidence in the hallway, that this was an assault, not a fire. It also seemed likely it was the half-dragons. He had already seen how much good the 9mm was going to do against them, but it was a small comfort all the same. When he was clear of all of this he would resolve that problem. This would be the last time he was this under-armed. He shook some of the water from his hands, inhaled a calming breath, aimed the pistol ahead of him, and prepared to follow the nurses into the only exit.

As quietly as he could, he shifted around to the front wall of the lab to see what he could of the hallway and the offices down the hall. Black, acrid smoke was starting to fill the hallway even though the sprinklers were filling the floors with water. When he reached the farthest corner of the lab where he could see all the way down the hall, he saw several half-dragons celebrating the fire that was consuming the cubicles in the office space. The bright flames were melting plastic and generating more black smoke. A single female that was closest to him was gyrating her hips to unheard music that reminded him of another memorable woman from the orient. He could not help thinking how inappropriate it was for her to be doing that.

As the water tried to put out the flames around her, she conjured a fresh stream of fire from her fingers. This was new. He had never seen them conjure fire. He had heard that some of them had breath abilities like legendary dragons, but he had never witnessed that, either.

He counted the moving heads down the hall again before he evaluated his chances of getting out. The only exit would be the stairwells. Partials were blocking any path he had to them. His mind flipped through every plan he could think of between silent curses about the water running down his back and out of his shoes. There were no scenarios that ended with him alive. He raised the pistol ahead of him and placed the single white dot of the middle sight just below the gyrating partial's bobbing ear. His finger disengaged the blade safety on the trigger as he began to squeeze into his death stand.

A sudden feeling that someone was standing beside him caused him to spin and point his gun at the center of Xue White's chest. His mind fought with instinct as it called back the pressure already on the way to completing the squeeze. His mind won. He released the trigger and raised the pistol up and away from his target.

Without a word, she reached out and took his tool roll from his waist. She rubbed a finger across the symbol on the leather before she reached out and touched him. The room surrounding them and the water falling over them vanished and was replaced with threatening gray skies and billowing acrid smoke. They were on the other side of the river, looking back at Washington from Arlington.

Silas hated to ask obvious questions so he kept the one he wanted to ask to himself. "Why did you come back for me?"

"A debt."

"You don't owe me."

"I didn't do it for you. I did it for the Folkvarder. If you were Chinese and in less trouble than you already were, your trick with the tranquilizer would have brought you a lifetime of bad luck. I can bring you no more suffering than is already ahead for you, but I can save you so that you may enjoy every moment of your interesting life. Take my warning now. Never do that to a dragon again. If I had been a different breed, you would not be alive now. If you trap a European dragon like that, they'll kill everyone and bring the whole building down around them."

Silas just stared at her as she grinned and handed him back his tools.

With no more noise than before, she vanished from where she stood, leaving Silas alone with the silent observers that surrounded him. He reached into his drenched pockets to find his equally drenched cell phone. The screen was black. He would have to secure another phone, but first he had to get to his base. If this was what he thought it was, and Xue's comments made him think it was, the report and the alert level were too late. He looked across the river toward the seat of power of the United States. All that he could see was smoke and fire. As he sloshed across the open field toward a place where he could secure transportation, he played through what he knew of succession plans and wondered where the Vice President was today.

September 6 – 1000 EDT – Signal Mountain, Tennessee

"There. Stop there," Charles said over Elaine's shoulder as she was sliding images across the screen of her tablet. She lifted her finger and looked around at his face, which was hovering beside her ear. It was the closest he had been to her voluntarily, and, even though the images were troubling, she couldn't avoid feeling a tingle at the proximity. She wanted him to admit that he felt something for her, but she would take the closeness they had always shared working together in the library.

She was sitting cross-legged in one of the low-backed lounge chairs near the back window in the library where she had spent most of her time and felt the closest to Charles. She had selected one of the peasant blouses and corset combinations she had found in the attic along with a comfortable pair of blue jeans. Overall, it was an outfit that her mother would hate, specifically selected to draw Charles' attention. He was leaning over the back of the chair looking down on the tablet she was holding in her lap. As close as they were and using every tool she knew, he still remained focused on the screen. She wondered if he even saw her sitting beneath him.

"What do you see?" she asked, a little too playfully for the subject. He didn't notice.

"I'm not sure. Can you zoom in?"

With two fingers she pulled the center of the image into higher focus. Charles nodded and reached over her shoulder to point to the right side of the screen.

"It's over that way."

The resolution of the image allowed them to zoom in to two-hundred percent before it became hard to see clear detail. The close-up of what looked like bodies and burning airplanes resolved itself on the screen. She tried to not react to the rawness of the images.

"Why don't you drive? It'll make finding what you want easier," she suggested and handed the tablet up to him. She shifted around in her seat to make room for him. "Here, sit next to me, and I can help."

He stared at her like she had asked him to fly a plane without any training, but he still moved to sit down next to her in the overstuffed seat. It was a tight fit, and she ended up sitting mostly in his lap or up on the arm of the chair.

"It's not that hard," she said to relax him. "You've learned harder things."

He turned his left shoulder out. She nestled into his chest where he could still see over her head and reach the screen of the tablet she was still holding. With his index finger, he touched the surface and slid the image to his left. He pulled his finger away from the screen a little as he tried to work out the orientation of the image after it slid to the left. She let him puzzle through it until he finally pushed the image up and to the left. She felt a small twinge of guilt at using this to get him this close. Sitting in his lap made thinking about the subject difficult. She wanted to toss the tablet away and kiss him, but she knew better. Charles was very serious about his work and never mixed play in, no matter how much she wanted him to. It was his focus that allowed her to wrangle him into this position at all. If he realized where she was sitting he would already be standing over her on the floor. She looked down from the powerful chin to focus again on the image. The damaged runway slid out of view and was replaced with an area in front of a hangar that was mostly empty. He stopped and reversed the motion she had used to zoom in, and the image zoomed out again. He did learn some things quickly, she thought with frustration.

He stopped and stood up. His movement discarded her into the seat. She flopped against the stuffed back and looked up at him. He had taken the tablet with him and was staring at the image.

"What is it?"

"Nothing. Something's missing. I think."

"What? What do you mean?"

"I mean, what do you see in that picture?"

She stood up so she could see what he was looking at. All she saw was the area around the runway where all of the planes were parked. In the space he had zoomed in to, there was nothing parked and thankfully no bodies.

"Nothing?" she asked puzzled.

He leaned in and moved the picture further to the left to show her the nearby destruction.

She shook her head.

"That space has no damage. No aircraft that are destroyed. No damaged cars. No dead bodies."

"So?"

"There's nowhere else on the whole airport with the same undamaged area."

"Maybe I'm just slow, but I'm not following."

"That means there was no fighting in that space, or they cleaned up the damage in that space. I expect they were protecting what was there. I wonder what it was."

"That's a stretch."

"Not really. If the combat raged across the entire section, there is no way it wouldn't have damaged something within that very rectangular space. The equipment sitting around the space is not damaged, but no other equipment anywhere in the image is preserved. Look right here."

He adjusted the image again on the tablet and moved it until a truck was clearly visible sitting at an angle on the empty space.

"A truck."

"What kind?"

She looked closely at the squat camouflaged truck and tried to figure out what it was.

"It's a fuel truck. To the left of it is an auxiliary power unit used to power planes on the runway until they're ready to take off."

Elaine looked up at him, amazed at Charles' own version of magic.

"So, what? They took an airplane from Andrews Air Force Base?"

"Yes, and it was a big plane, probably a C-17."

"Why does that matter?"

"It's a cargo plane, a big one that can carry troops. When we deployed troops and equipment to a foreign theater, we used a C-17 or something like it."

"Which means the half-dragons and dragons were going somewhere. But why would dragons take a plane?"

"Several reasons. Modern planes are faster than a dragon flies, and this plane carries more than any dragon can. If they were taking equipment or other personnel with them, or if they wanted to take the partials, they would need this plane. If they took the president with them, that's how they got her out before the noose closed around Washington."

"So, you think she's alive."

"You do. Even though the news is not sure, the reporters saw them carry her out. They didn't do that anywhere else."

She stopped and stared at him. She was not used to anyone listening to her opinion. It took a moment for her to accept that he had. Without considering the consequences, she closed her eyes and reached out to find the president. She tried to remember how her mind felt so she could zero in on her.

When she failed to touch her mind, Elaine said, "Come with me."

She grabbed Charles' hand again and drug him down the stairs and outside to the side of the pool. Once she was standing in the same spot she had been in before, she focused on the water and reached out for the memory of the mind she had shared earlier.

The first emotion she felt was the familiar fear that had poured out of the president that morning, but there was another emotion now that was more acidic. The president was angry.

The surface of the pool again reacted as if the wind had picked up. Just as quickly it calmed. The image cleared on the surface, and all Elaine could see was a dark cargo space where the president was lying along a wall next to the five boys she had seen in the earlier vision. The president was not asleep. She was lying among her enemies and collecting information.

Elaine slipped away from the president and looked around where she was. Behind her were rows of utilitarian seats filled with people in various states of rest. The plane was full. She pulled out farther on the image again to try and figure out where they were, but all she could tell was that the plane was over the water.

Charles was walking around her and watching the water of the pool. His face seemed confused and concerned, so she released the image and looked up at him.

"What are you doing?" he asked when he saw her looking at him.

"She's alive. I was just watching her."

"Watching her, where? How?"

"The pool. It's like a crystal ball. If I focus, I can see things that are happening in it. That was how I saw what happened this morning." She was a little nervous sharing what she could do with him because of years of high school bullying. Her friends would not hesitate to shame her for being different, but it did Charles no good if she kept this a secret. He nodded and waited for more. He was living in a house with two dragons and someone who said Wodin sent him visions to find them. She suddenly realized he was not likely to judge her for seeing images in the water.

"So, where is she?" he asked.

"I don't know. She's over the water, that's all I can tell."

"Which way were they flying?"

"Wow, you really want some details."

"Well, I don't know if this is like satellite images from overhead or sitting in the room with them. I'm just trying to figure out what information you can give me."

She nodded as she realized he had no idea what she was seeing, but she also realized she could do better to find out where they were.

"Okay, fine. Let's see what I can find out."

She focused on the surface of the pool and reached out to the president again. In far less time, she was in the plane. This time, when Elaine connected, the president opened her eyes. Elaine jumped as the woman reacted to the connection. It surprised them both, and the president quickly shut her eyes to avoid letting her captors know she was awake. Elaine could not help but laugh.

"What?" Charles asked.

"The president is playing possum. She's watching her captors without them knowing it."

Elaine scanned the area around the president. She forced her mind to widen the scope of her view and suddenly the image in the pool flipped outside of the plane again. She could sense more than see the other minds in the plane. She grabbed one near the nose of the plane, and the image shifted again to the cockpit. She could see all of the gauges and a flat panel where the aircraft was represented in the center surrounded by blue. There were boxes on the screen that held constantly changing numbers. She recognized the compass rose and figured out they were flying roughly northeast. With the information she needed secured, she released the mind of the pilot and floated out of the plane.

Aldrich, who had not been with her the moment before, was now standing next to her looking at the pool. She was so connected to her image that she had not heard him walk up or felt when he had joined her viewing. She started to release the image when she felt a spike of worry and fret fill her mind. It had not come from the plane. It was farther out, but it had touched her. Aldrich placed his hand on her arm, and she could feel a disturbance in the flow of magic. It smoothed out quickly as did the image in the pool. The powerful mind that was searching was drawing her somewhere different. The pool churned as they moved around the globe. When the water calmed the image began to clear. In a moment it was as flat as a mirror. The image of a badly beaten dragon, lying on the ground in a dark cave, resolved before them.

"Kaliastrid," the tortured mind asked her. *"Is that you, Kaliastrid? If it is you, stay away. Don't come after me."*

The force of the warning and the flood of emotions that came with it threw Elaine out of control even with Aldrich's help. The image dissolved into a turbulent ring of waves. She shivered as the fear and anger pulsed through her body and sent tremors of emotion though her. The thin blond hairs on her arm stood up. Static crackled in trembling waves of Saint Elmo's fire that washed over her. It was a disturbing combination of pleasure and agitation.

"You saw that, right?" she asked Aldrich, trembling and fighting to reign in the magical explosion wanting to burst forth from her body. She was suddenly glad she had been so strict on her practice.

"I did. I think that was Valdiest. He is trying to reach out to Kaliastrid."

"She doesn't want to see that." She shivered as she shunted the magic into the ground instead of letting it out.

"She doesn't have a choice," the small man answered and turned to walk away.

"What did you want, Aldrich?" Elaine asked.

He stopped and looked at Charles before he answered.

"As important as my duties here were, this changes that. We can fix the other problem later. I must tell Melissa and Kaliastrid about this."

Confused by his comment, she let him exit and looked at Charles. "They're headed northeast over an ocean."

"What was that last part about? What did Aldrich want?"

"I'm not sure what he wanted, but we both picked up a message for Kaliastrid. It was from Valdiest. He was warning her not to come after him."

"Ah," Charles responded and turned toward the house as if he needed to get back to something.

"Wait. Stay here." She chased after him and grabbed his arm. "I need your support."

"You don't need me. You're doing fine on your own or with Aldrich. I should get back to running this manor."

"I thought she told you she wanted your help, as a friend."

"She did, but it seems that my help has limits, and I need to get back to what Helena brought me home to do. I'll protect Melissa and make sure she has everything she needs to fulfill whatever Helena needed her to do."

His words hurt a little because no matter how she treated him, he was not going to stop watching out for Melissa.

"Then if you won't stay here for me, you should stay for her. I think she's going to need you shortly."

"Why?" Charles' concern was genuine. Elaine couldn't tell if it was love or just duty. Either way, it hurt.

"Her father is not in good shape, and she's about to find that out."

~~~~

Melissa pressed through the French doors onto the patio and immediately turned toward the pool deck. As soon as Aldrich had told her they might have found Valdiest, she had to be sure. Her emotions were on edge. The promise of finding her father forced the memories of being Melissa to the front of her mind.

"What is this that Aldrich tells me? You may have found my father?"

"I think he found us," Elaine answered.

"Hmm," Melissa hummed as she walked onto the pool deck to join Elaine. As she approached, Charles dutifully shrank away from the pool and dropped back to the wrought iron fence that surrounded it. Melissa noted that she may have reversed all of the progress she had made with him in one mistaken comment. Kaliastrid joined them, followed by Aldrich. Her face showed the conflict Melissa felt. She wanted to find Valdiest, but that would mean learning where he had been and why he had not contacted them yet.

"Do you think we can find him again?" Melissa asked, looking at her mother and then Elaine.

"I'm not sure how I found him in the first place," Elaine answered.

Kaliastrid nodded. "She can find him. She found him before. We have to trust her magic. They obviously don't think there's a reason to waste effort blocking something as fundamental as scrying." She was managing her own emotions and fulfilling the supporting role she had promised to hold for her daughter.

"True."

"Scrying," Aldrich commented to Elaine. "Until I experienced it this morning...I had never known it was really possible. Based on what I know, we should be able to search for him using his magical aura as a beacon."

"That's what I did with the president, but it wasn't her magical aura. It was emotions that made it possible for me to find her. I remembered what she felt like from this morning."

"Correct. They are basically the same thing. Her emotions are intertwined with her magic, just like yours. That's why you've had to learn how to focus your magic, separate it from your emotions."

"This may not be a good idea," Melissa suggested to her mother, realizing how right Aldrich was. The power of the emotions they might be sharing could overwhelm Elaine's ability to control it.

"I don't think there's another choice. He's not reached out to me using the gems in a while. He obviously no longer has them since another dragon used them this morning. At least we know he isn't dead. We need to know what he's trying to tell us."

"You forget what we saw when Nethliast came for us. What if those were real memories and not fantasies?" Melissa warned.

"I've not forgotten," her mother sighed.

"Oh, my God," Elaine exclaimed. "I'm not sure I can take that again."

"You're not going to have a choice, I'm afraid," Kaliastrid said "We're going to need your help to find him. You will have to be strong."

Elaine visibly shivered with the warning. Melissa tried to suppress the flash of fear she felt for the young girl. No reason to make it any harder than it already would be. She looked at her mother for verification. Kaliastrid was the strongest of them all, as she seemed to set aside her own fear even knowing that her mate might be in dire condition. She was focused on helping Elaine. Melissa hoped she had not drawn the curtain on this ability back too soon.

"What, is this some kind of séance?" Charles asked. "Are you sure this is going to be safe?"

Melissa felt awkward as she tried to answer his question without further damaging their current status. "The origins of what people think of as a séance, but real. Scrying is never really safe. The target can, in some cases, possess the watcher if they are magically stronger. There is a fine line between scrying and possession."

Charles nodded but showed no change in his guarded reactions.

Aldrich was watching her every move as Kaliastrid walked over to the pool. He looked unsure of where he belonged but anxious to be of assistance.

"Of course we will require your help as well," Kaliastrid said as she nodded toward him. She indicated a position at the end of the pool across from where Elaine was standing.

Melissa looked at each of them again as Kaliastrid prepared the circle.

Elaine crackled with live mana as excitement of what she was about to experience flowed out onto the surface. It was going to be a monumental moment in her magical adventure if she didn't lose control and kill them all. Melissa considered exactly how close to full-blood she had to be to have as much power as she did. One of her parents was pure-blood and didn't know it, but pure-blood what? She had thought about her own direct lineage in human form back in time which had enabled the spell to protect her ancient soul, but she had not considered what it would be like to be an entirely new magical being spawned by a relationship between an old soul and a human. Melissa quickly referenced what she considered her "safe" memories to decide which race Elaine probably was. Convinced she knew, Melissa kept that fact to herself.

Kaliastrid motioned for Elaine to remain at the head of the pool. Melissa nodded reassuringly. Kaliastrid had made the same evaluation: Elaine belonged at the head. She stepped up on the side of the pool opposite her mother and closed the circle.

"Charles..." Her tone still came off commanding. She paused to alter it so that it sounded more like a request. "Charles, would you please sit with Elaine? She may need your support during this."

Charles nodded without smiling or showing any emotion. He simply walked to the end of the pool and knelt beside Elaine. He was appropriate because he would act as a magical synch. He was not, as far as she could tell magical, although he had something magical about him. He would be able to help her unless she lost control completely. If he was magical, he would get drawn in. What Elaine needed was a connection to the non-magical in case she needed a way back.

Elaine sat down on the tile and crossed her legs. She floated above the ground on occasional arcs of energy. Melissa was amazed at the energy she could channel. She had never seen anyone as powerful.

Aldrich was already grumbling some oddly aggressive prayer to Wodin. He was always ready to go.

Kaliastrid sat down on the other side and nodded to her. Their eyes met, but Melissa paused.

"She must lead this. We can help, but I cannot. It's going to be hard enough to keep my emotions level," her mother said.

Melissa calmed her mind and thought of Valdiest. She could see that Kaliastrid was doing the same thing while fighting her own demons. She brushed the pendant hanging around her neck with her left hand and felt the surge of power circle them.

"Elaine, Aldrich, you have never met Valdiest. I'm going to try something. I'm going to send you a thought image of Valdiest. It may not work. If it does, it should help Elaine find him again."

"I don't think I'll have trouble finding him—"

Melissa formed the thought of her father in his dragon form in her head and then passed it to each of them the same way she would send her thoughts to Kaliastrid.

Elaine screamed.

Charles reached out to support her and flinched as an arc jumped from her back and struck the palm of his hand. He pressed through the strikes and placed his hand on her back. The muscles in his arm twitched involuntarily.

Aldrich harrumphed as the image settled into his vision-battered mind.

Tears flowed out of Elaine's eyes. Charles held his hand against her back even though the blue sparks were flowing up his arm. Melissa could see the muscles trembling, and she knew she had made the right choice. He would hold on until it was over or he was dead. When Elaine regained control and the magical wave passed, he pulled his hand away and massaged his tormented muscles. Melissa smiled a thank you at him, and he returned a dutiful nod.

"Wow—that's—wow." Elaine was handling it. She wiped tears from her eyes. She looked from Kaliastrid to Melissa and smiled a child's embarrassed smile. Then she looked back at the pool and inhaled a deep breath. She released it in a long hiss as she braced for what was next. Her arms trembled as she grabbed onto the tile on the pools edge.

"Focus on the image I sent you."

"I have more than that. I have emotions. Anger, love, fear, how do I deal with all of that? I'm shaking," Elaine said through clenched teeth.

"Calm your thoughts and just absorb it. If the emotions aren't there, you may not find him. Now focus on the pool and think of Valdiest. You may sense a shift in the power around you. Just relax and lead us there."

The water in the pool shimmered like a breeze blowing across the face of a lake. Elaine's eyes grew wider than Melissa thought possible. She shivered as the power rushed around the circle. Aldrich was struggling with the emotions and the sudden increase in the flow of power. Although Elaine had experienced this before, she had never absorbed the emotion she was about to experience. Their distraction caused the connection to waver, but Melissa helped focus them with another touch of the pendant.

The shimmer settled and for a moment all was calm until her father's mind blasted into hers.

He was searching for them. After the sudden explosion of his existence, pain poured from his connection and flowed through her into the circle. There was no way to stop the emotional spring he had filled while searching for them. She focused on it. The surface of the pool turned mirror smooth, and an image formed in the water.

His huge blue form was chained to the floor and walls of a cave. There was no light in the dark hole, but the magically enhanced view brought him into focus in the darkness. His wings were obviously broken. His skin was a gray shade of blue. Both eyes had been damaged, almost gouged out. Tears streamed down Kaliastrid's cheeks, and her powerful emotions rushed through them all. Aldrich absorbed it without a sound as Melissa felt the heat wash over her. Neither of them could stop the flood as it struck Elaine from both sides like solid walls of crashing water. Her skin flushed as she gasped and trembled, but she held her focus. Flames flickered over her skin and icicles grew from the edge of the tiles on either side of her white knuckled hands.

"Focus it, child. Ride it, don't resist it. Control it or we will all be killed," Kaliastrid growled across the pool.

Elaine swallowed strongly to force down panic that was raging through her. Charles reached for her and again shuddered as the blue bolts of magical static rushed up his arm. His support seemed to settle her.

The dragon in the watery image moved, and the waves cleared fully to form a flat screen. Valdiest raised his head and looked up at the roof of his prison with sightless eyes. An orb of light appeared over his head. He shook his head when he realized it would never pierce the darkness in which he was immersed.

"Does he know we're watching him?" Elaine asked as she took in a breath and shakily exhaled it. Tears flowed down her face and onto her peasant blouse. She trembled as her lungs emptied. Lightning arcs raced across her skin. A single bolt leapt from her head and shattered a sconce atop the wrought iron fence.

Charles ducked as it passed over his head. Melissa winced, not at the loss but the danger they were all in. She had known there was a risk. Charles shook his head but held his place. This was going to get worse before it got better.

"It's rare that the target senses it," she answered. "Humans are very sensitive to scrying. Even today, people talk about feeling someone watching them, but most other races are so in tune with the magic around them that the light brush of scrying is lost. They're desensitized." She hoped the conversation might calm Elaine, but it was having no effect.

"Force the emotions you're holding back into the pool. We can all take a portion of them. You'll feel less of the load."

Kaliastrid nodded at the advice.

Valdiest stirred in the image again and stood up. His chains rattled as he pulled at them. He had to be badly injured for the chains to hold him, unless there were magic bonds she could not see.

"My love? Kali? Is that you? I've been deep in my thoughts reaching for you. Have you finally come? Please tell me that is you," he asked.

The two-way connection would be far worse. Melissa wanted to reduce the risk, not increase it. She could feel the pressure her mother was applying to reach out to him. She tried to block it, but it was too late. The emotional response filtered through them all, and Elaine looked at Melissa to explain.

Valdiest nodded at the wordless reply. A sorrowful smile filled his draconic face.

"You shouldn't be seeing me this way, my love. I'm sorry. I've failed you. I've failed all dragons. My pride has destroyed us." He shook his blind head at the ground.

"He does, he senses us. We're talking to him," Elaine cried and trembled.

"He's insane, Kali," Valdiest continued. *"Nethliast is going to get us all killed."*

The battered dragon paused to look around the cave as if he was being watched.

"Don't come for me. That's exactly what he wants. He knows you'll come for me. That's why he has kept me alive. He thinks you'll bring Melissa. He wants her to come here to fight him on his grounds. Don't come after me." Valdiest shook his head violently.

Kaliastrid gasped as tears ran down her cheeks.

"If she comes here, we are in far more danger. You know why—maybe you don't. It doesn't matter. Don't come for me."

Powerful fear ripped through Melissa's mind as a long forgotten concern about losing control of the talisman overcame her. Elaine had no idea what to filter, so it flooded out over everyone else before Melissa could stop it. A sharp pain and brilliant flash of light exploded in Melissa's head. Everyone else flinched as the sensation filled their minds. Once the pain barrier was broken, Melissa understood that the fear had always been there. It was shared by all dragons. It had nothing to do with Nethliast.

That fear was reserved for someone that all dragons hated. It was a fear of the other one Melissa had released—the human wizard. Elaine looked at her through tear-filled eyes and nodded. Aldrich swallowed the pain and fear, but nodded as well. Kaliastrid stared at the turbulent water as if she had lost something at the bottom of the pool. The image was gone.

Elaine focused back on the water. Melissa reached toward the amulet again, but before she could draw power from it Elaine increased her concentration. The image refocused.

"...there's something he needs. He knows it has something to do with Melissa and her amulet, but he doesn't know everything. He doesn't know what she is. I have no eyes, but he is the blind one. I will do my best to keep him that way." Valdiest smiled with a pride Melissa had never seen as his thoughts of her flooded the pool.

"There's no reason to rescue an old man who is trapped by his own mistakes. I'll pay for my pride. Don't risk her by bringing her here."

Again he sniffed the air as if seeking some disgusting odor nearby.

"He knew you'd try and contact me. I did too, but I'm older and perhaps a little wiser than that young fool. He's forgotten what he should know and remembers what he shouldn't. We are all suffering from our fragile minds." Valdiest paused to breathe. The rattle of fluid in his lungs echoed off the chamber's walls. Melissa cringed at how much pain he must be in. *"Tell Melissa that she was right, Kali. Tell her, I should have listened. The humans are not our enemy."*

It was Melissa's turn to cry. Her father was saying goodbye. She wanted to tell him that it was okay, but she could not stress Elaine with more emotions. She swallowed what she wanted to say.

"Listen," he continued, *"you may already know, but Nethliast has aligned with the half-breeds. He's using them to attack the humans. What he's doing is not all diversion. He wants to control the world. If he realizes there is another way. If he realizes the power he could have, he will come after you in force. Once he came back from wherever you sent him, he was convinced I knew more than I was telling him. He's still waging his war to control the humans. I failed our kind, love, but I will not give this power to him. I will take what I know with me into death. If you don't know what I'm talking about, trust me. He won't need hostages to control dragons if he finds The Heart of the Dragon."*

A feeling of awe rushed through everyone.

"Once he has used it to align the dragons behind him, he will step into the vacuum he has created in the human world. I was fooled by my passions and didn't realize what he was doing until he and his witch had overpowered me. Watch her. She's a devil. She has ancient powers passed down to her."

He turned his head and looked past their view toward what might be an entrance. He sniffed at the air. They could see his muscles relax a little.

"That one has practiced her art without the power behind it. She is as strong as any innate, stronger since she understands what power she has. Don't underestimate her."

"Kill her," he repeated.

"Kill her when you get the chance."

"Kaliastrid, hear me. Kill her."

Malice, hatred, and fear rushed into the message and washed over them all like ice water. Kaliastrid punctuated those emotions with her own contribution of rage in response. Elaine's fingernails dug into the tiles, creating unequal furrows from the edge to a point just in front of her knees. Magical flames flickered and sizzled in each gouge left behind, blackening the edges. Tears streaming down her face froze into icicles. The face in the pool relaxed more at the reassurance her reply gave him.

Elaine could not keep this up much longer. The agitation she was feeling now was more than she had ever contained. Melissa was amazed that she was able to keep the power from exploding from her. She had grown over the past few months, and she had not noticed.

"He'll know if you come here. If you do come, come to kill him, not to rescue me. I'm a trap. You have to stop him; he'll destroy us all. Don't come for me. The humans are not going to lie down. They're fighting back, but he was happy today. The humans have lost these first attacks. He knows they will come back at him hard, and he is hoping for that attack so he can show them what power he has. He'll destroy us as sure as I'm chained here. Don't come for me. He cannot have that much power."

Kaliastrid stood up abruptly, breaking the connection, and walked off into the back garden. Tremors of anger and pain flooded over Melissa. Elaine dropped the few inches onto the ground. As Elaine trembled where she sat for a moment, staring into the water, she poured the power still rippling across her body into the pool. Steam rose from her as she flopped back into Charles' arms, spent and unable to move. The water in the pool exploded into a blast of steam that rose from the center. The geyser rushed into the air and dissipated itself into a rain that fell back around the pool. A cloud of steam rose into the sky from the remaining water.

Charles looked to Aldrich as if the priest could guide him on how to help Elaine, but he was dealing with his own emotional backlash. Elaine looked unconscious. Tremors still raged along the muscles of her body. She was lying back against his chest with her eyes wide and unmoving. Melissa could tell that the Marine who had faced so much was unsure how to treat her.

Suddenly, Elaine inhaled strongly and sat up. Unable to control her emotions anymore, she started crying in huge uncontrollable sobs.

Charles put his arm across her shoulder, and she collapsed back into his chest where she continued sobbing and trembling.

Aldrich was mumbling and pacing along the edge of the pool as if the argument he was having with himself was purging the power that still filled him. They were recovering as well as could be expected. Melissa stood from her place and turned to follow her mother. The message from her father had convinced her of her course of action. There was no way they were following her father's orders. There was no way they were letting Nethliast get away with his crime. But, she also knew from the results of their including the others, the humans, that they would be destroyed if they tried to help her stop him. She would not bring that on them.

Halfway down the yard and standing looking at the gray of the rain that was coming over the mountain, she caught up to Kaliastrid. Heat emanated from her in waves.

"Did you see him, Mel?" Kaliastrid asked as Melissa walked up next to her.

She knew she had, but the question allowed her to share some of the pain.

"I know how you feel. I hated to see him that way," Melissa said. "He's fighting, though. He's on our side now, and he's fighting. That's more than we thought. Remember those feelings. We can use them to convince the others."

Kaliastrid turned and looked at her. "I was never this emotional as a dragon. I'm not sure what has happened, but I hate him, Mel. That black-scaled runt hatchling has hurt me as much as he's hurt Valdiest. Did you see his eyes? He might as well have killed him. I'm going to kill Nethliast. I was wrong before. He's going to destroy us all. His war is not just about the humans anymore. I have no choice. He's out of control, and I'm going to kill him."

Melissa felt no sorrow for the statement. Even her normally argumentative dragon mind was settled on the fact that Nethliast had created his situation. To be the target of Kaliastrid's intent was not where Melissa wanted to be. She had thought, fleetingly, that she had already killed him. Maybe it had been wishful thinking, but it made thinking of killing him again easy. Nethliast had abandoned hope of survival when he had attacked her, but to see what he had done to her father was the capstone. There was no way she could protect him even if she wanted to. Any number of dragons would kill him for what he had done to their king, but Kaliastrid was whetting a serious desire for his death. Melissa shared in her infectious desire to be the first to exact justice.

"I saw it. He's hurt us all just as bad or worse. We can't let this continue. We have to stop him."

"What about the other? What about Renard?"

"Renard didn't just attack all the sovereign nations on the planet. I don't even know if our theory is right. I don't know if Renard survived to come back. If we focus on him, we may all lose. Nethliast is going to make us hunted all over the world. I can stop Nethliast, though, or we can. If we do this, we may stop Renard as well."

They both ignored the memory that had exploded through them all while they had been connected.

Kaliastrid nodded. "Where do we go from here, then?"

"We go to him."

"What about them? What about your father's warning?"

"This is between dragons, don't you think? They can't help us with this. Humans who get caught between dragons do not fare well. They can continue searching for the talisman while we clean up our own problem. Father is right. Nethliast wants me to come to him. He wants to control dragons, but he can't control the amulet. He has to control me. That, I will never allow him to do."

Kaliastrid grinned back at her. Melissa felt a warm glow from the ancient connection between mother and child and a shared desire to see this to its end. They turned together without another word and walked back toward the house. Instead of returning to the pool or entering the house where they would have to explain their plan, they followed the path to the garage. She would call and explain this to Charles from the air. Maybe by then he would be able to forgive her.

September 6 – About the same time – Signal Mountain, TN

The flood of emotions had stopped, and Elaine was no longer wracked with other people's anger and fear. Charles' strong chest supported her, and his arms enclosed her in a caring shield. Although she was starting to feel normal again, she refused to let go of him. Why should she? It felt right for this strong man to finally be holding her. She knew he needed her comfort as much as she needed his, even if he couldn't admit it. Something had changed in the scrying circle. His embrace felt real and honest now. Had she finally breached his fortress walls?

She knew she was young for him. She knew he was too proper to ever approach her. She knew he had a duty to fulfill, and he would die before failing that. Lying there in his arms, she knew that she loved him for all of that. Somehow, she had to let him know how she felt. More than the high school games she had played so far, she had to show him.

Right now she needed his strength. She was finally in his arms. Even if it had taken a unique event to get her there, she was not going to let him go easily. When he realized she was no longer sobbing, he tried to pull away, but she tightened her grip and snuggled closer into his chest. She could not be sure that all of the feelings coursing through her were her own, but she knew how she felt about Charles. Did he share anything close to the same feelings? She knew she was out on a dangerous edge now.

"Please tell me I don't scare you," she whispered as her biggest fear rushed into her mind.

"Scare me?" He looked down into her eyes, giving her the first indication that he shared her feelings. "I live in a house with a dragon and her mother. An impossible war between humans and dragons has just started. Magic, which didn't exist a few months ago, is wreaking havoc around the world. I've been in situations where really angry people were actively trying to kill me. No, you don't scare me. I actually feel more comfortable around you than most women. I mean, I thought I might have to shoot you the first time we met, but you've grown on me." He grinned down at her, using a joke to break out of the verbal spiral he was in.

"I'm learning how to handle this, magic stuff, y'know. It's not like school. It's not like engineering and science. I have fire, ice, and lightning flowing out of my pores when I get angry or excited. Maybe you haven't noticed, *Mister Stone,* that I get excited a lot. There's no manual for this. I'm working through it."

She looked up into his eyes to make sure he was still relaxed and not turning into the stone soldier. She smiled at him when she could see the softer edges of his face and the sincerity in his eyes. She was still inside the fortress.

"I'm used to formula and fact. I'm trying to control it, but I'm just not sure I can. My morning exercises had been helping, until today."

She gazed at the pool, remembering the most difficult experience she had ever had and shivered against him. He hugged her close to him, keeping his strong arms around her.

"That," she said, as she pointed at the half empty pool, "was just awful. I mean, it was exciting and cool, but I felt everything. I felt rage like I had never known. Kaliastrid wanted to kill. I wanted to kill. I still do." She shivered as a tremor of hate ran down her arms with a bolt of residual electrical energy. "That feeling is so exciting— and terrifying— all at once. It's like standing on the edge of an abyss that I'm afraid I might get swallowed by."

Her eyes fell from his to the gouges that ran from the edge of the pool back to where her legs were tucked under her.

"Did I do that?"

"Yes, you did," he answered with no hint of judgment.

She snuggled into his chest and again he squeezed her back. It felt good to feel him care for her. She knew he cared about them all, but he held everyone at a distance. He was close to her now.

She sighed. "I thought the girls I went to school with were emotional. Those ladies, dragons, whatever, are carrying some baggage."

For a moment they just sat beside the pool. A light rain had started to fall. It was the type of rain that lasted all day and soaked everything. In seconds it became a hiss emanating from everything around them. She refused to release the comforting grip of the man she wanted to love, and he had stopped trying to let her go. It seemed right, and before it became awkward he inhaled and offered a suggestion.

"Maybe you shouldn't try to understand it."

She looked up at him as he spoke. Rain was soaking into his shirt, and his black hair dripped. He never moved to complain about it. He was not looking at her. He was somewhere else.

"I knew a guy in AIT...training, that was such a great shot on the range, but he couldn't explain the ballistics. He knew them instinctively. He had grown up shooting, and he took to a new weapon like it had been in his crib. He stressed over every written test because he couldn't translate what he knew innately to paper."

He had dropped back to a place that was so comfortable to him that he could talk without worrying about what anyone thought. This was the real Charles. He was the warrior who thought of everything from the perspective of battle strategy and tactics. He knew about the softer world he lived in. It was the reason he fought so hard. But he was not part of that world. He was the warrior who was allowed to visit it. She smiled into his chest as he talked freely.

"We worked with him on the written stuff, because we knew how good he was. We called him Cracker Jack. It was kind of a play on words because he was from the middle of Georgia. He was really southern, you know, a cracker, and he was really good at shooting."

She could feel his smile just before it broke across his face at the memory, then she felt every muscle in his body tense like someone had stabbed him. A shadow crossed over his eyes. The smile vanished in granite that blocked the same rage she had seen earlier. She was still within the fortress, but whatever he had just remembered exposed a layer within his fortress that even she was not allowed into. With obvious effort he doused the rage and went on.

"Anyway, he was like you with your magic. It's just an ability that you have. Try to let it happen. Try to feel it, not understand it."

Charles paused. Elaine knew he was somewhere else watching a memory of a happier time. The utter peacefulness of the reverie made her tremble with an energy she rarely felt. The contentment of where he was in his mind filled her with peace and calm that she never wanted to let go.

From the far off memory he started again. "He would sit out on the range with his cover off, looking down range for a long time before he even touched his rifle. It was like his hair sensed wind direction, temperature, and pressure. He knew it all without looking it up or reading the briefs. Once he owned the range— that was what we called it— once he had tasted, smelled, and touched the environment, he could shoot anything, anywhere down range."

Charles returned from his trip to a past memory and looked down at her again, remembering that he had a point.

"Keep exercising your magic. Give yourself to it, and I think you'll be more powerful than you can imagine. Start owning it. It's part of you, not something you have to learn. I have no doubt you can do it."

She snuggled into his calm.

"You can do anything you put your mind to. Look at what we've done here."

He smiled a genuine smile down at her, and a thrill traveled up her body in a shiver.

"You must be cold," he responded. "Let's take this inside."

"No, I'm not. Really. Don't make me move, please." She paused and focused what little energy she had left. She carefully thought about Charles to make sure she didn't hurt him and then she released the energy she had collected in an envelope of fire that burned just above their bodies. The warmth was immediate as the flame vaporized rain drops and started to dry their clothes.

Charles jumped a little when the flame rushed across his body. She could feel the thump of his heart as his pulse quickened.

"Don't worry. You're okay," she whispered.

He grunted an acceptance of her comment but still stared at the blue fire that flickered just above his clothes but didn't burn him.

"I'm not sure, but I don't think this is going to get better," Elaine commented. "I think about it, and it makes me very afraid. There's something dark at the root of all of this, and it's not Nethliast. Every time I look at those books, every time I dig deeper into Heliantra's past, there's a cloud hanging over it, and that cloud is always the point where Melissa and Kali's headaches start. We got a clue in the connection with Valdiest. There is something the dragons all fear. It ties back to Renard, the wizard that was released when they emerged. I don't think we'll be able to solve this without the dragons, but I don't think we can find much more here. The more I think about it, the more I think Valdiest is wrong. We can't solve this without going over there. The answer is in Germany and France You didn't feel it, but the memory they shared is important. The real threat to dragons is not Nethliast, and it's not here."

"At least we know more now than we did."

"I'm telling you, we have to go to Germany. We only have a glimpse of it here. It's fractured by time and distance. We need to get to the root of all of this. That's where Nethliast is, and I think this is why he's there, even if he doesn't know it. Renard is there too, and I'm worried that he's ahead of us. He may even already be resuming his efforts from before he was trapped. Why do you think they've stayed here? Why haven't they gone there yet?"

"I don't think they know as much about it as you do. I think they need our help to find their way. Like you said, every time they try to break through the cloud, it hurts. They doubt themselves. Tell them what you're thinking. Tell Aldrich. See what he says. I'm convinced, together you and Aldrich can convince them."

He was looking down into her eyes. Their conversation was almost in whispers. She shivered with the last release of the agitation from the encounter with Valdiest. Charles brushed a few drops of water that persisted within the flaming bubble from her forehead and pulled her closer as if her shivers were caused by the cold. She still felt weak from her experience, but a desire she had resisted for weeks overcame her. She leaned up as his embrace drew her nearer to him and hoped, for the first time, he wouldn't pull away.

In an instant of perilous hesitation her soul trembled on a precipice, waiting to find out if he felt the same way. The delay was torturous. She was not prepared for the eventual refusal. Her soul would not be able to take it if it came. This time she was sure his avoidance would actually kill her.

His head finally dropped closer and their lips brushed. Fire rushed up from within her and she felt goose-flesh rush across her body. She allowed the euphoria of the moment to fill her. The magic that enveloped them both flared, reminding her that she had to maintain control of the fire. As always it was synchronized with her emotions and she fed it with the passion she had wanted to feel for weeks.

She could feel his hot breath on her cheek, and a shiver raced down her back as the hairs on her neck rose. She wanted him to hold her forever. She arched her back, pressing herself harder into his chest and captured him again in a deep kiss. In her mind she knew he was still bound to his duty and responsibility, but she abandoned her fears to the passion of the kiss. This time she held him to her and didn't allow him to slip away. He responded by pulling her closer. Steam rose from around them as the excited fire vaporized the moisture.

September 6 – 1130 EDT – Signal Mountain, TN

Kaliastrid nodded to the guard in the shack, pulled out onto the main street in front of the estate, and turned right toward the foot of the mountain and the airport. Melissa had her cell phone out and was dialing the hanger.

"They'll have to organize a plane that can make the trip. Nethliast has had the Gulfstream in the air since we emerged. It may take a while. Do you need anything?"

"We'll need our passports. It's going to be hard to get through customs after this."

Melissa had not considered the possibility that they would not let them fly out. There could be flight restrictions that would force them to find another way to Germany, and she had not thought about it. She didn't let that bother her. She would figure out the details along the way. She continued the conversation with what facts she knew.

"My passport is at the airport. We keep them filed there in case we have to leave in a hurry. Isn't yours on file there too?"

"I don't know. Valdiest always took care of that." Her knuckles turned white on the steering wheel.

"You really want to kill him, don't you?" Melissa sighed.

"Yes. I want to kill him. Do you want to talk me out of it?"

"No, I don't. I just don't want you to lose control of your emotions. It's just like the magic you warned me about. It is an all-consuming thing. We need to stop him, but I don't want to lose you in the process."

"I und—"

The back window exploded into thousands of pieces and showered them with shards of broken safety glass. The impact propelled both of them against their seat belts. Kaliastrid fought with the sudden turn toward the other lane the impact caused. Melissa was surprised she was able to keep the car under control at all. Kaliastrid started to brake and pull over. Melissa's mind screamed, and she followed suit.

"Don't stop! Keep going."

Melissa looked back over her seat, but there was nothing to see. The trunk was wrinkled into the back seat. Bright lights framed the destruction and filled what was left of the rear window. She heard the acceleration just before the vehicle behind them hit again.

The sound of rending metal filled the car. The front wheels lurched to the right. Kaliastrid fought for control, but the chase vehicle was pushing them. Nothing she did had any effect. Before she could get the tires to turn them away, the edge of the road and the mountain loomed up in the windshield.

The front of the Mercedes hit the cable barrier designed to keep vehicles on the road. In the chaotic impact, the seat belts clutched at them and held them in place. The bumper buckled, and the world in front of Melissa exploded in a silvery white explosion as the deploying airbag slammed into her face.

Melissa couldn't see. She was dazed by the impacts, and the crazy motion around her disoriented her more. She thought the car had flipped. Glass was showering all over them. She thought they were upside down. The sound of grinding metal indicated they were sliding down hill on the roof of the car. Magically, she reached out to slow their slide without really thinking about it. They slowed down and slid up against a tree that otherwise the car would have struck.

Silence descended around her. She could hear the hissing, angry sounds of the tortured engine and the dripping, tinkling noises of everything continuing to come to rest around her. When she took the first breath she remembered since hitting the barrier, panic raced into her mind. Someone had hit them intentionally.

She reached up to her belt to release it and allow herself to drop to the roof of the car. It resisted her attempts because of the weight straining against it. They had to get out. What had happened? Who had hit them?

An arm appeared in the shattered window of her door. Someone was going to help her out. The hand turned toward her, and she could see something in it. Her mind screamed that it was a pistol. She could feel the reactive transition starting when the silent puff from the pistol shocked her. She screamed as the round struck her in the chest. Sharp pain rushed out from the impact and was followed by an amazingly fast rush of warm relaxation. Her vision clouded. She couldn't think. It seemed her instinctive transition had been stopped. The little light that filled the car was getting darker. A bright flashlight crossed her face, but even that light failed to hold off the darkness that swallowed her into the silent, black abyss.

~~~~

The sound of rending metal and breaking glass jerked Charles violently back from his passion. His pulse was well beyond control, and he was shivering from a combination of her magic and his own abandon. Elaine's hands were on the back of his neck and head trying to guide him back to her.

He pulled away to listen, and he felt a chill as the fire around them fell back to a low simmer. Elaine looked up at him with an agitated question on her face.

"What's wrong?"

"Did you hear that?"

"No, what is it?"

Agitation chilled him more as he set his passion aside and listened to his danger sense. He needed her help to figure out what was wrong. He had shifted entirely to a state of combat alertness.

He slipped out from under Elaine, careful to help her stand. With each move she tried to maintain a connection or to keep holding him. He fought with the agitation it caused. He didn't want to break away from her embrace. He hated the necessity, but the air told him something was wrong. The interruption of their embrace caused her to release the magical shell that had surrounded them, and the rain now pelted down on him again.

"I'm not— "

Before he could complete his explanation, a screeching, crashing sound filled the night air. The noise lasted longer than the first. Her face showed that she had heard it this time as well. His gut wrenched, and he was moving toward the front gate and the road before he really knew why.

The resistant tug of her hand as she tried to hold onto him paused him. He looked back and saw the crushing disappointment in Elaine's eyes. As their hands separated, he watched the disappointment morph into tendrils of anger. He hoped that she would be able to understand, but he could not wait to find out.

He turned away from his peace to face the unknown of war and ran for the gate.

When he reached it, the man in the shack passed an M-4 carbine out to him.

"Sounded like an accident. I was about to call 911, but that second hit sounded more like an intentional ramming," the guard said.

Charles slung the rifle sling around his neck and nestled the butt against his shoulder to check the configuration and sight picture. The M-4 carbine didn't have the range of the longer rifle it had been created from, but it was good for securing the property, not to mention that it looked wicked to anyone who was watching them. With practiced ease, he dropped the thirty round magazine from the bottom of the rifle and checked the load. Satisfied with the quick glance, he slammed it back into the slot, thumbed off the safety, and yanked the cocking lever back as he walked through the gate to look down the road toward the noise he had heard.

"I guess you agree," the guard said to his back as he charged his own rifle.

He hadn't forgotten everything he had learned as a Marine, and the Boy Scout in him never rested. He'd deal with the paperwork later. It was action time.

He took a moment to feel the air, thinking again of his buddy Cracker Jack. It felt tense. The accident, if that was what it had been, was probably not more than a mile down the road. His stomach continued to support the nagging feeling that something was wrong, and he had learned in combat that his gut was his best counselor. He looked back at the gate guard.

"Lock it down. Nobody in or out."

The guard stepped into the middle of the road leading into the estate and blocked the entrance with an ominous stance. Elaine, who had followed Charles to the gate, stood behind the guard, staring at him.

The look on her face had changed again. This new look he regrettably recognized. It was the look his mother used to give him when he had broken one of any number of delicate trinkets scattered around the estate combined with a more troubling gaze he had seen so often when faced with civilians in a war zone. It was the painful glare of "what are you" that no soldier could ever avoid when the soft side of life abruptly met the violent side of man.

He shrugged at the sadness that overcame him whenever he saw that look. It ultimately appeared whenever someone finally saw him for what he really was. It was universally disappointing. The thought that the one vocation he felt very comfortable with scared her hurt him, but as he had done so many times before, he compartmentalized that pain for evaluation later.

Something foreign to him made him bring his hand to his mouth and toss her a kiss.

"Please tell me I don't scare you," he whispered to the rain in an echo of her own fear and hoped she would be as understanding as he was.

She smiled a weak smile, but the disappointment still showed behind her failed attempt to comfort him across the distance.

He repositioned the rifle, shifted the weight of her disappointment onto his shoulders, and focused on what he had to do. No time to second-guess now. He would deal with whatever remained when the threat was over.

As he was preparing to walk away, Aldrich rushed up the driveway on his short legs.

"I heard a crash. Kaliastrid's car is gone. They're not on the estate. I can't find them. What's going on?"

Charles nodded, gave the gate guard a look that said *we will talk when I get back*, and added that information to his deck. He had no time to worry about what that might mean until he was down the road.

"Take Elaine back to the house. I'll let you know what I find out. Make sure you both stay in the main house."

Aldrich nodded and went to Elaine. She hesitantly accepted his proffered hand and turned toward the house. Her eyes never left Charles as he turned away from them to focus on what was waiting for him down the road.

Charles took two steps and broke into a run that would cover the mile quickly without wearing him out completely. He couldn't discount the fact that he might have to fight when he reached the scene, and for that he would need energy and breath. He was wearing a pair of quarter height urban style combat boots along with the tactical pants and shirt he had started wearing instead of his formal suits after Melissa's emergence. After the fight with Nicklaus and the encounter with Agent Loxley, it made sense to be ready to react in case something else happened.

The cool September air and the rain helped keep him from overheating as he ran. All along he hoped it was just an accident and he'd be pulling some kid out of the woods. But, something about the way it sounded, the two hits, made the hairs on his arms rise and heightened his combat senses, dulled some by inaction but not forgotten.

He reached the first crash site in a few minutes of running and quickly scanned it. His pulse was slightly elevated, and he was working to get his breathing back under control as he took in the scene. He instinctively dropped into a crouched advance, stepping carefully forward with his rifle at his cheek. His right eye took in the scene with his sight picture overlaying it. His left eye took in the scene without obstruction. Either way he was ready. He edged along the road barrier while covering an area against the mountain that was a viable ambush zone. Glass sprayed out toward the edge of the road. There were no skid marks. The chase vehicle had hit without warning and without stopping. There was some braking from the front vehicle, but the wet ground had rendered it useless. There was no evidence of over-controlling. The chase driver was a pro. This was no accident. Charles paused one last time to scan the area for unseen observers or ambushers left behind to mop up, but saw nothing.

He abandoned the covering stance and ran beyond the initial impact. Because of the speed they were traveling, a few seconds separated each impact, but, on the ground, the distance between them was much greater.

The next scene was worse and immediately eliminated any remaining doubt. He again slowed his approach and brought his rifle up as he scanned the area. The rear vehicle had hit again at a point where the front car could not recover before striking the barrier. They had tried. At the edge of the road, more glass—from the headlights and possibly the side windows—spread out around the cable where the front car had smashed into the barrier. The car had not stopped. Given the speed it was traveling when it hit, Charles guessed it had flipped as it continued over the edge. He could smell the mixed odors of a hot engine, anti-freeze, and oil still hanging in the moist air. At the edge of the road above where the vehicle had impacted, he saw the still smoking Mercedes at the bottom of a long sloping draw that descended away from the edge of the road. Again, he scanned for anything hiding in ambush around the car.

It was a perfect spot for a non-fatal crash. The impact with the trees farther down the hill would have hurt, but the long slide would have slowed them down enough so that it would not be fatal, assuming the speed was controlled and the occupants were wearing seat belts. The setup was well planned and probably practiced. This was no accident. This was a grab.

The broken headlights of the car faced him. The crumpled front end that tried to stop at the edge was upside down. The doors had been wrenched open. He couldn't tell from where he stood if there was anyone still in the car or not, but it wasn't likely. A sick feeling filled him. This was not a dragon or half-dragon setup. Charles paused before he let his prejudices cloud his judgment. Based on everything that had happened that morning this could be a dragon hit, but it didn't feel that way. They had tried to take Kaliastrid in a night raid and failed. They had never tried to take Melissa, so why lay in wait like this? This had all of the indicators of a special forces snatch, and the more he thought about it, the more it felt like something an irritating spook from Washington might try.

He spun around, looking for any more evidence. There were tracks in the soft ground on the side of the road. The wheel base was wide for a car, and the wheels that made the impressions needed power. It looked like a Humvee. He replayed the scene in his mind as the car reached the edge and the Humvee stopped. In Charles' mind he could see the face of the over-confident, puzzle-working agent in the black SUV watching as the soldiers executed his plan. Whether he had been there or not, this was his play.

He jumped the barrier, still hoping he was wrong. His feet hit ground just over the edge, and his knees flexed to take the landing. He brought his rifle up immediately and scanned the mountainside for anyone left behind to stop him. The rain made the ravine treacherous. He found himself sliding and hopping down the initial drop until he was following the shallow draw. When he reached the car he scanned the area for threats like a machine, following the barrel of the rifle with his eyes. He could see signs that others had proceeded him through the fallen leaves.

When he reached the driver side door, he checked the interior. It looked like there was a little blood but nothing to be concerned about. The hit had been hard but not deadly. He didn't smell cordite, so no one had been shot here recently.

Something was lying on the inside roof of the car. He slung the carbine over his back and reached for it. His fingers found a cell phone and pulled it toward him. It was familiar. He didn't have time to verify it was Melissa's, but it was very similar. Whoever had done this had come for the people. They didn't need intelligence, or at least not what the phone could tell them.

He checked the car again to be sure he had not missed anything and then headed back toward the road. There would be plenty of evidence of who had snatched them in the area around the car, but he didn't have time to gather it. He had enough. Now he was focused on evidence that refuted his theory, and he was finding none. Close to the road he found more proof. In the rough briers at the last rise, someone had been caught in Tennessee "damn-it vines," the insidious wire-like vines that covered the mountains of the region. Once they grabbed something you either had to back out or surrender a tithe. Usually fabric was enough, but sometimes they had to have flesh. He hoped this had been one of those occasions, but there was no way he could tell from the strip of cloth left behind.

The torn cloth was hard to see, but it was there. They had been in a hurry or they never would have left it behind. This was a quick smash and grab.

He turned the material over in his hands to examine it. Summer weight, rip-stop, digital camouflage, gray; but who was it? The National Guard had the equipment and the men, but they had not been called up yet. They lacked the skill to execute a grab like this. Someone he knew in the guard would have told him if something like this was up. He scanned the edge of the road again and found the next clue he needed. The sharp heel imprint in the mud showed where someone in combat boots had stood and watched the extraction. Again, the weaselly guy from Washington came to his mind. If he had done this, Charles would have to break him a little when he caught up with him, assuming there was anything left when Melissa was done.

He jumped up onto the edge, over the cable barrier, and started his run back to the estate. There was no need for caution. Whoever had executed the grab was gone. This was not designed to draw anyone else in. He needed to find out where they had taken Melissa.

As he ran he considered who he could contact. He suddenly realized Melissa had been right. If the government thought she was a dragon, they would just take her. They knew she was ready and protected in her estate, so they had waited for her to leave. Standard tactic for high profile targets. Grab them on the move when they're vulnerable. He suddenly felt ashamed of his continuous agitation about her keeping secrets. He should have been prepared for something like this. He had to remember, the government was not a moral entity. They would use her just like any other asset to accomplish their goal. In cases of war it was too easy to suspend a person's rights. He had seen it happen often enough. She had been right to believe they would take her if they knew. Charles chewed on his crow for a moment longer before grinning.

Talk about having a tiger by the tail. They had no idea what they had just taken into their midst even if they thought she was a dragon. If they didn't know it would be even worse. Melissa would probably die before she hurt anyone, like she had said, but the car in the woods was Kaliastrid's. Both women were running on emotion since their encounter with Valdiest.

The idea of them being captured by anyone made him angry, but then he thought about what they could do. He didn't wish that on his worst enemies. None of that changed the fact that he was going to talk to Melissa as soon as he found her. She had to know it was stupid to leave without telling him. For a wise old dragon, she acted like a twenty-something girl far too often.

CHAPTER 3 - BY THE TAIL

September 6 – 1900 EDT – Signal Mountain, Tennessee

Elaine leaned back from the edge of the pool to stretch her back. She had been staring at the blank pool waters for several futile, angry hours. In frustration she released her control over the liquid. With a single push of her mind and a motion of her hand, she released a forceful blast of magical energy into the water, driving a hole into the depths. Water exploded from the lowered surface of the pool as the fluid collapsed around the void.

Ever since they had taken Melissa, Charles had been a different man. He was focused on finding her. Nothing else could distract him without making him angry. It had been hours since their lips had touched, sparking the passionate kiss that she was afraid they would never repeat, and yet she could still feel it. Frustration lashed away from her in another forceful blast and spray of water.

Elaine was agitated by how he could see details in a picture taken from forty-thousand feet, but he couldn't see how his sudden focus on Melissa following their kiss hurt her. Over the past twelve hours he had contacted every friend he still had in the military and a few who worked on the fringes. None of them had any information on who had taken Melissa or where. While he had talked he had loaded enough gear into the Land Rover to capture a small island in the Caribbean. That was the kind of dedication she wanted to inspire. Melissa had no idea, but she inspired crusade. Helen of Troy would be jealous. Elaine's shoulders slumped as she surrendered. Tears, which she normally shunted away, streamed down her face. She was invisible to him now, at least until they found Melissa.

Elaine hated being jealous of Melissa. She knew, even without her mother wandering around in her head telling her, that it was counterproductive, but it was how she felt. She had been in his arms, beyond the boundary of his damned emotional fortress, and now she was looking up at the outer walls from among the peasants. The ache of jealousy ate at her for a few minutes while she fought to hold back the magical energy that wanted to blast a hole in the side of the manor house.

She stood up to stretch her tight muscles and shook off the chill seeping into her from the edge of the water. It was the first time she had really moved since Charles had locked himself away to his phone calls, planning, and brooding.

She zipped the gray MIT fleece warm-up over her corset to fight off the cold and laughed at the outfit she was still wearing beneath it. What had she been thinking? She had no chance. There was no way she could even begin to compete with Melissa's charm. She was a dragon, for God's sake, and gorgeous as a human. No matter what Elaine chose to wear, she couldn't compete with that. She wanted to charge into the garage where he had locked himself away and give him an opportunity to make his choice final, but she knew the result of that. Why accelerate the inevitable? She laughed out loud at the situation. It wouldn't matter if she was naked. He had made his choice.

There was a cool breeze blowing across the top of the ridge after the rain had cleared. Stretching her arms over her head and looking up she saw the twinkling stars in the disturbed atmosphere. She watched them for a moment as she tried to get the thoughts of Charles out of her head and thought back over what had actually happened the day before.

Dragons and half-dragons, what everyone was now calling partials, had attacked the world. They had successfully driven most countries into a corner with a blitzkrieg worthy of the name. Magic was proving a potent weapon against modern armaments, as Melissa had noted to Charles when they had first emerged, but her own magic had not been able to stop someone from capturing her and her mother. Now, they were all searching for her in their own way and waiting for some sign of what to do next. In twenty-four hours, dragons and partials had stopped all progress on her search for Helena's legacy and completely derailed her relationship with Charles. She felt a twinge of embarrassment at her childish thoughts, considering how much worse things were in other places, but she could not hide from how she felt.

Her thoughts lingered for a moment on the fleeting closeness they had shared only a few hours before. It seemed so far away now that she questioned if the kiss that still burned on her lips and in her loins had actually happened. She felt the sting of tears at the edge of her eyes returning and could hear her mother in the back of her head telling her how useless crying was. Crying had never been allowed, it never solved anything, but at the moment it felt good to cry. With each hot tear that streamed down her cheek she felt the emotions she had never allowed out.

She could be angry at her mother. She touched the tear and let fire consume it.

She could feel attraction for Charles. Another tear immolated on her finger tip.

She could feel aversion for Nethliast and his plans. Fire leapt a foot into the air from her finger.

She could feel gratitude for Kaliastrid's kindness and motherly concern for her. Another plume of fire consumed a tear.

She could feel rage at Melissa for letting all of this get out of hand, for losing control of Nethliast, for getting between her and Charles. A fireball leapt from her hand and climbed into the air, consuming that tear.

Elaine released the last emotion and let the rest of the tears flow. Her mother would be embarrassed. She didn't know how her father would feel. She looked at the pool, which had been her refuge. It had given her a calming control that she had been lacking. Now it was nearly a foot low and scarred for all of its efforts. She shuddered as the emotions, some that seemed foreign to her and driven by the earlier scrying, forced tears out. Her mother was again in the back of her mind telling her how much of a waste of time this was. On a whim she focused on the pool and her mother at the same time. She was working, as always. She was alone. The delicate touch of the scrying mind caused her to look around as if someone called her and then she looked at the picture frame on her desk. It held an old photo of her father that Elaine had not seen in years. Nestled next to that photo was a recently printed image of her winning the high school collegiate bowl the year before. A tear, condemned as a waste of time, slipped from her mother's eye and hung on her chin. Elaine inhaled an emotional breath as she watched her mother's hidden soft side cry in her office.

"Wherever you are, my sweet elf, I hope you're safe," her mother whispered to the picture. "I hope you're happy. I hope you can forgive me for not listening." She stroked the image along the edge of Elaine's picture before wiping the tear from her chin and turning back to her job. Elaine sent a gentle nudge of reassurance at her mother and released the connection. She would need to tell her she was okay. Maybe she would go visit her as soon as they found Melissa.

With new resolve to find an answer, Elaine focused her mind and channeled her emotions back into the search. There had to be a way to find Melissa. Maybe if she found her, Charles would see her again.

Feeling a little relieved by the stretch of her body, the catharsis of her cry— *see mom, it does serve some purpose*— she settled back onto the edge of the pool, the cauldron of her recent discoveries. She repeated the search she had used to find the president twelve hours before and every hour since Melissa had disappeared. In her mind she conjured thoughts of what she knew of Melissa, but as usual there was no response. She changed her search to try and find Kaliastrid with the same results. Frustration agitated the waters of the pool as she brought her focus back to herself. The image settled as she watched herself stare into the infinite mirror over her own shoulder. With a frustrated burst of mana she smacked the water, dispelling the agitating image. She could feel the power she had control over course out of her, and it was a feeling she never wanted to be separated from again. It was distilled emotion that she controlled. No one else controlled it. It was hers, more than anything else ever would be. How had she ever lived without the connection to the magic? The sudden feeling of elation made her think of Charles and the kiss again.

She focused the thought as it formed. She had invaded his agitated space nearly every hour as well. It was not hard to find him. He was loading something else into the cargo area of the Land Rover while he was pacing and talking on the cell phone. It was clear from what she felt when she tuned into his emotional and mental signature how he felt. It was clear he loved Melissa. Elaine swallowed the ball that formed at her throat as she experienced that feeling from him.

Crates of ammo for his rifle and pistol, an overstuffed bag of gear, and two unmarked Pelican cases filled the back of the SUV. He was dressed in black nylon tactical pants and a matching shirt. A tactical vest filled with pointed and angry-looking tools topped off his outfit. Watching him focused on destroying whoever had taken Melissa gave her a thrill. It filled her body with the same feeling that had burned in her when they had kissed, and she wanted to feel that again. She allowed herself to think, as she had each time before, that he was looking for her. She knew it was a fantasy, but it was a way to keep the pain of his abandonment under control.

He stepped back to review the load in the car. He checked off each item and even walked through unloading it to verify that everything was in quick and easy reach. Although he was agitated, she did not sense any of the rage he had suppressed earlier. She thought about why as she watched him check off his list like a machine. This was war. This was what he did, and he did it well. Although his actions were driven by a fear for Melissa's safety and a love he denied, there was a beauty to his preparations, violence focused. It reminded her that she had to have control of her emotions to be effective, but she was not sure she could control the pain of his rejection.

An occasional comment to the phone was the only real indication that he was waiting on something.

"You have no intel on him at all? How is that possible?"

Elaine couldn't hear the response on the phone, but she immediately knew who he was looking for. Charles believed Agent Loxley was behind the abduction. What if she could find him? She had not tried that route yet. If Charles was right, and he was involved, then wherever he was, she would find Melissa. She had only met Loxley that one day. She wasn't sure it would be enough to find him. She focused on what little she remembered of his presence and channeled her emotions into the search.

In her mind she recreated the day they had met with all of its thrills. The agent was looking down on them from the second floor of the library. She embraced the fear. Charles was on one knee aiming his rifle at him from the lower floor where everyone else was watching. She pulled the desire out of that moment. She could feel her own magic spike as the memory of her agitation filled her mind. Kaliastrid's patient assistance was keeping her from losing control. He had scared her. He wasn't supposed to be there. He was going to find out Melissa's secret. She could see him in her mind clearly. With that image she reached out for him.

Faintly at the edge of her mind she felt him and then lost him. He was not resisting. How could he? She just needed more of something. What emotion was she blocking? She thought through the scene again and realized she was not allowing her desire for Charles to fully blossom in the thought. She refocused, forcing herself to feel the painful desire and reached out to find him again. This time the waters churned and then flattened with his image.

He was in a dark car driving alone. Melissa was not with him. Elaine let the frustration of not finding her break the connection, then she thought better of it. Maybe he was heading to where she was. She reached out again, much more confident of reconnecting.

He gripped the steering wheel with an intensity that told her he was upset about something. His hand shot to his waist, and she thought he might be reacting to her, but he pulled his cell phone out and scowled at the useless black screen.

He had thrown a couple of Pelican cases in the back. A printout of Google Earth directions sat on the seat beside him. She zoomed in on the printout and recognized some of the roads. He was in Tennessee.

He was preoccupied by his own thoughts and appeared to be in the same focused state as Charles, but she couldn't tell why he was agitated. Like she had with the president, she slipped away from him and looked around where he was. The signs on the freeway indicated he was near Knoxville, which matched the directions he was following. If he was on his way to them, he was about two hours away, but why would he be coming to them? She zoomed back in on the car and the papers. It was hard to tell, but it looked like he was close to his destination.

"Any luck?"

She jumped as Aldrich's question advised her that she was not alone. Another hour had passed. She lost her connection as she looked at the cleric with an angry scowl.

"I'm sorry, I should have waited until you were free," Aldrich said as he realized he had broken her connection by surprising her. "But, that means you have something. This is an improvement. Progress." The ever-positive lilt in his voice agitated her for a moment, but that emotion she squelched.

She relaxed from her surprise and answered his question. "No, not really. Like Charles said, she's probably sedated and will be until they're ready to talk to her."

"Can I help?"

His honest interest reminded her of the first day they had met. He had helped calm her and showed her how to better manage the magic she still could not control. He had given her the secret to controlling it and living in the magic rather than fighting it every day. He was the reason she could feel emotions again.

"Maybe—I don't know. I'm new to this and have no idea. You helped with the search for Valdiest. Maybe you can."

He smiled at her like he had that first day, and she suddenly felt calmer. "Where should I stand or sit?"

"Just sit next to me. I'm not sure there's a pattern we have to follow."

He nodded and sat down next to her. He looked troubled.

"What's wrong?" she asked.

"I never like it when Wodin thinks everything is happening as it should be."

"What? I thought you worshiped him?" She couldn't help but find his comment humorous.

"Worship? No. I'd never survive such a passive relationship with him. He's a god of the Norse for a reason. The All-Father does not have worshipers." He paused to let his comment sink in before continuing. "When I wander from Wodin's way, he uses suffering to teach me, but when he's happy, there is no telling what kind of pain is about to befall the world. It is interesting that a god of all wisdom, finds humor in us learning it."

She looked at him to let the thought settle, and he gave her an appropriate moment to do so.

"Anyway, no matter how I entreat him for Melissa's situation, he advises me that everything is going as it needs to. That is not good news for her, and you can not imagine how disappointing that can become over several hours of searching."

"It sounds like there's no easy way with Wodin."

"To follow Wodin, one will be strong." He grinned at her in the light reflected from the pool. "To have his interest at all means your life is difficult. Some days, I would much prefer if he simply ignored my inquiries. That would mean he doesn't care about what I'm asking about. That would be better for us all. I could go back to the silence before the emergence. Although he has always found a way to touch and control my life, lately he has been brutal."

"I see. I think. I could never go back to my life before this. The feeling of having magic flowing through you is euphoric. I would miss that feeling even though there is always a risk of losing control."

"Be careful of that feeling. There's a danger in letting emotions get involved in magic. That's a risky path. You would be better off to find the path of pure magic and leave the emotions out of it."

She felt like a child who had said something wrong. His comment made her scowl momentarily, but she let it pass and routed their discussion back on topic. "You want to see if we can find Melissa?"

"Of course. Lead us to her."

She smiled at his gentle gesture and focused on Melissa again. This time, a distant whisper that had been absent appeared and drew Elaine to her. She paused to make sure she had not made a mistake. Aldrich looked at her puzzled by her delay. He had felt the connection as well. She focused again with his help and found the thread of consciousness. They were in a small room that reminded her of an examining room in a hospital, but not as comfortable. Melissa was lying on a cot. A blond woman in some kind of uniform was looking at her. The woman was writing notes on a clipboard as Melissa rolled over. They had found her. Enthralled to have a clue, Elaine quickly pulled back to find out where she was. It took a little searching to find any solid indication, but then it all made sense.

She was in Oak Ridge, Tennessee. Agent Loxley was on his way there now. She had to tell Charles. This was her ticket back into his life. Maybe he would remember she existed. Maybe he would see her again. It would be too much to ask for him to love her, but she had not given up entirely on that either.

September 6 – 1925 EDT – Signal Mountain, Tennessee

"I've found her!" Elaine's words fired off in Charles' head like a starter's pistol. "She's in Oak Ridge, and she's alive."

Charles grabbed the strap of his rifle, hung up his phone, stepped across the floor of the garage and into the front seat of the Land Rover. He stowed the rifle in the seat behind him at an angle and looked back at Elaine and Aldrich, who were still standing where they had entered the garage.

"Let's move. We have to get there if we're going to help her."

Shock and another emotion he recognized but didn't understand registered on Elaine's face as she realized he was really ready to go. Charles chafed at the delay that was elongating as they both still stood staring at him. She should have been ready, and Aldrich should have helped her.

"I need—"

"Five minutes, no more. Meet me at the front door." He cut her off. She scowled at him. He puzzled over how she could be mad at him. She was the reason they were not on their way. She turned in a huff toward the house.

Aldrich slipped into the back seat on the passenger side, and Charles drove out of the garage into the circular drive. He noted how Aldrich adjusted the rifle where it was not in his seat but still reachable. He was not afraid of weapons. That was a good sign for the strange little man.

"You have time if you need to get something. I don't know how long this is going to take."

"She will be quick. She's been busy looking for clues. I travel light." He patted the never far off messenger bag. "I can count on Wodin to provide whatever. Whether I need it or not." He drew three bone tiles from a bag at his waist. He laid them out on the console beside Charles.

Charles nodded at his decision to stay and let the man continue with his devotional. He stared back out the front windscreen to let the news of Melissa's situation settle into his mind. He wanted to know more, but the fact that she was alive and near meant there was something he could do immediately. The rest of the intelligence, if there was any, could be reviewed on the way. He could feel the adrenaline pulsing into his mind and chasing the cobwebs of fatigue away as he worked through the possible scenarios. He drummed his fingers mindlessly on the steering wheel.

"This is good news, I expect," Aldrich said from the back seat, having retrieved his tiles. "The Norns say that this difficult situation is exactly what we need to move forward."

Charles grunted at the comment without really hearing what Aldrich said. Glancing at his watch and then at the door, he counted the time down before he could start getting angry. He didn't want to be upset with Elaine.

For some reason she was suddenly angry, and complaining that she was not ready would not help. She should have been ready. They'd had all day to prepare. What could she have been doing? She had more than enough time to be ready. Aldrich was ready. Each thought made him more angry, but he had to control that. He turned to Aldrich to get his mind off of it.

"Did you see her?" Charles asked to keep from letting his irritation turn into anger.

Aldrich looked up into the mirror and into Charles' searching eyes. "Yes, for a moment, before we broadened the search for a location. She was okay."

"What does that mean? Tell me her condition. Had they hurt her?" Charles realized his questions sounded panicked, and he changed his tone after taking a breath. "How many captors were there? Did you see who was holding her?"

"I'm sure we can find out, but we didn't linger long on the image once we found her. Elaine wanted to get this news to you as quickly as possible, because it had taken so long to find her. The location was secluded. It was away from town in what looked like an area that was long deserted. We didn't see anyone else around her."

Charles looked at his watch again and back at the door.

"She'll be here soon. She knows how important this is."

"She should have been ready."

"Perhaps I was not clear," Aldrich snapped. His eyes grabbed Charles' attention and held his gaze as he spoke. "She's been trying to find Melissa for hours. Maybe you should consider that and be thankful for the help."

Charles felt the impact of the chastisement and held the gaze of the powerful eyes in the mirror. It was almost as if he could not look away. Charles nodded at the castigation. Aldrich's stock went up. He knew how to protect his team.

"Point taken. Anything else I should know?" Charles asked, accepting the guidance from the wise man.

"She loves you."

For some reason, the last statement punched him harder than the fatherly warning about his patience. He didn't have time to linger on his emotions or hers. He had to focus on the mission at hand. How she felt was not a secret, not anymore, but to have it reinforced from Aldrich was enlightening.

"I care about her as well, but this is not the right time to get involved."

"When is?" Aldrich asked him with a knowing smile. "There may never be a perfect time in your life."

Charles looked into the eyes as Aldrich delivered the advice with no malice. Charles started to respond with another excuse when the front door opened and Elaine rushed out carrying her backpack and a glass of water. He glanced at his watch and was impressed that she had made it out in three of the five minutes he had given her.

"What is the glass for? I have bottled water in the back. Why did she take time to do that?"

Charles continued to analyze her as she ran down the steps, across the headlights of the car, and opened the passenger door. He realized he was inspecting her the way he would a new recruit. Nothing else increased his irritation, but the glass of water was a puzzle. It wasn't even full.

Her pack was in the floorboard before the door was completely open. An instant later she was in her seat and the door was closed.

"Go," she said as she settled into the seat. No other explanation or comment. She became a silent passenger.

His eyes met Aldrich's in the mirror as he turned his head to look at her. His foot was on the accelerator, and they were moving as he nodded to her. He stared at the half full glass.

Elaine noted his attention. "I expected you would want more information than just the location. I need a focus to keep track of her. They could move her. It will be easier to keep track rather than trying and find her when we get close."

Charles felt the knife of his own judgment and prejudice in his side. She had been prepared and even thought ahead about what he needed. The eyes in the back seat were smiling at her and deepening Charles' embarrassment. There was still an edge to her voice.

"Aldrich, can you focus with me? I don't want to lose her," Elaine asked with less acid.

"Of course," he answered.

This was the second time he had watched them do this. The first time had left Elaine an emotional wreck on the side of the pool and had led to her sharing her feelings for him. He was not going to have time to console her now if it had the same effect.

"I can't stop right now. Are you going to be okay doing this while I'm driving?"

Elaine looked up from the glass in her lap. Her gaze avoided his eyes.

"Just drive," she said.

"Do you need a light?" he asked as he reached for the dome light.

"No, don't worry about it. I can see what I need."

Charles returned his focus to the curving road that descended into the urban business districts of Signal Mountain. He didn't need any more indication that she was angry with him. He would have to figure out what he had done.

The traffic at the light on Taft Highway was non-existent at two o'clock in the morning. He paused just long enough for it to look like a stop, then shot through it. That was the last delay before he reached the base of the mountain. As they were passing the landmark Spaceship House on the side of the mountain, Elaine was sharing information with him. Charles raced into the early morning darkness of the rural roads between Chattanooga and Kingston on the most direct route to Oak Ridge and Melissa.

September 6 – 1937 EDT – An unfamiliar room in a strange place

Melissa came to on the canvas of a surplus cot. It smelled of storage and long ago wars. Senses struggling in the fog of her mind told her she was not alone.

"Kaliastrid!"

She rolled over expecting to see her mother but was shocked when she saw a blond female in a light blue shirt and black tie sitting next to her on a stool. The black name plate on her shirt said "Simmons." The single golden bar on her collar indicated her rank, but Melissa had no idea what it was. They were in an old block room that was as surplus as the cot. The woman was sitting on a small stool with her right leg crossed over her left and her foot dangling at Melissa.

Melissa sat up. There was no way she was facing this, whatever it was, lying down. Anger bristled at the back of her neck as she tried to figure out where she was and why.

"Welcome back, Helena, or do you prefer Melissa?"

"Melissa. Where am I?"

"You've been in an accident, and I need some information, Melissa."

Melissa paused to process the comment. She did not connect what the two had to do with one another. Shouldn't a nurse be asking her questions if she had an accident?

"Who are you?"

"You can call me April. You say you're an ambassador to the dragons. Why did they attack us?"

The direct questions came immediately, and Melissa suddenly realized this was not about the accident. Her mind struggled to find an answer, and April tapped her dangling foot quickly as if she was impatient for an answer.

"I warned them. I told them I needed their assistance in stopping it." Melissa felt light-headed and immediately tried to figure out the cause. Was she under a charm? No, this was chemical. A gentle surge of her dragon blood into her human system burned up whatever it was. Her head cleared instantly. The anger hung around, though.

"Kaliastrid?" She reached out to her mother to see if she was also being interrogated.

"Yes, you did say something about that. Why did you tell us to look for them in Germany? Why didn't you tell us of the threat here?"

Melissa adjusted herself on the cot before answering. She straightened her back and pushed her chest out to send her subliminal message of resistance to her captor.

"You should check your transcript. I warned about this very possibility. I don't think I'm going to answer any more of these questions. I am an ambassador, recognized or not. I am not required to answer you. I'm also a citizen and have rights. They have been violated by these actions."

April reacted to the sudden clearheaded response and wrote a note on her pad. She sat upright on her stool, dropping her dangling foot to the floor, and paused.

"This is not about your rights. I need to know why you didn't tell us about the threat to the president. I need to know why she was targeted and taken. You must understand that your knowledge about this is why you're here." She maintained her professional and unemotional air, even though Melissa knew she had thrown her a little with the last comment.

"Kaliastrid?"

"What?" Her answer flooded Melissa with anger and a little pain.

"Are you okay?"

"Do you intend to ignore me, Melissa? If you'd like, I'll go get Charles and see if he has some answers."

Melissa ignored the threat. If they had Charles, they had more trouble in one place than they wanted.

"I'm sore and they've given me something. I'm going to kill this little boy."

"No, you must stay in human form. They're trying to question us about Netbliast. Clear your head."

Melissa maintained her emotionless expression as she returned her attention to the woman on the stool. She was trying to use emotions Melissa had no need for now.

"No, you'll leave me and go get your commanding officer or a representative of whatever remains of the government. I don't have to speak to you. You're being belligerent, not to mention using drugs on me to extract information. Leave me and only come back if you have someone from the State Department. Or you can release me."

April paused. She must have thought the drugs were still going to work. Melissa smiled at her.

The door opened, and a man in fatigues walked into the room. He stood as Charles did when he talked to the men at the gate and walked the estate grounds. Melissa stood from the cot, stepped around April, and put out her hand as if they were on equal ground. He ignored her hand.

"Miss Schwendemann, you've told my superiors some things that were difficult to accept. Now some of what you suggested has been proven. We need more information. We need your assistance."

The games humans played just never ended. "Funny way to ask for help. Please. I came to you. I put myself in danger to warn you, and this is how you treat me and my assistant? You could have simply asked me for what you wanted to know anytime between then and now. But you've proven that I can't trust you. I'll assure you the dragons are not going to appreciate your actions."

"And which dragons are you representing? Are you not, in fact, a distraction? Did you not come to us to hide the imminent attack? Were you not used to throw off our investigation?" With his attempt at kindness blown, he dropped back to the mental assault approach, apparently still believing the drugs were going to kick in at any time.

"I don't know how to address you, sir. However, I'm not a distraction. I had no idea the depth of Nethliast's plans. I warned you because I expected you had more resources than I did to stop him."

She was not going to get anywhere resisting them. They thought she was a spy sent to feed them false intelligence. She needed them to believe her instead of fighting her. She could use magic, but it often backfired when the spell's effect wore off.

"The records say you told them to look for him in Germany. He attacked here."

"He attacked everywhere. You cannot possibly be unaware of that. I had no idea he was preparing anything this large. I told you what I knew, when I knew it, and warned you of his final goal, which was global. His goal had been and probably still is to recover control of his homeland. The rest is probably just a show of force. We never calculated that he would use mixed-bloods at all. It's surprising to us that he was able to organize them on this scale. It's not common for dragons to work with them. It surprised everyone."

"How did they get inside our security? Who are all the humans supporting him?"

"First, dragons are magical." She paused and smiled at him to let her condescension settle in. "They aren't limited by what you think is possible. As always, humans are arrogant and refuse to think anything can happen that they can't explain."

The cot behind her lifted off the floor and hovered in the air. Melissa allowed her little show of power to imply to him what his situation was. Although she had protected her cover up to this point, she was losing patience with their approach.

The woman who had been sitting on her stool beside her commander stood up quickly and brought a pistol up from behind her clipboard. The movement and the whiff of the small gun triggered Melissa's protective instinct. Trained by her previous experience, she transformed. Scales spread across her body beneath her clothes. She stopped the transformation before it covered her face and hands. A dart impacted her chest and stuck. The needle bent against her scales and flopped back to lay against her breast.

They all stood staring at the feathered dart. Melissa reached up, pulled it free, and dropped it to the floor before continuing.

"You see, you think you act from a position of power because you don't know the depth of your weakness. I need to be out there trying to stop Nethliast, not in here answering your questions and playing these games."

With as little effort and no hands, she grabbed the shocked woman in a magical grip and lifted her off the floor. The captive officer squeaked as she left the ground and looked at her commander for assistance.

The commander's eyes grew a little, but he quickly recovered.

"Please put the lieutenant down. She's fragile."

"I know, sir. I don't intend to hurt her or you, but your assumptions that I do are wrong. If I meant to harm you, I could and you would never know what had occurred." She gently placed April and the cot back on the ground.

You may hurt him a little. Nothing that can't be treated easily. Do not transform.

In response to her order, Melissa felt a slight surge of satisfaction.

"However, you may want to assist the young man questioning my assistant. She's not as patient as I am, and she will likely wake up angry. If she thinks you're going to hurt us, she might react before she thinks. Too many war movies."

The officer looked down at April and nodded toward the door. He felt the tide changing. He was smart enough to see a power play and understand this was no bluff.

The lieutenant turned and left the room. Neither of them said a word until she returned. She nodded discreetly as she entered the room. Her commander's shoulders slumped a little and then he straightened.

"We could have you killed."

"No, you could have killed me, but now you can't. I will not be drugged again. You may fool us once, but not twice, and we have very long memories." The old dragon inside of her smirked. She was still struggling to remember anything useful from those lost memories.

She wasn't sure if he was understanding what she was admitting. Maybe he just thought she was a witch. Either way, the conversation, and who controlled it, had changed.

"Can you please release my assistant and bring her here?"

"I don't think we can do that."

"I can't control her if we're separated like this. I will not be responsible for what she does if I can't speak with her."

I need you to act a little crazy. Break something.

Noise from down the hall drew the attention of her questioners. She turned to the door.

"Lieutenant, would you see if you can go get the lady down the hall?"

April nodded and left the room again.

"How are you doing that?"

"I'm not doing anything."

"Right, and we didn't drug you."

"I guess we understand one another."

"If I don't listen to you, this will get worse, right?"

"It could. I don't want to have to escalate this in order to prove that I'm on your side."

He rubbed his chin and waited. The door opened. He looked toward it expecting his aide, but Kaliastrid walked in dragging the lieutenant behind her in a headlock. She released and pushed the girl away from her while blocking the door. April smashed into the wall with a wet smack as her nose broke and blood streamed down it. She was unconscious before she hit the floor.

"Everyone in the hall is subdued. We can leave whenever you're ready."

The suddenly out-of-control officer stepped back from Kaliastrid, raising his hands to his shoulders. Melissa took a moment to check on her mother. Kaliastrid's clothes were torn in a few places from the accident, and her head looked like it had hit the door frame, but there were no signs of damage from getting into the room.

"There's a whole division outside. This room is monitored. They're on their way," the commander blurted. He was still trying to recover, but panic was starting to edge into his voice. Even as things were falling apart around him, he was still trying to force their acquiescence.

"Do you think he means it?" Melissa asked. Kaliastrid nodded back.

"Go out into the hall and make sure no one lives who dares to enter." Melissa said the words, and Kaliastrid paused for just an instant before she grinned mischievously and turned toward the door.

"Stop her. Bring her back and we'll talk," the trumped officer said quickly.

Kaliastrid didn't stop to see how the argument ended.

"No, I don't think we have anything else to talk about. Like I said, we're trusting, but we learn fast. You're less trustworthy than I like. We'll be leaving. Do I need to subdue you too or take you with me?"

"This is above my pay grade." She had heard the same comment from Charles and knew what he meant.

"That's what I told April when she started questioning me. How fast will your men arrive? I don't really want to kill anyone, but you're pushing me."

"What do you want?"

"I want out of here. I need to call my friends and let them know where I am. I need to speak to someone who can approve what I ask for, and I need a comfortable place to relax."

"I can make that happen."

"Kathy," she shouted at the door, not because she had to, but to cover any hint that she could communicate without speaking. The door opened, and Kaliastrid walked over to her.

"I don't want this to be a continual negotiation. Are you going to trust that I'm not your enemy?"

"No, that's above my pay grade as well. I'm going to let the men above me decide that."

"Then I guess we understand each other. But I've done what you asked. It's your turn, and I won't back down as quickly next time. Don't attempt to cheat me."

"This way." He motioned to the door.

Melissa stepped next to him. "After you. I'm the guest. I don't know where we're going."

Melissa had no choice. She could transform, but it would be very difficult to break out of the building even as a full dragon. She still hoped to hold back her true nature until she had to expose it.

He took his place and led them out into the hall. The building they were in was industrial and old. It had obviously been built in the forties, and it looked like it had been deserted for most of Melissa's life. At the end of the hall, they entered a plain yet functional elevator.

They stepped into the old car and closed the doors. He pressed the button for the ground floor, and the elevator moved. A fleeting glance to the left told Melissa where the camera was.

"You know this is a trap, right?" Kaliastrid asked.

"Of course I do. I can smell the lies as well as you can. Be ready at the top, they're going to try to take us again."

"At best. Why are we not just ripping this building down around them?"

"I still believe there is hope we can communicate with them."

When they reached the ground floor, the doors opened, exposing a line of five soldiers kneeling with rifles. They were backed up by more soldiers bracing rifles in ten doors on each side of the hall, proving that Melissa may not have been right. Bright lights filled the corridor with simulated daylight. Melissa stepped closer to the officer and cleared her throat to make her voice heard.

"I don't think you want them to die," Melissa said, looking out into the hall. "I hate to keep threatening you, but you're not trustworthy at all. I've kept every promise I've made. I've not tricked you. Do I have to hurt someone, or perhaps you, to make my point?" She looked at the side of his face where he stood in front of her at an angle. He had raised his hands to give a sign for them to hold. "You keep testing me. You don't think I can do it, do you? You saw the unconscious men and women downstairs. What kind of demonstration do you require?"

"I don't need a demonstration. These men are doing their duty. If they had not been here when I came up, it would have been their asses."

"I understand, I do, but I don't seem to have a choice. Which one of these brave men do you want to sacrifice to me for this?" She pointed her hand out and moved her finger from man to man. Not caring which one would be the example, she stopped at one of the front five soldiers. With a wave, she knocked his rifle from his hand and lifted him into the center of the hallway. Rifles snugged into shoulders and fingers tightened. She knew she was pushing her luck. Her prisoner raised his hand higher to signal them to hold their fire. "So far I'm being nice, considering what you've done to me. Don't you think?"

"I don't see this as nice."

"He's not in flames. This is no worse than how you've treated me. Would you like that, then? Should I start up the barbecue?" A ball of fire appeared in her hand where he could see it. He flinched at the heat. "You and I are going to have to come to an understanding, and I can't continue getting the long end of the skewer, so to speak."

"Step out and fall back, that's an order."

"I'm sorry, sir. We cannot follow that order. The prisoners are to surrender and come with us," a very young soldier in the front rank said, looking up slightly from his rifle sights to stare into Melissa's eyes.

"Or what, soldier?" he demanded.

"I don't want them hurt."

"I get that, but I don't like it. They want us dead. There may be no way to stop someone from dying. This has already gone too far."

"If they wanted us dead we wouldn't be talking. This is a test. Someone wants this to escalate."

"Then there is nothing we can do to stop it."

Melissa visually shrugged as she surrendered to the fact that they were forcing her hand.

"Or they don't leave the elevator, sir."

"Then I suggest you follow your orders."

Melissa's throat tightened as his words lit the fuse.

Each soldier's finger tightened on his trigger.

Melissa cast her shield across the elevator door to protect everyone in the cage just in time.

Fingers finished their traverse and the loud staccato of ragged three round bursts assaulted her ears.

Stunned somewhat by the excruciating noise, the suddenness of their assault, and the overwhelming force of it, Melissa felt overwhelmed for a moment. She released the soldier she had been dangling over them. He crashed to the floor behind the front line of soldiers.

Each burst struck her shield.

Each impact felt like a battering ram slamming into her arms.

The first fusillade forced her to take a step back against the wall and threatened to drive her mind to panic. She had never held back such a crushing onslaught with a magical shield. She could feel the impacts draining her strength.

A surge of dragon transformation gave her renewed power and stabilized the panic she was feeling. Beneath her clothes, her scaled legs and newly strengthened torso muscles resisted the beating she was taking.

Some of the deflected rounds buzzed back toward the soldiers holding the front line. If Melissa didn't stop them, there would be casualties that she wanted to avoid. She focused on a place among the first rank and released a blast of magical energy. It exploded upward and outward, throwing the cluster of soldiers toward the walls in all directions and stopping their assault. Some of them were injured in their hard landing, all of them were disarmed, but to Melissa's satisfaction, all of them were still alive. The supporting soldiers lining the hallway paused as an invisible force took out their front rank, but only long enough to refocus.

The new onslaught of rounds striking the shield ricocheted into the ceiling, blowing out the lights over their heads and the spotlights they had aimed at the elevator. Sparks and shattering glass added to the chaos of the confrontation.

With the front echelon down, Kaliastrid stunned the officer who had escorted them into the ambush. He slumped against the wall. Unburdened by their hostage, they could move out into the hallway and defend themselves.

Kaliastrid cast her own shield overlapping Melissa's to take some of the battering. With a nod of understanding, they turned back to back, keeping their shields overlapped as they stepped out of the elevator.

The fire had fallen off some since the front line had collapsed. Soldiers in the doorways were falling back to reload and maintain a field of fire. Each side paused long enough for the front soldiers to fall back before they took up the covering fire for the opposite side.

Melissa could see that the trained soldiers could keep this up as long as they had ammunition and hallway. Sooner or later, they would bring up a weapon she could not resist. She had seen the evidence in several news reports since they had emerged. She was not interested in resisting their fire long enough for them to kill her.

"Stun them all." Her order was passed in the silence of their minds.

When the next group stopped firing to fall back, Kaliastrid picked off the individual running men. The next burst of fire from the remaining soldiers was smaller. With each successful cycle, they reduced the assault force until silence filled the halls again.

Their ears rang from the unbearable noise of the gunfight and their lungs stung from the smell of burnt cordite. Cries of pain from the men of the front echelon reached out to her, reminding her of ancient battlefields she had walked before, and she suddenly felt sorry for their ignorance. They would all live, but she hated that she had to hurt any soldiers.

"What now, my daughter?"

"We find their leader."

The young soldier who had ordered the attack among the discarded group pressed shakily up onto his elbow. A trembling hand leveled his pistol at Melissa's head. His finger was squeezing the trigger as a warning formed on her lips. Kaliastrid was moving to stun him as the loud report shocked Melissa. She watched the single round slam into her shield. The impacting slug and its unstoppable results stunned her as much as the cacophony of the automatic fire had. An instant after the sound registered, a single red hole sprouted in her attacker's forehead. Recognition and surprise froze forever on the young man's face. His dead eyes accused her as he collapsed to the floor. All she could do was accept his judgment.

She stood for a moment and stared at the dead man who had thought his chance had come to stop them. She looked at Kaliastrid's face and could see the same shock. No other soldiers among the front rank moved.

"We didn't choose this battlefield."

Her mother's wise words goaded her forward. They reminded her that she was not responsible for his life.

With her shield still up, Melissa selected the first stunned soldier down the hall, rolled him over, removed his weapons and gear, took his radio, and dragged him out of the hallway. Kaliastrid covered their flank from further attack.

"What are you doing?" Kaliastrid asked.

"I want answers."

"Do you really think they're going to talk to us? Do we have the time to waste on this? We can get out of here now."

Melissa released the harness of the soldier, kept his radio, and didn't look back. She was looking for a stairwell other than the ones near the elevators. They should be able to get out now without as much resistance. As they headed down the hallway she noted the cameras that had been installed since the building had been built. She directed a blast of magical force at each one and destroyed them.

The small bit of violence kept her anger from boiling over. She was angry that someone had pushed her to take a life, even though it had been at his own hands. She whetted her anger a little as she walked to avoid thinking of the young man. If she focused on the image of his final moments, she would not be able to continue.

"I'm really beginning to believe we are wasting our time with the humans." Kaliastrid said, breaking the silence and giving her an outlet for her anger if she wanted it.

"You don't mean that."

"Right, I don't mean it. My mate is being tortured in the Black Forest by a maniacal dragon, and these idiots want to play soldier knowing we could wipe the floor with them. I don't mean it at all, but I am starting to change my mind."

Melissa was not yet convinced she was right, but she was tired of wasting time, and angry they had forced her to be violent when she had tried to maintain a peaceful, diplomatic conversation.

Melissa pulled the headphone from the captured radio over her ear and positioned the mic. There was no traffic on the line. She looked for the transmit button on the radio and pressed it.

"I need to speak to whoever's in charge here."

There was silence on the line.

"You've heard all that I've said so far. You were watching me and probably still are. You know that I can and will kill if I need to, but I don't want to. Enough have died here already. You've pushed me, and I've pushed back. His life is on your hands. I warned you. I just want to talk to whoever is in charge. You can continue this fight if you want, but understand me now. If you escalate again, I will not hold back. You will lose. I don't want that, and neither do you."

"We don't negotiate with terrorists," a voice said over the mic. A familiar voice was talking behind him. She could not hear what he was saying, but it sounded like he was in control. She had half expected he was the man in charge, but she had hoped she was wrong. Agent Silas Loxley was behind this. He was as brutal as Charles had warned.

"Okay, I'm not a terrorist. You know that, but now that I know what this is about, I'll stop being careful at all. I'll make a way out of here— through you if I must. You brought me here, wherever here is, and now you're playing games. I'm done. Agent Loxley, I know you're there. If you know half as much as I think you do, you know I can."

She smelled them coming. There were a lot of them, and they were trying to be quiet. Melissa stopped and pointed toward the intersection down the hall. Kaliastrid nodded.

"Call them back, Loxley, or I'll roast the first few as a sign of my dissatisfaction."

"If you're interested in talking, you'll not kill anyone," the strange voice responded.

"Were they always this arrogant? I don't remember having to kill them before to make a point," Melissa commented silently to her mother.

"Maybe they're just stupid now. You shouldn't do this. I'll do it. There is no other way."

"I've already killed. Why does it matter?"

"You know the answer to that."

"Okay." Melissa nodded. *"Maximum damage to the hall and really hurt the first few. Try not to kill them."*

"Fine, but I don't have to like it. Could you have made it a little harder?"

Melissa grinned. The noise and smell down the hall told her they were about to move on them. A new noise came to her ears. It was mechanical. She recast her shield and waited.

A tracked robot cleared the corner and turned on them. It was a small black rectangle with tracks and a pair of rifles mounted on a swivel that could target anything in a circle around it. The rifles were adjusting to point at them.

Fire belched from the twin barrels. The rapid staccato of its cyclic rate sounded like tearing material, only extremely loud. The impacts to the shield were pushing her back and threatened to knock her over.

A feeling close to terror rushed over her as she wondered if she had waited too long. She had obviously underestimated Loxley. She mentally castigated herself for letting it get this far as she wondered if this was her end.

"Destroy it and take some wall with it. Maybe even some flesh. Hurry, I can't hold it much longer." She could not keep the panic out of her message.

A flash leapt from Kaliastrid's fingertips. Thirty feet away a ball of flame exploded where the robot had been. The fireball consumed the ceiling and the wall. Flame belched down each hallway as the blast escaped the best way it could. Two soldiers who were directly behind the corner fell into the hallway. Chunks of metal clattered down the tile floor. Smoke rose from their gear and they curled up into balls, protecting burnt flesh.

"Cease fire! Cease fire!" the familiar voice said from down the hall.

Silas stepped out from behind the corner. He was a little out of breath, and he was wearing a casual Hawaiian shirt and a leather jacket.

"You want to talk now?" Melissa literally growled at Silas. "Are you done?" She put her head down, placed her hands on her hips, and walked toward him. "Have you seen enough? I'm really tired of this."

Silas backed up a step, raising his hands to his shoulders. "Yeah, I've seen enough. Did you really hold back on that?"

"Do you really think I'd tell you?"

"No. I guess not."

"Why should I not burn you down where you stand?"

"This is a misunderstanding."

"Help me to understand. You had these soldiers capture me and my mother. You wanted to interrogate us. You probably intended to run a few tests while you had us here."

"Okay." He shrugged and dropped his hands a little to a spot just in front, as if he were holding off her accusations. "That part is pretty clear when you say it like that, but, I tried to call them off on my way here from Washington. My phone was destroyed when the partials attacked my office, and I had no way to get through."

Melissa shook her head in disbelief at such a lame excuse. "Your phone was dead. Really? That's what you're going with? You're not a child. Neither am I. You know exactly how that sounds. Try again."

"You would think I had other options." Silas shook his head and smiled at her, and she enjoyed his discomfort as he danced for an answer. "But that's not really true. These guys are really paranoid, primarily because I selected them so they would be. After the attacks, this morning— well yesterday— they locked the base down."

"So?"

"So, I couldn't get through except on a recognized line. No one could. I didn't have a recognized line anymore because— " Silas pressed his hands toward her to emphasize that there was more to his explanation when Melissa's face told him she didn't believe his excuse. "Honestly, I was standing under a sprinkler while trying to avoid being killed by partials. My cell phone was destroyed in the deluge, and I didn't have a backup. I had to get here in person. I was on the way and out of communications when they captured you. I had no idea. I couldn't stop them until I got here. How was I supposed to know you would choose to leave your manor today, for the first time in months?"

"Charles wanted to hurt you when we first met. I should have let him. You never should have given the orders in the first place. How do I know you're not lying to me?"

Laughter burst out of his chest. He sensed that she had relaxed a little when he explained. "That boy scout would have gotten himself hurt. I know when I can't win, though. Truce. I'm not lying about this, and I don't want to fight with you anymore. It was a mistake to try and capture you. I made that same mistake twice if it makes a difference."

"You don't learn very fast then, do you?"

"Both of my mistakes have become quite clear to me in the past twenty-four hours. I'll assure you, I've learned my lesson."

For some reason she believed him.

Loxley made a motion down the hall behind him. At the same time a group of men came around the corner carrying rifles and wearing large rectangular backpacks. Kaliastrid's hand shot up at the approaching men and before anyone could stop her the first man was on the ground. He was not dead, but he was unconscious from the defensive push she had used to knock him down.

"Wait!" Loxley shouted. His face froze in a grimace of real fear.

The other men stopped at his order. Rifles that had been pointed at the ground were now pointed at Kaliastrid.

Melissa squinted at him as if he was pushing his luck.

Kaliastrid started to pull energy into a stronger attack.

"They're medics. They need to get to the wounded."

She reached out to her mother at the same moment. *"Don't! Kaliastrid!"*

They both dropped their hands.

Melissa felt the mana dissipate into the room around them with a snap of magical backlash. They both absorbed the pain of the squelched spell.

When the instant of tension passed the soldiers moved. Two dropped to their knees between her and Loxley. Another pair rushed to the other medic, who was down and struggling from broken ribs, at least. They sat him up, handed him his IFAC, took his med pack, and patted him on his shoulders before they grabbed their gear to head down the hall. A fifth medic dropped next to him and lifted him up to walk back the way they had come. A private conversation of whispers started between the two men working on the wounded soldiers from the fireball attack. One yanked open his pack while the other moved to triage and help the injured. They went straight to work treating the men at the corner, ignoring anything going on around them.

"You're a long way from Washington, aren't you, Loxley?" Melissa asked, cutting into the action that had dawn their attention.

"Call me Silas, please. Washington's a little hot for me this time of year. I didn't like the tourists that have recently arrived. Thought it would be safer here amongst friends." He motioned to the four soldiers helping two others on the floor.

"So you came south into a warmer climate where you have no friends. You're such a liar. Why do I always feel like I need a bath around you?"

The man in the hall smiled a big smile and rolled his shoulders back as he raised his hands out to either side. "I get that a lot, actually. It comes with the job."

"Where are we?. Why did you wait? Why didn't you keep me in Washington when I met you there?"

"I would have, yep. I wanted to, but no one believed you. I was sure the president would see what I saw, but she didn't, and it cost her. If she had listened to me, we probably could have stopped the attacks."

"Not if your approach was to capture and interrogate me."

He shrugged. "I watched the video of our interview again recently. You know what I saw on that tape? I saw someone who was scared and worried. But, I don't see that today. I see someone who's mad. I get that you're mad at me. But, there's more. You're not being as careful as you were then. Why the change?"

"You're still trying to treat me like someone you get to question, Silas."

He grinned and tilted his head to the side in an admitting shrug.

"You think I know more about Nethliast's plan. You think I'm the key to something. You want to stop him, but I'm not sure you're the patriot you want everyone to see you as."

"Ouch, now that wounds. I'm exactly what people want to believe. I never meant for them to put you into this situation. I got here just in time to see the show in the hall."

"And you let it continue, escalate, even?" Kaliastrid asked.

"Not exactly. I was taking charge as you were heading into the second trap."

Melissa wanted to hit him.

"You let me kill that man!" she shouted and stepped toward him.

"I'm not the bad guy here," he said. "I've called off the dogs. We're all friends now. There was nothing I could do to save him. It was already out of control when I got here."

"How do I know that?"

"You don't, and sometimes you just have to accept bad situations to get what you need. We invented the concept of collateral damage for that very reason."

Silas' words struck her and revived memories of other similar alliances that were not blocked by pain.

You've made worse arrangements, with worse people.

Melissa listened to her older self and felt her real age settle on her shoulders. She could see the benefit of having the help of someone like Silas. Someone with the ability to organize things like this while the government burned around them could be helpful. She physically shook off the lingering desire to kill him by clenching her fists in front of her.

"So, why are you here again?"

"My first mistake gave me a second chance. She could have left me to die in the partials' attack. I realized I wanted to use my second chance for something important. I want to help the president, my friend. I had a little time to listen to the news and review the information on my way here. I think she's just missing in action, not dead. She survived all of this. For some reason, when everyone else was killed, she survived. That's what the evidence says. I'd like to know why, and I'd like to find her. I thought, since she will probably end up near your ex, you might actually be interested in helping me find them."

"You know for a fact that she survived?"

"I have reason to believe it."

"And what makes you sure I'm interested in helping you? I don't really need your help."

"Hmm, some others might agree with you, but I'm not so sure. Dragons can't hide out forever. Sooner or later, we will find a technological advantage, if we haven't already. Washington's a wasteland, true. So are the other capitals. But I don't care how much of that magic you can do; there's something equally magical about an M1 sitting just out of the range of your magic and slamming spears of depleted uranium at giant lizards."

Melissa felt Kaliastrid's anger at Silas' threat. She was somewhat angered by the comment as well, but that had been his intent, or at least part of it. He wanted to see them react to his remark. She smiled back at him, not letting him know he caused any reaction at all.

"They chose their side," Melissa said. "With that comes responsibility for their actions. But, you're right. I can stop them. I know I can. I may be the only one who can without a great deal more bloodshed."

"Maybe, but they're not doing a lot of talking right now. They did a number on Washington and then, from all reports, disappeared. They dropped their ultimatums, laid waste to the brass, and evacuated. I don't think the cherry blossoms will be too nice next spring."

"You really don't seem too upset about it," Melissa countered.

"Honestly, I prefer to spend most of my time out of the country, not in Washington. I've just been back in town to complete a little paperwork. They actually did me a favor on some fronts. I'm only concerned about one person besides myself right now."

A memory from an earlier conversation with Elaine around the pool reminded Melissa that she might have a powerful piece on the board. She chose to take a chance. "How patriotic. What if I can confirm your belief? What if I told you the president was alive and she was not in Washington anymore?"

As well trained as Silas was, he could not hide the brief expression of relief he felt from her news. "You know that? Where is she?"

"I can do better. I know someone who can find her."

He nodded to her point. He didn't try to hide his interest in what she was offering. "We need to talk more. Let's go up to my office. I think we can both help each other."

Melissa looked at Kaliastrid. Her mother visibly rolled her eyes and shrugged. She did nothing to hide her impatience with the delay. Melissa decided, against her mother's dissatisfaction, to take another chance with Silas and nodded at his offer.

He motioned for them to follow him.

"You have quite a setup here. Why? What is all of this for?" Melissa asked.

"When the president took office she called me with some outlandish idea that someday she would need my help because of some surprise threat. Most people would have told her there was no threat, but I'm not that kind of person. She knew that. We were friends. I took an office post. It came with the understanding that I might have to do some unusual things. I bet it would never happen. Turns out she was right. It doesn't go any higher here than me anymore, and I'm alone with no real command or oversight. The Colonel who was in charge of these troops is probably dead. He was following my lead as much as he could. He was in Washington when the attacks started, sitting in the White House waiting to meet the president when the place was torched. I've not heard from him. It hurts us if he's dead because I'm not a soldier. His command is probably still intact, but they're looking to me and the president for guidance."

He pointed toward a staircase entrance and walked through it. "As I said, Washington's a mess. The military's functional, but they don't like working on their own turf. Without strong civilian leadership to tell them Posse Comitatus is suspended, most of the top commanders will wander around until someone grows a pair and tells them to move. It's sad but true. They knew how to hurt us."

"Time passes, but the basic rules of conflict never change. Take the head and the beast dies," Kaliastrid commented coolly.

Silas looked back and paused to consider her first contribution to the conversation.

"Nice. Try not to antagonize him."

"Perhaps you should share the rules of this game with him as well."

Melissa visibly frowned at her mother. She simply pointed to him with an expectant look. Silas ignored the exchange and continued.

"The strike decapitated our government, but worse than that, no one knows where the battle lines are since the dragons and partials merged back into the crowds when they were done. Any actions underway are at the unit level and are mostly defensive while they try to stabilize the situation. Worse, a lot of people don't know who to trust anymore. They're pointing fingers at everyone they didn't trust before and feel vindicated for their lack of confidence. Everyone could be a traitor. We've lost the momentum in this first action. It's going to take some time to get it back, unless you have some secret way to help us."

Melissa shook her head at the search for information and let him maintain control of the conversation as they climbed the stairs to the next level.

"I have my orders, and now I need to figure out how to help my fr— the president."

Melissa ignored the slip as they walked out the door into a heavily guarded nurse's station. Kaliastrid recoiled from the number of men standing behind it. Melissa noted the soldiers as well but tried to remain calm. Silas was not trying to kill them, at least that was what he said. He was still trying to gather information from them, but something told her, that never stopped. Everyone behind the counter seemed focused on a job that did not include harming them.

"Relax, this is not a trap."

"Are you sure? I don't trust him."

"And you never should."

Kaliastrid nodded toward a man standing next to the counter staring at them. His eyes tracked Silas across the room. Melissa could feel his angry intent like ice crystals in the air. The officer was monitoring the progress of a pair of technicians while failing to hide that he was not happy with Silas.

Silas looked up to acknowledge the angry salutation, but continued without addressing the officer any other way. The obvious display of territorial dominance surprised Melissa. Hundreds of years had passed and not much had changed when egos where involved.

"If what you say is true, I'm not so interested in staying here much longer," Silas continued as they walked around the barrier and into a massive communications center. He held up a finger to pause the conversation.

Melissa looked around while they walked past the soldiers. The lower floors of the building, which Melissa could now see used to be a hospital, seemed surplus, almost as if they had been hurriedly set up. This floor, however, had a distinct layer laid across its surplus face. There was a mobile military setup filling the space. Plastic shipping crates had been set up in the horseshoe of the old nurse's station. Each crate contained a complete computer station or other mounted equipment that was part of the monitoring and command center. The portable setup looked like something out of a NASA mission video. It was mission control meets garage band.

A pair of soldiers was rapidly modifying mission maps on one computer while listening to something on headphones that completely blocked them from the conversations in the room. Another group was going over several clipboards holding half-inch stacks of paper grids that Melissa could not read, but they were intimately interested in.

Several soldiers in a darkened corner of the station were scanning video on four monitors. A digitized stream of a man played forward on the screen at normal speed as he shifted from human into the scaly, protected form of a partial dragon. The video stopped and jumped back as the technician spun a wheel on the console and scrolled the video back to the point where he was human. The same technician played it forward slowly through the transformation until the man was again a scale-covered partial with a menacing look on his now alien face. On the other screens, a wider view of the same event showed several others who had transformed at the same time. She cringed at how many of them there were and how well they understood their magical abilities. Nethliast had been busy. A printer next to the men spit out a very detailed head shot of the man and dropped it onto a stack of others that had already been captured.

Silas did not slow down as he passed through the technical center. The officer with the scowl and matching black bars on his chest watched them until they entered a small hallway. Two doors past the video team, he motioned Melissa into what had once been an office. The room had a bathroom to the left that again seemed like it had last been used in the fifties. There were signs that it still functioned independent of the dirt and stains of age that covered it. As the tension of the situation was falling off, and she was beginning to feel the first signs of the nervous shakes that came from a massive adrenaline rush, she thought of Charles. Interesting that her first thought of him was how he would react to the bathroom. She smiled to herself even though she realized she had left their relationship strained.

Beyond that door, the office opened into a utilitarian space filled with a functional green metal government desk and two utilitarian metal-backed chairs that seemed to have been left when the building had been abandoned.

"Like I was saying, I think you're right. I think she's somewhere other than Washington. I think we need to go find Nethliast. If he has my friend, I think we should go visit him. You say you can stop this? You mean everywhere, don't you?"

"Yes, I mean everywhere, but it will take a few steps. First, I have to stop Nethliast. After that, I think it may be easier to talk to the rest of the dragons."

Kaliastrid nodded her agreement to the original plan. She seemed glad that Melissa still shared that goal.

"Well, I may be able to help you with that."

"How do I know I can trust you?"

"I work for the CIA. You can't, ever. How many more times do I need to tell you that?"

"Finally, honesty." Melissa laughed aloud. "I might be able to work with you after all, Silas." Melissa paused and pointed a menacing finger at him. "But, you double-cross me, and I'll burn you."

"Quite literally."

"We have an understanding, then?"

"For the moment, yeah." He nodded and flopped down in the government-surplus, metal office chair behind the desk and tossed his feet up onto the work surface.

"Let's talk candidly. No one's listening here. They know better than to bug me." He grinned again and threw his hands back over his head. "You're both dragons. I've seen the video. You can't tell the difference, but I know you're dragons. You can lie to me if you want to, but I think I know the answer, and, if you lie, I'll believe what I know anyway. Save me the effort and just admit it."

Melissa sat down to the left of his desk and thought about how to respond. She didn't answer him.

"So, Ambassador Helena, who goes by Melissa, and represents a dragon named Meliastrid, I take your silence as an admission that I'm right. I can understand why you protect that secret. I know why you didn't tell me about this in Washington. I bet that really bothered the Boy Scout-cum-Marine. I wouldn't have told you either, even if my bed-buddy-butler gave me a hard time about it." He winked at her, and she realized he had probably bugged the manor when he visited and had some evidence to support his accusations. "I can see how much of an advantage that ability can be. No one, at the scene — that survived— remembered seeing the dragons arrive. They were just suddenly there. That appearing out of nowhere is a powerful trick, but, they didn't really appear out of nowhere, did they? How many centuries have you kept that secret?"

Melissa knew it was a waste of time to lie. He had done his homework, which included spying on her. "I can't confirm that you're correct. But, what if you were?"

"What if I'm correct? Well, that just makes this conversation easier, that's all. I can stop saying they, and you can stop using the royal we. We can agree that you have skills I need to know about, and I can help you. We can all agree that you really want to help stop Nethliast. Then the middle man is out of the way. And as a free gift, which does not come often, I will tell you that no one else knows what I know about you."

"But, I'm not sure we need or want your help."

"Are you willing to decide that without first hearing what I can offer?"

"It's not what you can offer that I worry about. It's how much it will cost me."

"Right now, I only have one goal: getting the president back," Silas reiterated. "If, in the process, we kill Nethliast, that's a bonus."

"If we can even get her back."

"You said you knew where she was."

"I said, I knew someone who could find her. She was the target. They went to kill her like the others."

"How do you know that?"

"It's what a dragon would do."

"Always straight for the head?"

"Like she said, best way to kill the beast."

"So, why isn't she dead?"

"I don't know. It's also the best way to control the beast, but that only works when a government or a people can't survive the loss. Modern governments are not like that, and the U.S. Government would not negotiate for her."

Silas nodded. "Right. She's so much baggage and ceremonial now, until a new government is formed. Why take her?"

Melissa shrugged. "I don't know. Maybe something happened when they tried to kill her."

The conversation paused for a moment before Silas went on.

"Okay, so I can assume all dragons can take a human form. What about the others, though? There are reports of some with wings, but still human-sized. It seemed the dragons were leading them."

"No, Silas, this is not going to happen. I'm not going to give you all that I know so you can lock me in a cage somewhere. We're going to have to work together on this."

Silas held up a finger and tilted his head to the right, nodding. "Okay, as a sign that I can help you, and that I want your help outside of a cage." He pointed toward a large Pelican case sitting in the corner. "Although initially I did intend to bring you here to hold you and run experiments on you, I realized that I want—need— your help. You have a problem flying because of our modern radar and aircraft, more specifically the firepower we can put in the air."

"Maybe."

"You're almost as cagey as I am. Look, it was just after an encounter with a helicopter that you came looking for me. It scared you, how hard it would be to avoid or even fight them. Nethliast takes on a couple of fighter jets over Germany and does a job on them, but when he moves on us he raids armories around Washington to capture anti-aircraft support. Don't get me wrong, Ho Chi Minh would be proud, but it tells me a lot. So, just doing what they pay me for, I figured dragons feel a little confined and need space to literally stretch their wings."

Melissa made no signs, although his evaluation was very accurate. She had not actually been afraid of the helicopter, but she didn't want to hurt the crew. It was a difference that other dragons would not have struggled with. That was not a point worth discussing here.

"Now, you need to be able to get around without getting shot at every time you take off, so I think you might want these."

Silas stood up and moved to the case. He flipped the latches open and exposed several rows of powder-coated black boxes in black nylon cases. The boxes resembled large cell phones with two buttons and a small screen on the narrow side sitting up in the case. The black nylon cases held the boxes in place and could be strapped to a pack with a grid of nylon straps. Clipped to the case was a wireless earplug and throat mic. He pulled one out and handed it to Melissa. It was heavier than she expected.

"Outer shell is Kevlar and carbon fiber, so it's tough and should stand up to combat conditions. Inside is a military-issue transponder/transceiver. Each one is assigned an ID that will show up on radar as friendly. You can't change the transponder code, but you can transmit and receive communications on all of the military air bands. There are even a few tactical and command bands included in there. I'm not sure if the earwig and throat mic will work on you in your dragon form, and I don't know how you'll be able to carry them. But the guys outside can probably figure out an answer to both of those questions. With these, the wearer will show up on any American or allied radar as a friendly. So, no more 'duck and cover' trying to get around, and you can be in the form that is the most efficient. I can't assume trying to take on a dragon in your human form is very safe."

Melissa sat the package down on the desk and looked at Silas. He seemed to understand. There was more to him than he showed on the surface. The laid-back-company-man stereotype was an act to cover something else. She suddenly felt a little more respect for him, and then reminded herself that she couldn't trust him. He was slick. She looked back at the box of transponder radios. This was a key she needed. She could fly all over Germany, while Nethliast was limited in both altitude and duration of flight. It would be an advantage.

"So, we have a deal." It was not a question. Silas moved back to his desk, sat comfortably back in the metal chair, and laced his fingers behind his head.

Melissa looked at Kaliastrid quickly and made up her mind.

"They're not dragons, not totally. They're part dragons, like half and quarter. I'm not sure how small the division can be before the abilities are absent. A quarter or less may only have magical ability, but that's trouble enough for you. Some used to believe that's where the most powerful wizards came from." A twinge of pain reminded her of the penalty of clarity.

"There're thousands of them?" Silas did not seem surprised at her answer. He already knew what she was telling him. It was a test to see if she would lie to him, but she was already in, so the additional information would not hurt.

"Yes, probably more than there are dragons. It depends on how badly our lineage has splintered. We've not been able to figure that out. The ones in your footage appear to be fairly well trained or aware. I'd never have expected that level of skill from half-dragons on their own. They've been helped."

"They're calling themselves partials. The Partial Liberation Army. So we have two levels of threat, dragons and partials. And, yes, Nethliast has helped train them."

"It's not that simple. You have several levels within the partials. There are other species that are worse than these human blends. They are less intelligent, but worse. If he has any of these at his disposal, assuming they can understand what happened to them and remain sane, then you will have problems. They are more powerful than what you've seen."

"So how do we fight them?"

"You don't. You can't. We fight *him*."

"If we kill him?"

"Most of his dragon supporters will think twice if he's dead."

"You're sure?"

"No, I *think*. I'm not sure of anything. It depends on how convinced his followers are that humans are to blame and deserve to be subjugated. I know that some of them are being coerced with hostages. If we can find the dragons he's captured, his followers will listen to me. I represent something to all dragons. I'm their ambassador. If I can get their attention, they will listen to me."

Don't forget the mixed breeds, her inner dragon reminded her. "The partials are another problem, however. We had to eliminate them in the past because they could not be negotiated with. We may be able to reason with them now, but they're not going away. They probably don't remember what we did to them, before." She grimaced with the memory and rubbed her temples.

"Why do you say that?"

"If they did, they wouldn't be fighting with Nethliast. The others, the less intelligent, will vanish into the forests and jungles to become legend and superstition if their leader falls. Then we can hunt them down, again."

"So, we're talking about assassination and genocide."

"Yes, but we start with Nethliast. If we take him, the others will not have a leader anymore. There will be others who want to lead, but the power vacuum will work to our advantage. We're all suffering from memory problems. If I take away the head, the others will listen to me while we look for a way to fix our memories."

Kaliastrid didn't move or react, but her thoughts were with Melissa quickly. *"Are you sure it's wise to tell him about this? Why are you bringing him into this?"*

"I don't trust him, but there's more to him than the show. He could help us."

"I thought we were going after Nethliast. Why are we wasting time with this man?"

"Maybe we were wrong to think we could do this alone. I am an Ambassador, after all."

"Hmmmm." Melissa could sense the irritation and impatience from her mother, but the elder dragon kept any additional thoughts to herself.

"So when do you prove to me that the president is okay and not in Washington?"

"I need the others up here."

"All of them? Do I have to bring the Boy Scout?" Silas joked.

"Yes, you have to bring Charles. I need him to protect me from you." She grinned at him.

"Stop by the desk and ask for a clear line. I was actually going to reach out to him and bring him in on this anyway. He won your trust, and I might need that. What are you working on besides finding Nethliast, anyway?"

"What do you mean?"

"Well, you told me about Nethliast, but then you didn't keep after him. It's like you had something else to find."

"I told you. We're looking for what has our memories messed up. We need to solve that." It wasn't a total lie, but it was also not the truth.

"Get Charles up here quickly. I don't want to wait too long to move on this. If Nethliast is going to ground with hostages, we need to be on his tail fast. That means we're going to Germany, right?"

"I feel used," Kaliastrid said as she brushed her battered clothes off.

"You'll get used to it," he replied without looking at her.

She growled at him, which made him look up and raise his hands from the desk in a sign of surrender. Once the moment passed Silas tossed a small envelope to Melissa. She looked at him to explain before she opened it.

"Welcome to the State Department, Ambassador Schwandemann."

Melissa opened the envelope and extracted two IDs and associated paperwork.

"Official?"

"Of course. Well the president and congress have not approved the appointment, but that's only a formality. We'll resolve that as soon as we have either. Right now, it's going to be the easiest way to move around."

She took the IDs and Kaliastrid's arm and walked out of the office. As they left Silas, Melissa considered exactly how Charles was going to react.

I wondered how long it would be before you thought of him, her inner dragon stated. *What makes you think he has waited to react? I've known him the shortest and I know he's not waiting for you to call him.*

She stopped at the desk to organize the call that she was suddenly regretting.

September 6 – 2035 EDT – Kingston, Tennessee

Just south of Kingston, Tennessee, Charles' phone rang. He pulled a Bluetooth receiver from his vest and inserted it into his ear before he pressed the button to take the call.

"This is Charles."

"Charles, it's Melissa."

Although he knew from Elaine that she had just finished a meeting with Silas, Charles was still relieved to hear her voice on the other side of the connection.

"We're on our way! We'll be there in less than an hour."

"How? Elaine?"

"Right, she found you." There was no way to disguise his relief at hearing her voice. "You've had an adventure."

"A little," she replied.

"You can't trust Silas. He set this all up. You're in his control. This is not what you want."

"Charles, you're wrong. Listen. He wants me to bring you all up here. We're working on a plan. I have a code word for you to give at the gate. This is exactly what we needed."

He was too late. She trusted Loxley.

"How can you say this is what we needed? You're joining forces with the devil. No matter what he's promised, he's not going to deliver. This is not safe for you."

"You have to trust me. I'm not in danger. I proved that trying to double-cross me is dangerous, and I have Kali here with me."

Charles was not going to win this argument. All he could do was listen and get to her side as soon as he could. He didn't answer.

"I'm going to take your silence as an indication that you're at least listening to me."

He remained silent.

"Okay, say something so I know the line isn't dead and I'm talking to no one."

"I'm sure Silas is listening in. You can talk to him." He knew the words were childish as he said them, and he felt ashamed as they slipped out. "Give me the details."

Melissa read out the instructions on how to find them and then gave him the passcode. "Charles, trust me. This is not what you think it is. We're stronger working with him. Get here as soon as you can. I'll tell you the rest of the plan then, but have Elaine find exactly where the president is now."

"We're on our way. I'll tell her."

The line died, and he pressed the ear-piece again.

"That was professional and adult," Elaine said from her seat next to him.

He shook his head. "I don't trust him. I don't know how she can."

"I didn't see anything wrong with his plan. He didn't seem to be deceiving her."

"He's always deceiving. He does it so much it seems like anything he says is the truth."

"Charles, I think he's on our side in this."

"He's on his side. We just happen to align with his current goals. Spooks don't change."

"Wodin has sent him to us. He's the sixth. This is what my casting meant. This is the path forward."

Charles looked back at Aldrich through the mirror and again saw his eyes. He looked convinced. Charles was alone in his concerns about Silas Loxley and his plans. He nodded into the darkness and focused on driving.

"Find the president," Charles growled.

"What?" Elaine asked.

"She wants you to find the president again. She wants to know where she is."

Elaine nodded and looked into her cup.

As they sped up the cloverleaf entry ramp onto I-40, Elaine was quietly staring into the glass. The conversation descended into silence as they both focused. Aldrich leaned back against the seat and closed his eyes. Charles squeezed the wheel as if it were the only being in the car he could argue with. Rather than trying to win the argument, he focused on getting to Melissa and let the road marshal his thoughts.

Several minutes and more miles passed before he had his plan organized. They were minutes from the turn onto a back road into what had been part of the Y-12 plant. Melissa had sounded relaxed, but it could still be a trick. He wished he could tell if she had been under duress, then he reminded himself that she was a dragon and wondered how anyone could put a dragon under duress. His hand passed over the pistol on his hip again, and he resisted checking the rifle that was nestled behind Elaine's seat where he could reach it quickly. He knew this was likely to be dangerous.

"Listen," he broke the focused silence, "when we reach this place, I want you both to stay back at the rover until I get a feel. We're going in blind."

Elaine released whatever had been flickering over the surface of the glass and looked at him. He could tell she was surprised by his comment.

"This is not a trap," she mumbled

He could tell she was still angry at him.

"We don't know that."

"You mean you don't know that. They are not trying to hurt her anymore. She's safe. We're safe. You're like a dog with a bone about this."

He ignored the remark and continued his briefing. "Okay, but I still want you to stay back until I know what we're facing."

"Hmm."

This was not going well. He needed her on the same page so that he could keep them safe, and her anger was not allowing that.

"Look, we're all there is. We're going blind into this. I don't know what's ahead. They've captured two dragons, so they're a resourceful bunch."

"Oh, believe me; I know who's been captured. Right now, you're a prisoner to your passions. You won't listen to us when we tell you they're not holding her anymore. She's waiting for us to join her. In this case, *Mister Stone*, you're not listening."

When he didn't answer she continued, "Go on. Tell us what's going to happen. We get there. You throw on your armor and race at them baring your teeth to save the damsel. I stay back at the castle— I mean car— until you call for me and Aldrich. Should I bring up the wine then or wait until you've saved the day and rescued her?"

"Look, I'm just trying to get the plan ready."

"I think you're overreacting. I think we're guests, not combatants. You've been working that conversation over and over since she hung up. There really may not be anything hidden in it. Have you ever considered that? Every time you review it, you get more agitated. You just don't think clearly at all when it has to do with her. And I thought I was being a little immature."

He looked over at her, a little confused. For a moment he was not sure what conversation they were having.

"She's just a young girl," he continued. "She's never dealt with someone like Silas. I knew his mold as soon as I saw him in Washington. He's slick, and I don't trust him."

"With her, you mean."

Charles almost missed the turn and growled as he crossed the light morning traffic to take the exit ramp. What had she meant by that? He needed to focus, and this argument was not going anywhere useful. Gripping the wheel, he accelerated into the turn at the end of the ramp. There was no hope of getting a plan out of continuing the conversation, and he was beginning to wonder if he was having the same one. They both let it drop.

The suburbs of Knoxville, where the Y-12 plant and its supporting neighborhoods had been, had grown into a southern Appalachian forest over the years since much of the civilian quarters and support units had been absorbed into the city. Among the modern neighborhoods and strip malls, there were occasional glimpses of old structures and foundations. He had driven through the area a few times, but he had no idea what kind of building he was looking for or where it might be.

The next landmark Melissa had given him appeared, and he took a left turn onto an old road heading up a hill. There was a new sign next to the road that warned that this was government property and listed specific fines and imprisonments. Charles wasn't worried about fines. He was focused on preventing an ambush on the narrow gravel road. He reached behind Elaine's seat, pulled the rifle across his lap, braced it between his legs, and charged the cocking handle. The mechanical clashing of the bolt as it fed a live round into the chamber woke Aldrich, who sat forward and put his head between the seats.

"Something wrong? What's going on?" the drowsy passenger asked, gaining as clear a view of the situation as he could. With one glance at Charles he relaxed some. "We must be close."

"How could you tell?" Elaine asked acerbically.

"Would it help you any at all if I repeated that Wodin thinks they're on our side?"

Charles looked at Elaine and then at Aldrich. They were serious. Was he so wrong about this?

He followed the road through the bleached bones of an old neighborhood and turned onto a long forgotten four-lane avenue. At an intersection, the avenue turned left onto a two lane road that, according to a well-preserved sign, led to the old hospital. He took the right turn, scanning for any sign of the enemy. Ahead of them, a zig-zag of water-filled plastic barriers led to a sawhorse barricade and a single armed guard. There was no ambush, but there was a manned security post. He was already on top of it.

Charles pulled to an angled stop twenty yards from the barricade. They were already alert to his approach. Stopping like he did only heightened their readiness. Charles considered his options, all of which were bad. They probably had him covered. The young man at the post did not approach. He watched for Charles' next move. He did not raise the barrel of the rifle, but Charles did note that his finger was on the trigger. He would be on target before Charles could get out the door.

Charles laid his right hand on the carbine, placed his index finger just above the trigger, and wrapped his thumb around the grip until he felt the safety. With his left hand, he reached to roll down the window.

"Charles!" Elaine cried. "Stop it. They have you covered from two directions." She pointed at the second guard he knew would be there. "You must stop and think. She said she was safe, and you can't take on an army alone."

He considered her warning and realized he was not in a strong position. How had he gotten this far out without backup or support?

He released the grip of his rifle and rolled down the window. He rolled forward through the switchback to the barricade. By now the soldier had his rifle just inches from on target.

"This is a restricted—" The youth saw the rifle in his lap and shifted his weight away from the car. His own rifle was tracked up the last few inches until it was focused on Charles' chest.

"Dragon's claw," Charles croaked and lifted both hands from the wheel so both soldiers could see them.

The young guard visibly relaxed. The rifle returned to a resting position, pointing at the ground. He raised a hand to wave off his partner. Charles watched the shadowed warrior relax his rifle but not drop it from the front of the car.

"Yes, Mr. Lehman, we've been expecting you," the soldier sighed his relaxation into the greeting. "You may want to safe that rifle, sir. We're a little jumpy. Don't want anyone getting hurt."

"Right." Charles slid the carbine toward the back seat. Aldrich took it as it passed back and set it between the seats. The click told him Aldrich had safed the weapon. Charles' pulse was starting to fall off. "Where is Miss Schwendemann?"

"We're in the process of loading up to bug out, sir. Proceed to the back of the building. Since you're packed up, they'll probably just insert you into the convoy. You'll be briefed at the loading area. You'll find your party there, I expect." The guard stepped back from the door and saluted. It was an odd thing to do to a civilian, but Charles returned the honor out of habit and with slightly wooden movements. He drove past the guard toward the road leading to the back of the old building.

"Will you please lay off the emo a little?" Elaine asked as he drove.

He didn't respond.

The building was long and squat with three floors, a military style hospital from the 50's. He followed the road to the rear and pulled into a parking lot covered by camouflage netting. It was filled with Humvees in numerous configurations. Several were being packed with gear and others were acting as cots for soldiers breaking until the action started. Charles recognized the relaxed tension of prepared waiting. He felt it in his own body. He had been in that mode from the moment he heard the crash the day before. He looked over at Elaine, who was stoic.

He pulled the rover into an empty space near the edge and opened the door as he was applying the brake and killing the engine. He reached for the rifle. Her hand met his.

"Don't. They're all alert here and ready to take down dragons. I don't want you hurt, no matter how ignorant you are."

He released the rifle to grasp her hand, but she disappeared out the other door. As she exited she tossed her familiar backpack over her shoulder. The stuffed bear stared back at him. For an instant, he thought it was shaking its head.

She paused just beyond the front fender and turned to look at him. "By the way, you're welcome."

Elaine left him standing where he was and walked toward the main building. She swayed her hips in a provocative walk reminding him of the playful girl of a week before, but with an edge of something new and concerning. There was still a prevalence of anger in her walk. She was way too young for him anyway. Charles ran the palm of his hand over his forehead to get his thoughts to clear.

"Just go with it, son. Wodin brought this together, and you're a key part of it. Some folk just ride the waves of fate instead of fighting them. You and I will likely drown trying to fight the tide," Aldrich shared as he walked past him to follow Elaine. "There'll be plenty time to fight later, I expect."

With one last glance into the backseat and an internal struggle to decide what to do, Charles left the rifle and trotted after them. His hand rested comfortably on the grip of the M-9 on his hip.

When he caught up to them, Elaine was already hugging Kaliastrid, who showed no outward sign of being in an accident or being a prisoner. Elaine had totally avoided Melissa. Was she jealous of Melissa or just more attached to Kaliastrid? Charles wondered if that was why she was so angry at him. There was no reason to be jealous of her. He would have done the same thing to save Elaine or any of them.

Aldrich greeted the ambassador with great formality as always.

Charles walked up last and extended his hand to Melissa. The young woman he had been raised to guard, but whom had become a friend over the years, stepped up and threw her arms around his neck. Surrendering to the surprise, Charles wrapped her protectively in his arms. He wanted to hold her safe from any harm. He had to protect her. The comfortable heat of her body against him felt right and wrong at the same time. His father's voice in his head reminded him of his place, and he immediately started to pull away. She held onto him and turned her head until her lips were next to his ear.

"Thanks for coming for me," she whispered and then released him. "I can always count on you."

An odd noise from behind him caused him to look at Elaine and Kaliastrid, but the source and purpose was not clear. Kaliastrid pulled Elaine away from them as if she wanted to talk to her privately.

Reminded that Melissa was still standing in front of him, he turned back and stood for a long moment just looking at her. Where he expected a broken and trembling little girl, he found a powerful and in-control woman.

"How are you? Is everything all right?"

"I'm fine, Charles. We had a tough night, but I think we pulled through okay." There was a lie in there somewhere, but Charles could not decide what it was.

She was wearing a casual red business suit that looked comfortable for travel. An ID clipped to her pocket looked like an official state department ambassador credential. He recalled that Kaliastrid was dressed the same way, and they were both equipped with throat mics and oddly shaped flat earbuds.

"What's going on here, Mel?"

"We're going after Nethliast." She set her jaw as she said it. She expected an argument.

"You're going to kill him?"

"If we have to, yes."

"Wait, what did you say?" Aldrich asked, suddenly stepping forward to hear the conversation.

"We're going to stop Nethliast. Silas, Agent Loxley, is going to help us."

The answer stymied the elder professor. He simply raised a lone finger but said nothing more as he processed the change. Once he had the information, he shoved his hand into the small pouch at his hip.

He drew three tiles in sequence from it and consulted them before shaking his head and putting them back. For a moment Aldrich was speechless.

"Mr. Lehman, welcome back to the service." The irritatingly familiar agent's voice overrode the vitki's search for answers and drew everyone's attention to his arrival. All of the anger Charles had managed since Melissa's capture suddenly returned. He was filled with a white-hot rage. He marshaled it so that he could remain in control. The opportunity he had wanted was at hand, and he would not allow the moment to pass without the lesson. With just a glance over his shoulder, Charles pivoted in a smooth spin on his rear foot. The stance and position of his opponent was clear in his mind. His right foot was behind Silas' leg before the agent could react. With just enough force to warn him, Charles drove the heel of his right hand into the space just below Loxley's ear.

Charles watched the agent's eyes roll back as he crumpled from the blow that starved his brain of blood flow for a disabling instant. Loxley had already started a retreat as the blow struck. Those two things combined to send him sprawling to the ground. Charles smoothly continued his forward movement, stepped with the falling man, and placed his back knee on the ground. When the full move was complete, Charles was kneeling over Loxley with his left hand on his chest and his right hand cocked at his ribcage ready to strike out and kill the agent if his next move was not peaceful. He had pulled the first blow, but he was ready to escalate. It was all up to Loxley.

A young blond lieutenant with a very broken nose and newly formed black eye rushed toward the conflict in an inappropriate show of emotion for a subordinate. Two nearby soldiers who had accompanied Loxley drew their pistols.

As consciousness returned to his eyes, Silas slowly and carefully raised an arm to stop the soldiers' reaction as soon as he could. Charles didn't move.

It was obvious Loxley couldn't speak. Elaine gasped from where Kaliastrid had sequestered her.

"Wait." Silas could finally talk and he nearly shouted the word. "I told everyone to expect this. He was just quicker than I expected. You, my friend, are lucky Melissa warned us."

"I'm not your friend."

"No, I guess not, but I hope this is not a sign that we can't work together." The look on his face was sincere as he brought his hand slowly down to request help up.

Charles said nothing. The weasel deserved more, but that would do for now. He'd pay him back later. He ignored the hand and stood up, leaving the man where he was.

"Charles." Melissa touched his arm and spoke to him as privately as the situation allowed. "I appreciate your chivalry, but I need for you to work with Silas. First, he's not responsible for what they did to me last night. He has corrected the situation that led to that. I think we've come to an understanding."

"I see."

She looked into his eyes and seemed disappointed.

"I don't trust him, Mel. He's a snake."

"He is that," Melissa agreed. "But he's good at what he does and sometimes that's more important."

Charles saw the logic and hated it. It made his teeth clench, and he despised that Melissa was saying it. He also knew that he didn't have to like it. He'd learned that in the desert. He could feel the smothering blanket of his military training pouring out over him like a shell.

Aldrich, who suddenly found his voice, added punctuation to the conflict. "We cannot deviate this way. This adventure will not end well if we change our course like this. We must remain focused on the search, not revenge. This cannot happen."

Everyone looked silently at the priest. He said nothing more but prominently displayed a set of runes that he must have expected to explain his point.

"Okay, the drama's past," Silas said. He rubbed his neck and shook his head as he stood up without help, ignoring Aldrich's warning.

Charles smiled inside. He had shaken the bastard. Good. He knew how things would go if he moved against him. That's what he deserved for endangering Mel. No matter what Melissa believed, he had orchestrated the whole event. Charles was sure of it.

Aldrich harrumphed, "So the hard way it is, then. You've all been warned. None should listen so much as you." The priest pointed at Silas. "Your vengeful pursuit may cost you what you seek, if not your very life."

Melissa looked at Aldrich with a puzzled and troubled stare. They had never heard him be so direct. Charles looked at the bones he was still showing. He could not tell which rune was which, so they meant nothing to him.

"You must listen to me, all of you. If you pursue this path, you will face great loss and suffering."

"I'm decided, Aldrich. We must stop Nethliast to know peace enough to pursue what Helena wanted us to find," Melissa said with finality.

Aldrich shook his head and turned to Kaliastrid, who looked resolute. He looked to Elaine, who was also no help. With no support for his argument, Aldrich shook his head. "Perhaps, after this, Allfather, they will understand and heed my warnings. But, then again, it's never stopped me, has it? I shall continue to grapple with human nature. I see you feel I have earned this lesson." Aldrich fell silent.

"All right, that's settled," Silas interjected into the awkward silence. "We're almost packed up. We clear out in twenty."

Aldrich walked over to stand next to Elaine while Loxley continued. Charles was distracted for a moment by the look on Elaine's face as she watched Silas direct those around him confidently. It was his turn to be a little jealous.

Silas handed him an envelope.

"Charles, or should I say Captain, here are your papers. You're reinstated. I fixed your rank. Good thing you got that out of your system before I gave you those."

Charles opened it and looked the orders over. Captain was a promotion, sure, but who did he report to? His eyes caught the subdued gold cluster on Silas' chest. Surely, not this puke. He rankled and started to speak.

"That's about right, isn't it?"

"What?"

"The rank. It's where you would have been if you had stayed in?"

"Probably a few grades higher," Charles answered quietly. The alarms in the back of his head told him to watch out for what was coming next.

Loxley pointed at his own chest where the subdued gold cluster was sitting.

Charles shook his head. "No way. I might be able to pretend that I'm an army captain, but there is no way I can pretend you're a major."

"You don't understand, Captain. You're not pretending. Those papers are official. You're a captain, in the Marines actually, until you choose to resign the commission. I'm the one pretending, but that doesn't make these papers any less real. You've always wanted back in, haven't you? Did I read that wrong?"

Charles shook his head as he read the orders again, paying close attention to the details of the document. He didn't recognize the unit he was detached to. He didn't know what he wanted at the moment, but he suddenly felt like he was coming home. It didn't feel as perfect as he had hoped.

"Close."

A grin crossed Silas' face as he nodded.

As happy as he suddenly was, Charles refused to forget that there was a devil extending him the deal. There was always a catch in contracts like this. It was usually one's soul. But that was a deal he had made long ago. This was just a reminder of that long-ago contract.

Melissa smiled at him as if she always knew this was where he belonged. One step behind her, Elaine was scowling at Melissa.

"I don't know what this means, really. I'm not comfortable with all of this. What is this unit I'm detached to? I've never heard of it before."

"The president created a special joint forces unit on paper when she took office. It's designed to deal with odd and unusual situations that may arise. I don't think she ever expected to need it. She enabled it when the partials appeared. Colonel Holloway is...*was* our CO. He's currently MIA so you're assigned to me—" Silas raised a hand to delay the negative reaction. "—loosely, for this mission. There is no way we can deploy this entire force. They have a job to do setting up our base of operations while we're dealing with the current threat. We're to work together as a task force. The paperwork and the rank just give us room to work. Lord knows I need a competent XO. The system's a little messed up right now, and we're working it fast and loose. Have been since the president cut my papers. We're learning as we go. I expect things will shake out some when we are on the other side of this challenge."

"That could get us all killed."

"Could, but so could breathing nowadays. A few dragons and their partial friends have declared war on mankind, in case you hadn't noticed."

Charles put the papers back into the envelope and dropped the Velcro backed cloth insignia out into his hand. Silas had it all wired.

"We'll put the plan together in the air. You good?"

Charles nodded as he took a deep breath. A lot had suddenly changed in his world. It would take more than a few sheets of paper to make this real, but he would play at Silas' game for a while. If it was the only way to protect Melissa, he would wear the rank and follow the orders, but as soon as the scorpion showed his true nature, Charles would be there. Then he would break his stinger off and kill him with it.

"Okay. Captain Lehman, I want you to follow us in the convoy. You're on my tail all the way to the airport. I assume you're armed." Silas grinned. Charles nodded. "Augment from the armorer as you need. The bigger the better. Your M-4's useless so you're going to need to step it up a bit. We're short on anything you can carry that has much more punch. You should at least swap the M-9 for one of these." Silas pointed at the Desert Eagle on his hip. "Simmons, make sure the captain's side arm is exchanged. Wheels up in twenty, people!" The last was elevated for the audience.

Silas turned to look back at Charles as the blond lieutenant walked up next to Silas. She was carrying a folded set of Marine camouflage fatigues and a pistol belt to replace his.

"Captain, you're out of uniform. I think this will take care of that. Do you know how hard these were to find?" He winked at Charles before turning to look at Elaine. The lieutenant handed him a crystal sphere as he turned away "I hear you might be able to help me figure out exactly where they've taken a friend of mine."

Elaine tilted her head to look up at Silas. Charles could read the pride in her eyes as she nodded at his question. There was something else there as well, and Charles felt a new agitation settle into his mind. Silas reached out a possessive arm to envelop the young girl. Before the jealousy brewing at the base of Charles' neck consumed him, the blond lieutenant stepped between him and Silas and extended the parcel. She was oblivious to anything but her orders.

Charles accepted the uniform from the young lady. She turned away, always keeping one eye toward Melissa and maintaining a discrete distance from her, as if she were unexploded ordnance. He suddenly understood the damaged face. This was the woman Kaliastrid had tossed about like a rag doll, according to Elaine.

Standing alone in the middle of a suddenly bustling loading area, Charles thought about the morning's events. Silas knew he was armed and on edge from the moment he arrived. He had allowed him to knock him down. The diplomacy of that act was well played, but it was even more powerful that Charles knew he had allowed it. Weasel, sure, but smart. Charles nodded at the crafty move.

He looked at Melissa, who was still looking at him.

"You've made a deal with the devil, and apparently so have I," he warned.

"Sometimes you have to."

"What's his angle?"

"You know, I really think he cares. He and the president are pretty close."

Charles remembered how the two had felt like more than just friends in Washington. He nodded. "I don't like his methods."

"He's working the system, but he has to, right now. Charles, this may taint your armor a little. I'm sorry." She meant it, too. "Are you okay?"

"Yeah, I'm okay," he lied.

He looked at her. She was standing straight and tall. The suit looked good on her. She didn't have the hardened edge of a State Department insider, but there was something there. Her eyes showed wisdom he had not seen a few hours before. For a jealous instant, he wondered if he really was losing the innocent young girl to Meliastrid after all.

He brushed the childish concern away. No one could afford to be young right now. War had come home. She needed to be strong. It might not hurt any of them for her to be an old dragon for a while.

"Yes, I guess you are. You need to get changed. We're traveling as a special unit with orders to hunt down the leaders of the dragons. We have to look the part."

Charles nodded and turned to walk away.

"Charles..."

He faced her again.

"Listen, you never should have left the Marines. I'm sorry Helena did that to you. I don't know the whole story, but you're a warrior at heart. I've always believed that and— maybe this will make up, just a little, for the mistake of forcing you to be something else."

Her honesty touched him. He felt a flame of pride and joy rush through him.

"I've always been where I belong. Helena brought me home for this. I realize that now. This is just the next step in her plan." A long-lost smile crept across his face, and Melissa grinned. They were both getting back to what they should be. He felt a familiar fire in his chest that he had never dreamed he could entertain again.

"We'll talk more on the flight." She gripped his upper arm, squeezed it, and released it before she turned to let him deal with his new duties.

He found a quiet corner of the hospital emergency room and changed. When he was happy that the uniform was ship-shape, he walked back out and headed toward the Humvee he recognized as the mobile armory. They should have everything he needed.

As he approached the vehicle, a specialist and sergeant were counting boxes. The sergeant snapped to attention and saluted him. This time he returned the salute with all of the respect he had. It had been a long time, but he liked the feel of the uniform. He pointed to the manifest the specialist was managing and held out his hand. The sergeant handed it to him. He scanned the contents of the mobile armory and made a quick note of a several items that would augment what he already had.

"Specialist, help me load these items in my car." Charles pointed at the manifest and looked at the armorer. Both men looked at his Land Rover. The sergeant stepped up and took the clipboard.

"Sir, we'll handle that. Just leave the list with us and we'll get it loaded."

Having been an NCO, Charles had no problem working, but he recognized the pride the sergeant had in his job and nodded his approval.

"Carry on then, Sergeant."

He saluted them again and turned away.

He walked across the parking lot to join Kaliastrid, Elaine, and Aldrich back at the rover. They were talking animatedly about something. He left them to talk and sat down in the front seat to wait and rest while he could.

Soldiers and gear were loading all around him. He could tell as the tempo of movement slowed down that they would be pulling out soon.

The armory sergeant arrived with two large Pelican cases and a crate of ammunition. He motioned to the back, and they nodded. Charles moved to help them when Aldrich appeared beside him at the door.

"Charles, you must listen to me. I cannot convince the others. Melissa will not listen to my concerns. You're my last option."

"What seems to be the trouble?"

"This decision she has made to pursue Nethliast directly is not advisable. It deviates from the path woven for them. There will be suffering if I can't stop them."

"What's the threat? I can help if I know what the risk is."

"The course of action is the risk. I don't know the specific threat. Wodin never tells me the specific threat, but the runes say this is not the right course. No matter how I approach them, they tell me this action will end badly. That is not normal. When I cast the Norns, they hardly ever agree completely from one casting to the next because there is so much variability in what is, was, and will be. But today they all agree that there is nothing good at the end of this endeavor. That was different yesterday. We were on the right path then."

Charles stared at the man and struggled to keep his jaw from dropping open. He had to remind himself that the world was different now. He had to remember that this kind of thing was possible.

"I will talk to Melissa when we get situated and in the air, but you should tell her your concerns directly. She's listened to you in the past. Either way, Germany is where we need to be, right?"

"Yes, the right place, but for the wrong reason. I will tell her, but you must tell her this is the wrong way to go. This could lead to death for us all."

The small man grabbed his arm and squeezed it. Charles could feel how important this was to him. He would make sure he brought it up with Melissa if he could ever get a moment of her time. She was staying very close to Silas since he had convinced her of whatever it was that he had planned. He was the root of this change. Maybe Aldrich was on to something.

"You're all set, sir," the Sergeant called from the back of the Land Rover. "It messes up your combat load, but you'll be loading into the plane first so you can adjust when you get where you're going." He walked up to the door and handed Charles a helmet and a gun belt loaded with a Desert Eagle and extra clips. "From the lieutenant, and you'll need this for the ride, sir."

"Thank you, Sergeant." Charles accepted both and replaced his cover with the Kevlar, remembering the requirement that traveling in a caravan in uniform required the wear of appropriate head gear. He stowed the new pistol belt in the back seat. The Sergeant nodded and turned to walk back to his own vehicle. Charles checked his watch and leaned out the door.

"Load up. Time to pull out."

The group split up. Aldrich, who was trying again with Kaliastrid, followed her toward the forward vehicle.

Charles closed his door and started the engine as Elaine climbed in next to him. She was silent.

"Listen, before we get too far from this and I forget it, I'm sorry I didn't say anything when you told me you found Melissa. I had to find her. I was focused on that, not how you helped."

Elaine grinned at him and shook her head.

"What?" he asked.

"Nothing," she said, still shaking her head. "You can't take the knight out of the armor."

"What?"

"Never mind."

He frowned and continued, "Everyone's okay. I'm not convinced we're safe, though. Aldrich's irritation makes me nervous."

"Safe? No, I don't think we're safe, but that's why we need you."

Her grin turned into a frown. He knew there was more beneath that. He guided the conversation to keep it about something else. He didn't feel completely comfortable returning to their earlier relationship conversation.

"What do you mean?"

"It's your duty. Kaliastrid explained that to me. But, remember, Melissa doesn't need your protection. She's a full-grown dragon. Kali said she showed signs of realizing that when she was dealing with all of this. She said some of the things they faced would have broken the young girl Melissa was. She had to spread her wings, so to speak."

"I guess I lost sight of that until we got up here."

"A little bit, but it's what makes you such a great man." She blushed at her own words and looked away from him.

"I said I'm sorry."

"I know."

He gripped the steering wheel and stared at the bumper of the command Humvee in front of him, willing it to move. When it did, he felt relieved and followed it. Old training surged up into his mind, and he started scanning for any sign of possible ambush. He focused on the road and followed the leader until they turned off to head toward the airport. When they were on the freeway and clear of the closeness of the urban roads, he glanced over at Elaine. She had the small crystal sphere that Silas had given her in her lap. Her red hair was cascading across her right hand where she had her head propped against it and the window. Charles really was impressed with how well she could take apart the topics Melissa had thrown at her. Now with Aldrich's help they were getting closer to figuring out what Helena had intended, but this fight was getting in the way. Maybe Aldrich was right. They needed to focus on the search and ignore the rest. He knew that meant surrendering Melissa's father, and now the president, to Nethliast. It was not an easy decision, but Melissa had made it. The outcome would determine the wisdom of the action in the end. It was the same knowledge every commander took into battle. The time ahead of them would include conflict. Historians would decide if the battle really changed anything. Charles needed a break from thinking about it. He again looked at Elaine, who was twirling one of the errant strands of her hair that Kaliastrid usually chased.

"Whatcha doing?" he asked playfully, trying to lighten the mood a little. He was nervous where that might go.

"This is a crystal focus. It works like the water in the glass. I'm watching the president."

"Where is she?"

"Munich. That's where we're going."

"Is that easier to use?"

"Well, I can't spill it in my lap."

He smiled and realized she was not as angry as she had been. He would have to remember to ask Kaliastrid what she had talked to her about. He still didn't understand why she had been angry in the first place.

"The other stuff is still part of it, though. I still have to guard against their emotions and power. They could take me over if they know how, and I have to guard against that."

Charles nodded and turned his attention back to the road.

When they arrived at McGhee-Tyson, the caravan pulled through a secured gate away from the commercial terminal and drove directly onto the ramp in front of a C-37B. The military version of the Gulfstream G550 would make the flight to Germany fast and comfortable, if he could avoid making Elaine mad again.

September 7 – 0015 EDT – McGhee-Tyson International Airport – Knoxville, TN

Kaliastrid was sitting at the galley table staring into the darkness around the airplane as Melissa entered. She really wanted to sleep, but it was obvious that her mother had something on her mind. Now was the appropriate time to address it, no matter how tired they were. Unsure of how else to broach the topic that filled the small galley like a toxic cloud, Melissa flopped down in the seat next to her.

"What's on your mind, mother? Spit it out."

She looked away from the small window, and Melissa could see in her eyes that the subject was deeper and more toxic than she had expected.

"I hope the same thing that is on yours."

"I'm too tired for dragon mind games. Just say it."

"You've lit a powder keg between those two."

Melissa sat back for a moment and reviewed the most recent events, trying to synchronize herself with what her mother was talking about. When she failed, she raised her hands to her shoulder and shrugged.

"You're going to have to give me more than that. What two?"

"Fine, I'll slow down and walk you through it. Charles is in love with you."

Melissa started to deny it, and her mother warned her with a glance that left no question.

"He has risked his life more than once for you."

"Perhaps..."

"Stop being a human child. Think about just the past twenty-four hours alone. Now, you're risking all of their lives on something the two of us should probably be dealing with alone. This was not the plan. Ignoring that issue for the moment, you are blissfully unaware how your—our crusade is going to affect the others, particularly Elaine. You have thrown her at Charles continuously."

Melissa pulled back from her mother as each accusation struck her. She was tired. They were both tired. Melissa couldn't deal with the entire list at once so she took the one that struck her the hardest.

"How can he love me, mother? I've treated him like a servant. Now I've asked him to sacrifice his higher values to go along with this dark crusade and our deal with the devil."

"And yet he still follows you."

Melissa could not respond. Her mind refused to help her argue.

"He works side by side with what he finds reprehensible."

She started to argue that he had a choice, but knew her position was weak.

"More than that, he pushes away someone who might make him happy, someone you agree will make him happy. All so he can blindly rush to your rescue."

Her mother's arguments were strong.

"That's not healthy, for any of you."

Melissa felt the pain of truth in her mother's comments. She couldn't argue with any of her points, so she deflected. "I didn't need rescuing."

"And that makes it better? He didn't know that."

Melissa stared at the table surface and made small circles with her fingers as she considered her mother's arguments. He had already been on his way when she called him. The three of them had found her and had come after her knowing she was in a base surrounded by who knew how many soldiers. He had come loaded for war. She knew he cared for her, but she had never really considered it love. All of her life there had been a social barrier, but now, when she was in charge, she had automatically built onto the wall without thinking. How did she really feel about him?

Her mother was right about Elaine. Melissa had pushed them together. She made him laugh, and Melissa had not been all that successful with that lately.

When a thrill of passion tickled her mind at the thought of Charles laughing, really laughing at something she did, she quickly shut it down, but not before she realized what her mother had not said.

Why did she have to face this right now? She had been happy that Elaine liked him. She had tried to help her get closer to him. Following the attacks, she had treated him like a servant. She had shut him back up in the servant's quarters. How had that failed to run him off? She couldn't love him. It didn't make sense. Her argument did nothing to stop the feeling that warmed her inside. As much as she tried, there was no shutting it down.

"I'll have to speak to him. I need to make sure he's okay with all of this."

"What you need to do is leave them all right here, right now. We need to get to Germany. We need to deal with this situation ourselves, like we decided. Maybe we can find Gerliast and get him to help us. This is dragon business. You have no right to drag them into it. They have no idea what you're asking them to do. If you don't leave them here, they will all probably die trying to help us. Especially Charles, who would blindly charge into the underworld for you."

"It's not that bad."

Her mother's look clearly indicated her opinion.

Melissa thought about her warning and replayed it through what had happened over the last month.

"No, mother. I've considered this. Maybe not carefully, but I have thought about it. After they caught us, and as we fought to get out last night, I couldn't help thinking that we needed to reach out to the humans more. Work more closely with them. It's the secrecy of dragon kind that has caused this war. I needed their help before, and I need it now. I think it's important that I work with them. This has to be solved by both races, or when it's all over, I may not be able to change other dragons' minds about the humans, and I will surely not be able to convince the humans of anything."

"You're risking their lives for something you ultimately have to solve."

"No, they're risking their lives for something important to them. This is as much about them as it is us. Why else would Aldrich have come to us? Even he thinks Silas is important. Don't you see? Charles is not the only one who came after me. He just led them. They won't stop because they can't. This is as much their fight as it is ours. I can't keep them out now."

A shadow crossed Kaliastrid's face. Melissa paused to consider what her mother had been thinking. She thought about asking her, but she knew they disagreed on bringing them back into her plan. For a moment Melissa wondered if it was still her plan. She waited for her mother's response.

"You are not considering Aldrich's warning?"

"He never said not to go," Melissa answered

"No, he didn't. But what if his warning is that we should not be taking the humans with us? That's the part that changed since he thought we were following the right path."

"That's not all. We've decided to go after Nethliast directly."

"There is that, but I'm not changing that even if I have to find the runt myself."

"With that clear defiance of my authority, I don't see any other options in this," Melissa said wryly.

Her mother blanched at her comment and dropped her head. "My apologies. If you disagree with my direction, I will of course defer to your guidance."

Melissa paused at the sudden change in character and mood.

"What was that?"

"What do you mean?" Kaliastrid asked.

"You just reversed everything because of what I said."

"I've decided my course, and unless you forbid it, I'm killing Nethliast. But if you forbid it, I will follow your guidance. I must."

Melissa swallowed hard as she was reminded of the power she had.

"I will watch how I say things," Melissa said. "I agree we have to kill Nethliast, or at least try. I've not succeeded so far. I just believe there is reason for the others to be with us."

"Your choice, of course. Bring them along if you want." Kaliastrid shook her head and returned to staring out into the night.

Melissa chewed on her comments about Charles and the unrequested meal of emotions.

Silas rushed down the aisle from the front door of the plane. He bounced with each step as if he was waiting in line for a roller coaster instead of preparing for a nine-hour flight. He stopped next to the table like a flight attendant taking a drink order.

"Everything all right here?"

"Of course it is, Silas. What would make you think anything was wrong? I go to war against my betrothed cousin while ignoring the warnings of a Norse god every day."

He tilted his head at her sarcastic response. "Great, sounds like we are all set then," he replied with equal irony. "We're loaded. Wheels up in 10 minutes, according to the pilot. Make sure you have everything stowed and you're ready to go."

She nodded and looked at her mother again. It was clear her father's situation haunted her. In a few minutes they would be back on course to resolve that and end Nethliast's reign of terror. For her father and mostly her mother, she would see to that. She could protect Charles, Elaine, and Aldrich by making sure they focused where they belonged anyway. They would continue figuring out what Helena wanted her to do. To do this successfully, though, she needed emotions out of the way.

"I'm going to find Charles and try to clear this relationship stuff up. I hope I can."

Kaliastrid nodded to the dark window but didn't look back at her.

Melissa paused before she stood up to look around the plane. Silas had already moved farther into the back to secure a seat in the rear. He moved a small Pelican case onto a pull-out table between two seats and patted it with his hand. Melissa wondered for a moment what keepsake he was carrying with him that required such care and protection. He sat down in the leather seat and looked up at her with a childlike smile as she stood up. She was not sure of her decision to work with him, and she shook her head as she turned around directly into Charles' chest.

He was slumped over slightly to fit in the small fuselage. The picture of the sharp new uniform rolled over in a stooped stance to slip by the table and down the aisle nearly made her laugh.

His arm shot around her waist to stabilize her as she rebounded off of his chest. His helpful movement pulled her tightly to him. She felt herself slide across his body. Each place she touched him seemed suddenly sensitive.

"I keep making jokes and not knowing it," he said to her in his semi-official voice. He was guarding himself. Formal Charles was in charge. She straightened up and regained control.

"It's not you," she lied. "Can we talk for a minute?"

"Sure."

She could see, even in the confines of the plane that he had stiffened at the request. Scaling his fortress was going to be difficult.

He looked around. "Maybe, you should let us get loaded and in the air. We'll have plenty of time to talk then," he said as the others backed up behind him.

She nodded and sat back down. As she slipped away from him, she felt his strong arm release her to the seat. The uncontrollable encounter shook her. It made her wonder if she could really face what her mother had told her.

Elaine followed Charles with the same backpack she had brought with her that first day. Melissa followed her as she walked by. The bear, which had also come with her on her first day, still stared out the back of the backpack. The girl had grown over the months, but she was still so young. The stuffed gargoyle seemed to scowl at Melissa, warning her not to hurt the girl.

When she turned back around in her seat, Aldrich was at her shoulder. She jumped as passion turned to concern and immediately shifted to fear. His abrupt approach almost set her defenses off. She exhaled as he took her hand.

Someone outside of the plane closed the door. A uniformed member of the flight crew secured it. The pressure inside the plane changed.

"You've now brought everyone together as Wodin predicted. We're ready to face the challenge, my lady." He squeezed her hand to emphasize what he said next. "But, you must reconsider this plan. Wodin and the Norns have warned me most gravely about this. Revenge will only lead to more trouble." To punctuate his point, he placed the three rune tiles on the table before her.

She had never been introduced to the reading of runes. The tradition had apparently formed after their disappearance, along with many other religious traditions that replaced magic. She could not interpret what was showing on the table before her. Kaliastrid looked over at the tiles as well. She could not read her reaction, and she was not sharing if she knew what it said.

Melissa looked up from the tiles and into his troubled eyes.

"Aldrich, I can't tell what this means. I've never been taught this divination. What are you telling me?"

"No matter how I change or focus the reading in my mind, the runes portend bad results if we follow this path to face Nethliast. This most recent draw was particularly bad." Aldrich pointed to the procession of eihwaz, naudiz, and isa through the positions of the Norns.

"Do they tell you how we can avoid the danger?"

Aldrich paused and looked at her as if she had knocked him off of a horse.

"Obviously, we must change our course away from this perilous chase to confront Nethliast."

"That is not so obvious to me, learned seer. Please consult your guides for better instruction. I cannot avoid this conflict. It has drawn me into it. Please help me discover the best path we can follow through this course, not around it."

He didn't speak, but gathered his tiles and slunk back into the plane. She hoped he would consider her point when he consulted his tiles again. She didn't want to discount his warning, but she had to be sure he was looking at it from all possible directions and bringing her more than dire warnings to turn back. She could not afford to stand still any longer. Religious warnings like 'Here Be Dragons' were not helpful.

"You shut him down pretty hard," Kaliastrid commented from her dark window.

"You disagree?"

"No. You know I am set on this course. But, you also know that I think they are at risk. His warning is dire, and he believes it. Just something to consider."

Melissa did just that as the plane started to roll back. While she was working through Aldrich's comments, her own emotions, and how they intertwined now with Elaine's, Charles stepped awkwardly up next to her seat to get her attention.

"I'm ready if you're available. They're running up, and we may have a short wait for sequencing. What do you need to talk about?"

Although he was coming across as relaxed, she could feel the emotional boundaries he had set up. Maybe after this was over she could relax and rest, but there was no indication this conversation was going to go any better than the last.

She stood up from her seat and motioned toward the twin couches that ran down the sides of the fuselage separating the forward galley from the back seats. Charles slipped back ahead of her and waited at the couches for her. He shifted as much as he could to maintain an open space between them physically, and again she nearly laughed as he seemed to shrink into the curved walls of the airplane in an attempt to roll around her without touching. It was a wasted effort. Her breast brushed his elbow as she slipped past him and sat down on the couch. He sat down across from her

She wanted to deny any feelings for Charles, but the crazy dance they took part in to get into the seats and the emotional flood that filled her as she failed to avoid contact with him shocked her. The feelings she had denied while talking to her mother flooded her body again and made her tremble like a frightened child. He could have struck her full in the chest with a war-hammer and it would have had less affect than her accidental brush against him. She looked at the hero sitting in front of her, and suddenly realized her mother only knew part of the truth. There was no way she could understand how bad it really was.

She was right. Charles might love her, but Melissa had cared for him since they were children. She had denied it for a lifetime.

You've lived a long time, maybe a human lifetime.

She fought off a smile at the comforting voice in her head that kept her from spiraling out of control. The sudden perspective did help a little, but it didn't change how she felt.

Because you love him. Time won't change that.

The sudden realization of her feelings and that she was prepared to push him away suddenly paralyzed her. She was afraid, for him, for her, for everyone. She suddenly had no idea what to say to him. Looking into his face for some sign of the same struggle, she found no solace. All that looked back at her was his professional detachment. Even as she struggled with what she wanted to say, he offered her no safety net. She felt like she was plummeting out of control.

"Charles—I've—I..."

As he seemed to realize that she was struggling to form her thoughts, he dropped some of his protection and showed her an interested and concerned look.

"You don't have to say anything, Mel. We're all here to support you. I'm just glad you're okay."

The emotional dam in her mind burst. She struggled with feelings she had never before admitted to having. They threatened to drown her in a flood she could not control. Did she love him?

How could you not?

Was that why this was so difficult?

Because you're fighting it.

She had never really felt this way about anyone, and she had never had any difficulty speaking her mind. Her chest tightened as she realized she was not breathing. She took a cautious sip of air and tried to speak.

"Charles, did you really plan on coming after me no matter who had taken me or where I was?"

The question rushed out in a single exhale. It was not what she had planned to say, but it was what she wanted to know.

"Of course."

His lack of hesitation stunned her again. She fought with a renewed rush of weakness that enveloped her body. He had planned to take on the army that had taken her. She had never been weak in the knees for anyone, but she was suddenly faced with the realization that her feelings for him were genuine.

I already told you that.

She tried, for a moment, to blame it on being exhausted. She looked around the plane for support. Her mother would be no help. She didn't think he should even be there. Everyone else, except Elaine, was still settling in as the pilot had started to taxi toward the runway.

Elaine was watching them as they talked. Melissa could feel the cold appraisal she was getting. The girl knew. Melissa could also see the resigned acceptance and pain of loss in Elaine's eyes, but Melissa was not ready to admit anything had changed. She choked back the emotional torrent that was racing in her chest and forced herself to return to her role as the Ambassador. To protect Charles and Elaine, she retreated behind her own armored walls.

Brilliant idea. Ignore your true feelings a little longer.

"Charles, I really appreciate all that you do for me. I'm grateful to have you working with me. I owe you an apology for the way I acted yesterday morning. Even after I was a twit, you continued to help and even looked for me after I left without telling you. I'm sorry for all of that. I put everyone at risk."

Charles watched her face as she spoke with that unwavering and presently unnerving professionalism. She wanted to cry, but refused to let it happen. He touched her hand on her knee as she finished and looked into her eyes. The physical contact blasted through her defenses and caused her to tremble. The immediate closeness his touch caused threatened to destroy her resolve not to break down right there. She suddenly had the unfounded desire to leap across the cabin and kiss him.

You should. That would solve all of this.

In her mind she rapidly considered how that would break through his rock-solid visage. She felt the giggle coming before she could stop it. She disguised it with a cough.

She resisted the urge and looked at his hand. For a moment they both looked at the contact and said nothing.

Charles broke the moment.

"Mel, listen." He cleared his throat and sat up a little. He did not pull his hand away. "I'll always be there for you. I'll always have your back. You will always be that little girl I have to watch out for." He looked at her like the brother she had never had, and the touch on her hand chilled. Again, she was plummeting. "Helena made me swear to her that I would never let you down, and I won't—ever."

The last words crushed her as the plummet became the crash. She could feel the torrent of emotions inside of her turn cold and shatter on the ragged crags. Now she could never share them with him. He had sworn to protect her. It was not his love, like everyone thought. It was his damned honor. The ice that rushed in to replace the passion became an ache.

As if the universe, or a Norse god, was looking out for her, the pilot advised them that they were preparing for takeoff and everyone should take their seats until they were at cruising altitude.

"Great," she said and patted his hand. "Excellent—So, we're good then?"

Ouch.

"Yeah, we're good. I'm here, for you, through this, no matter where it takes us." His words came with jarring honesty and commitment to the cause, but not to her.

"That was all I wanted to make sure of. Great." She stood up and slipped past him to head back to her seat next to her mother. As she sat down, she turned to look at him one last time before she put it all behind her.

"Charles."

He looked up at her, and a fleeting emotion disappeared behind his falling portcullis of emotional protection.

"Thanks again for always being there." She paused, wanting to say so much more. "I'm going to get some rest. It's been a long night. Would you mind making sure we're not disturbed? We will plan our next move when we get closer."

He nodded and moved toward the back of the plane where everyone else was spread across the captain's seats. She closed her own drawbridge to a relationship she had never realized she had wanted. She sat down with her mother and silently cried into the sky over Knoxville.

~~~~

Charles sank into the seat nearly a plane away from Melissa as the pilot pushed the throttles forward and the plane rushed for the sky. An odd ache he had last felt just before basic training fought with the takeoff forces, and he was glad for their disguising any look on his face. Elaine watched him settle into his seat without a word. He could tell from the searching look on her face that she wanted to know what their talk had been about, but refused to ask. She shifted the crystal sphere from hand to hand and curled up in her seat that was turned with its back against the bulkhead, enjoying her first flight in a private jet. He wanted to be honest with her, but the right words refused to come. As the forces settled down, she turned to him with the same questioning look.

"She wanted to apologize for running off without telling me and for ignoring my concerns yesterday."

"Good. She should have," she said, relaxing a little but not completely. "If that's all, then what's bothering you?"

"Nothing. Just coming down from the last few hours," he lied. "You should get some rest. None of us have slept in a while, and it's a long flight to Germany. A good soldier sleeps when he has the opportunity."

She stared at him for a moment, waiting for more. He let his head drop back against the headrest. The soft leather felt good. He closed his eyes. He heard Elaine lay the back of her seat down a little and curl up to rest.

"Charles," she said in a near-whisper.

"Yeah?"

"You're a good man, probably the only one on this plane. I've been thinking about what you said. You're right. We're headed into quite a fight. I'm not sure it's going to be a good fight. I'm worried about what that's going to do to you."

"There are no good fights," he answered with a finality in his voice he wished he had not shared. "Don't worry about me. There is one fact you can write in your journal, though. None of us will be the same on the other side of this."

With an understanding sigh she said nothing. She left Charles alone with his troubling thoughts. In a few minutes the plane settled onto their cruising altitude, and her breathing took on a regular pattern indicating she was asleep.

"It's not nice to lie to women like that."

Charles jumped at the whispered words and opened his eyes to again find Aldrich standing next to his seat.

"What do you mean?" he croaked quietly. "I never lied about anything of consequence."

"Probably right, but you have to remember that one of Wodin's gifts to the world was wisdom. He gave his eye for it, and he shares it with his followers. We don't always use it. We suffer from those choices."

Charles stared at the small man who was counseling him.

"Now, I can say I've learned a little from not listening to Wodin's will. He sent me here to guide Melissa and along with her, all of you. You're all making a dangerous mistake, and I don't want to see any of you suffer, but you in particular. For some reason he keeps to himself, Wodin likes you. He presents you to me as a type of Cavalier. I'm not sure if that's a joke or if he's serious. You never can tell with him. That probably explains Loki a little better."

"Why does he like me?" Charles let the unfamiliar man talk even though he had no real belief in what he was telling him.

"That, he will not show me. But he thinks highly of what you are to become. He warns me that you are bound to suffer if you don't change

Melissa's course. She's about to make a mistake, and we are all likely to suffer for it. But we've already talked about that. I'm here to talk to you about your heart and what horrible thing you are doing to it. It would be better for you to commit your feelings to the one you're meant to be with than to continue to flirt with both like this."

Charles thought of Melissa and their recently ended conversation. He thought about the moment when she bumped into him as he boarded the plane and the rush of suppressed feelings from childhood. Was she the one he was meant to be with. What was Aldrich talking about?

"And which one is that, master seer?"

"You flatter me. No, Wodin sent the warning, but as always he sent no more guidance than that. The answer to that puzzle is up to you to figure out. But as I warned you, your choice will decide if both of you suffer or not."

Charles gave Aldrich a puzzled and agitated look. He tried for a moment to decide exactly what the little man was telling him. Un-fazed by Charles' reaction, the priest walked away and returned to the couches where Charles had talked to Melissa. When Charles finally gave up on figuring out the riddle, and started to ask him, Aldrich was already lying back down. He couldn't ask the question without disturbing the others around him.

Alone again, and nervous that Silas might want to give him relationship advice too, he looked beside him at the one person on the plane Charles actually understood. The spy, the puzzle-master, was engrossed in his work and was not even aware of what was going on anywhere else on the plane.

Charles watched as the lights of the coastline descended behind them and the darkness of the Atlantic took over. The same darkness swallowed him and his mood as he thought over Aldrich's warnings, their ultimate destination, and what he knew of Melissa's plan. Charles accepted the one fact he had shared with Elaine. Nothing would be the same on the other side of this.

CHAPTER 4 - INTO THE DRAGON'S TEETH

September 7 – 1620 CET – Hotel Hirsch, Füssen, Bavaria, Germany

Elaine had told herself many times over the past few months that she had not asked for this. She knew, deep down, that she was wrong. She had more than asked for it, she had sought it out, stalked it, and wrestled it to the ground. In her own weak defense she could still point out that the one part she had not asked for was to be a sorceress. She had not asked to be innately able to control and manipulate magic.

At least now she was not alone. She was not the only human innate, although the other one she knew of didn't seem able to manifest enough magic to get herself out of trouble and was awaiting rescue just outside of town. Elaine was conflicted now. She wanted to help Silas save his friend and the only other human innate Elaine knew, but she also had to stay true to Helena's plan. She had not invited her in to lose focus.

Elaine collected her single backpack from the cargo area of the Toureg and left the others standing around shifting gear. The flight had allowed her to reassess her situation and have an honest conversation with herself. Helena had asked her to come to help Melissa. It seemed that her hero wanted her to figure out the clues she had left behind. She had gone as far as she could with the resources in the library, so it was time to look elsewhere. Everything said what she was looking for would be in Germany.

But it wasn't just the legend that was drawing her there, not anymore. It seemed everyone was racing there with blind abandon. At least she could no longer complain about not being where she needed to be. The challenge now was staying alive as everything was converging.

Elaine slipped into a chair in the lobby to wait for the others to get organized and took out her journal. From a front pocket she pulled her favorite fountain pen, a gift from her mother. Then she placed the crystal orb in Lancelot's lap for safe keeping. She pointed a warning finger at him as if he needed to be told to protect it. The admonition was not required as he had never failed her before, but she still felt responsible for giving him clear instructions.

Elaine set the bag aside before she opened the book and scanned the last entry. How would she gather the past forty-eight hours on paper? How would she tell herself that she had fallen hard for Charles just to lose him to the two-thousand year old dragon while witnessing the destruction of human government by dragons and their partial dragon compatriots? It was a daunting task, and she would not complete it in this sitting.

She knew she should capture the more important facts, but she could not get her own emotions out of her head. Between naps on the plane she had thought through what had happened and still could not believe it. Had she really ever had Charles? That was the question and the true story for her to capture. A morality tale of sorts to warn her not to do it again. She had fallen for a committed man, which was ten times worse than falling for a married man. She felt the tingle of magic and a tear at the same time and controlled the reaction with deep breaths. She couldn't afford to become an emotional wreck in the middle of the hotel.

Determined not to let her pain at his betrayal destroy her, she focused her emotions into the pen as she often did while writing in her journal. Without thinking about what she was doing, she continued to ruminate on Charles and Melissa while she doodled down the edge of the page. She often drew glyphs of unreadable illumination down the margins of her journal. She never thought about what they were or what they meant. She just allowed them to form as she thought about something. The images that formed never had anything to do with what she was thinking. There were pages of illuminated text throughout the journal where she had doodled her pain and anger away. That way she could focus the written word on the important facts and not the emotional garbage that littered her mind. The square boxes, ovals, and polygons connected by intertwined vines engraved with runes formed windows into her emotional world. As she allowed the pen to darken some areas and block others, the borders formed with runes she could not understand and never had.

She broke away from the illumination to write a few paragraphs of text about scrying for Valdiest and finding the president. She captured nearly a full page of text before her mind relaxed and her pen returned to the growing glyph. In the first box she drew a dragon in flight. Why not? It wasn't the first dragon she had drawn in an illumination, and the pen was in charge. The next polygon wrapped in scales was a tower steeped in evil portent. Every brick seemed to ooze evil slime. Line after line, dot for dot, the images formed as she allowed the ink to flow onto the page as the pen drove her hand. By the time she had finished the text and the illumination, she had an interesting triptych captured between runes and vines. It showed a dragon, a tower, and a village at the head of a valley that stood just below an earthen dam. She had no idea what the image or runes said. As far as she knew, it had nothing at all to do with the text.

Elaine flipped the page and started it with the obligatory date. On the left outside corner next to the date, she drew a quick octagon. Within the borders she captured a bald man from his shoulder up. His eyes haunted her as she highlighted his chin and strong nose with shadows. She didn't know who he was, but something in the one-inch portrait scared her. The lifelike eyes accused her of something, betrayal perhaps. In the gray scale tones of her stippling the face looked familiar but arcane. It reminded her of the enraged look of Charles' eyes the morning of the attacks. For an instant, she wondered if her emotions might be in control instead of the magic that usually drove her illuminations. With a shiver, she closed the book and shoved it back into her backpack. Whatever his story was, if it had anything to do with Charles, it could wait. At least she could wait.

She looked up from her book into those very eyes without the rage. He was standing at the counter looking toward her while the others handed out room keys. Kaliastrid looked up at her and put out an inviting arm.

"I need a roommate. How do you fancy bunking with me for a night?"

Elaine felt the smile cross her face before she could answer, and Kaliastrid nodded at the unspoken acceptance.

"While they're plotting and planning, we'll get some ice cream and popcorn, curl up in the blankets, and watch something emotional on pay-per-view."

Elaine could not help but laugh at the motherly effort she was making. The dark eyes she had illuminated onto the page refused to release her, though. The man with Charles' angry eyes had more to say, but she needed the rest Kaliastrid promised. Again she decided, he would have to wait.

Melissa broke into her planning for a relaxing slumber party. "Before the two of you run off and bond, I need to meet with everyone on the terrace. We need to discuss how we're going to approach this now that we're here."

Aldrich's frown appeared just beyond Melissa's elbow. Elaine could tell that he was not happy. Charles and Silas nodded their understanding and approval.

"So, let's get our gear stowed and meet in thirty," Silas said.

Everyone except Aldrich and Elaine broke from the huddle to scurry up to their room. Aldrich looked at her with an amazed look on his face.

"They're going to run full speed to their doom," he said.

"It's not all bad, Aldrich. We're on the right trail to figure out what Helena was trying to tell us. We're exactly where we should be."

"Sure, but we're not following the right path. They're on their way to devastation and death."

"Maybe—" She started to tell him about the man to see what he thought. Then she decided it might be best to keep him to herself. She was not sure if he had anything to do with this, and her journal was private.

"I can't even convince *you* that this is a mistake."

"No, because I don't think all of it is. We're supposed to be here. Maybe we're not supposed to go after Nethliast while we're here, but this is where we need to be. This is where it all started. How could we possibly come here and not conflict with Nethliast?"

Aldrich paused and considered what she said. "Melissa challenged me on the plane to find a safe path, a solution, and all I continue to pursue is their plan. Maybe you can help me find the alternative. I need a different approach if I'm going to find any positive outcome."

He paused and concentrated for a moment.

"Think with me on what path we should take here. Think only of what you want answered and try to be open to the direction. Keep your own wishes out of your thoughts."

She focused her chaotic mind and tried to narrow her concentration as Aldrich had described, but the spooky eyes fought with her for attention.

Satisfied that he had a clear picture of what he wanted to know, he reached into the pouch at his waist and drew out a tile.

"Put out your hand."

She followed his direction. He laid the tile face down on her palm. She had never watched a divination before, but she felt power rush into the tile in her hand.

With two more dips into the pouch he had two final tiles that he laid out face down in her palm.

He turned them over in sequence and considered each one carefully. Once he had them all exposed, he studied them as a whole.

"So, what we start with is obvious. We have a division. That will lead to conflict and danger, possibly even death. But it will bring us back together, stronger and focused."

"See, that's good news then." She didn't feel that the divination was as positive as he presented.

"Eh, the conflict and danger are still very dire. The final result is not as strong as it should be. It is not as sure as the conflict. We may not come through it."

"Wow, way to cheer me up there, Aldrich."

He moaned. "It doesn't work that way. It takes far more to get a positive result than you think. When you get one, you better believe it will happen because they are rare. The Norns most often come stacked against you."

"Well, we can take what we have and work with it. Let's go. We don't want to be late."

"No, Wodin forbid we make Charles wait again."

Elaine grinned knowingly and with a hint of sadness at Aldrich as she grabbed her bag and the sour-faced man in her illumination.

September 7 – 1720 CET – Hotel Hirsch, Füssen, Bavaria, Germany

Charles agreed that traveling in military transports and using their resources made their travel easier, but it was not the way to travel if you were trying not to stand out. He felt like an obvious outsider as he walked out onto the back deck of the Hotel Hirsch. Although the world was holding its breath following Nethliast's first attack and news of the Partial Liberation Army ultimatums was starting to settle in, it still felt odd to be in uniform among the civilians enjoying their vacations.

The terrace on the back of the hotel was empty except for Silas, who was sitting in a lounge chair with his Pelican case in front of him. Most of the hotel patrons were either out enjoying the city or were in the hotel restaurant. They would have the terrace to themselves for a while.

They had slept on the flight over. Everyone was rested, but they had also eliminated any possible jet lag. He had seen it work before. If your circadian rhythms are messed up before you start a trip, you spend the trip mostly asleep. When you land in the morning, you don't feel the lost time or out of cycle.

The sleep and relative peace of the trip had done nothing to improve his mood, however. He was still struggling with a truth he had refused to admit as a young man and with Aldrich's dire threat. On the other side of the ocean he could finally admit that he had feelings for both women, but that only defined one of his problems. That particular issue would have to wait until he had dealt with the other one. Aldrich's foreboding comments had not been as easy to resolve. Midway across the ocean, Charles had wanted to shake the little shaman awake and force him to explain what he meant, but Charles knew that would work about as well as trying to get Silas to give up any of his secrets. He also knew that he was just reacting to the agitation of inaction.

Charles' time on the battlefield had taught him that the quiet time between battles was nearly as dangerous to the soldier as combat. Those reflective moments always set the stage for the next battle. Mental demons could kill a soldier as sure as an IED. There was no room for him to take emotions, fears, worries, or any thoughts into battle. When a soldier had time to think about things, weaknesses inevitably snuck in. Charles had allowed doubts into his mind, the most troubling of which was Melissa.

Why? She had always been off limits. Nothing had changed about that. She was the daughter of the man his father worked for. Even as a child when they played together, he knew he was not like her. So much had happened since the day he announced he was joining the Marines. That day Melissa had been proud of him, and he had felt that pride. That was the first time he had impressed her, and it was the last day he had seen her before his father's deception had brought him back to the family. Since that one day, long ago, he had never had the opportunity to impress her again. A childhood infatuation had died. She was his responsibility. It was that simple. She was not someone he should be attracted to.

From the moment he had walked on the plane though, he had been compromised. He had been feeling better. Melissa was safe. Even if they were rushing across the ocean to find Nethliast, who had been dead or missing up until a few hours before, he had been pleased that everyone was safe. That was when the sapper made it into his defenses. That was when he first realized that he loved her.

After his conversation with her and his own realization that he could not do his job if he allowed himself to love her, he hoped that was settled. He could shift to thinking about Aldrich's warnings, and not the one about picking the right woman. He had to focus on the other threats to the team. He needed to figure out how best to protect Melissa and the others as they raced into the teeth of the dragons in Germany. He had to forget about how she felt pressed against him. His thoughts had to transition to how he would keep them alive and avoid the suffering Aldrich spoke of.

Silas was fumbling with the small puzzle box again. He seemed obsessed with it. Charles wondered if it was the same one he was focused on when they had met him in Washington. Silas had not slept on the plane while he wrestled with the obviously irritating box.

"You want some coffee?" Charles asked, pointing to the service against the terrace wall.

"Sure. As long as you didn't make it."

"You would like mine. I've had years since I left the Marines to perfect it."

Silas grimaced at a painful memory. Charles grinned.

With two cups of the black aromatic liquid in his hands, he crossed over the rooftop overlook to join the spy. Aldrich slipped up beside him and took one of the cups from his hand.

"Thanks. Smells good and strong. Just the way I like it."

Charles grinned at the small warrior priest. He seemed to be in a better mood than sixteen hours before.

Silas carefully set the puzzle box down in the Pelican box and took caution to place it so that none of the side panels touched anything. It took so long that Charles was becoming irritated at having to wait.

Aldrich rejoined them, having doctored his coffee with cream, eliminating the very quality of the coffee he had praised. He also handed Charles a new cup to replace the one he had taken. Aldrich stared at the puzzle box as Silas looked up at Charles and took the cup. The agent braced for a shock and sipped the steaming liquid.

"This is good coffee," he said with a jab at Charles, who was just trying it himself.

"I've made better."

"Careful. They may revoke your Marine decoder ring if they find out."

"My tea is even better. What does that mean for my future in the Marines?"

"It may be over before it starts."

Charles laughed and sipped more of the coffee. It was good.

"What's the ground truth, Silas?" Charles asked as he sat down in the lounge chair next to him. "Why are you doing this?"

"Why do you think?"

"A woman? You expect me to believe that? It's not your style. Don't agents like you have one in every country?"

"That's sailors and ports. Charles, I don't expect you to believe anything I say. Maybe that's better for us, but it would be easier if we could at least agree not to disagree just because of who said something. Anyway, why do you have a hard time believing that it's all about Tara? It's the same reason you're here, only it seems you're here for two of them. I do, or did, have a woman in every country, but none were like Tara. Well, that's not completely true. There was one—but that was a world away."

Charles was not able to stop the blush that flashed across his cheeks as the man seemed to zero in onto his vulnerability like every agent Charles had ever known.

"Fine. Agreed. But I don't think anyone else here has any idea what's ahead of us."

"You mean war?"

Charles nodded. "They may be dragons, but I don't think they've ever faced war like we've seen. Modern war is nothing like what they've experienced."

"Something about Melissa tells me you're wrong. I don't think we have any idea what the world used to be like. I don't think the history we have tells anything close to the real stories. She may have led legions of half-dragons over the walls of castles and massacred millions. There's a lot of knowledge behind those eyes. From what I've seen, magic makes for a brutal battle."

Charles cringed at the idea of Melissa leading legions and witnessing the horrible outcome of battle. "You can't really believe that."

"After how she reacted in the hospital and the brutality of Nethliast's attacks, I'm not sure what she's capable of. You didn't see the footage I saw. You didn't see her. You didn't see the focus and resolve I saw when she was pressed into a corner. She would have killed if she had been pressed any further."

"You never should have pressed her at all."

"You say that in the same breath that you ask if she's ready to face war. I've at least tested the temper of the metal. I know what she can do if she has to."

Charles started to argue and paused. "Either way, she's taking a lot of chances coming out here with you and putting herself within reach of Nethliast. I can't let her keep risking her life like this. I'm not sure this is the right way to be approaching this, and Aldrich has the same concerns."

Silas laughed a little too loudly, and Aldrich jumped from a shock from the puzzle box. Silas looked at the priest with a scowl.

"What are you doing? That thing could kill all of us."

"Really? Not if I follow these directions correctly and you stop startling me."

Silas looked at him cross-eyed before scanning the surface of the box for any clue of what he was talking about.

"You can't possibly see it," Aldrich said as Silas continued to stare at the box as if the words 'press here to open' would suddenly appear. "It's a magical script, like a glyph on the surface. Even if you could read it, it's not in the right sequence."

Unable to come up with an argument to Aldrich's point, Silas leaned forward to close the case. "Try not to get us killed. This is not some dormant dig somewhere. These boxes can have serious effects if you don't open them right. I expect they're worse now that all this magic is floating around us."

Aldrich looked offended at Silas, reopened the case, and resumed analyzing the box.

"What were you saying—Oh right. You're being as unrealistic as I am. How can you protect her? She's a dragon." Silas raised his hands in front of him to attempt to describe the magnitude of that fact as he sat back in his chair. "I'm still trying to get my head around that one. You," he pointed at Charles. "You can't protect her from other dragons any more than I can."

"Maybe not, but I can try. I will learn how, and when I do learn, none will touch her." Charles looked away from Silas and stared at the unfamiliar ground below them.

"You do that." Silas paused and let the comment fall into silence. Both men watched Aldrich as if he were juggling live hand grenades. Neither actually moved to stop him this time.

"You soldiers always get me," Silas continued. "You always think you can win anything. I guess, if there's a company of you, that may be true. But you're alone here."

"What about you, then?" Charles asked defensively. "What do you think you're going to do? You can't stand against one dragon, much less an army of them. We have a rough idea where the president is. We're here, at best, on a hunch, and you're leading us into this conflict blind."

"It's more of a bet, really. I bet Elaine can find her. She found Melissa. I bet she can tell us what we're up against. When we go after Tara, we will find Nethliast. Then this will all be over."

"Now who's overestimating their ability?"

"You're right. Maybe we're not that different. But I have a few surprises yet. And we have Aldrich, Elaine, Kaliastrid, and Melissa."

Charles sniffed, mostly at his point that they were not different. The conversation fell off again.

Silas seemed to visibly restrain himself from taking the polyhedron from Aldrich and clapping him on the back of the head.

"I don't believe in the impossible," Silas rejoined the debate. "That's how we're different. You identify the impossible, admit that it's such, and still rush in. I just don't accept that anything is impossible. How else are we so different?"

Charles shook his head without conceding the similarities. "Then what are we doing here?"

"Our duty," he answered, "plain and simple. You agree with that, don't you?"

"Wodin is proud of your commitment to your duty. In fact, it's why he knew each of you would be here in the end. But he would prefer if you would use your heads and not your hearts to solve this," Aldrich mumbled as he held the box by two of the edges and looked up at the bottom from underneath. Holding it by those same opposite edges, he lowered it to his waist.

"What is that thing anyway? Why is it so dangerous?" Charles asked, ignoring the comment about duty. He pointed at the puzzle box.

"That. That is truly the impossible."

"No, really. What is it?"

"It's an ancient puzzle that is not even supposed to exist," Silas finally answered. "I've been collecting them all of my life, and this is the last one a friend of mine sent me. I hope it is the first one I will succeed in opening. According to my great-grandfather, it's a gnome puzzle box."

Aldrich harrumphed. "You can't really believe in those crazy tales. If it's really a gnome puzzle box, which I can't believe—there's no evidence they ever existed—then why is this hidden message written in Norse runes?"

Silas stared at the scholar.

"You believe in elves. You're likely a throwback to actual dwarves, if I'm to believe anything about what's happening. But you can't believe in gnomes when you're holding a box that has tiny gears hidden under the surface plates. Where do you see Norse runes?"

Aldrich looked up and rolled his eyes at Silas.

"I told you, it's a magical inscription. You can't see it, and I can't give you any way to see it. But, believe me or not, the writing is runic Norse."

Charles stared at the metal polyhedron in Aldrich's lap. "It looks modern to me. It doesn't look like an ancient puzzle box."

"Very observant," Silas agreed. "That's because it's such a miniature device—to us. Not so small to a gnome."

"You're talking about the little dwarf-like guys people put out in their yards. Does your boss know you believe in gnomes?"

Aldrich guffawed, but didn't let his gaze leave the box.

Silas raised and lowered both hands in a physical sign of frustration. "Both of you are amazingly short-sighted. You're joking about me believing in gnomes, and we're in Germany with two dragons, a human enchantress, and this dwarf priest who talks to Wodin. Are you listening to yourselves, either of you?"

Aldrich looked over as if he was going to argue about the dwarf comment, but just shook his head and returned his attention to the box.

Charles grinned when he realized Silas was right. He was limiting his belief to what he had seen. The agent had reminded him of a lesson he had learned on the battlefield. It was a tactical mistake to discount any possibilities until you had proof. Charles took a moment to adjust his thinking so that a gnome puzzle box with his name on it didn't kill him or his team. "Go on, then. What's in the gnome puzzle box?"

"I won't know until—"

"Pixie magic," Aldrich interrupted.

"Where does it say that?" Silas stood to look down on Aldrich and the offending puzzle. Charles took a hint of pleasure at Silas' discomfort over what seemed to be a personal conquest.

"Right there. But don't believe me. Look for yourself." Aldrich pressed two plates, turned a lever that appeared from a slit between them, and then pushed it back into the slit. The box popped open, exposing a cluster of small crystal stones tied together with a delicate silver wire. The slender circlet glowed for a moment before what looked like fireflies flitted from the tips of the twelve largest crystals and spiraled around Aldrich in a rising column of brilliant streaks before they dispersed into the surrounding foliage.

Silas stepped back and fell into his lounge chair as the lights flitted past him.

Charles leaned back as well to avoid an imagined threat. When everything settled down, the three men stared at the jeweled diadem until Silas broke the enchantment.

"How did you do that?"

Aldrich looked at the incredulous puzzle master with a grin on his face. "Like I said, I read the instructions. Once I figured out how they were ordered on the outer skin, it was simple."

Charles grinned at the discomfited spy and stood up to leave them to their discussion. He could admit that they were both just doing their duty, in their own way. He needed to check on the others. It was past time for the briefing Melissa had organized. Just as he approached the entrance, the three absent women arrived.

~~~~

Melissa walked onto the back terrace of the Hotel Hirsch and into a cloud of fireflies. The swarm, which she had never seen with fireflies before, swept out of the greenery below the patio that formed the biergarten and encircled her. She stopped walking to allow them to settle or go away. As the cylinder of swirling lights encased her, she felt a sudden relief. She could not explain why it made her feel so relaxed since she was about to attend a war council long in the making, but it put her mind at peace for the first time since the emergence. It felt like the whole world had just sighed.

The door to the terrace opened again, and Kaliastrid and Elaine joined them. As they approached Melissa the cloud of what clearly was not fireflies spun into a swirling pattern that wove around each of them. It briefly encircled each woman before it burst like fireworks around them. Each individual light vanished back into the foliage. Elaine giggled at the experience and reached out to touch a single light that floated about her head. It encircled her finger several times before it dove into the waves of her recently washed and dried hair. Elaine giggled again as the mysterious light vanished. Then she looked up at Kaliastrid as if to ask where it went.

"That was interesting," Kaliastrid said. "Was that what I think it was?"

"I'm not sure," Melissa replied. "Depends on what you thought it was."

"Pixies!" Elaine said in unison with the baritone rejoinder from Aldrich.

The euphoric feeling and Elaine's giggle suddenly made sense. Pixies were known to inspire joy with their presence, sometimes to the detriment of the party they were affecting. Elaine's relaxation was stronger because she did not have the same magical resistance that Melissa and Kaliastrid had. But even they were affected when the cloud surrounded them. As Melissa watched, a single pixie alighted somewhere in Kaliastrid's black hair. She assumed a similar pixie was hiding somewhere near her. For the most part they were a positive force. They were part of the reason fireflies continued to maintain some level of romantic charm even in a world without magic.

"Well, we can rest assured we will have few secrets anymore," Kaliastrid moaned in one of her more agitated tones. Melissa swore she heard the pixie beside her whine sorrowfully.

"You know that has never been proved."

"I'll remain convinced until I see reason to doubt."

"Unless we dispel them..."

"We can't do that," Elaine cried emphatically and stepped up next to Kaliastrid as if she was asking her to keep a puppy.

Kaliastrid looked from the girl to Melissa. Melissa shrugged and looked at her mother with a prepared look and told her in her mind, *"You created that problem as well."*

Kaliastrid harrumphed and surrendered.

Melissa turned to face the three men, who were watching the events silently. They were all three smiling, obviously included in the slight euphoria that remained on the terrace. She was not sure if that was good or bad. Either way, she had waited and considered long enough. It was time to share her plan, for what it was. Their council might change her mind, but she had considered everyone's input on the flight over. Now she would see if she was an ambassador or not.

"We're heading into more danger than any of us can imagine," she started. They all settled in to listen. "There is no doubt Nethliast is expecting someone to come after him. In fact he's probably expecting me to come rescue my father. That is exactly what I plan to do."

Everyone, except Silas and Kaliastrid, moved to disagree first. Charles and Aldrich shifted their feet and turned a little toward her to make it clear they had an opinion. Elaine raised a finger. The twinkling pixie flitted about her head and finger, distracting her as Melissa raised her hand to stop the collective arguments.

"I don't care what rank you're wearing or which deity you represent; I don't care if you think this is a foolish thing to do. I'm in control of this plan and I have considered everyone's points. I have not ignored you. I can explain why. This is not an emotional decision. I have to stop Nethliast, now. He has already been allowed to get too far without redress. I am bound to react to his rebellion, if nothing else."

Silence followed her declaration.

"Good. That does not mean your opinions and suggestions are not important. I need your help, which is why you're all here." She looked at her mother, noting the dissatisfaction at her inclusion of the others. She went on without commenting on it. "So, with that said, I want everyone to understand, the search for the talisman and Helena's plan is still critical, and it will proceed. If I fail, you cannot. Nethliast must never find the talisman.

He cannot have that much power at his command." The sudden clarity of the situation in her mind felt comforting, even though she could not explain why everything suddenly made sense.

Aldrich nodded at her point and listened as she continued. She had at least mollified his concern, or they were all drunk on pixie magic, and nothing she was doing would make sense in the morning. A flutter of light in her periphery and a soft whine amused her. Could they read her mind? Was that why they could affect emotions so well? She grinned as the whine turned positive. Before the pause seemed awkward, she continued.

"Elaine told me back at the manor and again in Knoxville that the search for the talisman and Helena's plan probably needed to move to Germany. Aldrich, what do you think?"

"Well, in the past few hours our path has improved as things seem to be converging. I started feeling better when our path headed into Bavaria. I think Elaine and I may be in the best place to continue the research. There's a library here, at the Abbey of Saint Mang, that may have some clues. Based on what Charles and Elaine uncovered in their research so far, that may be our best direction."

"Elaine, you've been able to track the president. I've not asked you to track Nethliast because that could give our intent away. I don't want that. Where is the last location you have on her?"

"She was in Munich when we were flying in, but as we landed I found her on the way south into Bavaria. I tracked her to this area, but now I can't find her. I'll see if that has changed." She pulled the small sphere out and checked it again.

Kaliastrid shared a knowing look with Melissa. They might have started to block all divination. She kept the shared thought to herself.

"So, the plan." She paused to make sure everyone was listening. "I agree that we need to be here. Something is drawing us all here. Call it divine intervention, fate, or even pixie magic. Aldrich, you at least agree with that?" He nodded. "Okay. So as soon as we have found where Nethliast has the president, we will know where he is. I will need Elaine's help until we know that. After that, the three of you will continue without us. Charles, you have been an integral part of that search, and I need someone who can keep them safe. Kaliastrid, I want you to help."

The fire in Kaliastrid's eyes threatened to engulf Melissa. She knew the assignment would not go over well, which was why she decided the band-aid removal approach was best. As she had thought about the plan and Aldrich's warning, she decided she had to protect and continue the search for the talisman. She raised her hand again to forestall the protest that was about to engulf them.

"Wait. We have been in enemy territory since we landed. For this plan to work, Nethliast has to think we're coming for him. I don't want him to even think about the talisman; but, as soon as we know where he is and we engage him, you must find the talisman. They will probably come after all of us. I can't leave the searchers unprotected from partials and dragons. That means we must have a dragon with them. You are the only other dragon."

Whether it was because of the wisdom of her argument, respect for her position, or the soothing croon of the pixie at her ear, Kaliastrid nodded and suppressed her obvious irritation. Out of the corner of her eye, Melissa caught an appreciative nod from Silas. Charles was listening to her plan with an unreadable face. She hoped that was a good sign.

"All of my memories and every image I can access without pain include a castle in snow-covered mountains." A sudden image sprang into her mind, unfettered with pain. She felt a knot form in her throat. She had to swallow to clear it. Kaliastrid looked at her as if she saw it too. She continued. "It seems obvious that they were taking the president to Nethliast, so we will use her and my father to find exactly where. Elaine, I'm counting on you. Let's see if we can find them."

Elaine looked up from the sphere. "Something is blocking them both. He was clear earlier. Now he's gone. I'll keep searching." She returned her focus to the sphere. Another sparkling will-o-wisp joined a dance above Elaine's head. Melissa paused to watch the dance before continuing.

"We're not safe here. Based on this change, it seems Nethliast knows we're on our way. We expected this." Silas nodded in unison with Charles. "I would be surprised if he and his witch are not using the same tools we are. They could be watching us now. When we're close like this, it's easier. Remember, everyone's goal is the talisman, and you will have to move quickly once you have a clue in case they're tracking you. Any questions?"

Silence was her answer.

"Okay. We're on watch until Elaine finds a clue or we decide to change strategy." She looked at Silas to verify he was ready. He nodded. Everyone split up from the makeshift conference room.

When Charles stepped away to look out over the city of Füssen, Melissa motioned for him to join her and walked with him toward the rail.

Melissa could feel the distance between her and Charles like they were standing in a freezer. She ignored her own ache even though her fractured ancient memories seemed empty of anything similar for her to compare it to. She could not waste any more time on her meaningless emotions with everything that was ahead of them accelerating into a tight spiral.

"Listen, Charles, I'm going to be putting myself into some dangerous places. You can't protect me from that, and I can't ask you to."

She could see that he was preparing to argue. As much as the chivalrous sacrifice made her feel good, she knew, like she knew her own name, that she had to release him from any feeling of responsibility. She had to redirect his duty in case she didn't survive her guaranteed encounter with Nethliast.

"Stop. I know you feel responsible for me, but you've done your duty to Helena. You have made sure I made it here. Now you have to let Meliastrid do her duty."

He nodded solemnly.

"I want to keep Elaine and Aldrich's search a secret for as long as we can. I want Nethliast to think we came here after him. That's part of the reason we've not split up yet. The three of you will come up with some ideas of where to look. For some reason, I feel confident that we are close. I think Elaine and Aldrich already have some ideas. I need for you to take care of them. Help them find the answers hidden over here while I keep Nethliast's attention. We need it. We need the Heart of the Dragon. Can you do that?"

"So, you're what, the decoy? A distraction?"

"It's critical that we find the talisman." She started not to say anything else. "But, I'm not treating this as just a feint. I'm going to take the head off of the movement once and for all. I have to do that to protect my position with my kind anyway. He's stood up against me, and I can't allow that. If we can find my father and the president at the same time, that's a bonus. There's something special about the president. Why else would he bring her here?"

"I'm not sure I can let you risk your life like this."

"You can't protect me from this. This is not your path anymore. You, of all people, know the importance of using your resources in war." Melissa pulled the gold chain around her neck and extracted the amulet from beneath her blouse. "Heliantra passed this responsibility to me when she bound this to me. You got me here. Now, there are two missions. I'm leading one, and I need you leading the other one for me."

He nodded as his assignment shifted.

"Do this with the same focus you applied to protecting me, and we'll all succeed." She leaned over and kissed his cheek. The fire from the touch exploded through her lips and rushed through her body, burning for a moment in her loins. She cursed internally because she knew it had to be showing on her skin. She was glad for the darkness that had descended on the city. For an instant, in the golden light of the terrace, she thought she saw a similar flash of color on Charles' neck and face. However, he made no sign that it affected him. Melissa pushed her emotions where they belonged. Charles nodded and backed away from the rail to join the others. Just before he turned he looked up at her and caught her eyes with his.

"Come back to me, Melissa."

The look of concern and fear for her safety struck her like a spear in the chest.

"I will," she lied.

He completed his turn and assumed his new role. She had no doubt he would complete it or die trying. She trembled from her unavoicable emotions. Soon they would engage Nethliast. He would have the advantage. Now all she had to do was wait to see how he would use it.

CHAPTER 5 - AGAINST THE STRONGHOLD

September 8 – 0730 CET – Near Füssen, Germany

Valdiest could sense a presence in the cave. The witch had taken his eyes, so he couldn't see who it was, but his other senses told him everything he needed to know. The anger that filled the space in front of the cave beyond the doorway, and the aroma of the witch clinging to the tangy scent of dragon's hide told him his once trusted apprentice was standing before him. His full dragon form was towering over him in the small cavern. The witch had apparently left the barrier down when she was done. Valdiest did not sense that she was physically with him.

There was no threat of Valdiest leaving the cave in this shape. He could not fit through the entrance, and he could not transform in the protected cave. But Valdiest did not want to move. He had not eaten since they had chained him here. His chains didn't really allow him to move around the cave. So wasting energy trying to escape was senseless. A younger dragon may have been able to take the beatings and not succumb to the damage. Valdiest's lungs were filling with fluid. He suspected more failures he couldn't feel. He knew his time was limited now.

Ever since he had reached out and connected with the presence scrying him, Valdiest had known what his next step was. He would not be bait for Nicklaus, and he could not provide him any more information. He would not be responsible for giving that much power to this child. He needed his energy for what was next. Valdiest had made peace with his decision. Now all he had to do was enact it. Calmness filled him in exact opposition to the emotions pouring out of Nicklaus. He raised his head to point his nose at the dragon standing over him.

"You need to watch that anger, Nicklaus. You may wake up some day, wonder where your life went, and only have centuries of bitter rage to look back over. What do you want from me? I'm resting from a busy morning. I have no time for children."

"Your daughter's here."

Valdiest put as much strength as he could into pulling himself up to face the black bastard. The chains rattled slowly through their eyes and stopped at their maximum length. The action caused him to wince from some as-yet unidentified injury. He hated to show weakness. His lungs burned, and he coughed a ball of phlegm onto the cave floor. In regal defiance he pulled his shoulders back and faced Nicklaus.

He sniffed the air as if he might have missed a presence and tilted his head at Nicklaus.

"Ah, you don't mean that I have a visitor in this very human prison you've created for me. You mean she's come for you. You mean she's in her ancient seat of power." Valdiest relaxed his shoulders and started to slump back to the floor. He paused and turned his head back toward Nicklaus again. "Unless you've made your peace with her and brought her here as a sign of your desire to live, there is no one else here for me to waste my precious hours with. I do, however, sense your whore sneaking up behind you again." He shifted his head toward the female human who had walked up as he was speaking. "I could use a snack. Maybe you would share with an old wyrm."

He leered at her as best he could without eyes. He sensed her step back a little when his teeth showed. She still feared him, even though she had brutalized him for hours.

Nicklaus showed no sign of concern and didn't react to the barb about the woman.

"Your daughter has come with a small group of her beloved humans. I can't figure out why. Do you know, old one? Is there something planned I don't know about? Is it that fictitious talisman you were babbling about, or has she come for you?"

Valdiest could smell something else in the pheromones raging through the cave. It had been a long time, but he knew dragon fear when he smelled it.

"I've not spoken to my daughter since you trapped me here, Nicklaus. How could I?" Valdiest refused to call him the name he had stolen from their history. He was no Nethliast, and Valdiest would not insult the ancient dragon by calling the pretender that. "Perhaps she has come to kill you like she should have that first night. I never should have protected you."

The old dragon felt pride fill his chest, and he stood taller in the tiny cave. The chains pinched and pulled a little further out of the wall. He put everything he had left into the show.

Nicklaus' wings rustled angrily at the use of his human name and the implication that Meliastrid could kill him without much effort. Valdiest sensed the tension build in the air, but it wasn't enough. The anger was there, but so far it was focused on Meliastrid. Nicklaus laughed at him, and Valdiest cried inside. He would not be released so easily. He had more work to do.

"You know more than you're telling me, my king. You aren't being completely honest with your prince. I'll find out. What are you hiding? Why is she in Füssen, why is she so close? She couldn't kill me before. What makes you think she can kill me now? Her sorry band can't harm me either, not here. I'm taking back our country from the humans who stole it from us. Why can't she see that and give up this foolish love for them? If she comes after you—and why would she want to save your pitiful hide—I'll kill her like I should have. Then I'll snack on her human followers."

Valdiest sighed an unconcerned sigh and settled fully onto the floor. When he had shifted his scales about to find the most comfortable coil he could, he laid his head on the ground. His slow process of settling into position was chosen to make the move seem dismissing, like a king who was done with an unimportant guest.

"I'm hiding nothing, Nicklaus," he finally said. "I'm an old dragon who has seen everything he ever loved tainted. I'm sad and angry that I ever trusted you. You've taken my very old heart and eaten it like your New Year's feast. You've consumed me on your lusts. You've already destroyed me. Now you're demonstrating how human you really are. You don't have the compassion to kill me, so you're going to torture me with my family. You're holding prisoners just like that bastard Renard."

Valdiest's mind filled with suddenly clear memories of the old wizard. Why had he suddenly thought of him? Why was he important now? The dragons the vile wizard had tortured for information were the trigger. Valdiest had visited some of the hidden caves where the wizard had perpetrated his most egregious crimes. Those caves were very similar to this one.

He knew there was something important about that memory, but his old mind wouldn't release it. Perhaps if he spent a little more time in his own tortured memories he would dig it out, but he knew he would never survive another round of torture. So did Nicklaus.

His comparison of Nicklaus with the human wizard scored, though. Apparently everyone remembered that old wizard and his treachery. Nicklaus roared at the insult and dropped his upper body onto Valdiest's head. His foreclaws slashed at already blind eyes. Valdiest felt new wounds form and precious blood pour out onto the stone floor, but it wasn't enough. Even in his weakened form those wounds would heal. His head swam with lights and pain, but he could not surrender to unconsciousness. He had to remove the chance that Meliastrid would come for him.

The witch was cackling behind Nicklaus, urging him on. Valdiest summoned what little magic he could. With a silent thought he grabbed her small body. Her laugh cut off in a surprised gulp.

He wanted to crush her into a broken heap of flesh, but his weakened state robbed him of the ability to conjure that much power. All he could do was slam her into the cave wall. He felt a deep satisfaction as her breath rushed out in a huff. He had at least figured out the types of magic she had not blocked. She fell to the base of the wall.

"What's sad, Nicklaus," Valdiest continued to press, "is that you aren't even as strong as Renard. You have to rely on a human witch to imprison me, an old wyrm."

Nicklaus pummeled him again with a violent strike to both sides of his head, and Valdiest almost lost consciousness. It was still not enough. He had to drive him to rage.

"You're afraid aren't you? You're afraid of her. I smell it on you under that vile aroma of whore you're covered in. You're afraid of my daughter, aren't you? You fear Meliastrid. You fear the dragon ambassador, as you should."

Nicklaus shifted but said nothing.

"She's caused you more problems than you ever expected."

He paused.

"She was always more than you deserved, you runt spawn of a diseased egg. Even before we retreated, you paled in her magnificent presence. You actually disappeared in her presence. We had to remind dragons you were actually there. No one who saw you together, remembered you. But now..."

The old wyrm chuckled to emphasize how much less he was than before.

"You've had to find someone less impressive than you, and that was a hard search. You picked a human female that you can manipulate. And, no surprise, you failed at that too. Even this frail human whore has manipulated you. She outshines you, wallowing where she lies. Soon you will carry her about like a princess on an impotent horse, a gelding. You don't deserve that name you've stolen from our history. You do not even deserve your own dragon name. Learn our history before you pretend to be something great, you emasculated cuckold."

He chuckled again and tried to feel if any of his taunts were getting through. He knew pride would not allow much more.

"You're a sad dragon, driven by the basest emotions. You're far more guilty of what you convict Meliastrid. You will never stand against her."

Valdiest let a full laugh escape his tortured lungs.

"Your future is written in our history. You can't even see it because you're blind to the compassion we are truly capable of. I'm glad, in my blind and weak state, that I can finally see that much of our past."

Nicklaus roared and shifted around in the small cave.

Valdiest had found a nerve in the anger. He would never know what Meliastrid had done that had hurt Nicklaus so much, but he had found the trigger that he needed.

"You think she'll come here, don't you? You think I can draw her to you and make her submit to you. You want me to call to her so you can show her how powerful you are. Or perhaps you fear that I've already called for her, given away you're secret, told her about your witch whore? You're afraid of her, you pitiable beast. What if I have? What if I'm calling to her now? If I have, it won't be like you think. She'll do what a dragon should. She'll laugh at you as she rips your weak spine from your body through your chest. You should be afraid. If she comes for you, it will be to kill you."

Nicklaus roared again and paced in front of the old wyrm.

"Yes, she's going to beat you. She will win because she's doing exactly what she's supposed to do. Oh, it's so clear now at my end. You can't win. You've seen her color, haven't you? You've seen what she is. You know what it means now, we all do. Only the most deluded of us can ignore that sign. Every one of us knows in our bones, even if we lie to our minds."

He laughed a deep laugh from his soul at his old friend. His mind was clearing some as he was dying. The new memories of Meliastrid were important, and they were coming as he needed them now. He had not realized what the subtle color change had really meant until just then. Now it was clear that she had power even over the king.

The air was full of rage like gas vapor.

Valdiest could feel it building in Nicklaus.

He could smell it.

The enraged youth had gone over his edge.

All that was required was a spark.

"You'll bow to her, like we all will. The Great Wyrm requires it. You can't deny that. It's in your blood. You'll submit to her like the child you are. You'll grovel to her for your very life— your pitiful, sad, life. If you're lucky, she will let you vanish into obscurity. But I'm going to tell her to make an example of you and your human rider. I'm going to call her here to punish you for your failure of dragon kind."

Valdiest felt the surge and had enough time for one last thought.

"My Love!" He put all the feeling and knowledge he had into that final thought before blessed darkness overcame him.

September 8 – 0747 CET – Füssen, Bavaria, Germany

Kaliastrid screamed and jumped to her feet, upsetting the small table of teas and coffee they were enjoying for breakfast in Melissa' s room.

Silas jumped away from the disrupted table, drawing a short knife from his sleeve in reaction to the sudden unexplained disturbance.

Charles was moving at the same time. He had his side arm out as he dropped into his combat crouch and scanned the crowded room for threats.

Elaine rolled off of the bed and onto her feet. She had been sprawled across the mussed coverlet with her journal and a plate of fruit. Blue arcs of lightning ran over her hands. She stood looking back and forth between Melissa and Kaliastrid.

Aldrich mumbled something about Wodin and thrust his fist into the air. The pressure in the room increased noticeably as he completed his fist thrust and a wave of force extended around him.

The mess forgotten, Melissa stared at a space on the wall that looked east from where they were. A tear ran down her cheek.

Kaliastrid shivered into her hands and looked back at the others around the disturbed table. Tears streamed down her face, which was contorted with a combination of grief and rage. A ragged roar burst from her chest. She took a deep breath and exhaled slowly. The flood of emotions and images was still rushing through her mind. Her pulse was rapid in her ears as she tried to control her urge to kill. The rush was starting to ebb, but anger was welling up inside of her.

"That bastard killed him," she spat. Acid ate into the carpet next to a spilled cup of tea.

Melissa turned pale as she shook off the ripples of Valdiest's message.

"What's going on?" Silas asked. Charles shook his head.

Kaliastrid had no words for how she felt as she rode the waves of passion and memory.

There was nothing more to explain.

Valdiest's last emotions poured over her.

His pain and anger mingled with hers and amplified her own desires. Key facts filled her mind from the deluge of information.

Valdiest was gone.

Nethliast had killed him.

They were being followed.

Nethliast knew where they were.

She screamed again as the final release reached her and her anger spiked in her mind. In two steps, she was across the room and at the window. It opened onto a small balcony.

She flung it open, discarding the broken lock and frame. Scales were already rippling across her body. She became more dragon with each step. With a single bound and no hesitation she was through the opening and in the air. Her transformation completed as she fell.

Emerald wings burst from her back to give her support in her fall. Massive legs erupted out behind her, and her torso expanded. Her long neck pushed out of her back all before the snap-rattle of the membrane announced her sudden presence over the street below.

With a strong downward thrust of her wings followed by a rapid beat, she stopped her plummet before she smacked into the asphalt. With little wasted movement she turned, climbed into the air, and circled the building.

When she reached roof height, she looked back. Melissa was through the window, transformed, and following her.

Good, she thought. She needed to see this. Valdiest had sent her more than a goodbye in his last emotional mental blast.

"Show yourselves!"

She broadcast her command through the village and around the hotel to any partial that could hear her mind. She knew they would be there. She could sense them now, like rotten meat in a freezer.

In a break in the trees of the biergarten behind the hotel, seated at a table with other tourists, what looked like a human put down a newspaper and stood up as if he had been yanked from his seat.

Another stood from a table nearby.

A third, a female, stood beside the last. Unlike the males, she immediately ran, disappearing into the trees.

Kaliastrid flapped, turned, and dropped from the air, racing toward the three partials. The thick hedge would force the runner to exit toward the front of the hotel or into the parking lot at the rear. Her original course was toward the parking lot. Kaliastrid angled to intercept her where the garden exited. The female would have been smarter to stay in the cover of the trees. Neither course of action would save her, but she had obviously decided that she was not going to die standing still. The partial's flight instinct was driving her to get away, but it was not full retreat. She was looking for a place to stand and fight. The trees covering the garden were thick, but Kaliastrid saw occasional flashes of movement as the partial plunged toward the parking lot.

She emerged from concealment fully transformed. Dark green and yellow scales covered her body. Horns emerged from her skull. Darker green scales covered what had been red hair. Having left the cover and committed to the run, the partial was pumping her arms as she headed east without looking back. Kaliastrid could sense her pulling magic. She was preparing to attack.

Kaliastrid stroked the air harder to restart her dive and lunged after the running half-blood. She was upon her swiftly. Her claws were closing around the partial as she was turning to release her spell. Kaliastrid felt the magical blast strike her scales as her foreclaws wrapped around the squirming body. The half-blood's scales, between Kaliastrid's claws, rippled and pulsed as the female fought her inevitable death. Mana erupted between Kaliastrid's claws as the partial fought to survive.

Hovering over the parking lot, she held the partial, waiting for her magical energy to bleed off. As the energy ebbed and futility settled into the partial's mind, the small female pounded at the talons that were ripping into her scales. Resignation to her ultimate end rushed into her eyes as anger melted into terror.

Kaliastrid flexed her muscled arms, and the body stopped twitching with a loud snap. She flexed one last time and ripped it apart. Green blood and entrails spewed out onto the ground.

Kaliastrid threw the corpse aside like useless trash. The two halves of the dead partial rebounded off the trunk of a car and slammed into the back of a delivery van in the parking lot. Spinning around, she settled into the lot, looking back over the partial's entrails. A roar of anger exploded from her chest, shaking the trees in front of her.

Screams that were already filling the air in the garden suddenly reached Kaliastrid's ears. Humans who had been enjoying the cool morning in the Bavarian garden were already rushing out of the exit to the front of the hotel. Some who seemed to lose all sense of danger were running toward the enraged dragon.

The two half-bloods that remained had grown bold with their partner's resistance and had chased after her. Magical bolts of energy struck Kaliastrid's scales and dissipated uselessly. She knew they were among the humans who were charging for the exit, but she could no longer see her targets clearly.

"You will die as badly," Kaliastrid hissed over the discarded viscera. "You have aligned with the wrong side in this fight."

New bolts of lightning arced at her from the crowd. Disturbed humans shied away from the enraged caster. Kaliastrid deflected each with her shield spell.

Humans, tourists, and innocent merchants were too close for her breath. She wanted each of her targets to suffer for their part in Valdiest's death. Both had made it to the exit and were now facing her. The more distant half-blood, standing directly in front of the exit from the garden, turned to blend in with the crowd.

Meliastrid back-winged above the crowd, turning them like stampeding cattle, and him with them.

She roared at him and culled him out of the retreating crowd, corralling him in the parking lot away from the humans. Clattering chairs and dishes announced that the innocents were finding their way out through any path available. A few of the foolishly brave thrust cell phones out through breaks in the hedge to video the pair of dragons confronting the partials. None of them had ever seen anything like this. The videos would be on YouTube before the police made it to the scene.

More bolts of magical energy flew past Kaliastrid as her prey tried to work his way around her. As Meliastrid angled herself to shield the innocent bystanders, they successfully closed off any escape the two half-bloods might have had.

Kaliastrid whipped her tail around over her head and pointed her claws at her opponent. He was mostly covered with black and dark green scales and was calling more lightning to propel at her. Even fully armored, he was less than two-thirds covered. He couldn't outrun her. He couldn't fly. He was staying just out of her reach and occasionally glancing from her to the remnant of the female.

She hopped a car length closer over the discarded mess of his ally and lashed her tail at him. It caught him just below the knees and spun him into the air. He flipped around and landed on a foot and a hand with skill he had probably known as a human. She had hoped to drop him onto the pavement, but he was too agile.

He jumped away from her, throwing a bolt at her as he did. It slammed into her ribs, and she exhaled with the blow. The worst of it was absorbed by the scales, but his luck angered her. He was exposed in the open parking lot with Meliastrid blocking his exit to the west. She released a blast of fire that enveloped him and melted the asphalt where he was standing. He tried to continue fighting for an instant as the cloud of blazing gases engulfed him. The human portions of his body burned away. His lungs filled with ignited vapors. He tumbled to the ground into a fetal ball. When the fire cleared, she could see bone where his human weakness had been excised by flame. There was no hair or skin. Scales that had resisted the fire were charred at the edges. He was broken and unable to move limbs that had been nearly burnt off. He pressed himself from the ground slowly, obviously in a great deal of pain. Spasms rippled across his body as he tried to suck air into destroyed lungs. He collapsed back onto the ground and looked up at her with a defiance he would never physically be able to accomplish.

He was barely an eighth dragon, if his limited ability to transform was any measure, but she didn't care. He was Nethliast's pawn. She jumped at him again, and this time she speared him through the back and gut with her tail. His eyes expanded into huge orbs. She lifted him from the ground and pulled him close to her nose. He was looking down at her green tail sticking out of his armored chest.

She shifted him around to where she could look him in the face, careful not to disembowel him or rip him in half. She wanted him alive a little longer. It was a struggle to resist yanking her tail out of him and spilling his vital organs all over the ground. When he was close, she exhaled a breath laden with sulfur into his face. Pain clouded his eyes, but he was still in there. She grinned at him, smoke curling around her nostrils.

"Call to him. Cry to him. Summon your leader. Let him see me." She jerked the tail to get his attention. "Let him see who has killed you. LOOK AT ME!" She growled. "Tell him how it feels. Tell him! Tell him we have come for *him*." She shook him to make sure he got her point, and sent the message to Nethliast. When she was sure the message was sent, she clamped his head between her powerful jaws and ripped it from his charred shoulders. With a shake of her tail, she tossed his body onto the hood of a nearby car. She spat his decapitated head, covered in fresh acid, behind the corpse. It thunked into the windshield with the flat, wet sound of a slime-covered deflated basketball

Kaliastrid could feel the anger pulsing in her veins as she shook her tail to clean off the last remnants of the partial's residue. She turned to find Meliastrid holding the last half-dragon spy in her foreclaws. He was babbling something about loyalty to dragon kind and being willing to work for them. Kaliastrid's mind suddenly filled with a flood of images and information. Meliastrid's prisoner was dumping everything he knew into whomever's mind would accept it. Kaliastrid tried to control the flow, but she would just have to review it all later to understand the flood of images and emotions that he was sharing. Meliastrid looked at Kaliastrid. She knew that her message to Nethliast had been a challenge. If he was nearby, he might send other dragons instead of coming himself.

Images of a farm appeared in her mind with a feeling that the location was nearby. Roads and turns ran through her mind. He was still trying, but Kaliastrid had no doubt about this half's fate. Anyone who stood with Nethliast was an enemy: simple, unclouded, dragon logic. They were all going to suffer for Valdiest.

Kaliastrid looked at Meliastrid. *"I want him to pay."*

Meliastrid didn't respond, but her eyes showed understanding, not even a glimmer of doubt.

"You're going to die by her hands because of what Nethliast did." Meliastrid nodded over the half-blood's head at Kaliastrid. "But before you die, you're going to tell all of your kind that Nethliast has dealt badly with us, and when he falls, any who helped him will pay unless they leave him now. That message must be clear with no room for quarter. Show me what you will send."

The transformed and terrified partial shivered in her claws and nodded. Kaliastrid watched as he sent Meliastrid the message.

"Now, tell everyone you can reach. Tell them to send it to others. The message must be delivered to all partials. I want them all to know that they can stand with me or they can stand against me."

He reached out to all who could hear him. When his focus returned to Meliastrid, she turned him to face Kaliastrid.

Kaliastrid thrust her face into his and growled.

"Remember me in the underworld."

Staring into his eyes, she thrust her tail into his chest under his rib cage and twisted it to crush and tear all of his entrails before she extracted it. She watched the light in his eyes vanish. She roared her vengeance into the air as a warning to any who might be watching. It was a more merciful death than he deserved. When she turned away, Meliastrid dropped him to the ground.

The sound of rustling leaves still falling from the trees ripped into the roaring in her ears. The smell of smoke and cooking food assaulted her nose. She flapped her wings, ascended into the air, and flew away from the now empty garden. Looking back, she saw Meliastrid following her.

"Go back," she sent to her daughter.

"When I know you're okay."

"I will be. I need a little room to think."

"You know we'll pay him back for this."

"Yes, I will. They're nearby."

"I know, but we aren't ready. Go see what's out there, but don't engage them. Your rage could undo any advantage we have if we can't get in place."

She flapped harder and turned toward the east.

"How did you know they were following us?" Meliastrid asked.

"It was among the last emotions in his message."

With that final answer she was alone flying over the Lech River and into the Alps. To the east among the farms was a base that was important enough that the condemned partial saved it until the very end. What was hidden out among the fields of Bavaria?

~~~~

Meliastrid landed and transformed in a grassy field on the western bank of the Lech River. A walk back to the hotel would probably be advisable, both to avoid the attention of any officials and to help her calm down from the early morning fight. The last images that had washed over her as the half-blood had begged for his life were still filtering through her mind. Kaliastrid had seen the farm. That was important, but he had revealed much more.

The threesome that had been following them had left Washington after the attack and had come to Germany with the president. Silas would want to know that. It proved Elaine had been right. They were in the right place. She had not expected a conflict this soon, though. Her timetable was changing. Everything was moving faster than she had expected.

She looked to the east. Out beyond the borders of Füssen, in the flat farmlands at the foot of the Alps, there was a farm where they were staging and training partials. Nethliast had been there, recently. He had been there with two human women.

Melissa focused on that image in her mind. One of those women was the witch who had helped Nethliast torture her father. Melissa had no doubt which one was the witch. She had seen her face clearly in her father's death message. Something was familiar about the other one. She was wearing a shimmering robe that was embroidered to make her resemble a dragon. Melissa tried to remember why the robe was so familiar. Pain blocked the thought, and she abandoned pursuing it. What sounded like a whimper in her ear caused her to look around. There was nothing near her to explain the sound, so she ignored it and continued walking.

There were more partials on the way to the farm. It was their staging area. It seemed important to them. Maybe it was important to Nethliast. Kaliastrid was on her way there, and soon Melissa and Silas would follow.

She felt a sudden lift in her mood. If there was anything good about her father's death, it would have to be the clues about where they might find Nethliast and his prisoner. As of that morning, there had not been any public announcements about the state of the president. Most of the world was keeping the actual state of their governments secret. Many were under martial law. No one was reporting how bad the decapitation really was. Melissa knew that Nethliast's tactic was not new. It had been used for hundreds of years by dragons. The ultimatum delivered first and the punishment for not following it had drawn many a wayward government back in line. This time, however, it was not working. Although the top administrators of most were eliminated, the bureaucracies continued to function. It was interesting how inertia seemed to be keeping most countries operational. They had some time to deal with this. It also meant Nethliast might be feeling a little agitated already since no one seemed interested in admitting their leadership had been eliminated by dragons.

Melissa reached out to Kaliastrid again. She was angry, and with good reason. All she could really do was hope her mother would keep her head and think of the long game. In the face of a personal attack by half-bloods and now the death of her mate, Kaliastrid had held her anger. Melissa had to trust that she would calm down before she found the farm. She had to admit, though, there was a part of her that wanted Kaliastrid to level the place.

Melissa had not let her father's death affect her. She could not afford to be distracted by the emotions it would bring. She had shared a little of the emotional message he had sent Kaliastrid, but she would have to see him to really accept his death. Melissa sighed to relax, but her concerns would not go away. There was nothing she could do to stop Kaliastrid if she wanted to fly off on her own and go after Nethliast. She wasn't sure her commands as the ambassador would work in the face of such strong emotion. She still wasn't sure where the power came from to back up that position. She certainly hadn't discovered any special powers in her possession yet.

When she approached the hotel, she saw emergency vehicles and medical personnel recovering the strange remains of the partials. She turned up the street that ran along the northern side of the building. There was no activity on that side. When she reached the front of the building and turned toward the entrance, she noticed the two vehicles parked in the drive ready to leave. Silas was at the wheel of one, and Charles was waiting next to the second one.

As she walked up to join them, Elaine came bounding out of the back seat.

"Where's Kali?" Elaine asked with genuine concern on her face.

"She's working it out."

"We saw." Elaine pointed to the screen of her tablet where the videos from the cell phones were already playing. "You guys are popular Ten thousand hits already and no sign of slowing down."

Melissa cringed. She was surprised the military had not yet shut down the Internet to keep the news under control. Perhaps it was a way of keeping the people from realizing how bad it was. Either that, or it was a sign of how little control they really had.

"On the positive side, most of the comments seem to be on the side of the dragons, even though no one knows what this is about. A large portion can't wait to see the movie the footage came from and are asking what it's called. They think this was all a publicity stunt."

Melissa cringed again. She was not sure what was worse. The fact that the video was up less than ten minutes after the fight was over or that they thought it was a movie trailer.

"We have to go," Silas said as he walked up to join them.

He was right. The timetable was up. Nethliast was surely aware now that they were not going to just allow him to follow them around.

"We're exposed. They'll be all over us."

"We were exposed before," she said. "We were probably marked at the airport. We expected this. This is exactly what we wanted."

"Not exactly." Aldrich joined the conversation from his open window.

"The last half that Kaliastrid killed wanted to live," Melissa continued. "He gave us quite a load of images and information to filter through. The president was brought from the U.S. into Germany right after the attacks. That matches what we already knew. Those three were involved. She was in a base east of here. Kaliastrid is on her way to check it out."

"And you know where she is?" Silas was suddenly like a horse in the gate.

"No." She hated to crush him, but she only knew where she had been last. "She arrived in Germany with those three and more partials, like we knew. After the farm, these partials didn't know where she went. At least, they didn't share that part. Probably didn't know, because he dumped everything else. After that all three of them went to the airport to wait for us."

Silas pulled out his phone and hit a rapid dial code. His face showed his agitation. "Why did you kill them? We could have questioned them. Maybe we could have learned more. They are apparently shielding her. Elaine's not been able to find her since last night."

"Too late, Silas. They were dead as soon as Kaliastrid found them. More will die before her hunger is sated. They were complicit in the death of her mate. And no, he would not have told you more than what he told us."

"How are dead bodies of partials going to help us find Ta— Nethliast?" Silas asked angrily.

"He will come to me. He will come to his base when I burn it down." She grinned. She would find and kill Nethliast this day.

"It's time to split up. This was the plan. Now it's time. Charles, take them. Find what we need. Nethliast has other partials looking for us. Keep them safe." She knew there was no way Charles could stand against a force of partials if they came after him. "Don't let them find you. This is the most important mission. I need you with them, not worrying about me. I'll send Kaliastrid back to help as soon as I can."

He nodded. "Duty or not, I'll never stop worrying about you."

His eyes told her that the walls were down and she was hearing his real feelings. A ball formed in her chest. She couldn't let her emotions betray her now.

"I understand the mission," he continued. "Go, and be safe. Give 'em hell." In that small exchange she realized he was giving her the respect she needed.

"Time to go," Silas shouted from the idling car.

Charles slipped into his seat as Elaine walked toward the passenger door.

"This course of action is not advisable, my lady," Aldrich reminded her as she turned away.

"Can't be helped. Nethliast killed my father this morning. He has other prisoners. I'm not waiting for him to start killing hatchlings for sport. This is all part of the plan." She paused and looked over her shoulder.

"If we find the talisman, we can stop him."

"We don't know that. Go find me something I can use. Tell Wodin, sometimes you have to fight for what is right to save what is important."

He grinned at her and bowed his head. "You have found the one reason Wodin might support you. That doesn't mean he'll make this any easier for you, but I expect he will be with you. We will succeed, but there will be a cost."

She shrugged before she walked on. Her beliefs had never included human gods, but the sentiment was comforting for some reason.

The adrenaline of the fight and the walk back was wearing off. The reality of what had happened was setting in. She could feel the pain of her father's death leaking into her heart. Her father had loved her before. He had loved her as a human. He had been misguided and led astray by Nethliast. She could never blame her father for following what he believed. In the end, he had realized his error. She needed the other dragons to do the same.

Her thoughts turned back to her mother and the pain she had to be feeling. She knew she needed time to let it settle in. The flight to the farm might have given her that time, but now she had to reel her in a little. She needed her to protect the others. The search had to succeed.

"Don't attack, mother. We need them."

"I know. I'm okay. Your orders are well understood."

She knew that she was not okay, but she also knew, now after some consideration, that Kaliastrid would not do anything rash. Her mother would always be a pillar she could rely on.

September 8 – 0900 CET - A Farm Near Füssen

Kaliastrid reached the farm following the images the partial had spewed in hope of saving his life. She was flying in from the north, following the river. As she reached the outer edges of the fields surrounding her target, movement attracted her attention. She zoomed her vision in to see what was happening.

The property had been a farm, but it was obvious by the way the equipment was sitting abandoned along the edges of the fields, the unharvested state of some of the produce, and the convention of military trucks surrounding the farmhouse and barn that it no longer served that purpose. There were several recently erected prefab buildings around the barn that also indicated more was happening here than farming. The trucks were idling at the edge of the new parade ground as if waiting on troops to load up, but none of that drew as much attention as the melee that was underway in the middle of the open space around the buildings.

The partials were fighting each other. There was a clear split between the sides. Partials that leaned more toward the human form were facing off against snake-bodied naga. The naga seemed to have the advantage even though they were outnumbered four-to-one. Kaliastrid would have expected that.

Leaders from each group were flinging mental orders into the fray from the fringe of the massive clash.

Lightning and fire flashed across the field, striking clusters of naga. Two naga were carrying a partial impaled on a long metal fence post over their heads. They dropped the body on top of a cluster fighting near the trucks. Kaliastrid could not tell what happened in the center of that fight as the naga tucked in.

Kaliastrid opened her mouth and let the aroma of battle rush across her tongue as it poured in through her nostrils. You never forgot the smell of war. This field, with its odors of close combat blended with iron and copper tinged blood, burnt skin, and hair, and the ozone of lightning-scorched air, reminded her of another war. She refused to coax the time or location from her mind. Fear of pain combined with an actual disinterest in pursuing it allowed her to file it away for later review. Her olfactory scan told her what she wanted to know: there was not a dragon among them. Kaliastrid flapped higher into the air away from the center of the conflict and flew another pass over the battlefield. None of the beasts on the ground were paying any attention to her. She verified the groups casting mental commands were the principal leaders. They had not been trained as well as they should have been. Their commands were undirected. Like shouts in an open room, anyone could hear them, at least any dragon. That, and they should have seen her circling the battlefield. As she spiraled, she identified a faction of human partials fighting alongside the naga. Alliances were not split specifically along racial lines.

There was a semi-circle of partials guarding a pair of trucks. They were holding off attacks from all directions as if they planned to use the trucks to escape as soon as their leaders joined them. Hidden from their view behind a temporary building, a mixed group was flanking them. Spells silently lashed out from the attackers and cut them down. The attackers looked up as she flew over. The lead naga pointed and expressed something she couldn't pick out of the clutter, but overall she sensed he was happy to see her overhead.

She had not intended to pick a side, but her distraction had allowed another group of half-dragons to launch a counter attack against them. Frozen spikes, stone bullets, fire, and lightning rained down on the surprised naga and his force. Only a tenth of his squad made it back to cover. The building they were hiding behind was smoking as secondary fires spread. On the other side of her flyover, a group of naga in helmets carrying makeshift lances were sneaking through the woods that edged the fields. They were flanking the entire battlefield and would be behind the partial leaders soon. If they made it, they would crush the resistance. Kaliastrid really didn't care if they succeeded or not. They looked up at her as the leader of the flankers sent a message that a dragon was joining the fray.

She flew over their heads and hunted for a hill, in the amazingly flat countryside at the foot of the Alps, where she could land and observe without engaging. She picked a wooded rise, the best she could find, and settled on its north face. It had taken her nearly an hour to reach the farm because she was following roads. If she had flown straight it would have been much faster, but the partials did not fly so they had no reference to that route.

"I've found the farm, and it is certainly active," she sent the thought to Melissa with images from her overflight. *"They're fighting amongst themselves. There's nothing for me to do here. Looks like the human partials are trying to disengage and leave the farm, probably due to your order. The naga are holding them, but they're both taking losses."*

"I'm on my way, following the road. Silas has initiated the plan. NATO Reinforcements and air support are on the way."

"He's not here. This is not where Valdiest died."

"We'll draw him to us."

Kaliastrid nodded without answering and watched the naga charge the back of the partial leaders. The lances crashed into the backs of scaled bodies. Enchanted tips slipped between scales. Blood spewed into the dirt. The battle was shifting toward the naga. A group of five half-dragons that had been moving with the naga ran for an old van parked near the farm house. As soon as they reached it, the van roared to life, and the driver pulled away. The wheels spun violently as the van whirled around to head toward the road and Kaliastrid's vantage point. She thought they might be coming after her and braced for a fight. She refused to run from partials, even an army of them. At the moment when they would have to leave the road to come after her, the van continued toward the main road that led to Füssen.

"A van has left and is heading your way. May be reinforcements headed toward town. They may be going after the others. Are they safe?"

"Switch to the radio so Silas can hear."

She had forgotten about the little black boxes the spy had given them. With care she pressed the button to enable the radio and spoke into the modified microphone.

"Right, sorry. There's a van headed your way. I think they're headed back to Füssen. Where are the others?"

"They're out of danger," Silas answered cautiously.

Kaliastrid suddenly understood. Radio was not as safe as their shielded mental communication.

"Where are you?"

"I'm not sure," Melissa responded.

"How long have you been traveling?"

"Nearly an hour."

"You're almost here. I'm going to follow the van and see where they're going. The fight here is nearly over. The naga have effectively crushed the other side. They seemed happy to see me, so I expect they have called for dragon reinforcements."

Kaliastrid took a couple of steps before her wings took over and held her over the flat plain that paralleled the road. The van had no windows in the back, so she stayed behind them until she could climb above the road. The young face she could see in the side mirrors was intent and focused on the road. He was not looking for a dragon to follow them, so he did not see her rise from the field. She was above them as they reached the intersection with the main highway that led to Füssen. At the intersection, the van turned left and headed south.

It was as she expected: they were heading to Füssen, probably to reinforce the three that had fallen there. The fight must have delayed their departure.

"The van's on the way to Füssen. Do you want me to stop them?"

"No. We're almost to the last turn. Meet us there," Melissa called back.

Kaliastrid shrugged and turned back. She landed at the turn. To avoid too much attention, she transformed. The road had been empty most of the morning, but she never knew when someone might come along and see a green dragon sitting beside the road. She wanted to stay back and kill Nethliast anyway. Maybe Melissa had changed her mind.

A few minutes later the Toureg pulled up beside her, and she slipped into the back seat. Melissa gave her a knowing appraisal. Silas had the SUV moving again and into the turn before her door was closed. Kaliastrid squirmed a little in her seat as the mother-daughter role was suddenly reversed, and she considered her actions in the light of stern evaluation.

"I did what I thought had to be done." It was her only defense.

"I know. This has moved up our time table."

Kaliastrid nodded at the change to the plan, but felt no judgment from the statement. They had engaged the enemy. The plan must be fluid now.

"What's out there?" Silas asked over the headrest.

"Several hundred partials split into two factions. I don't think I remember there ever being that many of them in the world."

Melissa groaned.

"The naga were acting like dragon enforcers. They're keeping the other partials in line. They seemed tactically smarter. That van had five partials who were working with the naga on their way to Füssen. I'm guessing, but I think they're going to reinforce the ones that were following us."

"They're going to have a hard time finding us," Melissa answered.

"Part human or not, they still have dragon abilities that will make the hunt easier. Don't drive up to the farm. They'll never let you get close."

Silas pulled to the side of the road near her former perch. They all piled out of the car. Both dragons took full form. Silas opened the back and pulled out a backpack and a long rifle case.

Kaliastrid shook her head at him as he stepped over the fence and into the abandoned grain.

"What?" he asked as he continued toward the rise.

"You really think that's going to hurt a dragon?"

"Combat intelligence says .50 cal. and larger pierces dragon armor. Fifty has to be closer than most snipers are used to. I've added a few adjustments to my load, and I'm using a ballistic tip. Should be effective, and the eye will not stop the round anyway."

Kaliastrid cringed a little thinking about getting shot in the eye, then remembered who they were talking about. "You can make that shot?"

"You bet," he answered confidently. "From here, all day long."

"I still don't like this part of your plan."

"It's better than an all out dragon fight that risks the dragon ambassador."

Kaliastrid shrugged a very human shrug in her dragon form. She was not convinced.

When they reached the low rise, they watched the farm for a moment.

Kaliastrid stood among the trees, watching the partials still fighting despite the overwhelming odds. She had to admit they were committed, then she remembered the reason. Meliastrid had compelled them to leave. They were fighting because she told them to.

She started scanning the woods and found a few more naga that stood out along the perimeter. They were hunting some escaping partials. As she scanned the most distant trees, motion in the barn caught her eye. A single naga watched the activity in the field and checked the perimeter occasionally. There were naga in the barn leading the movement of the others.

Meliastrid moved up to her. "Wow, there are a lot of them, even after they killed each other off."

Kaliastrid nodded and watched the field in front of the farm house.

"Why do you think they split?" Kaliastrid asked.

"Maybe because the order came through the partial and the naga could resist better."

"Then why are the other partials fighting with them?"

An image of a woman in human form, wrapped in a cloak that made her look like a dragon sprung into her mind. The image from the dying partial's flood of memories gave her a clue to that puzzle.

"A partial enforcer?" her mother continued when she didn't answer.

"A high priestess," Meliastrid answered, looking at her with a knowing and troubled expression.

"Nothing to do about it now. What's your plan? Where do you want me?"

"Back in Füssen with Charles, Aldrich, and Elaine."

Kaliastrid felt the words keenly as a punishment and started to protest that she needed to stay and help face Nethliast.

Meliastrid continued, "I want them protected. Those other partials are heading for them. They can't stand against them. They're on the way to that monastery Aldrich and Elaine were talking about."

"Right, Saint Mang." Kaliastrid nodded. "Mel, you can't take this on alone."

"I know, but I don't expect to have to. If Silas is right, we can end this quickly."

"Bait?"

"Yeah, I'm going to see how much he really wants to face me. If the high priestess is here, he should come to defend her. Either way, I don't think he can ignore the insult of me attacking his little army out here. I wish we could lure his witch here. That would bring him in a hurry. But we know he's close, so all I really have to do is draw him out. I think I can do that."

"Be careful what you ask for."

"I think he's waiting for a face-off anyway."

"That's what worries me. You can't risk yourself this way."

"I'm not worried about me." Meliastrid reached up to her own neck and removed the amulet. "I want you to take this. I can't take the chance that Nethliast kills me and takes it."

"I can't. It protects you. It won't let me touch it."

"It will if I do what Heliantra should have done centuries ago. She may not have seen the wisdom in you because you were such close friends, but I can. When I die, I want you to be my replacement."

"You don't know what you're saying. I've let my emotions lead me today. That's why we're here. There's no wisdom in any of this." A sudden moment of clarity caused her to feel even worse for moving up the timetable.

"Maybe, but we all have emotions, and we all deal with how they control us. You're the wisest dragon I've met, other than Heliantra. If I'm unable to continue in this role that she gave me, I want it to fall to you. You are the only one who will do what is right."

Kaliastrid dropped her head even lower and nodded her acceptance. Meliastrid slid the chain over her head and settled the pendant on her neck.

They both paused, waiting for some magical sign of the transfer. When there was no reaction to her touching it, they both assumed the assignment had been completed.

"If I survive this, I want it back. But just in case, I want it a long way from here."

"I understand." And Kaliastrid did understand exactly how important this was. She was not sure how wise it was, but it was not any worse than facing Nethliast alone with a human sniper.

"Good. Now go on. I don't want you around when Nethliast comes. He's going to be wary of me as it is. The last time we met face to face, I did something bad to him. I'm not sure what because I wanted to kill him and he's still alive. That didn't work, so now we're trying this. If you're here, he may not even show."

"Wise." She nodded. Now that she knew where they were, the direct flight back would be faster and would give her a chance to prepare Charles. She would probably even beat the van back to town. "Call for me if you need me and watch the naga in the barn."

"If I need you, there will be no time. Get to the others. Protect them. Find that talisman." Meliastrid looked toward the barn and nodded when she spotted the naga watching on the upper floor.

Kaliastrid turned on her rear legs and leapt into the air. In a few down-strokes she was on her way, leaving her daughter to face her mate.

"Give him all he deserves," she thought to her as she flapped toward Füssen, leaving a fair load of hatred in her emotional rejoinder.

September 8 – About the same time - A Farm Near Füssen

"Get into position." Meliastrid prodded Silas. "I still don't think this will work, but we're going to give it a try. If he spots you, it's all over for both of us. I'm going to get his attention." Meliastrid continued to watch the sporadic fighting.

Silas opened the pack and pulled out the ghillie suit. He started smearing something out of a sealed jar onto his arms, hands, and face. Then he pulled out another bottle and poured it over his shirt, hands, and pants.

"*What* are you doing?"

"Covering my scent."

She sniffed the air and a rush of hunger assaulted her. She sniffed again and laughed. "You'll be lucky if you don't invite him over."

"What?"

"You've been watching too many hunting shows. Be careful whose urine you use next time and hope Nethliast's not hungry. The deer who provided that sample was virile."

Silas frowned, stopped pouring, and turned away from her. "You can tell that by smelling the urine? Either way, I won't smell like a human assassin."

"I have the sudden urge to eat you. I don't think that was your goal. I don't know how Nethliast will react to the smell of a breed of deer that's not commonly found in Germany. If we're lucky he may not even notice. The carnage on that field will overwhelm any random scent. If I do my job right, he'll be angry enough to overlook a tank sitting in this field waiting to kill him. That is assuming I can get him here."

He threw the suit over him and started to walk toward the edge. As added insurance, she touched him as he passed her, and he vanished. She liked her camouflage better. Silas would probably never notice the difference. Satisfied that he was not visible at all, she jumped off the mound and flew toward the farm. If he was as good a sniper as he indicated, he would be still. There would not be any of the tell-tale signs of disturbances caused by something invisible moving through cover.

The fighting beneath her was starting to break into individual fights. She didn't want them spreading too far apart. She needed them clumped together, but more than that she needed the woman she had seen in the image. She banked to the left and came around on the road side of the farm to attack down the battle line between the new buildings and toward the watching naga.

"Nethliast," she called. *"Come! We need to talk before this gets any more out of hand. Your army is in disarray. I have done this with a word. You can't win this."*

She sent him the image of her flight over the top of the farm and the blast of flame she blew onto the ragged battle line of fighters below her. She flamed the entire group. Then she hovered over the entrance to the barn, where she filled the interior with an expanding cloud of fire. The dry interior caught and dust from years of storing straw exploded out of doors on the ground floor.

She did not get a response. She flew to a height above the farm that would allow her a good view of all approaches and hovered there. The barn below her was engulfed. A handful of naga that had escaped before the heat overcame them threw bolts of lightning after her that she avoided. Her attack had stopped the fighting as both sides were now writhing in the dirt. The naga had not been as affected because they were better protected, but even they were injured. Most of them were not interested in continuing the fight. Once a dragon picked a side in a fight, the fight was usually much shorter.

"Why should I come to their aide? They are not worthy of my rule," he answered.

As she had hoped, he was nearby.

Intent on finding her target, she scanned the grounds from her height until she had narrowed it down. The farmhouse looked familiar. The woman would be there.

She bolted toward the trucks and buildings at the far end of the farm near the house and flared just above the last truck. Hovering there, she flamed the trucks and turned toward the house. The only full-blood human among the partials was standing on the porch staring at the carnage around her. Without hesitation she dropped to her knees in front of Meliastrid. The robe she was wearing covered her. The form of a copper and bronze dragon with wings extended spread out on the ground around her. Meliastrid recognized it and flinched in reaction to a bolt of pain that never came. The memory was suddenly available. She could see the robe worn by a human at the dragon king's court. She was the human counterpart to Meliastrid. A human ambassador to the dragons.

"What do you command of me, my lady?" a terrified voice filled her mind as the woman looked up at her. She could not remember what powers the robe conferred on her, but communication with dragons was an obvious advantage.

"Who are you and why do you stand with these abominations?"

"I am their priestess. I have led them here by Nethliast's command as king of the dragons. But your command is higher than his. I know that now, and I bow to your rule."

"When I am clear of this place, leave it and never return to Nethliast," she commanded. *"I will find you."*

"As you command."

Meliastrid broke off the attack and climbed to a safe altitude.

"You may not care about your army anymore, but I'm here to talk to you. and you only seem to understand violence. Is that true, my mate? Should I destroy all you have here and move on to the next site your half-dragon spy told us about? Face me now. This place may mean nothing to you, but the next may hold something or someone you care about."

She flapped in place over the conflagration, waiting for a response. This was the only place she knew about, so, of course, she was bluffing. But how would he know?

"You've come alone?"

He was watching. He wanted to see if she looked at her compatriots to give them away. She continued to look at the ground below her, where fire was consuming the trucks and the naga were slithering into the trees at the back of the farm.

"Yes, I'm alone."

"Where's Kaliastrid?"

"Exactly where I told her to be, doing exactly what I told her to. She's not happy with you. In fact she wants to rip your head off. I need to talk to you, and I can't have her killing you before I can. So do we have a meeting?" She carefully measured the emotions she allowed into that message. It was very easy to expose your own lies with the tell-tale emotions that infused them.

"What if I want to kill you?"

"You can try. You tried once before and failed, so maybe this time you will succeed." She filled her response with contempt. He would come.

"Silas, get an estimate on when your backup is getting here."

Their plan was underway. The military had never been part of her actual plan, but Silas had convinced her that they could clean up this nest when they were done. It would help Meliastrid look like a hero to the humans. Right now, though, the dragons needed a new champion.

"They're moving. Have been for an hour. The ground force is probably about an hour out. They have air support lined up. Best I can do working with NATO here. I have no real authority, but they're moving because I told them we found a dragon base. The pilots are not really listening to me, though. That could turn bad fast."

"It will have to do. I don't want him getting away once we get him here."

"What do you want to talk about?" Nethliast asked.

"Ending this. I want to talk about stopping this war."

"Why would I want to stop it? I'm winning."

"You're not even fighting it. You're hiding in the mountains while our kin die for something they shouldn't be fighting for."

"We owe the humans."

"For trapping us?" she asked.

"You know my answer. It has not changed."

"You don't owe humans, cousin. If you want to punish the one who cast that spell, you need only come here."

"What are you saying?"

"I cast the spell. Why do you think I had to cast it again? Now that I know why I cast it in the first place, I'd do it again, right now, if I could."

That was her ace. Curiosity or revenge would drive him to act now if he was still the dragon she knew. He would want to know why she had done it. He would want to know how the humans had forced her. He had to know just like he had to know why the President was able to use magic at all.

"Why?"

"I'm not telling you unless we're face to face."

Movement toward the mountains to the south drew her attention. He was flying in over Silas. She had expected that. She still hoped he wouldn't sense him as a threat. She refused to look toward the place where Silas was lying in ambush.

The black spear-point shape was flying low over the fields and roads to avoid detection. He became clearer as he headed for her at full speed. She didn't want him in the air. She needed him on the ground. This was the dangerous part. He could decide he had talked enough and just attack her. She was counting on his curiosity to overwhelm his rage.

"I'm landing. Like I said, I'm here to talk."

"I don't trust you. Why should I land? Tell me what you have to say."

"I can easily fly away. You can't follow me without attracting the German Air Force. Since your last encounter, they've changed their rules of engagement. Do you want to take them all on, alone?"

She landed among the burnt twigs that had been a field and waited. If he sensed a trap, he could decide to leave, but she was confident that he wouldn't. She had baited the trap with the one thing he would want to learn.

"Air support is inbound, we'll only have minutes before they get here. He tripped their radar. They are frothing at the bit to kill a dragon. Any dragon," the voice in her ear whispered. She cringed. If Nethliast heard the report he'd be gone.

"Your army isn't very strong," she spoke to his mind to keep his attention on her. *"They aren't very committed, either. We kill a couple of them, and they break. How do you expect to win with such a weak force?"*

"They don't like to have their noses bloodied like this. You've killed many of their kind today. Don't you recall the way they fought us before?"

"I've killed no one. Their blood is on your hands. You brought them into this. You sacrificed them for desires that are based on your fractured memories and hatred that is unfounded. You, however. You killed my father."

"I thought this was a white flag," he said as he approached the field. He looked around for a threat and took in the damage. Meliastrid read some anguish on his features when he saw the woman lying prostrate on the porch.

"How human of you. When did a dragon ever honor a white flag? When did I offer one?"

"No reason to be insulting. What did you do to my priestess?" he growled aloud.

"She fell down to worship me as I charged the farm house. I left her there, and she has not moved. Wrong me further and I will have no problem destroying her and you."

Nethliast settled onto the ground in front of her. He shifted from side to side, and his head moved in intricate S patterns in front of her. He was anything but relaxed. She ignored his aggressive stance. Her presence and appearance, which should have caused him to realize who she was, had no effect on him. He was quickly running out of chances.

"Why, Meliastrid? Why did you cast the spell?"

"I was told to."

"Which humans forced you to cast it?"

"I was only the conduit. All dragons actually cast it. We cast it for the humans, Nethliast. We cast it to save them and us from one human. But all dragons, even you, agreed to the entrapment, or it would not have worked. We all knew what was at stake, and we chose to do it, for the sake of humanity."

Nethliast reared back onto his hind legs and flapped his wings.

"I don't believe you. You would say anything to protect them from me. I'm on the verge of beating them, and you're telling lies to protect them."

Meliastrid shook her own head in a lolling left to right pattern. "I knew you wouldn't. The spell fractured our memories somehow. We can't remember the exact events. But I've found records that prove it, and my memories are starting to clear a little. Look into yours and see if you don't know the truth."

Nethliast dropped forward, brought his face close to hers, and held her gaze. He didn't move. He opened his mouth to show the teeth he would use to rip out her throat. She held his gaze and didn't back away. She had to maintain her stance. The sudden aroma of flowers seemed to rise off of him like steam. The odd juxtaposition almost threw off her focus.

"You're tainted. When did you take Charles to your bed? You never committed yourself to me, but you guard him like a lover. I can never believe you. You've lost—"

The bullet ripped into his left eye before she had to answer his challenge. Green blood and ichor showered her face and ran down her neck. The crack of the rifle roared over the field as Nethliast's head and body were falling to the ground. Meliastrid watched as he fell over onto his side, and his head bounced on the ground with a thump. A painful lump formed in her chest, and she wondered if she had done the right thing.

The second round struck the scales on his neck without effect. A cluster of naga who had returned when Nethliast had arrived moved toward her quickly. Their newly promoted leader slithered aggressively toward her with murder in his eyes. A mist of green exploded in an expanding halo above his shoulders as his head disappeared with the clap from the third round from Silas' rifle.

Still shocked at how close she had been when Silas had pulled the trigger, the death of the naga leader had snapped her out of it. She flapped away from them and the limp form of her mate before any of the others chose to approach her. As she moved out of the clearing, a jet passed over her head and released its entire payload of bombs. Another was lined up behind the first and plunging toward her.

"Melissa, get out of there! You've got to get out of there!" Silas screamed into her ear. "The air support is here. They aren't expecting any allies down there. I tried to tell them you were in the mix, but they don't care. Right now lizards are lizards to these guys."

September 8 – 1000 CET – Füssen, Bavaria

Kaliastrid landed on the bank of the Lech, transforming as her feet touched the ground. She was dressed in an inconspicuous green pant suit and emerald low-heeled slippers as if she was on her way to a morning meeting at the historical building. With a quick glance to make sure no one was watching her, she walked toward the towering walls of the Abbey of Saint Mang. She had beaten the van into Füssen, as she expected. They had killed both of the partials only a few blocks away. It would not take the searchers long to find their trail and track them to the monastery.

The tourist traffic was light. The entire town had the subdued feeling of a European town under siege a half-century before. Even the weather was aligning with the mood as the sky threatened an early snow.

Before she entered the building, she hid the claw amulet beneath her cream blouse. The others didn't need to know that Melissa had honored her this way. She cursed at the need for it and questioned the wisdom of trusting it to her for the second time. Something about the decision troubled her, but she could not explain why. In her mind she swore to do her best to live up to the honor and asked the Great Wyrm to guide her in making the right decisions. The weight of the new responsibility subdued her as she crossed the courtyard leading into the abbey.

There were so many faults in her character that made her a bad choice. She had to do better at controlling her anger, to start. Heliantra never would have given her this honor. She rightly would have told her she was too impulsive. The thought came with a twinge of sorrow but no pain. She ignored the ache of loss to pause a moment in the peacefulness of the memory of her ancient friend and remembered that they had discussed this. Meliastrid had been the right choice.

Her moment of introspection forced her to consider her actions that morning. Was she really responsible for rushing them into conflict with Nethliast? Maybe this was exactly what he wanted. She calmed the sudden panic that rushed through her. She would stay with Melissa's instructions and take care of the others. It was too late to change what was happening at the farm, but she could not deny that she had put Melissa at risk.

Kaliastrid shoved her feelings deeper into her chest and looked around again for signs they were being followed. There were others in the courtyard of the ancient structure, but none were paying her any attention. None stood out to her. She sniffed the air and reached into her magical sense to be sure. Everything smelled peaceful. None of the people in the square were magical, dragons or otherwise. There was no way for the partials in the van to know where they were, yet. But they could and would find them. Someone would remember them. Someone would talk. She pulled open the door and walked into the ground floor of the monastery.

The building smelled its age. She checked a directory to figure out where the library was and followed the map in her mind until she found the second floor entrance. It was blocked with a sign that said the library was closed to the public.

She stepped around the velvet barrier and through the door. The circular room was disappointing. She expected a grand library. It was smaller than the library back in Heliantra's manor in Tennessee. They had come all this way hoping to find something, anything. This room, even with its two floors, could not contain as much as they had already reviewed. She felt a sudden surge of fear that this was a waste of time. Once she was fully inside the room, she turned around to look behind her and saw that an entire wall was empty. Her shoulders drooped further, and she turned back to the center of the room. There had to be more. What if they didn't find anything here? What if Melissa was risking her life for nothing?

Walking toward the center of the room, she scanned the shelves above her. Movement to her right on the balcony that surrounded the third floor caught her attention. She sniffed the air and immediately found the others. Elaine was a few steps away from Charles where Kaliastrid could not see her, and Aldrich was behind her. She walked to the center of the room, where a railed hole in the floor looked down on the floor below her. She leaned on the rail and took in the rest of the library.

She could see the upper floor was a narrow balcony surrounded by a matching railing. Above their heads the intricate window arches held up a flat ceiling covered with relief vines framing Benedictine frescoes. In the very center of the ceiling a dome opened the room up by providing both space and light from round windows set in two sides. However, the lowering clouds reversed the attempt and subdued the space.

"How's it going?" she called up to Charles with as much of a positive sound in her voice as she could provide.

Elaine, who was actually up a ladder reading titles on ancient spines, looked back over her shoulder with a punishing scowl. Kaliastrid suddenly felt like she had broken some unwritten rule but ignored it.

"Lots of note taking and whispering." Charles shrugged and walked over to the rail where he could look down on her. "Not sure why we're whispering. We're the only ones here. Aldrich made sure of that. Where are Melissa and Silas? What's going on?"

She knew he didn't trust the man, but since the flight here, he was trying to treat him as part of the team. That was the magic of humanity that dragons had sacrificed to save. She felt a melancholy ache when she thought of the sacrifices that continued. The ache turned into a surge of sadness at her memory of Valdiest who would have, ultimately, loved this man. A wisp of nostalgia churned in her mind. She squelched it to avoid the inevitable pain, which was oddly absent. But there was no recovering the memory now.

"What's happened?" He had observed her pause.

"I expect she's facing Nethliast as we speak." Her answer caused Elaine to step off of the ladder. Her newest find was clutched in her hand. The motion drew Aldrich's attention, and he removed the never distant ear-buds from his ears.

His questioning face caused Elaine to whisper into her quiet sanctuary. "Melissa's already fighting Nethliast."

"Wodin, guide her and gird her," Aldrich said and thumped his chest when he was done. He stifled the roaring yell to send her off to face her adversary.

Kaliastrid smiled at him. It was beautiful to see such courage from a small man. She could see that he was still troubled by the choice to confront Nethliast, but he was doing his best to support it. He turned his attention back to the books.

Charles just stared at her. He knew she was throwing herself into danger to protect their mission here.

"So, where's the Heart of the Dragon?" she asked.

"I think we have to ask the specialists. I can't tell if we're making any progress."

He tapped Elaine on the shoulder.

"What's our status here? Anything new?"

She scowled a little at being rushed, but motioned for Aldrich to join her.

"We know we're looking for some reference to Renard and the Heart of the Dragon, but it would help if we knew more about where we should be looking. This is regionally close, but all of the books are even more subdivided."

"We delivered the talisman to his castle," Kaliastrid answered without hesitation as a memory appeared in her head. She took a chance on pursuing it. The absence of pain was refreshing. Somehow she could remember now. A flutter of light crossed her periphery, causing her to jump.

Aldrich and Elaine looked at her.

"Do you remember what it looked like?" he asked her.

The question drew her attention back from the agitating light.

"Maybe. The memories filter in and out, and some stay. If the right clues are present, they come without effort. I'm either growing used to the pain or something has changed."

Charles was staring at her hair. It made her suddenly self-conscious.

"What?" she asked harshly.

"Nothing," he responded and looked away.

"Can you try to dig a little deeper?" Aldrich asked, drawing her back to the conversation.

"It was sunset when I approached the castle."

"Was it a keep or a castle?" Aldrich asked. He and Elaine turned together to pull out her journal and his note pad and pen from his bag. Their hands stood ready to record what she said.

Kaliastrid paused and stared at each of them in turn. Aldrich was walking around to join Elaine where she had been searching.

"Go on, please. We need to hear whatever you remember."

Kaliastrid started to ask what difference it made, but quickly realized the details were critical to their search. She thought about the memory and braced for the painful hit that would come with it. A tingle instead ran through her head. At the same time she heard a descending whine just by her left ear. Although disconcerting, she ignored it to follow the memory.

"It was a keep. Now that I think of it, it was a small, dark tower surrounded by a curtain wall. But it was not a full castle." She faltered a little as a nauseating pain rushed through her head, reminding her of the penalty for remembering. She wavered and almost fell, collapsing against the rail in front of her. She grabbed at the rail to avoid falling to the floor. Charles rushed toward the stairs behind the book cases. What sounded like an apologetic whine emanated from all around her throbbing head.

"What's that?"

"Pixies," Charles answered as he continued to move to help her. "They've been with us since we got here."

"What?" Kaliastrid asked and then remembered the odd sensations she had never really enjoyed, and how they had joined them at the hotel. "Right. Irritating little buggers as I recall, but useful all the same."

Aldrich and Elaine compared notes and nodded. They both looked at Kaliastrid. She was still weak and clinging to the rail when Charles reached her.

"Are you okay?"

"Just weak. That last memory really hurt."

"Look at this and tell me if it's similar to what you remember," Aldrich called down from the balcony, handing Elaine's journal down to her.

"Charles, could you grab that for me, please?" She hated looking weak in their eyes. She braced herself and stood up from the rail. The vertigo that the headache had caused was gone. She could stand again. A whimper from beside her head came as an apology. The flicker of light rushed from ear to ear and eliminated the last of the pain.

Charles grabbed the book from between the railings and handed it over to her. As she opened it to the proffered page, a wreath of twinkling and singing pixies spun about her head.

The drawing was intricate. The keep it represented filled her memory. She was landing in the courtyard with a box in her claws. Lightning flashed in the image. She wasn't sure if it was part of the memory or a byproduct of the pixie magic. The setting sun was shining across the ground, highlighting the birch trees that surrounded the keep. It spilled through the arrow slits in the curtain wall in long golden fingers.

The inner ward was empty. An assault from the ground would be difficult, but the simple keep could not withstand an attack from the air. She was here to do a job though, not look around. The single door in the keep wall had a small window in it. She was sure there was an eye staring at her from within. She could sense both malevolence and magic seeping from under the threshold. She sat the box in the center of the courtyard, as instructed. It was facing the setting sun. Wings raised over her head, prepared for her down stroke to escape any trap, she spoke a final chain of words that had been given to her before she left. Meliastrid had practiced them with her over and over to make sure she had the exact trigger words prepared. As she spoke them, golden runes flared and vanished in smoky dust from the maniple wrapped around her wrist. Magical tendrils swirled around her and the box.

With full downward strokes she left the box below her as she turned to depart the keep. Looking back, she glided down a ridge to meet a group of humans who were waiting in the trees just beyond the range of potential defenders at the keep. The sun had been on the horizon, but it was dark where she landed with the others. The memory vanished in another flash of pain that put her head onto the rail and sent the pixies flying away from her in a streaking pattern of orange red light. She felt Charles' arm go around her waist, and her breakfast threatened to return. She looked up at him through blurry eyes and smiled. She wondered how bad that one would have been without the help.

Elaine's hand was furiously stippling on another tablet. Her eyes were unfocused as she channeled something. Scratching noises from the rapid illumination continued as Kaliastrid struggled to her feet with Charles' help. With a flourish of her pen, Elaine turned her own drawing around for Kaliastrid to see. The page was filled with black lines and runes that contained a very accurate picture of the keep from the base of the ridge. The intricate line and stippling work even brought out the highlights of the sun as it set behind the single tower. Caught in the final rays of the sunset, she could see the bald head of a man standing on the tower with a staff in his hands.

"Yes, that's the keep I delivered it to. He was there, and he came to take it as the sun was setting. It appears we planned it all to coincide. Melissa was casting the spell, but I triggered the final words to set the trap when I left the box. I was sent to deliver the ransom. It was on the Eastern face of a mountain in a long valley."

"So," Aldrich said, "that is the keep we seek."

"So it appears," Elaine answered. "Her description of the location matches what we know as well."

"How did you know?" Kaliastrid asked.

"Another dream from Wodin, some fairy guidance, and some interesting local legends."

"Then find this place," she said flatly. She pushed back from the rail, frustrated more by her own weakness than their progress.

Elaine and Aldrich paused to process the order. They had apparently been expecting applause, and her irritation at the pain made it impossible for her to be effusive. Another skill she would have to learn to help Melissa. Kaliastrid growled to herself. She would rather be leading an army over a wall.

"Listen," she turned to Charles and said in a conspiratorial tone that still seemed loud for the empty library. "We need to be ready to move. There's a van full of partials searching the town for us."

Charles tensed exactly like she expected him to.

"When they find us—"

Charles started to correct her, but she didn't let him speak.

"They will find us. When they do, they'll not wait. We have to remain ready to move. Don't let them spread out and get too comfortable. We may have to move with very little notice. I'm going to check on our pursuers' progress."

She turned back to look at Elaine. "What else do we have?"

"We've found a few tales about someone who could be Renard. The legends follow Heliantra's stories. We've even found a rough genealogy."

Curious about the genealogy, she walked around the center hole toward the edge of the balcony.

"Let me see."

She reached up as Elaine handed another sheet of paper down to her. The tree of names roughly scribed on the paper matched a tree she had seen on a tapestry ages before. Renard was listed at the bottom. Above him was his brother Eduard. She should remember these people. She had lived with them. She should have some recollections of them. Pain simmered in her temples at the same frequency of pixie lights that circled her head as she stared at the list.

An image in her mind formed. She was sitting by a river with Heliantra.

"You're looking at the future king of this realm, and the biggest threat to his kingdom, all at once," Heliantra had said about the young man and his brother in the field near them. The elder brother, by a mere hand's-length, was wielding a sword against his sibling in a training bout. The younger brother, identical except for his bald pate, was lying on his back, disarmed. "He should know better than to lord over him like that. He's a trapped snake, and he will strike. Watch."

Kaliastrid continued to watch the situation as Eduard circled Renard with the tip of his sword a mere inch from his head.

Kaliastrid watched the look on the second son's face shift from fear to fascination as his brother's gloating became disregard. Renard's spell was called up with a few simple, whispered words. Before Eduard could react, the sword was flung across the field into a tree. Renard's dagger was hovering just under Eduard's rib cage, and Renard was now standing.

"You see," Heliantra whooped with excitement inappropriate for a dragon. "Everyone always underestimates Renard. As if birthright makes the other more powerful! Eduard can't afford to do that."

Kaliastrid's eyes locked onto the surprised face.

She returned to the room staring into Charles' eyes. It took her a moment for her to realize she was not still in the memory. She handed the sheet and journal back up to Elaine. She pointed at the village drawn next to the keep.

"You're close. Stay on it." She looked back at Charles and understood why Heliantra had worked so hard to keep him near her. "You ready to make sure we're safe? It's a big place."

He nodded and looked at the door.

"Elaine, Aldrich, I'm serious. We have to be ready to leave at any moment," Charles called back as they walked out.

"I want you to secure the outside of the monastery. I'm going to the roof where I can see. You're looking for a white panel van with no windows in the rear." As Charles nodded, she pointed to her earwig. "Did you get a radio?"

He reached into his pocket and took out a wireless earplug and slipped it into his ear. He pointed to the hand-held unit on his waist. They matched frequencies and then separated. She had to find a way to the roof.

Walking along the deserted upper level corridors, she found another velvet rope blocking access to a short staircase. She stepped around the rope and up the stairs to a door that had been added to the old monastery to make roof access easier. The chain on the door couldn't resist her dragon strength when she partially transformed. She swung the door out onto the roof. There was nothing beyond the door except a roof plunging away to a courtyard below. The opening looked toward the river, across the courtyard. Her view of the road was partially blocked. For safety, she transformed the rest of the way as she stepped out onto the roof and then turned invisible. She had nearly as much area to cover on the roof as Charles had to cover on the ground. Keep an eye on everything was going to be difficult. She lifted off from the tiles and started flying a circuit around the building where she could see. She would be okay if no one else was flying five hundred feet above the old building.

September 8 – About the same time - A Farm Near Füssen

Meliastrid barely escaped the air assault that descended onto the farm after Silas took his shot. She lifted off as the first planes released their payloads and threaded her way through the plummeting destruction. She scantly avoided the conflagration that consumed the ground where she had faced Nethliast. As soon as she had enough altitude to maneuver, she turned directly toward Silas' hiding place and bolted for clear air. A couple of the attacking aircraft had chased after her with their cannons flashing and heavy caliber rounds chewing into the air around her. She heard Silas screaming for them to "Check Fire" and to consult their instruments before they fired on a friendly. Both jets, who were having a hard time flying slow enough to maneuver with her, broke off pursuit with colorful responses about a dragon being a dragon.

Silas forcefully reminded them to avoid the blue smoke billowing from the relative safety of the adjacent field. She landed there and transformed to watch the rest of the strike airplanes clearing the airspace.

An iron circle of helicopters flowed in as the planes departed and poured cannon rounds and rockets into anything that moved. As she watched the pirouette of death in the smoking remains of the farm, she felt a nagging disgust at the visceral attack she was witnessing.

She knew they had to be sure the location was pacified. Many of the pilots were reacting to the threat they had been told to expect. For many of them, this was their first chance to repay the violence meted out just days before.

In the initial confusion of her escape, she had lost sight of Nethliast and the priestess. It was hard to imagine anything surviving the aerial bombardment, but Melissa needed to be sure. Something she had seen as she was flying away prevented that. A wall of what Silas called Bradley fighting vehicles were rushing through the abandoned crops to encircle the destruction. They created a final cordon to keep anything that did survive from getting out. Occasionally a turret would shift and the long barreled gun would thud out destruction into the brush or rubble where a gunner saw movement. As she watched them close the final barrier, she started to believe that Nethliast had been contained, but the smoke was still clearing. Nothing more than knee high still stood where the farmhouse and temporary barracks buildings had once been. The largest cover on the field was the burning hunks of metal that had been trucks, and they were mere smoking heaps of their component parts.

Ancient memories and modern knowledge warned her that without a corpse she could never be sure. The last time she had assumed his death, he had returned and attacked the whole world. She needed proof this time. A spine and tattered wings lying where Silas had dropped him would be an acceptable verification. Melissa shivered at her own callous thought and wrapped her arms around herself to fight the chills.

"What's wrong?" Silas asked as she touched him to reverse the invisibility.

"Nothing, it's just a little surreal."

"You mean, disgusting."

"No, war is always dreadful, but I feel no remorse for what we've done. I should feel something."

"You will. Adrenaline is your friend until it goes away. Then it's worse than a hangover. You don't get the headache, but the regret comes in super-sized boxes."

She grinned at the spy standing next to her and turned back to watch the progress on the field. Soldiers were entering the edges cautiously and sifting through debris. Remotely operated vehicles like the one Silas had sent after her and Kaliastrid were leading the advance into the alien landscape. An aerial ROV circled over the field with missiles ready on its wings to take out anything moving in the debris.

Melissa stared at the crater where she had faced off with her former lover. Her gut flipped as it became clear the image she wanted to see was not forming.

"He's gone, again. He's not there."

"What?" Silas asked as he scanned the field with his binoculars.

"Nethliast. There's no sign of his body. Not even a claw, or tail. Nothing!"

"I know I hit him. He's dead."

"So, where's his body? There are parts of half-dragons spread across that field, but not even a tattered piece of Nethliast's wing."

Panic gurgled up in her stomach. She looked around for any sign that they were being watched. If she could not kill him, what hope did she have to stop his plan?

"That's the same arrogance that led us here. I thought I killed him before. We can't assume he's dead. I can't believe that wyrm dead until I see his corpse rotting in the sun." She could hear the panic in her voice, and it both scared and embarrassed her. Melissa moved to walk across the road toward the battlefield. Silas grabbed her arm.

"You can't walk out there. Those soldiers will kill anything that moves. They're not playing."

Melissa nodded at his concern and vanished without a word. Silas was still holding her arm until she pulled away and left him standing.

Something the gunners didn't see drew her attention to the trees on the opposite side of the battlefield. It was beyond where the barn had once stood. It was outside of the cordon of steel. The initial tickle of someone reaching out to her mind exploded with a panicked cry for help. The priestess' fear mingled with Melissa's and nearly made her run away. Instead she stood still and reached out until she felt the mind. She immediately knew where to look.

The panic transformed to terror as the tortured mind realized hope was gone. Doubt vanished as Melissa stared into Nethliast's malevolent eye as he drove his tail into the priestess' chest. Yet another flood of dying emotions rushed across her mind. Death dislodged another mind. For a moment they both hovered over the battlefield as they were forced back into their own bodies. Melissa felt the delicate scrying touch vanish and wondered if it was Elaine who was watching. Fleeting wisps of rage and surprise lingered behind in Melissa's mind from the anonymous watcher which told her it was not Elaine. Who else had witnessed this death?

With the dying scream of the woman fading in her mind, Melissa knew where Nethliast was and that he was alive. She could not rush across the field of death. If she hurried and disturbed anything, the soldiers in the APCs, the troops on the ground, or the circling ROV would kill her even if she was invisible. She skirted the farm, walking behind the steel wall until she was near Nethliast's last position.

With the sound of searching robots and clanking tanks behind her, she focused on the noises she could hear ahead of her. Nethliast was out here. He could be waiting to kill her the same way he killed the priestess. She moved cautiously forward as she made sure her armored form was fully protected. Each step seemed to echo in her mind as she crunched through leaves and twigs that had withstood the destruction. She would never sneak up on him like this.

How could he have survived a shot like that, followed by the bombardment Silas called down on him, and still be able to fight? He should be dead. She should have hung onto him and made sure he was done. It may have cost her own life, but it would have been worth it.

A trail of green blood was drying on limbs and the trunk of a tree. It was a single deposit followed by a few more. A few steps beyond, the green ichor was replaced by a large amount of red human blood. She could see two sets of clumsy human steps walking into the woods and pausing The pair them headed east, deeper into the wood. She followed that sign farther into the trees until it changed again. A clearing opened up from the woods and exposed a make-shift emergency room. A combination of red human and green dragon blood littered the ground among footprints that told the tale. Lying on the edge of the clearing was the priestess. She was face-down, covered by her ambassador's robe. He had most likely killed her because of her shift in loyalty when she had witnessed Melissa's color, but not before she had treated his wounds. The discarded first aid kit and the circling footsteps told the story. An empty ampule of morphine lay in the center of the field where he had transformed back into his dragon form and flown off. That was where the final strike had been delivered to the priestess. That was where she had called out to Melissa to save her.

She must have tried to drug him and get away. He had transformed, negating the effects of the drug, and killed her for her betrayal. Melissa felt partially responsible. The priestess had changed her loyalties, and she had paid for it.

The robe was obviously magical. Humans could not speak to dragon minds without help. The robe gave her that ability. It allowed her to seek them out as well. She was probably the reason Nethliast had been able to reach out to the partials the way he had.

Melissa stared at the intricate scales of the cloak draped over the body. The memory of the human liaison who had been allowed to wear the magical robe reminded her how close they had been with humans. She didn't have time to recover the robe, but once she found Nethliast and completed this, she would come back for it.

Nethliast had flown from the clearing, as small as it was. That meant she could follow him. Standing in the center, she transformed and looked into the air. There was barely enough room to get off the ground, but it was the only explanation for where he went.

"Silas! He's in the air," she reported over the radio.

"Roger, wait one. I'll see what I can find out."

There was a delay as she fought for any altitude at all.

"Melissa, they tracked something flying from the area low over the trees. They've vectored a flight of choppers to follow it. It's moving slowly south, toward the mountains. Looks like he's heading toward the Alps. He may be heading to another base up there. It's probably where he came from. We need to find it."

"Notify them that I'm pursuing. I don't want to get shot out of the air because someone up there is gun-happy for dragons. Tell them my markings, and make sure they understand that Nethliast is black."

"Wait one."

After a short pause he said, "You're cleared to join the chase. They're holding back to track him. Switch to 369.1 and contact the leader. His call sign is Blackjack. They've assigned you a call sign for ease of communications."

"Go ahead."

"When you call in, your call sign is Puff."

"What?"

"It's a joke. You're really too young. Puff, the Magic Dragon."

She smiled. At least they had a sense of humor.

"Got it. I'm Puff. I'm changing frequencies."

"Wait. When you talk to these guys, try to use terms they know."

"What?"

"When you understand something, say 'Roger'. Report only what you must in quick, simple messages."

"Whatever," she answered, a little irritated by his waste of time. She pushed the little button on the radio with her claw and watched the digital numbers increase until she was on the frequency. With everything set she dispelled her invisibility, stopped flapping to hover, and started tracking south.

"Puff, this is Blackjack. Radar contact. Do you read me? Over."

Melissa listened to the clear message obviously addressed to her and thought for a moment before responding.

"Puff, are you reading me?"

"Roger," she answered meekly like it was a question.

"Good. Relax, I don't bite." She could hear the smile in his clear, if accented, American voice. "You're 30 klicks north. Adjust heading to 165. Intercept in 25 minutes."

She struggled a moment with the short snippets of information, but, after she thought about it, it made sense. He saw her on radar. She needed to turn east a little, and she would catch up in 25 minutes.

"Do you copy the course correction?"

"Yes," she responded, forgetting Silas' instructions as the need to communicate overruled anything else.

"Good. Move smartly. He's taking his time and moving erratically, but you'll need to move to catch up. Looks like he's trying to throw off followers. He's staying low, near the radar floor and flying erratically. But he always goes back on this course."

"Thanks." She adjusted her course a little and flapped harder to speed up.

"Stick with me, Puff, and we'll get you on his track."

"Blackjack, he's hurt and learning to fly with one eye. He's probably a little panicked, but don't underestimate him."

"Roger. Keep coming. You're gaining on us."

"Does he know you're tailing him?"

"Negative, we're NOE and bunny hopping as he gets to the edge of our visual range. If he goes for altitude, we may reach our ceiling and have to back off. How high can a dragon fly, anyway? We'll call in the fast movers if he goes for altitude and have them take him out."

"What?"

Melissa tried to translate the message and failed. She had no idea what NOE meant, and she could only guess what a fast mover was.

"We can track him, and he can't see us."

"Okay. I can follow wherever he goes."

"Roger, Puff."

She pushed herself harder than she had since the emergence and aimed for where she thought 165 degrees would be. After twenty minutes of silent flying she was climbing up out of the valley and into the foothills of the Alps.

"Puff, have you in sight...and what a sight it is." There was excitement in his voice. "You made good time. We're below you at your 1 o'clock. He's just landed ahead of us. We're holding here to see what he does next."

She banked into a rising spiral on a light updraft from the hills to let her wings rest while she searched for Nethliast. She looked below her and found the muted forms of six helicopters just to the right. The five in front were combat helicopters with missiles and rockets on stubby wings on each side and a large gun scanning the trees ahead of them. They looked like angry, flying locusts. The sixth one behind the others was larger with guns pointing out of windows just behind the nose. It looked just like the one that had chased her into the caves near her manor the morning after Nethliast had taken his first flight. She scanned ahead of them for any sign of Nethliast.

"Blackjack, where is he? I can't see him."

"10 o'clock, 1000 feet below. 5 klicks. We've lost radar contact and have had only partial visual contact since he landed. We have possible civilians on the ground there, so we're waiting for clearance."

She turned her head to look for him but saw nothing except a set of cabins on the side of a low mountain climbing up to the higher peaks around them.

"Blackjack, how long ago did he land?"

"Less than 5 minutes ago. We wanted to wait for you."

"Is there a road down there?" She scanned the trees for any sign of him.

"Negative. We show nothing in the area."

"What are those buildings?"

"Damn, you have some eyesight: Retreats for the tourists who want to rough it or people who want to get away. It's a little of everything down there, mostly accessible by trails."

"Or air. I'm going to take a look. Consider any civilians a threat. He can take a human form, and he has partial support that will also look human."

"Roger, Puff. We're moving up to cover. Negative on the civilians. We can't do that without clearance or acts of violence directed at us. What are we looking for?"

"I don't know yet," she answered, trying to figure out why he was in these hills and what the cabins were for. "Can you pinpoint where he landed, exactly, for me? I don't have a map."

"I'll vector you in. Turn left and descend."

She banked and started to descend.

"Stop turn and descend. Increase descent... I have no idea what your glide characteristics are, or I could tell you how much."

She dipped sharply on the heading and held it.

"Half that."

She leveled out half of her descent angle and waited. A small cabin was off to the right of her current path. She held her descent and another clearing started to grow ahead of her.

"I think I see where he may have landed. Mark his last spot. There's a cabin up the ridge..." she fought with the metrics converting based on football fields until she had an estimate, "approximately 140 meters up the hill from his landing. 30 degrees right."

"Roger, Puff, we're right behind you. I've marked the building waiting for clearance to engage. Hang loose until we get a response."

She looked back and saw five arrow-shaped helicopters skimming the trees toward her.

"Sierra 1. I show active radar from that site. There's a SAM battery up there," an unidentified pilot called anxiously before his voice grew pinched. "They're firing, missile away."

"Puff! Turn away! Get out of there. They have you painted. Hostile fire, north of the cabin."

"I count two," another voice said.

Before she could react to the warning, she felt a blast of magic ripple down her side. It was mostly absorbed by her scales as it glanced off at an angle. She looked down where Blackjack directed. A small woman was standing halfway between the cabin and the clearing. Her hands were circling her body in an intricate dance, and her mouth was moving. Blue light formed in front of her. Another bolt burst from her hands. It raced across the distance quickly and struck Melissa again in the ribs. The electrical energy rushed around her but again caused no damage. Then she saw them. Two missiles were rushing toward her. She couldn't deal with both in time.

She climbed up, beating the air, and realized her first reaction was wrong. Both missiles converged on her from either side. The one to her left was above her. In what seemed like a distant place, she heard Blackjack order the flight to fire. She rolled her wings away from the closest threat to her left, craned her neck toward it, and released a fanning blast of fiery breath. It raked and engulfed the missile, setting off the armed explosive.

Continuing her roll to keep her wings safe, she exposed her chest and her strongest armor to the second missile. When she realized she would not escape it, she folded her wing into her back and fell away from it as quickly as she could. It passed near enough to activate the explosive as she fell. The concussion slammed into her chest like a battering ram knocking the breath from her lungs. Several searing pains across her chest introduced her to what it was like to have her armor penetrated. That was a new experience for her. She could tell that the shrapnel had stopped in her fatty layer under the armor and did not penetrate muscle. The concussion was another story.

Craning her head, she tried to examine her injuries as she expanded her folded wings to arrest her fatal plunge into the trees. She rolled over from her inverted dive to allow her wings to slow her down. She was having a hard time controlling them. Her chest muscles and her lateral abdominal muscles all refused to overcome what her brain said was pain. For some reason she could process the overload. Although the muscles were trying to work, she had very little control of them. Green streams of blood were running down her chest from the penetrations around the edges of her scales, but more threatening was the problem she was having flying. Her wings were only partially extended. The muscles were protesting. The trees were now too close to avoid. She pulled the wings back as best she could to protect them again and hoped she had slowed down enough.

She knew other explosions were going off around her and up the side of the mountain toward the cabin. She had not really paid any attention to what was happening as she handled her own emergency. The first tree she hit was a small pine that broke in the middle from the leverage force she applied to it. She grabbed it with her legs to slow her crash down. When it broke she lurched into the next few trees chest-first. She realized she could not really rely on her arms at all and thrust her legs forward to continue to try and arrest her fall. Talons raked bark from several trees and others slammed into her like dragon-sized baseball bats. It hurt, but with each impact, as bruising and punishing as it was, she slowed down. As her speed dropped off, the last of the trees broke beneath her. She slid down a sturdy pair of pines to come to rest with a painful thud.

She was still conscious, but sorry for it. The pain sensors were now able to clearly tell her what hurt. She knew now why her arms and wings were unable to work effectively. Both of her arms were broken from the concussive force of the attack. The muscles that controlled her wings were sympathetic to injury in her arms so they did not work either. Breathing was hard because of several fractured ribs. Lying against the tree, Melissa counted herself lucky. That was when the voices in her ear became clear again.

"I copy her down, Sierra 5, can you cover her? There's movement on the hillside east of her."

"Affirmative, Sierra 1. We're on it."

The thumping in her head matched the rotor wash that was beating the broken trees around her. Over her head she could see the arrow-shaped fuselage of one of the sleek helicopters that had been behind her.

"Puff, do you read me? Are you okay?" Blackjack's voice pounded her senses. She could not marshal her wits to answer.

She tried to inhale a deep breath to answer, but pain ripped through her side. She couldn't breathe. She couldn't fly. She had never felt pain like this before. She turned her head on her long neck, which still seemed to work, and looked up the hill. The witch was walking toward her chanting a menacing rhyme. Melissa forced herself to speak.

"Beware. Beware. Danger. The woman on the hillside is hostile. She's preparing to attack."

The helicopter above her spun to its right. The gun hanging from the nose beneath it jumped and slewed until it was facing the threat. What followed next was a confusing, loud chain of events. The gunner fired a burst that destroyed a tree near the witch but missed her, or perhaps the rounds were deflected. Melissa could not tell which. The woman released the spell. It struck the helicopter. Its nose raised up to avoid the attack, but it was too late. When the ball of lightning struck it, there were several popping noises like popcorn. Then silence reigned as the engine stopped. The blades continued to beat the air.

Melissa released a blast of fire up the hill, but she was too far away.

The craft above her spun around. The nose dipped as it started to move forward. She watched the pilot as he fought the suddenly powerless craft. In that instant, with his face obscured behind his helmet's dark visor, she could only imagine his expression as he stopped the craft's dive and spin to turn it into a controlled descent into the trees.

It took a few seconds for someone in the craft to get back on the air.

"Mayday... Mayday... Mayday... Sierra 5 going in. Complete electrical failure. Just like a lightning strike, but it burned through the surge protection and shunts." The voice on the radio was different and calm even though the pilot was struggling with the pitching and bucking craft that was suddenly silent except for the whupping prop.

"I'm on rescue radio relaying situation. It's like she hit us with an EMP. She fired some form of energy weapon at us," Sierra 5 continued over the frequency.

"Sierra 5 is going down," Blackjack reported to someone else.

"Roger Sierra 1, we've marked his last location based on lost transponder. Report when he's down with coordinates if able." A flight controller Melissa had not heard before responded tersely before the slowly descending helicopter reached the trees.

"All units. Weapons hot. Suppress that area and give five some support," Blackjack commanded. "Danger Close. Watch Puff's position and five's descent. They're in our line. Is the slick still with us?"

Rockets sped away from the wing pods of the four remaining helicopters before he had completed his call. They streaked over Melissa's head, trailing white smoke back to each helicopter. Each smoke trail blossomed into bright red and orange fireballs on the mountain side very near where the witch was standing. Trees and ground erupted into blossoms of fire and debris, but she was not there anymore. Somehow the witch had vanished just before the rockets struck.

The rotors of Sierra 5 hit the treetops twenty-five meters to the south of her and shattered. What lift the helicopter had, vanished, and it dropped sixty feet to the rocky floor of the woods. The pilot had successfully controlled the descent to keep the wheels level, but the landing still seemed very hard. The tail separated from the forward fuselage behind the stubby wings, and fuel spilled out around it. They were very close to smoking debris from the rocket attack and Melissa's failed attempt to burn the witch.

"Roger leader, Sierra 6 in position," a German accented voice replied.

"Do you have your insertion point? One hundred meters below the cabin. You're inserting hot. There are two ground units flanking the impact site. There has been effective anti-aircraft cover, although we have eliminated the radar-controlled site. We have no idea what's coming up at us, so try to keep their heads down."

"Roger. Our stick is ready. Starting run."

"Roger, Sierra 6. We'll cover your insertion."

Melissa rolled over painfully to see if she could see the other helicopter. She could not see it through the trees, but she could hear it.

"Blackjack. You can't send those men in. She's not hurt. She's still out there and unhurt. Do you hear me?"

"Roger, Puff. How do you know?"

An ominous whining noise emanating from Sierra 6 drew her attention for a moment before she could respond. She could see the hulking body of the larger helicopter settling above her. Fire erupted from the gun mounted in the window behind the cockpit. A stream of rounds slammed into the trees to the east of their position. Melissa focused on her thoughts and responded.

"She disappeared just before the rockets struck. She was not there when they hit."

"This is impossible stuff you're telling me. It doesn't happen. People don't just vanish like that."

The larger helicopter was holding over her and facing the opening in the forest that had just been bombarded. It was angled slightly to the left and skidding into the zone, keeping the mini-guns on either side facing the flanks. The other helicopters were now circling around it. The mini-gun in the gunner position behind the pilot continued to saturate the area to the east with fire in sweeping arcs. The whine doubled as the second mini-gun spun up and growled out rounds to the west. Melissa could see movement as partials retreated.

"It does now. There's a witch and an injured dragon in or near that cabin. I can't help you now. I'm injured. None of you can stand against her, him, and a platoon of partials. We have to go back. Get those other men out and pull back."

"Roger that, you're the expert. I'm checking with base. Sierra 6, hold position. Sierra flight, over-watch."

A voice from control called back. "Sierra leader, pull your flight back until we can move up support."

"Leader, Sierra 6, holding. Puff's down. We can't leave her. We can extract five, but she will need something bigger. Six can cover until they can get reinforcements up here," the German voice from Sierra 6 called.

Melissa couldn't see any of the other helicopters anymore. Sierra 6 was still visible directly above her. She rolled onto her rear legs with some difficulty and checked to see if she had missed any injuries. She was down and there was no way, even if she could fly, that she could fly out. She'd have to walk out, and she wasn't sure she could do that in her state. Each movement sent shocks and ripples of fire through her arms and side. As she reevaluated, it was possible some of the shrapnel had gone deeper than the fat.

"Negative, this zone is too hot. We're pulling out. Hold position and prepare to recover five."

"Puff, can you handle yourself there or get out on your own?"

She paused and considered her situation. She wanted to be brave, but she was surrounded and unable to defend herself. Even her magic was hampered. She didn't need her arms to cast, but they were important if she wanted to aim it and control it.

"No," she answered in a tone that sounded more defeated than she wanted. She could feel her human side wanting to cry and knew the pain and fear were making it across the line. She would heal, but not before Nethliast's witch found her. "Can Sierra 6 carry a small woman?"

"Sierra 1, we can make room for her plus Sierra 5 if she doesn't mind a crowd, but who's she talking about?"

As he was asking, Melissa transformed into her human form, dressed in fatigues like she had seen at the base in Oak Ridge. She remained armored underneath for safety.

"Holy sh—" The radio shut off before the expletive made it out. "Sierra 1, Puff just... changed. We have a single female in fatigues on the ground. Moving to extract. Sierra 5, are you clear?"

Melissa looked up at the large helicopter and then scanned around her. The panic in her chest was threatening to overcome her. Where was her dragon fearlessness when she needed it?

"Sierra 6, Sierra 5, we're out and mobile. Moving to you," the pilot from the downed helicopter called. Melissa looked back to see the two men in the broken helicopter moving away from the downed craft. As they cleared the circle of debris, one of them tossed a smoking flare back into the spilled fuel. The fumes lit and exploded up into the trees in a roiling black and orange cloud of fire.

There was silence on the air as Sierra 6 circled her location. A hand pointed down at her out of the window behind the pilot, and the mini-gun tracked onto her position. She could barely stand, but she refused to fall down.

"Puff. We're dropping a ladder. Can you climb it?"

"No, Sierra 6. My arms are broken. I can't hold on."

"Sierra 5, get to her. She's going to need help."

"Sierra 6, you need to speed this up. We have more movement heading toward Sierra 5 from around the cabin. I count six more tangos. Up-armored humanoids. Looks like an angry SciFi convention heading your way."

The heavy report from the front-mounted gun on two of the circling gunships ripped through the rotor noise. Melissa could not see what they were firing at, but she felt the sudden push to get up the ladder.

The pilot and gunner from the other helicopter were moving toward her in a combat crouch. One was facing her and moving forward. The other was retreating while keeping his rifle pointed toward the cabin and the smoke rising from the clearing. They had survived the impact and were covering the area as the ladder was being positioned.

"Sierra 1, cover us in case the hostiles want a cheap target."

"Roger, Sierra 6. We're already suppressing the movement near the cabin. Get up as quick as you can. We're hanging out up here, and they're proving difficult to kill."

The four remaining attack choppers skidded around in a chaotic orbiting pattern that looked like the atom at the heart of crazy keeping their cannons pointed toward the smoke and the hillside. She grimaced at how exposed they were, but no more spells came. Apparently, the witch had retreated from their last assault. Partials were moving in to cover their withdrawal. This was a major base and possibly where Nethliast was hiding. As one of the pilots from Sierra 5 reached her, a ladder dropped from the side of Sierra 6. The young pilot from the downed chopper grabbed it as it snapped open next to her. He secured his rifle and put his arm around her waist. He looked up to get a thumbs up from two soldiers in the hovering chopper. With clearance to climb, he motioned up with his head.

"Lean back against me. Step on the rung and just walk up the ladder. I'll support you," the soldier shouted into her ear.

She grimaced, grinned a grin she didn't feel, and turned to face the climb. He put his arms around her and let her lean back into his chest. Her partial dragon form would help her with the climb, but there was no form she could take where her ribs and arms didn't hurt. She tried to ignore the pain as she climbed. With each step up the ladder, she realized how exposed they were to another attack. It seemed like it took all day to climb out of the trees. When she reached the door, two soldiers strapped to the helicopter reached down and pulled her in. Searing pain shot through both of her arms as they helped her in, but it could not be helped. She had a momentary view of the other soldiers climbing in behind her before she passed out against the shoulder of a large German trooper with an amazed smile on his face.

CHAPTER 6 - A NARROW ESCAPE

September 8 – 1100 CET - Abbey of Saint Mang, Füssen

"Charles, go inside and see how they're doing. We can't hope for much more time here. Get them ready to go." A thrill of anticipation ran up Kaliastrid's spine. She didn't see anything, but she felt a change and knew something was about to happen.

After a few minutes, he called back. "Slow, they say, but they think we need to go to France."

Frustration filled her mind. It was not completely caused by their report. They were making progress. She couldn't stop worrying about Melissa. She knew the partials were getting closer. Füssen was not big enough to hide in for long, and they were not that far from the hotel.

"Stay with them, and get them ready to move. I'm going to check in with Melissa. Stay cautious."

She flew a little higher where she could ride a draft and switched her radio over to Silas.

"Silas, what's going on?"

There was a pause before Silas responded, which prompted Kaliastrid to check her radio. The screen said she was on the right frequency. She started to call him again when his voice cracked over the band.

"We thought he was down for good," Silas responded. "Melissa went to check. Turns out, he survived. He's injure, and she's chasing him down." Fear for her daughter filled her chest. "She's been pursuing him for about an hour."

"You let her out of your sight?" Kaliastrid clutched at the talisman.

"I wouldn't say I let her. She's bigger and meaner than me, if you remember."

"Watch her, Silas. We all need her. I can't replace her. Nethliast is dangerous." She worried that Melissa was really willing to sacrifice herself to stop Nethliast. Why else would she hand off the amulet? She had been humbled by the action, but now she questioned if Melissa had some fatal obsession with stopping her maniacal cousin.

"Roger, I'll get a SITREP... Wait, there's something coming over the air. Chopper's down. I'll get back with you." The channel went silent, and the frustration returned.

She clicked back to Charles in time to catch the last part of an excited report.

"Say again, Charles."

"A white van just pulled up across the street. An odd looking group of boys climbed out. They're young and a bit too American to be driving around in a van like that, alone, in a German town. The leader looks like one of the boys in the images from the White House attack."

Of course, she thought. Why should this get any easier? She looked down and spotted the movement outside the monastery. She considered controlling them, but, when she finally had to let them go, they would know a dragon had been there. She didn't want to give away any clues to what they were searching for if she could help it.

"Charles, do they know you're there?"

"They seem to know something is here. They're coming across the road and pointing up here at the library. I don't think they've seen us, though."

"Get them out. Go down the hall away from the courtyard. Head toward the cloister. See if you can find some way to get outside on the castle side."

"Moving. I don't think we can beat them to the ground floor, though."

Kaliastrid grinned at the calm report, even though she knew he felt the same adrenaline pumping through his veins that she did. The moment a soldier realized the battle was joined could cause some to freeze, but Charles remained calm and professional no matter the pressure.

"Understood," she responded.

She flew around the roof to watch the group spread out and cover all of the major exits. She zoomed her vision in on the van. There was another partial waiting there. The engine was running, and he was waiting for anyone who made it to the street. As the others reached the doors and disappeared inside, she called Charles back.

"We're out of time. Where are you?"

"A little delay. A discussion about what we can carry."

"You're still in the library?" She growled. She could see Charles cringe as he tried to follow an impossible order and was reporting why he had made no progress. She felt sorry for him but still had to get them moving. "If you're not out of the library in a few seconds you'll be explaining it all to Nethliast. I don't see a dragon with them. There's a fifth one in the van. Get them out of there, Charles, if you have to carry them."

"Copy."

They weren't going to make it. She turned back toward the door she had used to get out on the roof. When she reached it, she hovered and pulled it open. It fell away from the roof, leaving the hole of the framed doorway. She transformed down to an armored human form and fell through the opening. The transformation ended her invisibility, so they could see her, but she wasn't taking time to call it up again.

Over the short distance, she dropped her shoulder forward and landed in a roll across the tile floor. As the impact ran down her side, she transferred her force into forward motion and came up on one knee to stop the roll on her left foot. She stabilized quickly, stood up, and ran toward the library.

She was out of time. Three of the four half-bloods were closing on the library. She could hear them making their way up the stairs. She jumped the rope barrier and pushed into the door. Expecting to find Charles still arguing with the other two about what to carry, she was surprised by the empty room. The problem was still on its way and blocked her only exit out of the library. She transformed up into her dragon form without wings and towered into the room, filling both floors. She backed against the balcony and looked down on the only entrance to the room.

The door opened. Three half-dragons spread out in a wedge. Each one was covered in plates of carapace and scales. Spikes on their shoulders and down their arms made them look distinct and aggressive. In the instant of confrontation Kaliastrid noted how they seemed to be more aware of their abilities and how they could bend their forms to their will. They were not prepared for what they found waiting for them. The room was not occupied by three defenseless humans. Instead there was a full grown dragon, ready to pounce. Their advance faltered almost in unison.

"*Stop!*" she commanded in her mind to the three of them.

They froze in place and looked up at her. They could not resist the command. She jumped forward onto the rail around the hole in the center of the floor and butted the first one into the door where he crumpled and lay still. He was probably not dead, but she couldn't take the time to finish him off. The attack released them from the geas, and they moved to attack her. She smacked the one to her left with her tail and struck the one on her right with her forearm. They both fell against the wall where her strike had thrown them. If they had been prepared for her attack, it would have been harder to knock them out. She moved to finish them when the channel on her radio opened.

"He's found us," Charles called. "We're in the main courtyard at the entrance. He must have doubled back. He's blocking our escape." There was no panic in the voice, but it was stressed. She could hear him running. She had to reach them.

"You're very lucky I don't have time to kill you," Kaliastrid said to the three unconscious partials and transformed again.

~~~~

Charles had his pistol clear of the holster his uniform allowed him to wear in the NATO partner country. He wished it was the grenade launcher he had left in the car, but he would do his best with what he had. His shoulder hit the ground as he executed the roll he had learned years before. Aldrich was holding ground in front of the approaching half-dragon and chanting a menacing phrase over and over that made the hair on Charles' neck stand up. Elaine had moved in the opposite direction to form a triangle with Aldrich at the point. It did not escape Charles that he was the magically weak side of the formation. He needed to get them out of the door beyond the menacing partial, but he couldn't see how, not all three. If there was one who could be sacrificed in this encounter, it was him.

A ball of fire exploded from the half-blood's fingertips and raced at Aldrich. Charles cringed at the speed the conflict escalated. It slammed into an invisible barrier in front of the small man and instantly flew back at the caster. Charles dropped into a solid stance and aimed his pistol. This had to count. He held his breath and squeezed the trigger. The report from the up-sized pistol seemed loud after being out of combat for so long and compared to the relatively silent exchange of magical attacks. He ignored the difference and continued unloading the magazine in the controlled fashion his Sergeant had really liked. Seven rounds struck the armored youth in the center of its chest in rapid succession. None of them broke through the plating although they tore through his shirt. They did stagger his gait and attract his attention.

The fireball that Aldrich had redirected struck the partial in the chest as he turned to look at Charles with a sneer of superiority. The force of his own magic sat him down. As he hit the ground, Elaine's bolt of lightning struck him.

Charles took advantage of the partial's focus on the others to reload and adjust his aim up toward the head. It was a long shot, but if he could hit the eye, he knew it would end this fight. That was a small target at long range for the pistol. With controlled squeezes between little exhales to keep his lungs happy, he continued to empty the new magazine in double taps.

Each pair of rounds hit the target's head and snapped it back like a boxer's jab. He reacted to each pair, unable to focus on the others or stand up while Charles had him targeted. None of them came closer than an inch to the vulnerable eye, however.

Charles was beginning to think they might be able to work their way around him when he took advantage of his pause to stand back up.

He dropped the spent magazine and reached to reload as he moved. His hand found the final magazine on the run. A moving target was harder to kill, hypothetically. He had no idea if that rule still applied to magical combat. Standing where he had been and aware now that they were not unarmed, the armored partial was holding his position and blocking their exit.

He was summoning something as Charles slammed the fresh magazine into the pistol, released the slide lock, and dropped into a combat crouch. His knee dug into the grass as he brought the pistol onto target. He released his breath as he fought to control aim and squeezed into the trigger at the bottom of the exhale just as the blade and pips were lining up with the target's eye. The round struck the eye ridge, and the target's hand came up to protect the sensitive region. He was angry, and focused exactly where Charles wanted him.

Riding the recoil, he forced the pistol back on target two more times as the half-dragon backed up while covering his eye. Both rounds smacked into his hand, which he balled into a fist but kept over his eye. Charles felt ineffectual, but he did understand the importance of keeping an opponent off guard. That was his job while they continued to leapfrog toward the exit: Keep him off guard and focused on him so the others could do some damage and get away.

Aldrich was mumbling again. Elaine was moving toward Charles. He held his hand up to stop her and pointed at the partial that was now rushing at him. His menacing left hand was pointing at Charles and glowing. Charles held his place and emptied his last magazine into the face of the rushing monster. He had the bastard's attention and intended to keep it.

Another fireball erupted from his hand and flew toward Charles. He balanced in a crouch on his toes waiting for the last moment. Based on what he had seen of the characteristics of the fireball that Aldrich had deflected, Charles leapt across the opening between him and Elaine. The sphere rushed past and above him as he landed flat on his stomach in a grassy area in front of her. He could feel the heat wash over him, and he knew he had cut that one a little close.

Aldrich's chant stopped. His hands came up at the same time, pointing his palms at the half-dragon. An invisible force struck the attacker, stopped his rush, and even forced him back a few steps, but he retained his feet. Elaine grabbed Charles' shoulder as he struggled back to his feet.

"You're an idiot. Brave, but an idiot." She shook her head as they all joined up in a cluster.

Charles holstered his pistol and shrugged.

"It's what I know."

Elaine took a balanced stance in the front of their now tighter triangle. Aldrich stepped to her right in front of Charles and pushed both hands forward like he was shielding them. In unison they walked forward. With each step, Elaine executed a sweeping T'ai chi style hand block followed by a single open hand punch. Each stroke landed an invisible force on the body of their attacker. Each strike forced him back a step at a time. They had covered twenty yards but still had more to go when Elaine had to take a break.

The partial, who had withstood everything they had thrown at him, raised his hands above his head. Lightning crackled from his wrists. Bolts struck the ground all around him. The snarl on his face grew into a grin as his hands moved to point toward Aldrich. Just before they were straight out and the inevitable release of energy engulfed Aldrich, the half-dragon looked up into the air as if he had lost all interest in them. The lightning disappeared around him with a loud clap of thunder that seemed to shake only him, and the energy of the called lightning rippled over him. Following the loud clap and the force of mana that passed out around them, he just stood where he was like a possum with a car bearing down on it.

"Move!" A draconic growl filled the air as Kaliastrid flew over them toward the front courtyard. Without thinking, Charles pressed the others forward with his now-empty hands. After a half breath of irritation they all ran for the door.

Charles had no idea what she had done, but the partial in front of them was just standing there. Smoke rippled around him from the electrical discharge he had failed to direct. Charles didn't waste any time trying to figure out what he was seeing. Kaliastrid flared a foot off the ground, transformed, and landed on the run. She pulled open the door and rushed through it. Charles paused to hold the door for Elaine and Aldrich even though he had no weapon to use against their attacker. He would have to fix that, soon.

He looked back at the neutralized partial standing in the courtyard one last time as he closed the door behind them. He had not even turned around to see them leave. Charles turned his back on him and caught up with the others.

When they reached the door into the front courtyard, Kaliastrid stopped them.

"There's another one in the van outside. I don't think he's parked where he can see us. Where's the car, Charles?"

"We're parked out front."

"I'm going out to the van to distract him. Go get the car. Be ready to move."

She walked out the door and headed toward the corner near the river. As she walked away her armored form changed. A green dress enveloped her and highlighted her non-combat assets. Charles felt a twinge of pity for the young partial when he had to explain how he had been distracted.

The other two looked at him, waiting for his order.

"Let's move. Follow me. We're moving, quick, for the car." He opened the door before anyone could argue and headed toward the other corner. "Be prepared. There may be others we don't know about."

Aldrich growled something and brought his hands out in front of them, then nodded to Charles. They moved out together.

The courtyard felt like it would never end. When the wall was finally past them, and they were on the exposed walk to the car, he was suddenly aware that there was one advantage to where they had parked: the library was on the other side of the building. Anyone looking down from there to see where they had gone would not be able to see them. The van was on the other side of the building. He scanned all the possible places where someone could hide and checked to make sure Elaine and Aldrich were still with him. Elaine's hands crackled with her favorite spell, and Aldrich was pointing his hands out at his side as if his shield was now surrounding them. Again, Charles felt naked without any weapon, but the solution was a few steps away.

When they reached the car, he clicked the button on the key fob to unlock all the doors and walked around to the cargo area. A quick glance told him his weapons were not reachable. He mentally castigated himself like an angry drill sergeant. They might even be in the other car. There was no excuse for being so unprepared.

"Elaine, how powerful are those bolts of yours?"

She looked at him with a grin he had never seen before as she thought back over the encounter. "I knocked him down but not out. I'll see what I can do about making them more powerful. I've never used them this way, and I've been afraid of even trying them with any power until just now. I can make them stronger." She nodded when she realized she was babbling.

"Keep a lookout until Kaliastrid joins us. You see him again, give him all you have. If you have something that doesn't include thunder in this car, get it ready, Aldrich." He closed the cargo area and walked past Elaine to climb into the driver's seat. He started the engine and looked around. Elaine was standing in the open doorway watching. Aldrich was on the other side of the vehicle leaning out of his door. The passenger seat was empty. They were saving it for Kaliastrid. They watched, on edge for a few moments, when the radio in his ear came to life.

"Charles. Come get me. I'm around the side of the abbey."

"Get in," he called back and shifted the car into gear. Both doors closed, and he pulled out.

He cleared the curb and pulled around the building until he was beside the van.

Kaliastrid walked calmly across the road and climbed in. She looked unhappy. He ignored that for a moment and turned back to the others.

"Where am I going?"

"Head toward France," Elaine answered from the back.

"Alsace is the western frontier of the Swabian region," Aldrich explained. "As far back as we can figure from the stories we're working with, there was a border set up on the peaks of the mountains there, but none of the legal documents support it. We're sticking with the idea that fiction, folk lore, and legends are the homes of our fact."

Elaine climbed between the seats to set up the GPS in the dash. "No matter what you think of Silas, he gets good equipment," she said.

Charles shook his head. "So, we're following a legend?"

"Ya," Aldrich continued, "the actual histories don't account for the existence of any of the castles of Renard's family. In fact, much like you've faced all along, there are no references to real people at all. When we look at legend and myth though, we find the exact references everyone remembers."

"There, just follow the purple line," she said.

"Around five hours' travel time, I'll see what I can do about avoiding checkpoints so we don't need our passports. Get them ready all the same." With instructions given and their direction set, the conversation fell into silent contemplation of their escape.

Kaliastrid sat next to him with her eyes closed, clutching at something under her blouse. He noticed the chain and realized she was wearing Melissa's amulet. His heart raced, but he controlled the panic and asked the best question he could think of.

"How's Melissa?"

"Switch over to Silas' frequency and find out. It was unclear the last time I talked to him."

"Should I be worried?"

"Maybe." Kaliastrid was not one to avoid tough subjects.

Charles fumbled with the radio and changed frequencies.

"Silas, this is Charles. What's your status?"

"We're not really using good radio protocol today, are we?"

"Okay then, Spook, SITREP. We'll assign call-signs before we try this again, but this operation didn't really have a lot of planning. What's going on out there?"

"Boy Scout, we've set up a staging base outside the farm. Target is not down. Puff spotted his hiding place and encountered strong resistance. She's banged up and on her way back here. I'm trying to organize a counter-strike."

Charles translated the call signs automatically from context, grinned a little at the two choices. He gripped the steering wheel roughly when he heard that Melissa was hurt but controlled his anger.

"Charles, I need you to stay focused," Kaliastrid commented, and he felt himself settle.

"What do you mean by, 'banged up'? How bad?"

"Unknown. Unconscious. Medic on the flight says broken arms for sure, ribs too, and potentially some internal injuries. He's having a hard time treating her through the armor. He reports her as stabilized."

"Roger, keep me informed." He took a breath and repeated what was important to the others in the car. "Nethliast's not dead. I don't have any details."

"How's Melissa?" Elaine asked, subdued by the sudden violence of her first firefight and the news.

"She's hurt. Silas has no real information on how bad. She's being transported to the base. That's all I know." The words hurt as he said them. "If you guys have any camouflage magic or ways to keep them from finding us, you may want to use it."

The car remained silent. He looked down at the screen on the GPS, then out at the road. There was nothing he could do to help Melissa right now. He had to stay on mission. He just had to drive and get as much distance between them and their pursuers before they figured out where they were going. All they knew was where they had been, not what they were looking for or where they were headed. He wanted to keep it that way.

September 8 – 1218 CET - A farm near Füssen, Bavaria

Silas shook hands with Colonel Carlson as he joined the command center that was forming in the field near the road. The older combat veteran wearing the US Army NATO Brigade patch on his arm eyed Silas with cold interest as a voice on the phone became a real person. Neither of them was surprised by what they saw, but Silas could see that Carlson was congratulating himself for being right about something.

"Well, at least they didn't make you outrank me," the older man said. "How's Old Ironsides?"

"Professional courtesy only, Colonel. That doesn't change the power behind my orders. I've not talked to him since they hit D.C. He was in the White House, and she's in the wind up here somewhere."

Carlson nodded as he accepted the MIA report on both his friend and the president. They were both part of her network, but Silas was not sure how Carlson fit in her plan.

"Roger that. We barely have boots on the ground here anymore. I'm a coordinator mostly. These are German forces. They're ready to climb in there and kick some ass after Berlin. This is coming together fast and loose. The paperwork is going to suck."

"If they succeed no one will ask any questions."

"And if they don't?"

"The weather in Kansas's not that bad."

The old soldier nodded. "Well, they're Oh and One so far. What do we need to do about it?"

"I say we point them in the right direction, turn them loose, and support as needed. We need some armor and we need it now or this is going to be tough. I want to go back in there."

"It may be too late by the time we get anything heavy in here. Most of the heavy armor's tied up in Berlin. We'll be sending some of the Air Cav units back in as part of our support role."

"Why are they holding the armor up there?"

"To break the siege. They're not sure why the dragons are holding Berlin, but they want it back."

"That doesn't make sense. It's a feint to keep them tied up. They should know that. There's nothing left in Berlin. Analyze the data and see if I'm wrong. I think our target is up there."

"I wouldn't bet against you considering your record so far, but there's no telling them that right now. They can't get through the ring of fire to find out for sure, and they're not releasing the armor until they know. So, we're probably heading in with armored and air cav, and infantry."

"Great." Silas shook his head and surrendered to the eventuality. You fight with what you have, not necessarily what you want. "Any word on Puff?"

"The birds are on the way back. Your lady's as stabilized as they can get her. Medic says she's pretty banged up. He can't do much to treat her through that armor, and he can't get it off. I hear she took two SAMs and whatever else the witch was throwing at her. She won't be running any marathons any time soon, but she's alive."

"I think I'm going to need to get her out of here. I may need some air support myself."

"You don't think she can help?"

"Not in her state." Silas thought for a moment about Aldrich's warning.

"I just thought, well—she's a dragon and all. She might heal...different."

"Now that you say it, I can't say that I know. Doesn't matter. She can do more somewhere else. We need to roll back in, hard and soon. We can't wait for healing, accelerated or otherwise. If we hurry we can get this over with. Maybe we can get to them before they reinforce."

"Whatever you think. Like I said, the birds are support units for whatever happens here, but I think I can spare a Blackhawk for a few hours. I'll see if I can get a Predator retasked. That might help."

Silas nodded. "You think it's going to take that long to get back in there?"

"Well, it's a tough place to get into. There are caves and bunkers from World War II back in there. We don't have good maps or even good records of them. We can bomb them out, if we know where they are, but we don't. All we have is a point where we engaged them. I'm searching for any records of bunkers in this area. Like your lady said, there's no way we can send in troops to face them, not without armor support. They're using the terrain to their advantage. It'd be different if we could face them with dragons. Evenly matched, you know? We're going to miss her when we go in."

Silas had wished for more dragon support for a long time but had not been able to get any traction. Now with the dragon ambassador on his side, she didn't seem interested in pressing the fight once they found the hole Nethliast had crawled into. It seemed there were only two dragons on his side, and they didn't want to press this fight. That concerned him.

"I need to report back to my team, Colonel. Let me know when you have a plan for a counter-strike. I want to be part of it."

The colonel's response was blown away by the rotor wash of the Blackhawk settling onto the field, but he didn't have to hear it. Silas knew the colonel would do his best to accomplish the mission. They had dragons in a hole; he would not fail to take advantage of that.

Four Apaches flew overhead. Three hovered to cover the landed slick. The leader's chopper settled behind the Blackhawk. The commander of the flight, called Blackjack, was out of the cockpit and on his way to the ambulance before the rotors had stopped spinning. She did have an effect on people.

A large soldier with a full pack was stepping out of the Blackhawk with Melissa's wilted form in his arms. They had stripped her fatigues back to try and treat her injuries. He could clearly see through the flaps of the blanket they had wrapped her in that she was covered with the crimson, copper and bronze scales.

Silas felt a sudden surge of guilt that he filed away in the box in his heart where he always stored it. It was as treacherous as the puzzle boxes on the shelf in his office, and some day he was going to have to face it. She looked so weak in her partial form. They placed her on a stretcher as soon as one was available, and the medic went to work. They didn't have a hospital. It would be a little better than aid-station medical care at best. Her arms were already splinted, and compression bandages were wrapped around a couple of injuries on her chest. When the medic pulled back the blanket, he threw up his hands, took two steps back, and looked around for guidance.

"What is this, some kind of joke?"

When Blackjack and the soldier who carried her in scowled at him, he refocused on the victim. He couldn't even assess her injuries through the tightly stacked scales. He motioned for the corpsmen to take her on to the ambulance.

Silas followed the group to the back doors and pushed his way up to the medic. He grabbed him by the arm.

"Wake her up. You can't treat her in that form, but she can change if you wake her up."

"You've got to be kidding me. That could kill her. I have no idea what internal injuries she has. I can't assess them through the armor. I don't even have X-Rays available. Do you know what's under there? I don't, and I'm all out of O Dragon blood."

"If you don't wake her up she could die because you can't treat her."

The medic pushed Silas' hand away and stepped up into the back of the ambulance. Silas tried to follow him, but a pair of armed guards stopped him and turned him around.

"They'll come get you when she's awake and they have some idea of her condition," the smaller of the two told him while the larger one stared at him like a steak dinner.

Silas walked away to wait nearby. Nearly thirty minutes later the small guard called him over.

"Doc says she's awake. You can check on her now."

Silas stepped up into the ambulance where Melissa was lying on a gurney. She was covered from the neck down in a sheet, and the medic and an orderly were wrapping her arms in an air-filled splint. She looked pale, but she was awake.

"You gave us a scare. You want to tell someone about it?"

"Hey, Silas." She smiled at him. "Good shot, but it just didn't have enough power."

"Not really a trophy winner, I'll admit. It was a marginal shot. I never should have taken it. I should have waited, but things were getting dicey."

"He's gone now. He has a hole up there, and you won't drag him out. We have to find another way. There is no way to get in there. His witch and an army of partials are not going to just let us in."

"I heard. This her work?" He motioned to the ribs.

"Not directly. She tried, but most of this came from a pair of missiles I should have expected."

"You were close to being in Nethliast's hands."

She nodded. "That was always a possibility. We're not going to be able to take him this way. If this is his fortress or a part of it..."

Silas shook his head at that news. It didn't change his opinion or his plan, but it made the decision harder. "I've got to report to Charles. He wants an update on you."

"You told Charles?" She growled and cringed in pain for the effort. "He needs to focus. Where's Kaliastrid?"

"She's with him. She couldn't lie to him. I could. Maybe you should reconsider how you're promoting in this unit. Anyway, he's calm and focused, but he wants to know you're okay. All we could tell him was you were hurt."

"Tell him we're coming to him."

"Sorry. No can do. I'm not giving up here. You know my goal, and it has nothing to do with your quest for fire. I have a friend to save."

"We tried your plan. It failed. Now you help me. That was our deal."

She was pulling his plug. She was going to get Tara killed. He was not going to give up on her when he was this close. "I can't. I have to see this through. My only path to Tara is up there."

"You don't know that she's up there. Elaine can't find exactly where she is. You send those men into that mountain, they won't come back. I told Charles, right after the emergence, guns would not work. I can't believe I let you convince me that this might. You can't win this way. If there's one thing dragons know how it do, it's defend a hole in the ground. Even if this is the actual hole and not just a staging point. Aldrich is right.

We have to focus on finding the talisman or reverse the spell. Then I'll be able to stop this. I got distracted. Not anymore. A gun didn't bring down that helicopter." She grimaced as she tried to point. "A witch did. Did you have witches that could do something like that two months ago? Combine dragons, partials, witches, and a cave, and you have a full house of wild cards."

She had a point, but he wouldn't just give up on Tara. She deserved his best effort. Her country was reorganizing as if she was already dead. They were throwing her away, but Silas would not be part of that. "I can't. I have to save her. He knows where she is, and I'm going to find her. If she's up there, I have to try."

"We will find her, Silas," Melissa said with a comforting tone, "but not here. We have to combine our forces. We're split now. I really think we need to get back with the others. This is playing to his strength. I was stupid to do it. Dragons learned better long ago. I should have known better. Of all dragons, I am supposed to be able to rise above our base emotions and rage."

In his heart, Silas knew she was right, but it was his inability to give up that had gotten him where he was. He paused to think if that was good and then pressed on.

"How do you know you can save her chasing after some legend? How do you know it even exists? I'm close here. I can press this without you."

"I don't know, not any more than you do. I have to trust we'll figure this out before Nethliast gets any crazier or any stronger. He kept her alive when he killed all of the others. There has to be a reason. She's not dead yet, Silas."

Silas paused and thought about what she said. Maybe she was right. Maybe Nethliast needed her alive for some reason. Silas thought about her other goal for a moment and a memory of his grandfather came to him clearly. According to his tales, the Folkvardr had hidden powerful magical items where they would not be found. They had hidden them to protect the world. Her other search may not be as easy as she thought. It had taken two Folkvardr descendants to find the small puzzle boxes he had collected, and she was talking about a large talisman. He shook his head as he returned to thinking about saving his friend.

"I can't take the risk. I won't bet on the long shot. She's up there somewhere, and this is as close as I've been to getting her back. Even Elaine said she was down here, but she couldn't tell where anymore. I'm going to see this through."

Melissa frowned. "Where are they, anyway?"

"France, or they're on their way." Silas allowed the subject change to enforce his point.

Her eyes grew large. She leaned toward him, making the doctor shift and complain.

"We need to get there. They must have figured something out." Energy seemed to fill her eyes.

"Why?"

"I can't explain. It just feels right."

"You're going to force me to come, aren't you?"

She paused before answering him. "No—I think you're going to come on your own. You know I'm right."

"Not this time. I belong here. I'll get you back to your team, but I'm staying here to save Tara. I owe her that much. She trusted me." He couldn't look at her eyes. She really believed he was supposed to be with the nerd, the Boy Scout, and the miniature Viking. He'd join them if he had time after he'd splattered that lizard all over the mountainside and found Tara. There was no way they were going to save her by flying off in the opposite direction, no matter what they found in France.

Melissa's face showed her disappointment, but she didn't say anything else.

"Hey," he called to the pilot who had come over to check on Melissa. He was standing just out of range of their conversation. "You're Blackjack, right?"

"Yep, that's me. Captain O'Mallie." The tall pilot with the blackest hair Silas had ever seen called back. The dissonance of his name and his appearance threw Silas for a moment. His skin had an obvious red hint to it, and his facial structure was very strong to be Irish as his name implied. Silas struggled to identify the other side of his family tree, and it escaped him. It wasn't Italian. Silas stepped down from the ambulance to greet the approaching pilot. When Blackjack saw the cluster he snapped a salute at it and added, "Sir."

"Never mind that." Silas waved the respect away, making himself as close to one of the boys as he could. "Great flying. Thanks for getting her back in one piece and following him to ground. I think we have a good chance of taking him up there."

"Not based on what I saw, sir. With respect, sir." As the tall man talked, Silas was listening to his cadence and intonation. There was something about it that would explain why he seemed so out of place.

"Eh, don't sweat that. You don't have all of the intel. Look, I need to get her out of here and over to Alsace. Can you manage it?"

"Short hop, no problem. I'll have to clear it with the colonel, though, sir."

Looking at him squarely and factoring in the mellow tone that had kept everyone calm through the fight helped Silas narrow the pilot's heritage down. He couldn't resist the puzzle and refused to leave it unsolved. After a few more seconds of thinking he had it. He was Native American, probably one of the western tribes. He was not pure-blood, but he was not far from the reservation either. The blend was striking.

"No problem. I've already talked to him. You go get it cleared, and as soon as she's patched up, I want you to get her out of here. Oh, and tell the colonel that I need a Carl Johnson and some AP rounds."

The lanky pilot appraised his request with some respect for his knowing the slang for the Multi-Role Anit-Personnel Weapon System. He saluted again as he turned to follow his new orders.

"One more thing, Captain," Silas said and stopped his departure. "Navajo, right?"

Blackjack grinned. "Yes, sir. I wasn't sure what was puzzling you before, but now I understand. I get that a lot." He rubbed his hands through somewhat unruly locks. "My mother was full blood, daughter of a Code-Talker. She married the son of an Irish immigrant that fought with her father. They moved off the reservation. Too much patriotism in my blood to do anything other than join the military, and I've always needed to get out and spread my wings."

"Glad you were out there with her. You kept it together."

"I'm glad she was there with us. She probably saved us all." Blackjack nodded to Silas and turned to follow his previous orders.

Silas stepped in the other direction so he could find a place to think and to call Charles. He found his radio and switched back to the frequency they were waiting on.

"Boy Scout, do you read me?"

"Roger, go ahead." Silas heard humor in his response and relaxed. The conflict was breaking down the barriers years of distrust had built.

"I need a location. I'm sending Puff ahead in a chopper. Where should I send her?"

There was silence and then a crackle. "There's a chain of communes in the Saint-Amarin valley. We need a place to meet."

Silas thought about the area and assets that were available to them. In his mind he reviewed a rough map of France to find where he was talking about.

"Go to Colmar," Silas finally replied. "There's an airport on the north side of town. We have a safe-house there. I'll send specifics with Puff."

Another pause as Charles checked the location.

"Roger. We'll be there in about three hours. There's an airport, but it's pretty small. Is that the one you're thinking of?"

"Affirmative."

"Roger. We'll pick her up there."

"It's going to take them a couple of hours to get her there. She'll be on her way in 30 mike. You've shown great restraint, not asking, but I'll tell you anyway. She's got two broken arms, her ribs are a mess, and they've pulled some shrapnel out of her chest. Nothing other than muscle damage inside. Otherwise she's fine. She's out of this fight until she heals, though."

There was no response. Silas wondered if Charles had heard him and almost retransmitted the report when the carrier filled his ears.

"Roger, thanks for the update. We'll meet up with her there." There was relief in the distant voice.

"Boy Scout, listen. Take care of her. She put herself in some real danger up here. She's not feeling real good about any of this, especially since Nethliast got away and I'm not coming along. Try to get her mind off of it. Help her find what she's looking for and end this."

"Don't be nuts. He'll eat you for lunch."

"Maybe, but I have to try. I can't leave a friend in need."

There was another pause before the respectful reply came back. "OORAH! You keep it safe, soldier."

Silas took the admonition the way it was meant. "You too. I'll send the info on the safe house with Puff."

Silas turned off the radio. He'd finish organizing Melissa's airlift and then find Carlson. He had to find a way up that mountain.

September 8 – 1500 CET - Colmar, France

It was afternoon when the helicopter approached the airport in the medium-sized capital city of the Haut-Rhin Department of Alsace. The small terminal was not a bustling center of travel. That was probably one of the reasons Silas remembered it so fondly when he told her about the safe house.

A few charter jets waited for their passengers to load on the tarmac. The pilot of a single engine Cessna was waiting for someone to join him and was the only person to take any note of the helicopter approaching the edge of the taxiway. It was an odd enough occurrence that he was not sure what he should do. He obviously did not miss the escort helicopter that was hovering behind and above the landing transport. Unsure he should be watching at all, he turned his attention to anything else inside the flight bag he was preparing to load into the plane.

As the wheels touched the ground, it was easy, except for the pain in her chest and arms, for Melissa to forget that she had just tried to kill her ex-mate and nearly died trying. A combination of pain killers and regret induced a fugue where she could pretend she was not responsible for starting a war between dragons and the entire world.

In her own defense, this was her second attempt to kill him. She didn't understand why she had failed the first time. She had wanted to kill him, but now she understood that she had just exiled him somewhere and allowed him to return, stronger. Her failure this time was as clear to her as anything could be in her physical state. Her own hubris and abdication of her responsibility caused it. She couldn't keep failing to kill Nethliast. It was going to make her look weak to her kin. That could not be allowed.

As they had flown across Germany into France, Melissa had watched out the open window behind the pilot. The country she once knew as her own passed below her, and part of her could understand Nethliast's desire to reclaim what they had once ruled. It had only been a few years since she had left the region after spending her adolescence in a boarding school outside of Paris, so she felt close to it even as a young human. It was the same with Nethliast. He felt a deeper need to protect the legacy of dragons because of her father, who didn't understand that dragons had surrendered their reign for a reason. Half-way through the flight, she could no longer watch. She simply slumped in the seat and let the crushing fatigue, thrumming pain, and opiate-induced lethargy drag her down. When the pilot had announced over the headsets that they were close, she forced herself to look out the window at the peaceful French city again resting on the edge of war.

Colmar was, like many cities in the area, a collection of very old, romantic buildings snuggled into a modern wrapper. She could easily imagine that she was just a tourist, visiting the wine country or walking the historic old-towns. The young girl she had been a few weeks before would have loved a trip to Europe with no concerns, but the dragon remembered a very different world. She remembered an older civilization that seemed to have vanished from history completely. As she looked down into the town, she could see how quickly that had happened.

Suddenly, Melissa wanted to be that young girl with no worries again for a while. She wanted the freedom of her responsibility-free youth that had been ripped from her by her grandmother's will. She could visit Europe, with Charles along as a friend, or lover. They could repair the breach she only recently realized her family created to protect their bloodline. They could enjoy a peaceful walk in the beautiful lands that had been fought over ever since dragons had surrendered them to humans. Beneath her physical pain, Melissa felt an even deeper ache. She missed Charles and her life before the emergence. Drugs and romantic fancy painted those memories far better than she knew they were. Landing at the airport forced her back to reality.

The wheels touched down on the faded gray surface of the taxiway. The gunner had the door open as the shocks took the weight of the aircraft.

Blackjack circled their landing area in the single escort chopper as the door gunner helped her down. It was very difficult to climb in or out of the helicopter with no use of her arms and pain in her ribs and chest. She tried not to bounce, but it wasn't possible. No matter how she stood or sat the pain remained a reminder of her inability to kill Nethliast and end this war she had not asked for. The pilot and copilot looked back, sat up straight in their seats, and saluted her as she walked backward away from them. She had never been trained or even thought about military protocol, and she could not return the respect even if she knew how, but she nodded her head in the best salute she could produce. These men had risked their lives to save her and they were saluting *her*. Her movements were slow and matched both her physical and mental state.

The two men grinned at her, then returned to their jobs. They both looked forward and busied themselves with the takeoff ritual. Having shown their respects, it was time to get back into the war.

"Puff, this is Blackjack."

She looked up and spoke. Someone had set her radio to allow her voice to activate it. "Go ahead."

"You take care now. Sounds like I'm going a-dragon hunting, no offense, and I wondered if you had any advice." She could hear the stress in his voice that he could never admit. She thought she saw the eyes of the copilot dart to her as he asked the question they all wanted answered.

"Yeah. Keep him on the ground and stay as far off as you can. The closer you get, the easier it is for them. And Blackjack, don't underestimate them. They're as smart as any modern force with the added benefit of magic you are not trained to understand or fight. They've demonstrated that several times, but no one is paying attention. They're the worst combination of modern warrior and ancient beast. Your best and only hope is overwhelming firepower with no regard for any life near them. You can't give them a chance to fight, and never follow a dragon into its lair."

She had cleared the sweep of the rotors and was moving toward the single terminal building. The wash was beginning to pick up dust around her and buffet her clothes.

"Roger that. Any ideas on the Major?"

"Yeah, don't trust him with your wallet or your wife. Beyond that, he's all in. He's on a mission."

"Roger that. I'll see ya."

She looked up again as he flew overhead in the opposite direction. The Blackhawk, as she had come to recognize it, lifted off and followed him toward the east. She hoped they would be careful. She wished they would stay as far away from Nethliast as they could, but she knew that was too much to ask of a soldier.

On the flight out Silas had been busy. She had listened to the transmissions back and forth between both the base and Blackjack and the two helicopters. Even though they were soldiers and trained to fight, they were nervous about what the combined forces were planning. They had faced the witch once and seen what she could do. They had seen how hard it was going to be to defend against her, never mind that there was at least one dragon up there, too. She hoped someone would convince them to back off, but she knew, in her heart, they would not be stopped. Berlin was a smoking bloody nose given to them by dragons. Someone had found a nest of those same dragons. As far as they knew, they were facing only a single male and a woman. In their minds they believed they should be able to clean out this nest and move on. She shook her head. Even though she doubted Nethliast was even up there any more, she knew the outcome of this evening like she had written it herself. Humans throughout history had underestimated magical forces, and this was no different. She frowned and pushed open the door into the terminal with her hip and the help of a local traveler.

There was nothing she could do now in the shape she was in. She knew, after three more hours to think about it, that his plan was not going to work.

With difficulty, she changed the dial on the radio to call Kaliastrid and Charles.

"Kali, Charles, what's your position?" The pain made her sound as tired as she felt, and she did nothing to change that impression.

"We're on the outskirts of Colmar, heading north. Should be there in a few minutes," Charles answered. "It's good to hear your voice."

She could hear the chastisement in his tone and accepted it because just behind it was his honest concern. She had made a lot of decisions lately that had risked her neck, and she was wondering if they had really made any difference.

"I'll see you when you get here."

"What's wrong?"

"Nothing, Charles."

"Mel, come on, I know something's bothering you."

She had left the last hope of stopping Nethliast in a cottage on the side of a mountain knowing she couldn't do anything about it. Silas was going to sacrifice himself to keep trying what Melissa knew was hopeless. She still had no idea exactly what they were looking for. She had dragged them to the middle of Europe hoping to kill Nethliast while chasing legends and dreams of her dead grandmother, snippets of memories that could mean anything. Nothing had worked the way she had planned, and worst of all she couldn't tell him how she really felt for him.

By now, she had hoped, the rest of her kin should have been rallying to her side to stop the conflict with the humans. Instead more soldiers were about to charge in to kill or capture Nethliast and his witch—and probably die trying.

"Aldrich was right, Charles. I never should have taken this risk. Nethliast is too strong for me. I've done nothing but make things worse, and I'm probably going to get Silas killed."

"Nonsense Mel. Don't give up on yourself or this mission. We all face defeat. Sometimes we get a second chance to learn from it. Wait until you see what they've found. Your effort was worth it. It kept them occupied so we could find a clue, which was exactly what we needed."

She nodded but didn't respond. She was thinking about what Nethliast had been able to accomplish while she had been sitting around reading romance novels. That thought rushed the floral-scented witch to the front of her mind.

She shook her head at the memory of the young woman she had only seen briefly through the trees but would never forget. Where had she come from? Elaine was demonstrating innate magical abilities, but this witch was different. It was obvious, based on her ritualistic casting, that she was not innate, but she was more powerful than any innate Melissa had met so far. That scared her. Her father had warned her, but she had not expected the power and desire to use it that she had demonstrated.

Was Nethliast *involved* with her?

Melissa felt the blush flood across her face. It was a combination of anger and embarrassment.

Why did she care? The perfume that was all over him answered the question, and she felt a twinge of masochistic jealousy. When that passed, she wanted to laugh, even though she was wringing her hands together. If Melissa knew Nethliast at all, the poor witch was just part of his plan.

"Mel?" Charles called back.

"I'm fine, Charles. We'll talk more when you get here."

"I have the time. I'm just driving."

She felt the sudden weight of it all and nowhere to lay it down. The fact that Charles cared enough to push her to talk drove her over the edge. She had failed to kill Nethliast, and she had no other plan. Twenty-four hours before, she would have sworn it was the only way to solve any of this.

"I'm not sure I can do this, Charles." She felt the tears in her voice and wished she had the energy to keep them out.

"You're not alone. We're all working the problem."

"That's what worries me. Soldiers are about to die to stop Nethliast. The one thing I came all this way to do. They *will* die because they can't stop him, and I can't do anything about it."

"Aldrich and Elaine have a good idea that we're heading in the right direction. So far we've seen no sign that they're following us, and they don't know what we know. There's no way they can follow the clues we have. How many times have you had the guidance of a god? And you can't complain, it's Odin—sorry Wodin— after all."

He made her smile and chased her tears off a little. As a dragon, she remembered a world where that kind of devotion was common. She remembered a time when magic was all around. That memory made her very happy, but then she realized it was coming back. This world was not prepared for it. She sat down in the small terminal and watched the rest of the world try to live in the war thrust upon them for no reason they could ever understand.

"I have to end this. Too many are suffering for nothing."

"We'll be there in a few minutes. We'll go find some food and get some rest while we try to piece together where we're going next."

"You risked your life to stop Nethliast. You're doing your duty, daughter. We're all here for you and believe in you. Now stop scaring the humans."

Melissa smiled at the comfort of her mother's mind. The reassurance of her stability was what she needed, and the kick in the pants was helpful, too.

"You're right, Charles. I'm fine. Let everyone know that I'm fine." Her voice sounded stronger. "See you when you get here." She couldn't afford for Charles or any of the others to feel the defeat she was getting over.

"Why are we the only dragons fighting him?" she asked the comforting voice in her head.

"He has all of the males behind him. Their mates and children are his prisoners. Our memories are fragmented. They've been human so long they've forgotten that they would have torn him into little pieces already for the crimes he's committed, and he's stood up to lead them. We can't fight him without them behind you."

"Maybe it's time we changed that. Maybe Silas could help. We have to try something."

"The two of us? Think about what you're saying. We have no idea where he's holding them, and he has to be using magic to keep them. We can't hope to continue fighting these odds and winning. We need an advantage, and that's what you have everyone else looking for. The Heart of the Dragons is the key." Kaliastrid was not angry with her, and Melissa knew it. She had to be firm to keep Melissa focused right now.

"So, Aldrich was right. Wodin wanted us to go this way all along. We're suffering from a lack of faith?"

"Child, when have you ever known a dragon to listen to a deity, any deity? You are suffering because you have not faced a witch in a millennium. I'm suffering because I didn't chase that rotten brat down after we emerged and force him to respect you and your father. We may be suffering from bad choices, but we're not suffering from some curse of the gods. Get your head back in the fight."

Melissa smiled at her mother's strong chin that came through her thoughts.

"Thanks for keeping them safe."

"It's what we've done for centuries, isn't it?"

"What?"

"Watch over humans."

Melissa hadn't thought about it until Kaliastrid said it. She hadn't considered that her grandmother's novels had all been about that. Sure the newer ones were romances, but at their core they were tales of how dragons were watching over humans, helping them. All of the older books Elaine had found were the same way. That was why this all felt so wrong, and the answer had come without the tell-tale pain of a memory.

She pondered that realization while she waited for the humans she loved, deeply in her soul. She watched the other humans around her and realized that she loved them nearly as deeply. Nethliast had been right from the start. His anger, as misplaced as it was, had pointed out the truth to her that she had never understood.

She did love humans, had for centuries, and for some reason she had been placed in a role of watching over them. Sitting in the seat in that airport watching them continue to live while dragons attacked the foundation of their world, she came to understand, again. She didn't realize how long it had been when she was suddenly aware of someone standing behind her.

She stood carefully and awkwardly from the seats and turned to face her friends. Kaliastrid stood behind them, watching as she always would. She was better prepared for this. Melissa choked down the recurring doubts about her ability. It was what it was. She had to work with it.

Elaine was there and looking better for the chance to continue the role Heliantra knew she was meant for. She looked unsure of how to approach her, so Melissa smiled with pride to show her how important her success was. It seemed to relax the young woman. Charles was beaming at her like a proud brother. Aldrich was looking at her with the same pride he had always shown, but he also had the furrowed brows of a worried father.

"Sit down, Meliastrid," he said as he approached her by walking around the row of interconnected chairs. His voice was soft, and he was coaxing her to the seat. Warm hands on her hand made her relax and settle.

"There you are, child," he crooned gently as he placed his hand on her ribs. "Quite a bit of work you've made for me here. Wodin will not forsake you, even though you have willfully pursued your own path. The outcome is positive."

She had expected pain. In her mind she wanted to resist but for some reason she didn't. His right hand on her hand seemed to hold her in the seat and was somehow calming her. She could transform and stop his magic cold, but she didn't.

He looked up at Charles to ask for help. "We will do what we can here, but more will be required when we have a safe place to rest."

His left hand covered one side of her broken ribs, and ice shot through the pain. She shivered. His warm hand burned in the middle of an icy pillow. His fingers caressed her ribs gently. She looked at him. He was mumbling something she couldn't quite hear, and she could feel the power flowing from the hand on her hand to the hand on her ribs. His fingers seemed to be tracing a pattern of runes in her skin. As the pain vanished, she felt a flash of euphoria. Tears streamed down her cheeks. She had no idea how long he had been chanting when he stood up. He raised his hands to his face and blew into them. Black dust, like ash, rose in a cloud and then vanished. He dropped two gnarled chunks of metal into her hand.

"Those would have been a problem later. I've knit the ribs back together and fixed the bones in your arm." He removed the air cast on her right arm, and she stiffly helped with the left. "There's more to be done, but you're more than stable now."

The pain was mostly gone, and her mind was clearer than it had been. She stood back up and looked at her friends.

Elaine suddenly decided how to handle their greeting and threw herself around her neck. What would have been impossible, moments before, was a pleasant show of affection. Charles walked up and placed a hand on both of their shoulders. Melissa felt an absence in her group and looked around for the missing member. As she scanned the room, she remembered that Silas had stayed behind and was going along with the attack as soon as everyone was in place. Something in her head told her she needed him, now. She couldn't let Nethliast kill him. She needed to get him out of there.

She reached out and pulled the protesting priest into the embrace. These humans, in particular, she had to protect, including Silas. They were something important.

With everyone in her embrace, she looked up to Kaliastrid, who was still watching over them all.

"Go get Silas. He won't come easy unless he's nearly dead, and I hope that's not the case. Help him realize his hunt is here. We need him if we're going to solve this. They're moving in on the mountainside. You'll never get there before the fight starts. Bring him here, even if you have to subdue him to do so."

Her mother nodded and turned without a word to walk out and do as she had been told. The pieces were coming together. They finished their greetings like friends who had been separated for years, then packed back into the car to find the address Silas had given her.

"Aldrich, what did you do to me? I feel great."

"I healed you. Wodin gave me that power as soon as he appeared in my dreams. It's wonderful what I can do with his guidance."

"Well, thank you. I..."

"No, don't thank me. Thank Wodin. You're a worthy warrior. You faced death without fear. Wodin healed you because you fight for what is right, independent of your choice to ignore his warning."

Melissa nodded to him. There would be more advocates soon. There would be more healers. The face of the world was changing.

"I'll likely ignore your advice again, little man, but keep giving it all the same." She smiled at him. He seemed to glow in her respect. "So, why are we here? I've been out of the loop."

"Because," Elaine nearly squealed. She had been waiting for the question and pounced like a cat when it was finally asked. "We found a legend in Füssen. It was printed with a map. When we compared it to a local map and found that it matched a valley west of here. At the end of the valley there's an old castle. It may be Renard's."

"What makes us think that?"

"Because, it matches the tale, Renard's tale...well his name is Rinehard, but I thought that could be explained by it being an oral legend for so long."

Melissa turned to look back at her. They had looked for books that referenced him directly before and never found him. It was like he had never existed. All of the kings and people she remembered had vanished from history, just like dragons.

"Right. I see what you're thinking. Why is this different? Good question. Well, it's different because it's fiction. It's in a book of fairy tales from the region, written in the 1500's. It has some interesting stories in it. The one that got our attention was actually a tale of how a knight that was troubling the locals finally met his tragic end in the rivers flowing out of the mountains."

Aldrich held up the map from the book and the small atlas he had compared it to.

"It's a little thin, isn't it? Why are we even looking for Renard's castle?"

"It's no worse than what brought us here," Elaine snapped defensively.

"It is thin, but it matches what we know, mostly. It's the same reason the male dragons could never prove sovereignty over the Swabian lands. Their lineages were locked up in fiction, not history." Aldrich stepped in to defend the idea. "And, we're looking for Renard's castle because that's where Kaliastrid said she took the Heart of the Dragon. Her description of the location matches this valley. The illumination Elaine drew from her memories of being there is stark."

"Remember what I said about knights fighting dragons and how that was impossible without magic? It just fits with the legend of a knight that is plaguing the region and then just disappears. That doesn't happen either."

Memories were somehow starting to repair themselves, and the pain from each one was either lessening or she was getting used to it. She hoped Nethliast never got his memories back, or, if he did, he remembered everything.

"So, where to from here?" Melissa accepted they were convinced. She needed to follow for a while.

"Chateau de Wildenstein," Aldrich and Elaine answered in unison.

September 8 – 1900 CET - A farm outside Füssen, Bavaria

Kaliastrid flew in over the remnant of the camp set up in the field outside the farm she had first seen only twelve hours earlier. The buildings, trees, and fields had been transformed into a landscape of destruction. Fire still burned in a few places. Bodies of half-dragons, naga, and human soldiers lay abandoned all over the battlefield. Several helicopters lay across the field in different broken forms. Tanks and artillery burned, filling the darkening sky with black smoke and obscuring the battlefield. A trail of smoking vehicles leading from the south showed how the humans had tried to rally as they retreated back to their last position of power. From her initial scan, she couldn't tell if any of them had survived or if they had held their last stand at the farm.

"Silas, are you here?" She called over the radio again and, just like the last time, silence came back to her. She was going to have to do this the hard way.

She inhaled the horrible aroma of the battlefield, a combination of burning wood, plastic, and flesh, hot metal and cordite layered over the ever-present scents of blood and feces. At first it seemed impossible to distinguish a single smell, the scent of a single man, from the overpowering clamor of smells. But after a few minutes circling the field and testing the air, she was able to find an awful blend of Silas and death.

She circled the location twice more to make sure what she smelled was correct, choked down her bile, and then focused on that odor.

She flapped south toward the mountains, following the smoking trail of destruction that looked like the discarded toys of a giant child after a tantrum. She would start her search at the end of the trail, where the rout had begun and see what she found. Along the path from the farm there was no sign of his scent. He had not walked or left by vehicle.

Thirty minutes later she was flying over a massacre worse than what was behind her at the farm. Several heavy troop helicopters lay in crumpled piles that fanned out around a clearing in front of the smoking, obliterated remains of a cabin. Fifteen bodies lay immediately around the house. Nearly one hundred more were spread out around the surrounding area. Some were charred lumps, evidence of dragon's breath. Some were crumpled into fetal positions with their faces stretched into a rictus of surprise. Their death had come unexpectedly from powerful magic. Two of the soldiers that had made it to the cottage stairs were dispersed in a fan of destruction. The cause of their demise was drawn in an intricate magical ward outlined in blood on the ground.

She sniffed the air again for her target, letting the horrible odors fill her mouth. Tracking required her to almost taste the air for her prey. Focusing on the odors that were not strictly destruction was difficult and required her to circle the field. She was beginning to feel that it was hopeless until a hint crossed her tongue. Dragon, human, some odd flowery perfume that persisted even among the destruction, half-dragons, an interesting and confusing symphony of human and canine musk blended with flowers all merged in her nose and mouth. Hidden among that cacophony was Silas. Sniffing again and focused on that scent, she followed the wisp of it away from the smoking hulk of the helicopter. He had exited it alive. This was his initial point on the ground. Then he had moved up slope away from the soldiers.

Kaliastrid followed him until she found where he had laid down. His strong musk was all over the ground where he had watched the events unfold below him. A large tube-like rifle, different from what he had used that morning, was lying in the leaves. He had left it when he had run out of ammunition. He must have been planning to snipe Nethliast again, or maybe he was after the witch. He had not returned to this location. She flew off, tracking his scent.

The thought of Nethliast allying himself with a human spell caster had chilled her when Valdiest had told them about it. An ominous thread of fear tickled her mind about that out-of-character alliance as she focused on the search.

Silas' scent trail drove her back toward the house. He had tried to sneak up on the witch. Her nose was beginning to draw a map of Silas' part of the battle for her. She circled to sample the air again.

The images clarified in her mind. Half-dragons had been waiting for them. More than fifty had waited in ambush. They were hidden in redoubts among the rocks and trees. It was possible they were invisible until the attack started. Nethliast had expected they would come back in force. The soldiers had been allowed to reach the ground and close on the house before the trap was sprung. Partials had fired on the helicopters as they unloaded, guaranteeing that the soldiers were trapped on the ground. Nethliast counted on ubiquitous human arrogance.

She followed the scents for several more passes before she found what happened to Silas after he abandoned his sniper's nest to try to take out the witch. The next stages of the battle clarified in her mind as she circled. While the soldiers were being neutralized by the partials closer to the house, the assault helicopters had leveled the house and killed several squads of partials before they were finally shot down by flankers. Silas had killed several of them with his weapon. His final approach to the position beyond the house where the witch had led the fight turned against him quickly. This was where the part-human, part-canine creatures she had smelled earlier had taken the field. They were the answer to why the humans had had no hope of winning. Behind the cabin, nestled in a hidden cul-de-sac in the trees, was an entrance to an armored bunker where reinforcements were staging as needed. Silas was in a fast retreat into the woods pursued by the odd smelling human, canine creatures.

She followed his path and flew over the wreckage of the remaining choppers in two ravines on the side of the mountain. The last helicopter had covered Silas' retreat and had also crashed into the ravine. It was smoking but not aflame. She hovered. Someone was alive down there. She could see the faintest hint of movement near the shattered cockpit.

She followed the crash path the chopper had taken as it had flown into the trees. The pilot had gunned down two humans, who were splayed naked on the ground as if they were crawling away. A memory tickled her mind and threatened pain until the flickering guardian at her temple whistled it away. The beasts had each been a loup garou before the pilot had released them from the witch's control.

She coasted in to land without difficulty. She looked around cautiously for a trap because she could not take off from this spot. As her feet touched down she transformed, covering herself with scaled armor over her arms, legs and torso, before pursuing Silas' trail.

A loud crack accompanied a pressure in her chest that sat her down in the dirt. She rolled to her side and down the hill toward the fire as rounds chewed at the ground above her head.

"Friendly! Friendly!" she screamed as she recovered her knees and approached her attacker. She repeated it over and over as she crawled toward the smoking fuselage. The small rounds didn't penetrate her armor, but they stung. When she was covered by the helicopter completely and the shots had stopped, she tried again.

"Friendly."

"How do I know?" a decidedly angry voice asked. She could hear him reloading the rifle.

"You're still alive."

"You make a point. Why are you here?"

"I'm looking for Silas."

"Who?"

"Silas Loxley."

"The Major? Probably dead. Everyone else on this hill bought it except me."

"I see that, but he wasn't down there when it started. He was above them on the hill then."

She had stepped out where the pilot could see her and pointed to the ridge that she had tracked Silas to.

"Yeah, maybe then. He might have gone unseen. But when you find him, he owes me. Puff told him to stop the attack, and he ignored her."

"Puff?" She moved closer, showing her hands, and looked over the fuselage. He was holding his rifle up at her. The signs of shock were at the ragged edge of his attempt to stay conscious.

"Yeah, the lady—dragon—who flew with us earlier today," he replied. He took in her scales and shivered a little.

"A historically human fault. It's hard to get them to stop and think."

"Human, huh? And you'd be?"

"Decidedly not human."

"I guess. How do I know you're really a friend? If you're a dragon, which side are you on? If you're not, then what do you want with me?"

She smiled and waved a hand over the scales that covered her torso. "I'm a dragon, on your side, and I know Puff."

"Well, now days you can't tell. I saw things up here today that I never saw before. I'm certainly not assuming anything anymore. I'm especially not going to assume that any female is a non-combatant. Puff had already warned me, but when you see that witch standing in the middle of the battlefield in a business suit, you hesitate. She made a mess of those poor guys." He swallowed nothing and continued, "I know 20 mike mike stops most anything but 5.56 is useless. And whatever those huge wolves were, they were nearly as hard to kill as those half-dragons."

She stood up straight at the mention of wolves. "What wolves?" She sniffed the air again, remembering the blended smell of man, canine, and flowers. Her spiny back ridge twitched at the thought of what the creature was.

"Big ones, about as high at the shoulder as a man's waist, but big. I left two of them dead in my wake as we crashed, at least Smiley did. Last thing his silly grinning face ever did." The pilot pointed with his left hand at the shattered remains of his helicopter. Kaliastrid assumed the uniformed body slumped forward and unmoving in the front seat was "Smiley".

"We have to get you out of here. If they come back, you're dinner." She started looking around again for the loup garou prints or any sign of the large wolves. They were not fun to deal with, and she didn't want to fight them in any form other than her full dragon. That was what the witch had sent after Silas.

"My M-4 here scattered them well enough. Don't think I killed any, but they took off."

"They'll be back." She knew they were on their primary mission if they had left him alive. It was the reason they had been enchanted. "Can you walk?"

"Nope. Both legs're busted. I'd be half-way home if I could."

"What's your name?"

"O'Mallie, Sean O'Mallie. Captain, US Army."

"Sean, I'm going to have to carry you. I need to find Silas. The sooner I do, the better. He's probably the reason the loup garou left you alone."

"Loup garou?"

"Intelligent Wolves. What you might call werewolves, but not exactly like the stories that you grew up with. Large, mean, ugly."

"Yeah, okay."

She transformed again, letting her legs grow into the stronger dragon hind legs. The tail appeared automatically, her chest and arms bulked up, and her head transformed into her full dragon appearance. She was a slightly smaller version of her full dragon form without wings.

Sean grimaced as she transformed.

"Sorry, but to have the strength, I have to take on the full form."

"Right. You just look meaner that way."

Without responding, she walked around the helicopter and lifted him up over her shoulder. With him situated, she sniffed at the air and took off after the loup garou pack. It was exactly what she thought. They were following Silas, playing with him because, as a pack, they could have taken him easily.

"How long ago did they come through?"

"'bout twenty minutes before you did. I thought they were coming back when you walked up."

She started to run with long loping dragon strides. She could feel Sean clenching his teeth as she bounced over the rough terrain, and she was impressed by his silence. The scent was getting stronger.

At the crest of the hill she found a dead loup garou lying against the side of the hill. She knew it was another of the enchanted man-wolves of legend because of the way the naked body was still contorted into a four legged sprawl where it had fallen and transformed back exactly like the two Sean had killed. Its head was mostly gone. She sniffed carefully at this one and verified her fears. The witch was crafty. She had used partials, which meant they were volunteers for the charm required to create the beasts. They would be stronger than any loup garou she had ever faced.

"How many?"

"There were ten originally. They came off the top of the hill with the woman. We mowed down five of them back there. They weren't immune to the twenty."

That left four.

"What did the partials and dragons chase back to the base?"

"We brought a few APCs in. Tanks couldn't make it. The Bradleys had the bushmasters on them. They'd take a chunk out of a dragon's hide, no offense."

She shook her head.

"Anyway, the APCs dropped a few more of the partials and then the anti-tank rounds hit. About the same time someone lit us up with stingers. In seconds, there was nowhere to go and nothing to do. We were down, the APCs were smoking, and everything started looking bad. I hadn't really listened to Puff's advice. Sure enough, they were using modern tactics blended with magic. We never had a chance. The survivors, what few there were, hauled it for base. Probably tracked 'em all the way back, didn't they? It was a rout."

"That's what it looked like. Shh." She stopped and sat him down next to a tree. He still had his rifle. He checked his load and put it up to his shoulder.

"I got your back," he whispered.

She smiled and walked ahead slowly, completing the transformation to her full form as she crested the hill. There were three of them surrounding a still form. His fatigues were torn from his upper body, and horrible scratches crossed his chest and back. He was bleeding from several bite wounds in his legs and arms. The loup garou had not seen her yet, and she was downwind from them. None of them were directly facing her. The closest of the three had his back to her, and the other two were facing each other at right angles to him. They were standing over Silas, growling a conversation in their own language.

She wanted to let loose with a blast of fire, but Silas was among them. The closest one took a long sniff of the air and stopped talking. Hackles lifted along the back of his neck. He turned to look at her over his shoulder. His paws shifted around to face her. An odd leather mask crossed his face. It held a crystal gem over his left eye. Surprise was gone.

She cast a bolt of lightning into the masked one. He crashed to the ground before he could warn the others. Smoke curled from the charred hole in his back and side as the dead body transformed back into its original form. Her attack advised them that their pack structure had shifted fatally.

The loup garou on her left circled away from Silas to flank her. The one closest to Silas immediately lowered his head and placed his jaws around his prisoner's neck. Canine saliva ran down both sides of the prone man's shoulder.

"Come any closer and the human dies," the circling beast warned her.

She considered any reaction there might be to her attack and answered, "You can't kill him. You were sent to find him, to hold him. That's why he's still alive. Where's the last member of your pack? Your alpha's dead, but his second has gone to tell the witch that you found her target, hasn't he?" She growled at them and bared her teeth to maintain her position.

The growling conversation continued as well as it could with Silas' neck secured in one of their mouths. The two remaining loup garou were not a threat to her, not like the whole pack would be, but they could kill Silas and Sean. The roaming one was getting behind her. So far he had not smelled Sean, but he was curious. She couldn't stop both of them, and Silas was unarmed.

"We'll kill him and blame it on the one you killed."

Silas' attacker tightened down on his neck. She could see the canine's sink into the soft neck muscles but not break the skin. They were willing to kill him.

"You won't fool Nethliast that way. Run off now and I won't have to kill you. I just want the human."

She could tell he was wrestling with what she said. He seemed to be weighing what he knew of Nethliast and the witch.

She watched him make up his mind. His jaws started to contract, but her tail was faster. Like a whip it struck just behind the canine's ears and severed the spine as she decapitated it. With the rush of blood from the severed head, she had no way of knowing if she had succeeded or not. The circling loup garou was moving as well. He had sensed that she was protecting something.

"Sean, He's—"

A burst of automatic fire made her message unimportant. When the magazine was empty and the bolt snapped open, silence filled the air.

If Sean had missed, the loup garou would be feasting. That particular noise was unique. Chances were good that Sean was okay. She would check on him when she had Silas safe. She transformed into her armored human form and walked over to him. The dead loup garou's head had shifted back to its partial form and slipped off of Silas' neck. She kicked the now-human-looking torso away from the head. Regeneration had never been possible for the original loup garou, but she saw no reason to take a chance. There was no sign that the animal's teeth had broken the skin. A quick feel of the throat made her feel better about Silas' condition. He was breathing, he had a pulse, and he responded to her touch. He was not in good condition, but he was alive.

Before she collected him, she policed the two bodies. The one she had decapitated didn't have anything, but she slipped the leather mask off of the other one. There had to be a reason the enchanted creature was using the odd lens, and she might find a use for it.

Again she transformed and collected Silas. She tucked the gem and the leather mask into his ripped fatigues and turned back to see about Sean.

When she came over the small crest and looked down the hill at the tree, Sean was missing. She looked to the left and found him stretched out prone, bracing on a rock, and pointing the rifle at her. As he recognized her, he relaxed, releasing the rifle and sliding back onto the ground.

"I'm glad it's you. I was out." He pointed at the loup garou laying between them. "It took a whole magazine to kill 'im."

"Can you handle a thirty-minute flight? It won't be easy with both of you, but it's the only way I can get you out of here. There's another loup garou out there, and he's gone to find the witch."

"If it means I'm out of here, I can handle anything. Well, maybe not walking back."

"The flight may not be much better."

"I'll chance it."

She walked over to him and lifted him from the ground and positioned him into the crook of her right arm. She shifted both of them over her neck between the ridges.

Taking off would be difficult here, but she had to get them out before the witch returned. She had no evidence Nethliast had been there since he had escaped into the tunnels. She climbed back to the top of the crest where it was more open.

She inspected the trees and envisioned the required flight path in her head. She would have to jump almost straight up. Each stroke would be difficult between the trees, but she felt confident she could get into the air.

She paused to make sure she had each man secure, settled onto her haunches, and jumped. As gravity fought her launch, she flapped aggressively to climb out of the trees. Her single stroke took her most of the way, but she was not clear yet. She extended her wings out and up around the trees and stroked again. Finally clear of the trees, she hovered and checked the men to make sure they were still in place. She could feel Sean clenching his muscles at the difficult take off. Silas was completely unaware. She checked her position, turned north, and stroked forward. It was dark, but the fires leading back to the farm still burned, lighting a path.

Several times along the way she worried about potential partials on lookout with rocket launchers. She quickly discarded the thought. If they saw her and took the shot, she and her passengers were probably dead. There was nothing she could do about it. She flew on until she reached the Toureg, parked where they had left it in the neighboring field. It was amazingly untouched by the battle that had raged just down the road from it.

When she landed next to it, she set them both against the car, transformed, and helped Sean in. From the inside, Sean helped her pull Silas in and then secured him in a seat belt. There was no way she would make the flight across Germany into France with both of them in her arms. In this case, it was faster and safer to take the car, and it had equipment they might need.

"I'm on my way. Silas and Sean will need Aldrich."

A drowsy response came back a little later. *"Who's Sean?"*

"A pilot who knows you."

"It'll be midnight when you get here. I'll have him ready."

"Probably later. I'm driving."

Kaliastrid settled into the seat and prepared for the long drive ahead. Fatigue threatened to fog her vision and drag her into a nap in the comfortable front seat. With a flickering support that reflected in the windshield next to her ear, she fought it off and surrendered to the purple arrow on the small screen in the dash.

September 8 – 2015 CET - A farm outside Füssen, Bavaria

As the dragon's self-powered carriage pulled away from the roadway, Renard shifted Rich's odd backpack on his shoulders and continued to sift through what happened on the battlefield. In his search for magic to bolster his arsenal, his orb had drawn him to this field. There was no denying there had been magic here. His concern was if there was any magic still here and if it would help him. Dragons did not leave magical items lying around for humans to discover. At least, they hadn't in Renard's time. They had been very thorough.

When the dragon had descended onto the road, it had startled Renard. He had been waiting for any stragglers who might disturb his search, but he had not expected a dragon to return. He had hidden to see if she was after the magic his orb had detected. Overloaded with her human cargo, it quickly became apparent that she was not looking for anything else on the battlefield.

Renard had struggled with his desire to kill his first dragon in what he determined had been several hundred years. The part of his brain that had kept him alive for so long had won, and he had stayed his attack. Even when he had all of his wits about him and every magical tool at his disposal, he never engaged a dragon in a fair fight. Fighting fair with dragons was a fast way into a grave. He was not planning on risking his life so soon after returning to it. In the end, he decided he was not prepared to face a dragon yet.

This land or time that he had emerged in intrigued him, and he would rather remain alive in it. The opportunities were fascinating. The people were more superstitious of magic than the uneducated masses he had known before he was trapped. Worse, they were not as careful of strangers. Rich and Barb had proved that when he had finally caught up to the unfortunate pair of travelers who had witnessed his return. Their misfortune had become Renard's advantage in many ways, the least of which was Richard's identity. Renard was not sure what the United Nations was, but Richard's position there was intriguing and promising. It would be more so, once "Richard" overcame his "illness" enough to return to his duties.

Renard knocked burnt twigs and other detritus of battle out of his way with his staff as he crossed the open field of death. The cooler weather was keeping the stench under control, but many of the victims on the field had fallen to dragon's fire. The sulfurous smell left by dragons was all too familiar to Renard's nose. It was not a pleasant aroma. The stench saturated his soul and always reminded him why he hated dragons.

Their condescension, even on the field of battle where men had died at his father's command for their cause, made his bile rise. The only redemption he found in his sudden memories of war that floated just out of reach was his recollection of seeding the dissent that had led his father and the dragons to the battlefield. Many magical races had found themselves hunted for acts they had never committed.

Renard laughed aloud as he walked across the deserted field among the silent dead. None of them had ever laughed with him when he toured his father's battlefields looking for unwanted survivors. He always found that offensive. Why should they not laugh? He knew they were watching him. They knew his task as well as he did. They could have at least laughed at his jokes as he did his rounds as reaper. He had never cared if the survivors were offended by his laughter. Their suffering never lasted very long, and then they were among the snobby, silent dead.

At the edge of the destruction he found a set of tracks that drew his attention from the dead. They led along the orb's projected path. He didn't want to blindly stumble into a trap, so he looked closer at them. First he saw the large four-clawed tracks of a dragon. Dragons hardly ever worried about leaving tracks, but this one was less concerned than most. He had been injured in the fight but had escaped the bombardment. The delicate steps of a human female told Renard the dragon had not been alone.

A few steps along their path together, the tracks changed. Other trackers might have been thrown off by the change, but Renard was very familiar with dragons' ability to take human shape. This one had shifted from dragon to human and back as he tried to heal the injury, but it had bled badly in either form.

There was an overlay of new tracks that followed the first dragon. This set shifted from human female to dragon. The last set of tracks were more cautious. She was hunting. The paths intertwined and entered the woods. Somewhere down the path in front of Renard, there was sure to be more destruction. Dragons only knew how to bring destruction and death. They had convinced the world otherwise, but the Brotherhood knew the truth they had hidden from humans. Power and rule brought absolute power.

Renard took out his orb. With dragons involved, he would be extra cautious. He whispered one of several command words available in the orb, and it floated in front of him. With another magical command he attached the orb to his consciousness. With a third he engaged the spell in the orb that revealed magic wherever the orb pointed. He focused on controlling the orb and leaned on his staff. The view always took effort to adjust to, no matter where it was pointed.

He turned his head to his left and scanned slowly to the right. The orb followed his movement. In his mind he could see the gray-black landscape of the non-magical world. The fact that it was night did not make it harder to see. He had used the magical detection of the orb to see at night before because it highlighted everything with its base magical signature. Everything had some magic to it. Otherwise magic could have no effect on it.

Nothing stood out from the detailed negative image of the world as he scanned slowly across the landscape until he passed the center of his arc. Exactly where he expected to see it, ahead and to the right of the point where the dragon and both women had entered the woods, a brightly colored patch flared across his vision. That was what he had come looking for. It was extremely powerful magic. From its color and brightness, he could tell it had power that dragons rarely allowed humans to have. From this distance and through the lesser-magical interference, he could not tell exactly what it was. It was large, and it spread across the ground. His mind automatically spun through a collection of potential magical items. He would be surprised if it was a rug, but it could be a cloak, robe, or even a magical blanket. It was obviously fabric, based on how it flowed over the surface of everything around it. With these possibilities in mind he prepared to approach it.

He watched the glowing patch for a moment to see if it moved or if there were any of the hair-thin wisps of power that represented a connection to something else. That could mean that a trap was set on it. When he was sure it was stationary and there was no trap, he relaxed his focus on the orb. As his own vision returned, he commanded it to drop into his hand, and he placed it back into his bag. Gnomes had been amazing artisans. They could merge a lot of magic into a useful package, and the orb was a masterpiece among works of art. He was almost sad they had made the decisions they had. The race as a whole never ceased to fascinate him. They had been willing to work with humans. They did not completely agree with dragons, but they remained dedicated to the nearsighted dwarves that they considered cousins. The nonproliferation treaties both races had signed with the dragons had doomed them. The Brotherhood could not allow such power to remain if it was not to be shared freely.

Pain assaulted all of his senses at once, filled with bright light and high-pitched noise, and forced him to surrender the rest of his memories as he tried to recall specifics of how they had eliminated the gnomes. The obviously magical interference of his memories made him think of another meddling race that had to be dealt with, but he stopped just short of the pain before cursing the suffering he associated with the only race they had not been able to eliminate.

Renard stepped forward into the woods, resolute that he would solve that as soon as he could get back to his keep, once he could remember where it was. First, he needed to recover the first mistake dragons had made since releasing him. No one left such a magical item lying around unless they were dead. Worse, dragons never left anything with value of any sort. Magic like this they guarded jealously from humans. So, nothing but tragedy and continued conflict could explain why the item he had seen would be where it was, unless it was a trap.

With a delicate whisper of another power word, magic surged from his staff. A blue light surrounded him for an instant before it vanished. The clue was slight, but it was enough to tell him he was shielded from most attacks. With another whisper a reddish light pulsed from the end of the staff. The light allowed him to travel in the night that had settled around him without drawing attention or losing his night vision.

Renard followed the footsteps that told the tragic tale that had played out into the clearing. He stood still at the edge and read the events. The first female was not a willing participant. She resisted, but not a lot. There was some attempt to heal the dragon, then she tried to drug him. That had not ended well for her. Before the second dragon reached the clearing, the male had transformed and killed the first woman.

Renard was standing above the dead form of a woman who had died over half a day before. She had fallen in the magical robe that his orb had been drawn to. The male dragon had left it to flee from the other dragon. This was positive. He liked any world where dragons fought each other. In his lifetime, they had not returned to that level of their beast mind. Perhaps they had fallen from grace in this world. If they were fighting each other, they would leave him alone. There was no reason for them to believe he was alive. He smiled.

Renard checked his deduction. He nodded as his second review proved the results of his first when he found additional markings from the second dragon. She was hunting the male dragon, not the female human.

Renard stuck his staff into the ground and leaned onto it for a moment as he considered the possibility of a civil war among dragons. He hit a painful barrier quickly as his memories refused to tell him more than his first impression. It was still a good situation for him if they were fighting. He just needed to figure out how to help that fight escalate.

Both dragons had flown off from the clearing. The orb did not show any sign of their large magical forms hiding, invisible in the distance, so he would not be able to track them any further. They had both been so interested in their own conflict that they had left behind the woman's cloak. That added validity to the idea of some conflict, but was equally odd.

Renard knelt beside her body. Before he touched her, he took a moment to whisper a phrase he had learned from a very dark Brother before he disturbed the dead. They may not share in his humor, but he knew to respect them and the power they represented. Death and death magic was not a place to venture lightly. It was very unforgiving. When he had completed the rather long enchantment that required him to walk around the body, he removed the cloak carefully.

She had been a beautiful woman. A wisp of her dead spirit danced through the unclosed eyes and begged Renard. She had been a happy person who was very connected to her spiritual side or the poor ghost would have already slunk off to join the others that were watching him. In her case it was not too late. Renard paused for a moment and wished he had his tome of rituals. This woman could tell him so much, and she would not suffer much from the side effects, either. He cursed the magic that made his head hurt whenever he tried to remember where his keep was. With one spell, he would know so much more about this civil war raging between dragons.

He could not resurrect the woman, but he was not the type to waste an opportunity. Renard again whispered the enchantment to beseech forgiveness from the dead. He never took from the dead without requesting permission, especially when he was about to take their essence.

With the formality complete and what he thought looked like understanding from the aura that still surrounded the body, he removed an empty vial from the strap of his bag. From his belt he drew a thin-bladed, curved knife that closely matched the curve of her neck and sliced the jugular artery. The angst-filled blood of the dead woman filled the vial with blackness in the red-highlighted darkness. Powerful magic could be brewed from the remains of unforeseen murder, and nothing was more powerful than the victim's blood. Doubly so, since it had been appropriately requested and surrendered by the dead.

Renard completed his collection, and as a final safeguard he pierced his own vein to leave his payment to the dead. The murmur in the trees told him they had at least listened. They were never appreciative, but at least they weren't going to take him with them or plague him for ages for being disrespectful.

The final wisp of tenacious hope that lingered on the body settled into the dirt near his knee. A tremor of satisfaction flowed over him. The shiver threatened to double him over. He remained upright next to the body while the sensation filled him with a trembling emotional release. It grew until he could not remain upright. He slumped over with his head in the dirt, twitching. He could not regain control of his muscles. The dead had never interacted with him that way. It was an invigorating and terrifying feeling he was not sure he wanted to ever feel again. When he finally regained control of his body, he stood from the ground with his treasures.

The robe was an amazing elven invention. His mind refused to tell him why the elves had made it for the dragons, but he had no doubt it was designed to help them control humans since it was designed for a human to wear. Satisfied that he had removed a powerful magical tool from their arsenal, he smiled against the concentration-shattering headache. If he could find his castle he could stop the pain, he was sure.

Forced once more to the ground by his own search for answers, Renard dropped to one knee. He breathed in controlled gasps as the cold sweat flashed across his body. It was clear that his castle was the one thing the dragons who had cast the spell to trap his memories didn't want him to find. He had not given up on challenges far more difficult than that. He would not give up on reclaiming what was his and then finally purging this world of their corruption. He ground his fist into the fertile soil around him with his unending promise ever witnessed by the dead.

CHAPTER 7 - MIKHALA'S VISION

September 9 – 0012 CET – In the Swiss Alps

Mikhala was beginning to understand that sleep came whenever you could get it, and apparently they were not going to get any sleep tonight. Yesterday— barely minutes before— had started with their largest loss of partials and ended with what everyone was calling a victory. Her platoon of "Guardian Angels" had overseen it, constantly transferring the information from the field up to command. All without their high priestess, for the first time.

The images of war she had observed that day would live with her forever, but more powerful than watching the gruesome deaths of her friends, was the haunting murder of Ariela, her friend, mentor, and leader. She had been the only human she liked at all. Mikhala had never been drawn so closely into anyone's mind before. It was as if, in her dying realization, Ariela had taken over Mikhala's soul and shared with her emotions, beliefs, regrets, and convictions. It had been hours. Mikhala still couldn't shake the haunting feeling of Ariela's mind slipping away from her as her consciousness vanished from the fabric of the world.

A disturbance at the entrance to the barracks drew her out of her thoughts. She shivered in her bunk as Ariela's murderer railed in the open doorway.

Mikhala had watched, powerless to do anything but comfort her leader, as Nethliast had killed her. Now his raging madness was disturbing her sleep, the first in over twenty-four hours. It was all Mikhala could do not to scream, as revulsion at his presence exploded into her mind. She

249

could not be sure if it was her own emotion, residual from the priestess' final contact, or just so much time without rest.

Nethliast's loss of self-control and agitation were spreading through the cavern dormitory. Mikhala could feel her own agitation blending with the low morale of the troops trying to sleep around her. Many of them had been shielded from most of the worst traffic, but there had been no way to shield them from Juan's blast of angst and panic before he died. His ultimatum had hit them all directly, and each of them had to deal with how they felt separately. It was hard to know what to believe. They had been told in training that Meliastrid had forsaken her own kind to stand against them with the humans and that Nethliast had control of the dragons. She had believed that, broadcast that to her platoon as a buffer against Juan's message, and kept most of them from running. Now, after watching him kill Ariela, she was not sure that she had made the right decision. The other members of the communications company had not been protected by her controlled message. Most of them had fled. Mikhala was not sure who was better off.

Her emotional agitation at Nethliast's presence and the current situation was keeping her from understanding the chaos of what he was howling about. Her platoon was sitting up and looking to her to translate or at least show them what they needed to do.

"Aten-shun," she shouted as she catapulted herself out of her bunk and onto the floor in front of her appropriately policed foot locker. All she could hope was that he would get to his point when the troops fell in and the discipline of the action would pull her out of the funk she was in. Either way, the respect for the rank was trained into her, even if she hated the beast who wore it.

The rest of the partials in the mostly deserted barracks wing followed her example and fell in at attention. She could feel a troubling cloud of dissension in the ranks as she pulled them from the edge of sleep. They had all been through this type of treatment in basic at the academy, but that had been on the other side of what they had witnessed yesterday.

When all that remained of her company, a little over one platoon, was toeing the line, Nethliast calmed his verbal and physical torment of the room, but he continued to fume. He was in his fully armored human form. Even his head was transformed into glossy black scales. The gray white horns that formed a V in the middle of his head appeared as the first signs of the shape of his draconic head. None of his normally regal appearance remained in the angry visage, and the grotesque socket where his eye used to be added to the madness. It glistened in the light cast by the florescent tracks suspended from the higher cavern roof as if the ichor still flowed from it. Even with their telepathic communications, rumors still traveled faster than reliable intelligence. Although none of her team ever shared the information in their communications, the fact that someone had attempted to assassinate the king of the dragons had been rampant, even as she was sending messages to rally troops at the northern tunnel entrance. Some of the tales that had ultimately filtered up to them were wildly exaggerated. The one she liked the most, that she had heard in the latrine as she had prepared to sack out, was where Meliastrid had actually ripped the eye out with her teeth as she sat on his body and held his neck down. Remembering the absolute impossibility of that tale almost brought a smile before she remembered she was at attention in formation and squashed it. She pulled herself together and waited for him to post before her. She could feel the anger pouring off of him as he stepped up. He was as close to her as he had been when he had killed Ariela. She avoided cringing exactly like she had avoided smiling a moment before.

"Are you the senior member of this company?" he asked when he reached her.

"Yes, sir!" she exclaimed. There was no time to explain that she was the senior enlisted of the platoon, not company, and considering the size of their remaining force that distinction was not important.

Spittle was running down his chin, and she could see the glistening white teeth beyond the hint of reptilian jaws that were just forming in the semi-human, mostly-dragon face. The anger in his remaining eye was apparent. He vibrated from a failed attempt to control his rage. Incongruously, he smelled of flowers and cordite. His breath huffed out of his twin nostrils before he spoke.

"Come with me," he growled menacingly.

"Yes, sir," she shouted again.

He looked back at her with a sneer.

"You can stop that and just follow me."

She was already falling in behind him when his crushing disrespect for the military protocol she had been taught smacked her. She simply nodded and maintained her poise as her entire being wanted to drive a spike through his head. As she walked past the bunk next to her, she nodded to Kara.

"Take charge, get them bunked and rested. This is not over. We will be needed soon and must be rested."

Kara nodded. Mikhala could see the shock blossoming on her face.

"Get a grip soldier," she sent with a mental slap. *"Don't crack up. They're depending on you."*

Kara nodded again and seemed stronger when Mikhala lost sight of her.

"I don't want to see you in that form ever again," Nethliast croaked as they walked down the aisle between the bunks. "Unless it is required for a mission, I want you and every other partial on this base in their *dragon* form. I want no chance that human spies have made it into this base."

"Yes, Sir," she said and followed with a command to the room, "trans—form!" She and all of the other partials in the room immediately transitioned into their draconic forms.

With a sudden relaxed air of appreciation, Nethliast nodded and walked out of the dormitory without another word. Mikhala followed without hesitation as she had been trained even though she had no idea where he was taking her. Although she doubted it, considering the losses they had seen between desertion and the mess at the farm, he could be making an example of her. There was no valid reason for it, but then she was not aware of a reason why he had killed Ariela either. A shiver of fear raced up her spine at the thought of it, but she arrested the panic before it could engulf her.

They walked in silence through the bunker system last used as a defensive barrier against Germany. It had been re-purposed as part of Nethliast's plans, developed in the conclave that had officially started their offensive. The command center was centrally located and a floor above the barracks and entry points to give it a layer of security from invading forces. They entered it as another group escorted out a woman Mikhala recognized from their successful raid of Washington. She had flown to Germany with her. The President of The United States looked stoic considering her situation. Mikhala had to respect that.

The partial guards escorting her into the room walked her in front of a line of dragon officers that Mikhala had ordered to report to the base several hours before. She knew they were to be the new commanders of the partial troops. Until Meliastrid's ultimatum had cleared the decks, partials had mostly been led by partials. Nethliast no longer trusted partial commanders. The previous ones had failed to stop the desertion in the face of Meliastrid's commands.

At midnight the rest of the command center was lightly staffed. A completely untrained adjutant was standing at the priestess' podium, looking as lost as he surely was trying to route traffic into and out of the center. As soon as her troops were rested, she would prepare a rotation to man the command center at all times and start looking for replacements. Mikhala felt an ache settle into her heart as she automatically started to review Ariela's duties. She was not even sure she would still be on the base in a few more hours. Why was she thinking about the duty roster?

A pair of subordinate partial commanders was present to manage the transition of control to the new command. Along the opposite wall, Nethliast's new personal guard were formed up by their newly promoted leader. Oddly enough, they were all partials promoted from the ranks of the Washington assault platoons. Her heart jumped at her first sight of Adrian since landing in Germany. She had kept loose track of him as he had fought through southern Germany and had raced to face the rest of Meliastrid's team in Füssen. Since he had departed the farm she had only heard rumors of his team. It was good to see him alive. He controlled any outward sign of recognition. Standing next to him was Nethliast's human witch, the exact opposite of Ariela. The strong aroma of flowers proved that some of the other rumors swirling about the caverns were true as well. Mikhala did not engage in gossip among her troops, but she could now file one particular rumor appropriately.

For a moment she thought of her love and the situation they were in. She could not suppress her genuine pleasure at knowing he was alive, but equal to her happiness was a darker fear that they were on the wrong side and would never get away. She focused on the positive. After the day they had experienced, counting anyone she knew among the living was a bonus.

"Good to see you," she sent to him even though it was technically breaking protocol. She could not fully contain her excitement, and she could, quite honestly, use the moral support.

"Good to be seen."

She understood his meaning and made no sign of reaction. His response came loaded with emotion that she would parse later. The two she felt most was his love for her and a fear of what was to come.

"Captain Valdez," Nethliast addressed the highest ranking partial in the room who had only hours before been Colonel Valdez. "I'm not sure why I had to give this order just now, but I told the company of observers where I retrieved..." He looked her over for a moment and apparently realized she was not in uniform anymore so he could not find her rank or name. "...anyway, this partial, that all partials will be in their dragon form unless otherwise required to be in human form. I want no surprises. No humans among us without our knowledge. Is that clear?"

"Yes, sir," he answered.

"And, see if you can find some way that their rank and names can be present in that form."

Mikhala thought about the need for a moment and adjusted her transformation. The slate blue and emerald scales on her chest shifted. Black letters appeared on her breast plate. Subdued stripes appeared on her bicep scales as well.

"Yes, that's what I want, sergeant. There you are, captain. See if you can't get that uniform change applied. Now, Sergeant Salenko, you are the ranking officer in the observers company, correct?"

"No, sir," she answered. "I am the ranking NCO in what remains of the observer's company." She could not avoid correcting him and felt wrong even as she said it.

"Whatever. You are capable of performing the same duties the priestess could perform, correct?"

"Yes, most of her communications abilities, sir."

"Can you find someone by scrying?"

"Absolutely, sir."

"No matter where they are?"

"We have not found a limit to its range yet, sir, but I expect there is a maximum limit."

"Within Europe?"

"Yes, sir. We can find them in Europe."

"And they can't hide from it."

"These bunkers block it, as do caves. I've heard of magical blocks as well, so it can be blocked. It can't be totally eliminated. For example, they can't hide their thoughts completely without magical help. The same is true for any scrying. However, some personal knowledge of the target is required to find them when the search area is so large, unless they are also looking for someone to contact them. If I know where they are I can look for them in that area. If I have previously scryed them or if I have extensive knowledge of them, I can look for them anywhere. Looking for someone I have never connected with over the entire landscape of Europe will be—difficult." She wanted to tell him impossible, but that would not be useful.

A massive assault of emotions ripped into Mikhala's mind as Nethliast delivered the conglomeration of sight, sound, and emotion that was Meliastrid to him. She doubled over, dropped to her knees, and stumbled to the floor as her mind lost all focus. He raged about in her mind like he had in the dormitory. Nothing was organized as he shifted randomly through emotions he felt for Meliastrid. Mikhala shuddered and tried to manage the overwhelming flood of information. When she cried out from physical pain caused by his assault, rather than controlling the flow or backing off, he released the rest in a flood that exploded in her mind as a white-hot blast of malevolence. The final blast included the human years, the emergence, her spurning him for the human, the fight in the cave, the transport to some distant desert, her deception to draw him out to the devastated farm and hold him in the sights of the sniper, and finally the excruciating pain of the bullet ripping into his eye. Instinctively her hand rushed to the left side of her face. She screamed as he released her mind. When he was done she was on the floor in a fetal ball with her hand over her eye and whimpering slightly.

"Can you use that?" he asked snidely.

She had never before thought anyone capable of as much hate as Nethliast had just shared with her. She shivered from the violation of the event and slowly uncoiled from the floor and pushed herself up onto her knees.

"Yes," she managed to choke out, "yes, sir."

No one moved to help her as she used trembling arms to press herself up until she was kneeling in front of him. She could tell he thought she was weak, but she moved as quickly as she could to regain her feet. When she was again able to face him, she resumed a shaky at-ease position and waited for his further orders.

"I want you working directly with Sergeant Fieldman and his team. You've been reassigned as his communications specialist. Is that clear?"

"Yes, sir."

"Good. Go find her and her human lovers. I want to know as soon as you have anything. Fieldman, you will report to me everything you find, is that clear?"

"Yes, sir," Adrian answered.

"And you will not act without my direct orders, understood?"

"Yes, sir," he repeated and tried to hide his surprise at the question.

"Get on it, then. I want results. Now. Don't let me down like everyone did yesterday."

"Sir." Valdez drew Nethliast's attention. "Sergeant Salenko had just come off duty. Her platoon was bunking down for the night. We were expecting to start rotating them through the comm center in the morning. Would it not be—"

"She can sleep when she's found Meliastrid," Nethliast said He looked directly at her. His intense single eye told her that this mission was life or death for her.

With his orders complete, he turned to focus his attention on the other officers waiting for him. A brief look at the line showed her a gray dragon standing at the end of the line of officers. He looked like an older version of Nethliast. She filed the face away so she could ask who he was later. She was interested in him not only because of who he looked like, but also because he looked very unhappy with what he was observing. There was more to him than most of the others in the line. She would need to see what was behind that. Her view was suddenly blocked. She looked from the officers to who was standing in front of her.

Adrian, who looked as tired as she felt, sighed

"So, am I starting the search here?" She pointed at the podium. "Or is there somewhere else we'll be working?" She could not keep the hope from her voice, and Adrian picked it up.

He seemed to relax when she focused on the duty instead of complaining.

"Let's find somewhere we can all relax a little, unless you need something specific."

"I can scry in a cup of coffee, or a large bowl of water, but one of our observing spheres will be better for this." She pointed to the abandoned consoles.

"Size of the focus makes a difference?" Jay asked wryly as he stepped up and looked at her in his normal, discomfiting fashion. She had even missed him and felt a sudden closeness that would require a long bath to clean off if she survived the night.

"Thanks for being an example and not griping as soon as the brass were out of the room," Adrian said as they turned to leave the command center.

"I'll talk with you after we've found Meliastrid."

"Technically, no," she answered Jay as she politely returned to his point, "but detail is easier to see in a larger focus unless you have a high quality crystal."

Jay was still grinning at her. She finally realized he had been baiting her. She smiled back at his juvenile joke.

"Child," she said dismissively.

They left the Command Center and walked back toward the dormitories. The old bunker system had been carved out of the Alps by the humans during World War II. It had been abandoned shortly after it ended, but partials and dragons had reclaimed it and turned it into a stronghold.

The cantonment area had been set up in a large central section of caves that served as a hub to several other smaller caverns. Most of them paralleled the central cave. The large hub naturally became the dining hall and was used as a mess and meeting area. There were a few smaller rooms on the sides of the common area. They were being used as alcoves for private meetings. Some of them had been sequestered as unit ready rooms. As they entered the mostly abandoned hall, Adrian motioned to one of the private areas that he had commandeered. A guidon presenting his new unit's colors was stuck into a hole that had been newly drilled into the wall. She had no idea that Nethliast had planned on standing the unit up as a company, but she nodded at it and looked at Adrian with a combination of pride and a little fear.

"So, are you the senior NCO of this unit now or is there a field promotion I was not aware of?"

"He's working on filling in the unit. No, I'm not an officer. We should be getting a CO as soon as he picks the dragon he trusts enough to be in charge of his personal guard."

"Speaking of that, who was the gray dragon standing at the end of the line? I don't recognize him."

"You won't," Jay said with some unspoken remark on his lips.

She looked at Adrian for an explanation.

"That's Gerliast."

The name was all that she needed to understand.

"See?" Jay asked.

"Yes. Interesting."

Everyone except Jay left the unspoken history alone.

"Yeah, Nethliast wants to make sure he has someone he trusts leading his brownshirts. It won't be Gerliast. Following the screw-up yesterday, it wont be a partial either," Jay splurted. Nothing about the last few days had dulled his generally jaded nature.

Adrian's head turned toward Jay in a flash with a look that would have withered flowers.

"May as well be honest about who we are, and the reality of what's happening since that message was shared," Jay said.

"This is a position of honor. We've proved we're reliable."

"That's true, Jay." Chip joined the conversation as they walked across the mostly deserted chamber toward their room. "We could all be lying in a field among those other units that failed to distinguish themselves. Remember, there are always alternatives."

"Right, and frozen to our spots in an abbey is so much better?"

Chip shook his head.

Mikhala could not deny that the punch to the morale from the previous day had been universal, but it surprised her that they were willing to talk so openly about it. Especially considering how quickly Nethliast was cleaning house around him.

Adrian was struggling to find the right words to say to his squad that had just been promoted to the honorable position of king's guard. It was obvious, to her at least, that he was finding their king difficult to like. She chose not to share her knowledge of his callous disregard for Ariela's life and her own, based on how he looked at her.

"The mission hasn't changed," she said, giving Adrian the boost he needed to shift the conversation back to the positive.

"Right," Adrian said. "The mission is still the same, and this is how we support it. We have to find the threat to Nethliast's plan. Right now we're all there is to this unit, but soon we'll be reinforced. I want to find Meliastrid and stop whatever they're up to."

"He doesn't want to stop them," Jay shared. "He wants to know where they are. Didn't you catch that in his orders? I think he wants to know what they're after. Doesn't it seem strange that he no longer wants her dead? What happened today to the fire of the dragons?"

"What makes you think they're after anything? What makes you think Nethliast's focus has changed?" Mikhala asked. All she knew was that Nethliast wanted her to find Meliastrid. She was not aware of why or of what Adrian's team had already done. She knew from rumors that they had been sent to find the rest of Meliastrid's team when the fight at the farm had broken out, but another Guardian Angel had been monitoring them.

"Let's take this into the ready room. I want to brief Salenko so everyone is up to speed. Walt, Garrett, go get one of the large spheres they stowed from Washington."

The brothers nodded and walked toward the back of the common area where the warehousing spaces were set up.

"Jay, give them a hand," Adrian said, a little more powerfully than Mikhala had expected. Jay raised his hands and dropped them to his sides as he nodded and turned to follow the others.

"What's that all about?" Mikhala asked as all of Adrian's lower ranks were sent off to collect what she needed to do her job.

"We failed to catch Meliastrid's team in Füssen," Chip answered. "While she was trying to kill Nethliast. We were still searching for a lead when they assaulted the northern gate. Everyone's feeling a little down because we failed and missed the fight. Jay just has a tendency to see any authority as bad."

"I'm trying to keep the team functional," Adrian added. "This new assignment is a compliment. I wish everyone could see that."

"Jay's not completely wrong about the posting you've been given," Mikhala commented.

Adrian looked a little hurt.

"We know that," he answered, defensively. "But Chip and I have to keep the team focused. Right now, all of our orders are legal and aimed at the enemy. If we start getting orders to police our own, we may have to reassess our position."

"What about orders to police the dragons?" Chip asked.

They were all senior NCOs in the squad-sized company, so Adrian took a moment to think about their concerns before continuing.

"I've heard rumors that some of the dragons are starting to dissent since Meliastrid's message was shared. They're just rumors, but I hear the dissent goes pretty high. Until we have more concrete information, we can't engage in spreading them."

Mikhala had been in the command center as most of the news they were referencing had been received. She could verify that particular factions were not happy with things since Meliastrid had told everyone they were on the wrong team. There was something irresistible about her, not just her message. Mikhala kept her information to herself and noted that they seemed to have information she didn't.

"Wait," she said. "What dissent are you talking about?"

Chip and Adrian shared a knowing glance and a silent conversation. Chip turned to watch for the others as Adrian motioned for her to enter the company ready room. He stopped at the curtain and closed it behind them.

"A private meeting?" Mikhala asked and felt a little uncomfortable for some reason.

"Mikhala, listen. I'm sorry about the way Nethliast handled that. He's a little rough around the edges, but he is the king now."

"The *dragon* king."

"Yeah, and most partials aren't astute enough to catch that difference. We don't have a king, though. In fact we don't have anyone except Nethliast watching out for us at all. The fighting yesterday at the farm was bad. A lot of things happened there that surprised us. None of us realized that dragons could command us directly."

"That's what they said happened to the team in Füssen," she said.

Adrian nodded seriously. "Yeah, the dragon froze them in their place, then they tore them apart. She did the same thing at the farm to the priestess somehow. Her mother almost did it to me."

Mikhala controlled her jaw to keep it from physically dropping open. Nethliast was not sharing the whole truth about the priestess. It was very possible that Adrian didn't know. She may have been the only witness. She might be the only partial who knew. Even the story from Füssen had details that had not been shared. One partial had been able to resist the mental control and fought back. She never should have tried to fight. Three partials against two dragons is not good odds. She didn't correct Adrian's story.

Adrian took a seat at the table and pulled her to a chair in front of him. He looked directly at her as if he needed to make sure she understood what he was about to tell her. She could see that it had been a long time since he had slept. His eyes had a manic shimmer to them, and she suddenly felt nervous. She took his hand and interrupted his thought.

"How are you holding up? You need some rest."

Her concern touched the soft side within him. He was a good leader. He could be an officer and would be if Nethliast could ever trust them again. He softened with her for a moment.

"I thought it was me. I thought I froze. Then the others told me what happened in the library, and I felt better. She froze us all with a command."

"Are you all right?"

"I'm fine. We all need rest. We've been backtracking Meliastrid's team all the way back to the airport since we lost them. We thought we could find some clues if we knew where they had been."

She nodded and listened to him talk. It seemed he needed to share. She knew he was concerned how he might deal with stress. She was proud of him, but she was troubled with how much he seemed to trust Nethliast and his dragon officers. She needed to know how he really felt.

"Do you think we're still okay?" she asked.

His face crumbled before her, and she realized he might think she was talking about their relationship.

"No, I mean the partials. Do you think we're okay here. You know?"

"That was what I was about to tell you. No, I don't think we're safe. But the big threat to us is not dragons. It's our own kind. We can't trust most of the ranks of the partials. Not since Meliastrid got to them."

He didn't go where she thought he might. It was clear how committed he was. She would have to tell him what she knew, but not now. In his current state, it might push him over the edge. He did think of Nethliast as a surrogate father, a father who had not shrunk into his own mind to avoid the problem. She nodded and let him continue.

"When Meliastrid's order came through, there was an immediate split. I felt it. I wanted to run. If it had not been for the time I had spent with the Lieutenant, I might have. We already had a dragon command structure. It should have been that way through the whole force. That and how much Nethliast had done for us kept me from being on the wrong side of that fight. Can you believe that so many of us would just turn and run like that when she gave us an order?"

The depth of his commitment became painfully clear. He would require a lot more convincing. She would have to figure out how to give him the information in a way that would not destroy him.

"I knew there was a division at the farm," she said, "and that local commanders were trying to get control."

"Some of them were, but most of them were ordering general retreat. They told us to run and surrender to the humans in Berlin. If we had done that, they would have killed us."

He was right about that. If the commanders had surrendered all of the partials who had just helped kill the entire German government, the mass execution would have been historical. She shuddered.

"If it had not been for the naga forces and the orders from your Guardian Angels, we would have lost the whole force to desertion."

"We still lost them, Adrian."

"To enemy action. They died fighting the enemy, not each other."

She knew that was not entirely true either, but the dragon attack at the Farm had stopped a mass desertion.

"Things may look a little different, given time and space."

Adrian paused and looked at her with concern that chilled her.

"What are you saying?"

It was too late to take it back now. "Not everything you're saying is accurate. I was overseeing a lot of it. I'm just saying there are two sides to every conflict. This one has its fair share of gray on both sides."

"Such as?" he asked, forcing her hand.

She could see him struggling with his anger. She didn't want it directed at her, but she had already made a tactical error. She was the only one who could do this, and now she had to.

"Nethliast killed the priestess. He murdered her. It was not Meliastrid who did that. In the woods behind the farm. She had tried to help him with his injuries. He killed her in cold blood. She was unarmed."

"He had to have a reason," he said forcefully. "She had changed sides or something. He had to know there was a reason."

He was right that she had changed sides. Mikhala had observed that as well, but it was like she had no choice. There was something bigger behind the division and how easy it was for dragon, partial, and human to follow Meliastrid.

"He killed her without cause. I witnessed it through her eyes. I can share it with you if you like."

Adrian looked at her face. His anger dispersed a little when he saw the pain she did not hide.

"That must have been awful."

"It was not the worst thing I witnessed yesterday. It probably won't be the worst thing I see before this is all over. But I can tell you that what he did felt wrong to me, no matter what reason he felt he had. There's some reason all of those partials turned on that field. You know they were good men."

"They were not men at all."

"You know what I mean. They were good males, then."

"If they had been, they would not have turned."

"We're not going to agree."

"No. Not on this."

"Keep an open mind. Let me find proof. Keep us safe from both sides while I find the proof we need. What you don't realize is that we are now caught between two sides in this fight and we don't have one of our own."

"How do you intend to do that?"

"It may be better that you not know exactly."

"You're going to have to do what Nethliast has ordered. You can't refuse. I can't allow that."

"I don't intend to disobey a lawful order. I'll find her. I have to in order to figure out what's really going on here."

"Why do you think it is more than what Nethliast has told us?"

"Because, I looked into his eyes—eye—when he killed Ariela. Because he's losing his connection to reality and mistreating his troops. I can tell you he had no care or concern for how brutal his mental attack on me."

Adrian winced at the memory of that. At least he still cared about her. She had not destroyed that yet.

"Let me find out what's going on. While I'm doing it, you keep doing what you have to. But believe me, Nethliast is not concerned about you or any other partial."

Adrian didn't answer, but she could tell he was willing to let her do what she needed to do.

"Adrian, would it matter to you if I told you Nethliast was in a relationship with a human?"

"That's just a rumor."

"Yes, but would it matter to you?"

Adrian stopped his argument and thought about what she was asking. "I don't know."

"He argues that all humans need to be punished for trapping dragons and partials in whatever betrayal they engaged in."

"Right."

"Then why is one of his key advisers a human female? Why were two of his principal leaders human females until he killed one yesterday?"

Adrian didn't answer, but he did think about what she said.

"How can a dragon not know about an ability they've had for thousands of years?"

"You're saying Nethliast and the other dragons held back information we needed to know. You're saying they knew all along that dragons could control us. Our command knew the team in Füssen was at risk and didn't tell them about it."

Mikhala nodded. "Why tell us when there's no defense?" She could see that the thoughts were now circulating in his mind.

"You can prove it, can't you?"

"Not yet, but I believe it. But you knew that at some level already. That's why I'm here. You had your doubts, so you told Nethliast about me to get me in here didn't you?"

"I knew I needed to protect you. I didn't know why. That's not all, though. I thought, if we could find Meliastrid, we could end this fight."

"You can see that there is no safety right now. You know, we're among the enemy."

"I'm not as convinced as you are."

"I'll prove it to you, but no one else can know about this."

She pointed at the curtain and Chip, who stood beyond it.

He shook his head.

"You had better keep it that way."

"They think I'm bringing you up to speed on what happened today, which I am."

"You get me some time and private space, and I'll see what I can see."

"You find Meliastrid first, and you'll have as much time as you can stand."

"Get that sphere in here," she said.

A plan was forming in her mind, and she had known earlier that it would be a risk. Now she was wondering if she could pull it off. She would be spying on the current king of the dragons. Earlier that day she could scry within the bunkers. She knew scrying into them was not possible, but within had worked. There was no reason to think they were blocking it magically. If she was caught, there would be no trial. The most powerful dragon in the world, that she had just seen raging in her dormitory, that she had watched murder a defenseless woman, would find her and kill her. Based on their experience with Meliastrid, Nethliast could manipulate her mind without her consent. That meant she had to stay away from scrying him directly. A sudden burst of fear pulsed a massive dose of adrenaline into her system. She was awake and probably would be for a while.

The curtain slipped back when Adrian reached out to Chip. The whole team stepped into the room. Chip sat down at the table. Garret, Walt, and Jay carried a pedestal and crystal sphere into the room and set it down before they all patted her on the back and welcomed her to the team. Chip grinned at her with a look that told her he was not so out of the loop as Adrian thought.

"Listen up," he said to the room. "It's been a long day, and none of us have had any rest. I want everyone that doesn't have to be awake in their racks. Chip, I want you down especially because I need for you to be my backup. Once we have a line on the targets, we'll be moving. Get some rest."

Everyone except Mikhala and Adrian stood up to leave.

"Jay, before you rack out, can you check the status of that radio van we need? I don't want scrying and eying to be our only way of tracking them. I want everything in our tool box out there."

Jay nodded and gave him a thumbs-up before slipping through the curtains.

Alone again, Mikhala braced for the work she had ahead. She stood up at the crystal and checked her pocket to make sure she had her compact. Adrian grabbed her wrist. She looked up into his very troubled face.

"Mikhala, listen..."

"This sounds serious."

"Yeah. Look. I can't risk my squad by getting involved with a member of it. We have to..."

"Give me some credit, will ya?" she growled and pulled her wrist away from him. "We're about to do some pretty bad stuff, but even I know that we have to stay professional until this is over. No sweat, trooper. But once this is all over, you're mine." She smiled at him to remind him of the last day they had shared before leaving the school.

He transformed before her into the youthful human, breaking Nethliast's new rule as he did it. He looked exactly as he had at the academy after she had spent several weeks trying to hunt him down. She relaxed her own form as well and he pulled her up to him. Their lips met and rekindled the passion she had felt so long ago when they had shared that rare day without duty or assignments. They held each other for a few minutes alone in the room before Adrian broke off and walked toward the entrance.

"That has to be the end of it, for now," he said to the curtain.

"Of course," she agreed.

"Prove your point to me. Don't take it to anyone else. I'm still not totally convinced. I'm going to take a walk and check on the others. Let me know if you need any more of your gear, and as soon you get a line on her, let me know."

She nodded, and he walked out.

September 9 – 0210 CET – Colmar, France

Headlights turned down the long driveway from the main road. Melissa froze. Nethliast and his partials would not come by the road. She reached out into the darkness with her enhanced vision to identify the vehicle.

It was them. Kaliastrid was driving. The pilot she had met the day before was sleeping in the back seat, and she did not see Silas. Kaliastrid looked like she was pushing the car toward them with the pure force of her mind. When the car finally stopped in front of them, Kaliastrid sank into the seat and didn't move. Melissa felt a renewed stab of shame at having rested while her mother was threatened.

"I'll check on them. Get some help. You still need to be resting," Aldrich said as he rushed past her.

Melissa turned toward the house to find Charles as he rushed out. He apparently had not been resting, either. Was anyone following her instructions? Frustrated, she turned her attention back to the arrivals.

Aldrich swung open the door behind the driver. He shook his head and grimaced at the unseen passenger that must be Silas.

When Charles joined him, the priest took charge.

"Get Silas back to the room I've been using. Everything is prepared. I don't think carrying him will hurt him any more. He's beat up pretty bad."

Charles nodded and pulled Silas smoothly into a fireman's carry. He used both of his hands to roll him over his shoulder and down his back as he carefully stood up avoiding the door frame. He turned immediately toward the house.

"I'll be right behind you. I can fix this fellow here while you're moving Silas. Then he can walk in on his own."

Melissa watched them efficiently execute the steps as if they had practiced them.

Kaliastrid finally pulled herself out of the car and stood next to it. Unable to control herself any further, Melissa ran across the yard to grab her mother in a tight hug.

"You're letting your emotions get to you again," Kaliastrid said. Her eyes were sunken. Bags were forming underneath them.

In the car, Sean woke with a start at the small man removing his seat belt.

"Trust me," Aldrich advised. "Wodin heals those who deserve it, and any who work to his ends deserve it."

Before Sean could respond, Aldrich placed his hands on his legs.

The man's face constricted. A scream started in his throat as he reacted to the man's touch, but it never formed fully. When the pain vanished and the chilling warmth Melissa remembered from her several healing sessions throughout the day rushed into his leg, his face relaxed.

Kaliastrid grabbed her elbow before she started to manage everyone again.

"You look as bad as I feel. We need to eat, really, and then we both need to sleep. Come, let's find some food. Leave the healer to his trade. They have this under control."

"There's food on the table inside. She refused to eat until you were here. Please take her in and feed her," Aldrich urged over his shoulder. "My effort today will be undone by her stubbornness and fretting if you don't."

Melissa didn't resist her mother's insistent grip. The urgency was obvious even though she looked too tired to stand.

"Not exactly what I had in mind," Kaliastrid shot back at the gruff healer.

"Tell me that after you see what Wodin provided."

She nodded and turned them both toward the house.

Melissa had already seen the spread of food Aldrich had somehow prepared for them between healing sessions, but her nerves would not allow her to eat. He had nursed her back one step at a time, leaving her to rest while he entreated Wodin for energy to go on. When he finally released her to heal the rest on her own, she had seen the spread he had laid out on the dining room table. There were several rare meats that would satisfy their dragon tastes while also providing for the others in the party.

"Wait, first things, first," Kaliastrid said, pausing outside of the house.

She reached up to the chain around her neck and pulled the claw scepter over her head. She handed it over to Melissa with very little ceremony.

"I understand why you gave me this, but its job is to protect you. You're not an acceptable sacrifice for any reason. We have to protect you and everything this represents." She looked at the jeweled claw with reverence as Melissa took it back from her. She had done what she thought was right. If she had fallen with the amulet, Nethliast would have recovered it. She could not chance that even though the amulet would not allow him to wield it. In hindsight it seemed like a mistake. She hoped she would learn how to stop making those. A twinkling light that had kept pace with Kaliastrid as she had walked from the car flitted around the amulet and vanished into one of the stones. The stone glowed briefly as the will-o-wisp vanished inside of it.

"You must remember that you have led armies before. You are not a child who has never sent someone to die. I know its what you remember most. I've had a long drive to think about things and, for the first time in ages, my mind is clear. You're more important to dragons than I ever will be. Do not ever endanger yourself for me again."

Melissa took the chiding that she deserved and tried to let her mother's advice set in. She did not feel like the dragon warrior her mother described.

"Now, let's see what the priest has organized for us to eat. You can't rightly lead us on an empty stomach," Kaliastrid added.

The front room of the house had been a living room with a dining room attached. Aldrich had extended the dining area into the main room and spread a feast table around it. Kaliastrid nodded appreciatively.

Charles followed them through the doorway with his burden and excused himself around them to carry Silas into the room in the back. Sean stumbled through behind him, still not used to having working legs. Aldrich rushed past them all to catch up with Charles.

"Everyone, eat. You too, son. Wodin's blessing for his warriors." He paused his pace only slightly to grab a stone growler and a large bowl. "Spirits for the healer, or else this will be a very long night."

Sean nodded at the instruction and didn't pause. Like any soldier, he knew you ate when food was available.

"Where did all of this come from?" Kaliastrid asked.

"He made a trip to a local store, locked himself in the kitchen where he argued with himself for a while, and then it was here," Elaine answered as she descended the stairs.

"Does no one in this group know how to rest?" Kaliastrid asked. The young girl obviously had not slept.

"I tried, but I couldn't sleep. It feels like someone's watching me. It's creepy in this place. It made my skin crawl. Even when I did get to sleep, I couldn't get away from them. I guess that's what I get for running from half-dragons all day." Elaine rubbed her arms as if they itched and there was nothing she could do to stop it.

Kaliastrid and Melissa's eyes met in a snap of recognition.

"Someone's scrying us," they both said in unison.

"It was sure to happen sooner or later. They cannot hear our thoughts," Melissa continued.

"We must remain cautious of what we share aloud."

"That means they already know where we are. Do we need to move? Do they know where we're going and why?"

"No way to know, it's too subtle to know when it started. We must move quickly whatever we do. How long will Aldrich need with Silas?"

"We need to find out."

"I'm really starting to hate when you do that, you know," Elaine said to their silence.

"Can't be avoided," Melissa answered.

"Someone is watching us, aren't they?" She looked around as if the someone were hiding in the corners or she could find the hidden cameras.

Neither answered her. Melissa smiled comfortingly at her with little effect.

Sean, oblivious to what was going on, sat down on a couch to eat. He watched the conversation but chose to stay out of it and just learn. Melissa felt another human tug of guilt at dragging him into this. Then she remembered her mother's admonition. He was a soldier who knew the risks he faced. She had not caused his suffering. Nethliast and his witch had.

She filled her own plate with what looked like rare venison and thought about what to do. She knew from the conversations in the car that Charles was familiar with what they had found and where it was.

"So when are we going to—"

"Stop!" Melissa shouted.

Elaine stared at her with her mouth open and then realized what she was saying. "Oh-kay. No talking about the secret thing. You could have just said that. It's not like they don't know we're not talking about the thing they want to know about."

Melissa nodded as she realized they were stumbling through this new ground. She had to keep what they knew a secret, but she had no idea how long they had been watching them.

"How long have you felt like you're being watched?" Melissa asked. Elaine was the most sensitive to it at the moment.

"Only since Aldrich finished your last healing session. Before that I was too busy looking for the president to notice it. When I tried to sleep, I just couldn't."

Melissa nodded and considered what that meant. She had no idea who the scrying was focused on or how skilled the diviner was. At best it would be a guess. She thought about her options.

Charles was healthy and the least likely person anyone would be able to track. Nethliast would underestimate him like he always had. She would use that to her advantage, but she needed to make sure it made sense first. Elaine was the second option since she was not well known to anyone who would be scrying them. If the diviner could tell she was magical, it would be hard to keep her from being found. Aldrich had to stay with Silas as long as it would take to heal him.

"Tell Charles I have an errand for him. Ask Aldrich how long he needs with Silas."

"We seem to be in a hurry again," Elaine said, turning serious.

Melissa looked at the ceiling, hoping the message would be clear enough. Elaine nodded at the orders and the silent message that their watchers would be on their way soon. She moved to find Charles.

"Oh. Wait," Melissa said as she turned away. "Are there candles in this house?"

She shrugged at the question and continued toward the door.

Kaliastrid looked at Melissa with a puzzled look as she filled her plate with equally rare meat.

"They can't read dragon script. We've used it for secret messages before," Melissa answered her unasked question. *"How did I remember that without pain? Why am I not hurting with every thought? What did we do?"*

A light flitted from the edge of her vision and then disappeared back into her hair.

"There is more for us to worry about than just being watched. We're not alone. There are more magical creatures than dragons now," Kaliastrid said. *"Magic is returning. We were not the only magic to emerge when the spell was broken. Good things of course, and bad things. Some that this world is not ready for."*

"Something worse than dragons?"

"There is so much worse than dragons, and you know it."

"Not to humans. Not right now."

"And they have no idea. Nethliast's witch is a problem."

"First father, now you. How bad can she be? What have you seen that you have not shared? I know she's deceptive and powerful, but I've not seen anything that make me that nervous."

"First she drew you into a trap that nearly killed you without a lot of effort. But, if that's not enough, she conjured loup garou from partials."

Melissa couldn't stop the intake of breath.

"She enchanted them yesterday to track down Silas. Don't underestimate her. Your father did, and it cost him his life."

"That's powerful magic for anyone and old for someone so modern," Melissa said.

"Even more for a human witch. It took humans generations of dedication to learn that type of magic. That's exactly what we worried about if humans were ever stronger in magic. In the history of magic, human scientific magic was the worst combination. They merged magic from all disciplines and forms. It's a bad sign for what is to come."

Melissa and Kaliastrid both paused and stared at each other, somewhat confused at how easily that memory had come to her.

Melissa continued. *"Is she an old soul? Did she somehow emerge when the spell broke? Who is she?"*

"I have no idea where she came from, but she has demonstrated she knows powerful magic. Maybe she just has access to an old Grimoire. She scared a dragon. She killed your father."

Melissa paused to think about that and chew on her meal. The food was a sudden and pleasant source of needed energy. She knew she was tired before, but she had not realized how low her energy was. After a few bites and some thought about what her mother had described, she started to understand why her mother was so concerned.

"Nethliast killed my father. The witch helped, but he killed him. I agree she is a threat, but she would never have had access to him without Nethliast's help. It takes a dragon to trap a dragon. Something he and the others have forgotten. Something I should have reminded him of that first day."

"True, I can't forget his guilt in this. But, legends and night terrors from human fairy tales are emerging, the good and the bad. The bad seems to be returning faster. It seems more powerful. We lived in this world before, and it is not as fun as human fairy tales draw it. We helped to establish and maintain a magical balance before so that humans could live safely. We worked to keep powerful evil magic like this in check."

"Others will rise up to help us stop them. They did before." The memories of centuries were hard, this time, to wrangle in her head. Pain flared again. The light flitting about her head whistled an apologetic whine, and her pixie fire dimmed noticeably.

"I believe that too, but so far all I've seen are the malevolent ones. We're not getting any help."

"We'll have to be ready then."

"If Nethliast is able to build an army of creatures that mankind can't defend against, we can't stop him alone."

"The human fighters have always been powerful. More powerful than our magical kind ever really believed possible. We cannot underestimate them now. Look at Elaine. Look at Aldrich. Maybe even the president, based on what we've seen. Innate humans didn't exist before, maybe there are more of them."

"Yes," Kaliastrid said. *"And I hope we continue to find them, too, but who's going to train them? We're going to need help. But hundreds of years ago we needed more than humans to stop the evil creatures that nipped at the heels of humanity. We're already behind in this war."*

Melissa cringed, not in pain from the memories, but in her realization that her mother was right; they were behind. *"Our memories are improving, at least."*

"It's the Pixies," Kaliastrid answered without thinking.

"The what?" Melissa asked.

Kaliastrid paused to review what she said that surprised Melissa. The answer surprised her as well.

"You asked earlier what we had done. Your question didn't make sense because the answer was obvious to me. Pixies have been helping us since that cloud assailed us in Füssen."

"I hadn't noticed. Why didn't you tell me? I should have reached out to them by now."

The rejuvenated glow beside her temple flitted out in front of her and whistled. Melissa raised her hand, and the miniature creature of positive, if mischievous, magical power circled her index finger. Somehow Melissa understood that as a sign of their support and felt a warmth of magical buttressing rush through her mind.

"I just realized it. I guess it was something I was just so used to that I didn't even think about it. They were with me all the way back from Füssen. They kept me awake and focused."

"Is there anything else we've just been ignoring? Maybe there are others like us who are already trying to help."

"No, but, now that I've reminded myself, I need to tell you what I was thinking about on the drive here. I should have stood beside you sooner. I could have helped, but I had forgotten what it was to be a dragon. I had forgotten what we all have forgotten. You're the example, the ambassador. You're the one who will bring us all together. That's the way it works."

"Our kind looks to the female, and we're the only ones that Nethliast hasn't trapped."

"One female more than others. The others will stand up, my daughter, when they can feel you. They're trapped and scared, but your presence in their minds is missing. Until tonight, I hadn't realized what was wrong. I've felt odd since we emerged. There was always some presence in my mind before. Heliantra's presence. We're all missing that."

Melissa stood up from the chair. She finally remembered the importance of the complete talisman. It unified dragons behind the Great Wyrm. It helped lead them because whoever possessed it and the pendant was present in all dragon minds. That was the absence she had been feeling in her mind. Heliantra's presence was gone. She had thought she was just missing her grandmother, but it was worse. Someone needed to be there to help maintain sanity within the race. Without it they fell to their base emotions and acted on their never far-off rage.

"We have to get the talisman. I can't believe we ever let it out of our control."

"I don't think we really ever did."

"What do you mean?"

An image filled her mind from Kaliastrid's memory. A tall keep stood in front of her. A man was walking on the battlements. She couldn't see what was happening, but the memory was filled with anticipation. A cluster of dragons stood around Kaliastrid. They all looked to the west as the sun was setting.

As the last rays disappeared, all of the dragons changed into humans. Just before the memory ended she looked again at the tower to see the man standing staring into the sunset. A reassuring rush of emotion swept over the group. The observer was caught up in it for a moment; but, as the memory faded, she felt the last hint of the observer's emotion. It was anticipation. There was more to be done that night. What was it? She looked to Kaliastrid for the answer.

For the first time, Melissa saw and understood the twinkling light next to her mother's ear. It looked like a small diamond earring, but it was alive with magical power just like the one that had circled her finger. She had no doubt now that it was being helpful. The light beside her mother's ear flitted out to meet the one hiding in Melissa's hair, and they circled in a dazzling ring that formed into an unbreakable circle of light. Her mother's eyes softened slightly, and Melissa felt a draw on her own energy as well. Her mother's face changed and looked like she was enjoying a decadent French chocolate that her father used to bring when he came back from his business trips. Her eyes closed over the pleasure and then opened again with clear resolution.

"You're with me. It has been ages since I felt this. How is it possible without the Talisman?"

"The pixies are doing it. They're acting like the connection the Talisman provides?"

"To everyone?"

Melissa tested the connection in her mind and found only her mother. *"No, it is only between us."*

Kaliastrid frowned, and the pixie ring whined a sorrowful cry.

Melissa reached out to the pixie in her mind to tell her it was okay. What she had done was good. The whine turned into a whistle and Melissa knew she had found or remembered a way to communicate with the sprite. The whistle came with a feeling of acceptance. The ring split, and each pixie returned. Her mother's continuous presence didn't stop. It filled an emptiness Melissa had subconsciously recognized, but had never tried to fill. She enjoyed a longer moment of the comforting pressure of her presence.

"So, what does this mean?" Kaliastrid asked.

"Based on what Aldrich and Elaine shared with me from their time in the library, and the clear thoughts I've had since the pixies have joined us, I think there is more to our entrapment than I first thought. It is far more connected to Renard. I think we, or Heliantra primarily, had a plan for what happened after we became human. I don't think she believed the spell would work, or if it worked at first it would not last, but she followed her directions. She has carried the spell forward through all of the generations we have lived as humans until now. So in some ways she was wrong, but in the end she knew the spell would fail. She had some kind of backup plan. I don't know what it is. I can't remember it, but I don't think it's because of the spell like the other things I can't recall. I think it's because she never told me."

"So what do we do now?" Kaliastrid asked.

"We figure out what the plan was."

"How?"

"We seem to be on our way to discovering that already. We're collecting quite a group of skilled humans. They can help us figure this out."

Kaliastrid nodded.

"Let's see if we can't figure out what her plan was. They seem to think it has something to do with this castle they found. Heliantra left clues."

Melissa paused before she went on, thinking carefully before adding, *"I'm going to send Charles to investigate it,"*

"Alone?"

"Yes. He can handle himself. We need to keep the attention on us. I don't want our spy to track him, so we have to keep their attention on us as long as we can."

"You can't send him alone. Not without magic of any sort. I should go with him."

"They have to think we're planning here or looking for something else. We have to keep their attention away from what we've found. If he disappears, they may not notice."

"Wait. I'm not sending him out there with nothing. I found something else the witch had. It may help, and there are other protections we can give him." Kaliastrid stood from the table and her food to walk back to the room where Aldrich had escorted the pilot and Silas.

In a few moments she returned with a leather wrapped bundle, Elaine, and a box of candles. She handed the leather bundle to her, but Melissa didn't open it.

"What is it?"

"I'm not sure. I think it's a sort of divining lens. One of the Loup Garoup was wearing it in the leather harness while he was searching for Silas. He will need to test it. It may help him identify other dragons and partials who are following him without them knowing it."

Melissa nodded at the thought and set it aside.

"It can't hurt. So, we send him to see what he sees."

"It does seem to be our only option," her mother agreed. *"If they go after him..."*

Melissa raised her hand to stop the thought. She had already considered that possibility.

"Aldrich says that it's going to take hours to get Silas back to a stable state. Then it will be up to him," Elaine reported and handed off the box of candles.

Melissa nodded. The unspoken message was that Charles would come to see her when he was free.

"Good. Two things. Elaine, I want you find where Nethliast is hiding. It's near the farm, He was close when I called him, and they were able to muster a defense. Kaliastrid will give you the location to search near. Find him. If you need any help from us let us know. I need a location as soon as possible. I'm tired of hiding out from him." Melissa winked carefully as she gave her the instructions.

"We're the decoy then," Kaliastrid asked, getting her plan.

"I want them watching us or at least unsure of what's happening."

"Second thing, figure out how to block their scrying. I don't want them spying on our planning meetings when the others get here."

Elaine nodded and pulled the small crystal sphere from her pocket.

Melissa took a candle from the box and lit the wick. In a small bowl she let the wax drip and harden. Each drip she charged with her own magic power.

"What's that for?" Elaine asked.

"Even innates use ritual magic from time to time. Sometimes the innate chains are too long to string together without dropping something. We use rituals when that's the case. I'm going to prepare some enchantments for our assault. It will make us more powerful."

Her answer was not false, but the enchantment she was preparing was a way to deliver messages that could only be read by the intended recipient. To anyone else, they would be in draconic. Later she would use the wax medium to carry out her will. When she had enough wax in the bowl, about an ounce by measure, she selected a sharp knife from the table. With the tip of the knife she pierced her forearm and let her blood drip out into the bowl. As the hot blood flowed into the bowl, the wax melted again and merged with her vital fluids. When the bowl was filled with an even mix of wax and her blood, she wrapped the wound with a towel to stop the bleeding. Even as she wrapped it the injury closed, causing her to look up for the Norse healer. When he was nowhere to be seen she returned to her work, confused a little by the rapid healing.

Kaliastrid, who now understood her plan, handed her some parchment they had brought with them from the library.

"I need a quill," she said to no one in particular.

Elaine pulled a fountain pen from her bag and handed it to Kaliastrid. She stared at the new version of the ancient writing implement, then held it up to Melissa, who considered how it would affect the magic. In the end it was the best tool they had. Melissa nodded.

Kaliastrid unscrewed the nib from the barrel and discarded the ink cartridge while Melissa focused on closing her wound. Then she screwed the pen back together and spiraled the last of the ink onto a sheet of paper. Once the pen was dry, she handed it over to Melissa.

She dipped the nib into her blood and started scratching symbols from the ancient language of dragons onto the parchment. With each stroke she worked the magic into the blood and parchment. As she wrote the message she thought of her grandmother. She had done the same tedious exercise to create the spell she had asked Melissa to cast on that longest day that still had not ended.

With her first and most important message complete, she wrote the next two quickly while everyone watched her. When they were all finished, she folded the parchment of the first message neatly around the others, laying the bottom of the parchment over the middle and then creating a flap with the top that overlapped the bottom to the middle of the fold. With it closed neatly, she poured the hot wax and blood mixture onto the parchment. It pooled and hissed into a cooling dome. With concentration on each mark she pressed a glyph into the wax with the nib of the pen. The glyph would guard the letter and only allow Charles to open the seal. When he opened it, the magic in the script would release, allowing him to read the message. If anyone else tried to break the seal, the magic in the text would incinerate the message and the parchment. It might even take the hand of whoever tried to read it.

Satisfied that her enchanted message would work, she handed it to Elaine with the leather bundle.

"Take this to Charles. Tell him I want him to go to the store. He should get what's on this list and follow the instructions in it." She handed the folded parchment and the leather bundle Kaliastrid had given her to Elaine.

"What about—"

"That's all that I need right now. Once you've delivered the message, find Nethliast's base. I want to be on our way as soon as we can move and the others arrive. Aldrich will stay here to heal Silas. He can follow. That's all we can do until Silas is better and can help us."

Elaine nodded, confused, and followed the instructions. Now Melissa had to set up a council to keep the attention of their spy while her other instructions were delivered and Charles could follow his.

"I need to finish eating and rest, after I've checked on Silas. We may have time to catch a couple hours of sleep, but that's all. I want everyone back in here in two hours to plan our assault based on what you find. That should be long enough for our allies to get organized and out here to meet us."

Kaliastrid nodded at her as she gave her instructions. Melissa knew she had read the messages she had written. She knew the plan and would follow it without question. There was no way the others could know without letting the spy know. Now, all she could do was figure out how to sleep while she waited for the time to tick away. Charles had to get to the mountains as soon as he could move. He would figure out how to get out without drawing attention. It was a good guess that they didn't have a physical presence in the area yet. If they did they would have to react.

"See if you can find someone watching us," Melissa sent to Kaliastrid, who nodded and stepped out of the room.

"Hey, Sean. You think you could help me with something?"

Sean looked up from the couch with an amused look on his face.

"It's not every day I'm drug out of a crash by a dragon. I guess I can give you a hand."

"Good. There's some gear I need before dawn."

Melissa focused on the list in her neat dragon script before she sealed another parchment message. When she was done she handed it to Sean and smiled. ""When you're done, let me know."

Sean looked at the folded parchment and nodded. "My horoscope told me to expect some surprises. I really should have listened to it this time."

He set his plate aside and stood up to leave the room. He turned just before he reached the front door.

"How do you know you can trust me?"

"You didn't leave my side before. We're fighting the same war."

He tossed her an informal salute and walked out the door.

September 9 – 0255 CET – In the Swiss Alps

Mikhala cursed beneath her breath. She had found them, and they knew it, so she had no idea what they were planning. Meliastrid knew how to keep information away from someone scrying them.

Mikhala had enough of what she needed to get started, though. Based on what she saw they were not moving right away. They had time to get a force out to Colmar.

"I've found them," she sent to Adrian. *"They know we're watching. We probably need to get moving. Meliastrid is dividing the team. Looks like a possible diversion, again."*

She would let Adrian decide how to deal with the tactics Meliastrid was using. As soon as he had the information, she turned her eyes to treason.

September 9 – About the same time back in Colmar

Kaliastrid felt around her with her magical senses for the gentle brush of scrying. At that moment she didn't feel anything, but it was never guaranteed that she would. The touch of scrying was so light that it was very difficult to sense, but Elaine could tell her if the eyes were still on them. There were simple ways to block scrying, but most people grew tired of the continuous refreshing of the blocks. Most often the watchers only had to be patient. Dungeons and deep caverns had free protection based on their location and depth. If you were in the caves with someone, you could sense them, but she had never known anyone who could find anyone in a deep cave without going into the same cave system. It was different if they were actively seeking, like Valdiest had. She shook off the agitation and doubt of being followed and made up her mind.

She walked up behind the conversation as Elaine delivered the leather bundle and message to Charles in the back room were Aldrich was ministering to Silas.

"Before you go, I could use your help," she said to Elaine. Then she pointed at Charles. "I also have something for you, so don't leave until we've talked."

Charles nodded. He pocketed the note and turned back to make sure Aldrich had what he needed. Elaine closed the door and looked at Kaliastrid.

"Are we still being watched?"

Elaine reached out to see if she could sense the light touch while rubbing her arms. She shook her head without saying a word.

"I'm going to share a spell with you. You'll need to focus on how I do this and then you will do the same around this house." Together they walked to the front wall of the main room on the first floor.

"What are you going to do?"

"I'm going to hide us from the scryer, or any divination, for a short time."

"How?"

"By making the house resemble a dungeon."

Confusion swept across Elaine's face.

"Just follow my lead and watch what I'm doing."

Kaliastrid focused on the walls and roof of the front of the house. Magically the walls did not exist, and she needed for them to look like something significant. She pulled energy from around her and pressed it into the top left structures of the wall and roof and then pressed it between and around the wall as she drew a line to the other side. If Elaine could not see the magic in the room, she would only have seen Kaliastrid drawing a line from the top left corner of the front wall to the bottom right, but Kaliastrid could feel her magical draw as she watched her.

"So you see what I did? Can you repeat it?"

"Yes, I think I can," Elaine replied and started to point at the same corner.

Kaliastrid touched her hand before she started and moved it to the opposite corner. "Overlap from the other direction to create an alternating lattice of depth."

Elaine nodded and focused on the right corner. Kaliastrid traded places with her and focused on her power to watch the process. When she could see that she understood, she stepped back. When she completed the line, she looked back at Kaliastrid as if she needed more instructions.

"Every layer makes the structure thicker to the magic that is trying to find us. Do the same process around the entire building, including the roof and the floor. The scryer will not be able to see through the wall."

"Is it permanent?"

"No. It will only last a few hours before you have to add more layers. To stay hidden you have to add energy regularly. You should actually add a layer to the whole building every hour once you have it strong enough. That is why most people do not do this."

Elaine nodded and built another layer on the wall. When she finished Kaliastrid nodded.

"Change the pattern as you feel. You may find one that creates a stronger layer that may last longer."

"Can this shield us from anything else?"

"Shield walls are similar, but you have to focus on what you're trying to block. It depends on many things. The general shield wall is good for stopping anything striking it because it translates force into repelling energy. You can't use that here. It would have no effect on the mental magic that is allowing scrying to happen."

Elaine nodded even as she tried to understand what Kaliastrid was telling her.

"You learn very quickly. Don't feel bad when some of this doesn't make sense to you. It will. It will not take you long to figure it out."

Elaine smiled.

"I'm going to do something a little more arcane while you're taking care of this. When you're done, join me upstairs. I need a flat surface and privacy. If you learn what I'm about to do, rulers will flock to your door. Or at least they used to."

Elaine gave her a confused look. Kaliastrid smiled back to comfort the young woman then turned to find Charles. He was still helping Aldrich. When she opened the door and stuck her head in, he looked up. She motioned for him to follow her. He looked to Aldrich who nodded silently that he could leave.

He followed her out of the room and up the stairs. At the top he stopped her with a hand on her shoulder and a look on his face. He pointed at the folded and sealed message in his hand.

"Nope, you'll have to read it. We were being watched. I'm not taking any chances."

He nodded.

She pointed to one of the bedrooms and held up the other supplies she had collected. When he saw the candle, needle, knife, and small ramekin, Charles blanched.

"I have a gift for you," she said with a uniquely draconic grin.

"I'm not going to like this, am I?"

"No, not receiving it. You will like what it is. Read the note first. It will make more sense."

As he looked at the leather bundle and the parchment note, Kaliastrid ushered him into the bedroom. With her help he might be okay, but Melissa's plan was a big risk. He would need all the help she could give him, and they didn't have enough time.

September 9 – 0300 CET – In the Swiss Alps

"She tried to kill me— she admitted that she cast the spell…"

Nethliast wandered the tallest chamber of his new empire cogitating on Meliastrid's two revelations. It was the only chamber in the abandoned bunker system that was big enough for him to take his preferred form, and he needed to be a dragon just then. It had apparently been a gymnasium. There was an attached room with an olympic sized swimming pool which they had filled and warmed for his comfort. Other rooms provided sleeping quarters and offices for staff. The main entrance was a pair of double doors guarded by a partial who was sworn to the King's protection and would not allow anyone in without clearance. Nethliast turned at the far wall and swiped his tail across the floor as he changed direction, oblivious to any who might be standing near him. Rebekka had learned to time her movements to place her near one of many alcoves where equipment had once been stored whenever he came near to her side of the room. She was mumbling on her phone quietly as he ranted, and her lack of attention was not helping him solve his problem.

The two revelations continued to plague him.

He swished his tail against the near wall and walked back across the floor. In her protected alcove, Rebekka was swamped by the size of the chamber and Nethliast's equally large size, and she was the only other being in the room. Her business suit was stained with blood, soot, and dirt, which told the tale of exactly how long she had been unable to change. She hung up the phone and crossed her arms over her chest. As if she was considering his points, she dropped her chin against her chest. As she thought about his agitation and the reason for it, she scowled. The incongruous blend of the business suit, the cave, and her agitated look made her normally attractive face seem completely discordant. He knew that her appearance was a particular irritation of hers, but it was not the only cause of her agitation.

"She tried to kill me," he said again, somehow feeling the need to highlight his complaint and defend his own mood against her brooding. He wasn't sure, and didn't particularly care, how many times he had repeated those words. To him it was a momentary salve to the idea that Meliastrid had tried to kill him. It was as if saying it again reset the thought that he just could not reconcile.

This was not the first time that she had tried to kill him. It was the first time she had plotted to kill him. Her last attempt could be excused. It had been a half-hearted attempt, and in reality it had been a defense against his obvious intent to kill her. He could excuse that, but this was different. She had intentionally planned and manipulated him into an ambush. She had baited him out. Not so that she could strike him down, but so that her human assassin could kill him. How could she do that to him? That was low, unacceptable, but very draconic. It was still treason to his throne.

She had loved him, once. She had really loved him. That was one memory amongst all of the pain that he never doubted. This was no way to treat a mate.

He had only ever wanted to make her his queen. His only dream had been of reclaiming their lost power and the glory of their families— for her— mostly. Why couldn't she see that?

"She really tried to kill me," he said with another swish.

Rebekka groaned, and pushed off of the wall. "You are such a child. For an ancient dragon, you're a child. Would you please get over it and act? Bida would not be brooding here in his room. He would be out sweeping the countryside for his enemy and putting them to the flame."

She walked out of the niche and into the middle of the room to face him and stop his pacing.

"You have the whole world's attention. You have decapitated their governments. They're scrambling around trying to recover. They can't organize any force strong enough to stop you. You rule the world, if you could just see that. All you have to do is stand up and take it. But you're chasing your own tail over your lost love like a damned teenager. I think I backed the wrong dragon."

"Be careful," he growled. "Don't think your presence here protects you."

"That's the anger I'm looking for. That's what I want to see from you. Don't lose sight of the goal now. Tell the world what you demand!" She stomped her foot and shouted. "Why are you crying over this insignificant irritation that refuses to leave you alone? Just let me kill her! When you find her, and the partials will find her, let me take your elite guard and end this."

With a subconscious straightening of her new suit, she calmed herself. When she was done, a placid look returned to her face and with it the razor of her wit.

Unbowed by her show of force, Nethliast bent his head down until it was level with hers. The rest of his bulk towered above her. He placed his single good eye directly over her face. She did not even flinch. He didn't expect her to.

"You— have—no—idea what it's like to live with a mate for as long as I have known Meliastrid. In your short, meaningless life, you cannot possibly understand the depth of the relationships of dragons. Do not pretend that you can counsel me. Do not compare me with any other dragon. I carried that conclave, and not a male in the room doubted my resolve or power. Otherwise they would be ruling now."

Nethliast wanted to strike the arrogant woman down before him and protect her from her own foolishness at the same time. It wasn't so much her misunderstanding of their relationship, but her pure lack of knowledge about dragons. He could forgive her ignorance.

His own ignorance worried him more. He should know all there was to know as a dragon, and yet something in his painfully fractured memory still eluded him. A fleeting memory laced in pain warned him that trying to kill Meliastrid was likely to fail. He didn't pursue the memory to its painful conclusion. Too many other failed quests for clarity had taught him there was no benefit to the struggle. He didn't know the reason that he thought she was protected. He simply accepted the memory and didn't argue.

A quick reminder of the penalty for digging too deep into his memory for anything made him growl again. He transformed the snarl of pain into anger at the human that had caused the pain, in her own way. Why did he even care about the future of the pitiable creature before him? The guttural rumbling continued at the idea that he was worried about her life. She would expire in a tenth of his lifespan. Suddenly, he felt an urge to kill her where she stood. That pleasant thought was balanced against his desire to caress her skin and protect her from her own ignorance.

In that short-lived thought she chose to press him harder rather than see the patience he was exercising.

"You were obviously so worried about that *relationship* when you were in my bed," she said with no expression whatsoever. "You can't even remember if dragons were monogamous. Please don't pretend at fidelity now." She goaded him as if she wanted him to kill her.

Nethliast raised his foreclaw to strike her across the face.

She stuck her chin out to take the blow.

He turned away from her and roared his frustration into the height of the gymnasium rather than give her the satisfaction of manipulating him. She had to scramble to avoid the mindless swish of his tail.

"I don't know why I waste my time with you. I never needed you. You're here because I find you amusing. That's all."

"Right, that's why you came crawling to me, quite literally, when your lifelong mate had a human sniper put a bullet in your head." Rebekka stepped back against the wall but followed his pacing. "She came close to killing you. An inch to the right and it would have missed that ridiculously hard bone in your head and destroyed that minuscule brain of yours. You were an inch from dead at the hands of a human. Then you were betrayed by your high priestess of the order of Nethliast, who had been devoted to you since she saw you. At least until the very moment that she saw Meliastrid. Was Meliastrid the second real dragon she had ever seen? Never mind, it doesn't matter. So, deserted and attacked by both of your other women, what did you do? You crawled to me to save and protect you." She circled around to face him again. "Stop lying to me. You can lie to yourself if you want, but I know you need me. You've needed me since the beginning of this. You would not be here, in this bunker, without me. Your own kind are deserting you, turning against you, and you still believe they're the superior beings." She laughed. "Your partial army is more superior so long as you keep your former mate from inciting them to mutiny. If you don't watch it, she'll tell them the truth just to foment a rebellion and leave you to deal with it. That's what I would do. Then I'd stand back and watch the fun. Trouble is, that would be just too easy with what you've told me. Of all of the races in this little war, the partials are the only one with a valid complaint."

Nethliast could feel the rage building in him. His desire to strike her across the face drove his scaled and spiked fist out before he could stop it. To avoid killing her, he tried to draw the strike back and transformed. His dragon form melted into his black suited human form. As he emerged from the transition, his balled fist struck her across the face in a wet cracking sound that he had seen completely fell a man twice her size. Her lip split from the force. Her head snapped to the left, trailing an arc of blood that erupted from the cut. She didn't fall. She had expected it—invited it. She simply shuddered from the force she had intercepted and held her ground as she magically dissipated the strike into the air and earth around her. He felt his lust flare. It made him dizzy with sudden desire. He couldn't believe she continued to challenge him. Some day she would make him kill her.

She grinned and wiped the blood off of her lip. Her finger caressed the split. She mumbled a long stream of familiar words that he knew were only the trigger words for a much larger spell she maintained in her mind. The bleeding cut closed and disappeared into her flawless skin.

"Just kill Meliastrid and be done with it," the woman said very calmly. "If you would just kill her, we could get on with your plan in peace. She's a distraction from what's important. She's like a scab that you can't leave alone, and she will figure out your weakness someday. She can't be that stupid. I'll kill her. Just let me find her."

His initial arousal flared into an uncontrollable flame as she demonstrated more of the power hidden in her weak human body. Even as the desire overcame him, he growled at the control Rebekka had over him.

"I can't kill her. Neither can you," he rumbled.

The look on her face was incredulous.

"You don't understand. She's protected. I know that she is, but I can't remember how. That old wyrm," he said as he pointed toward the frozen crypt where he kept the body of the king. "He knew. He goaded me into killing him too soon, or I would know. That's why she's here. She didn't just come here to kill me. She came to find what he told her to find. She's after something that he knew about. They're hiding it from me. It's important to securing our kingdom. I know it. It's just beyond my memories, shielded by that cursed pain that I think she's responsible for. I want to know what she's after. Even if I could kill her, I want to know what she is here for." Pain lanced through his head as he tried again to remember why she was so important. He screamed aloud, "Why can't you do something about this pain?"

Rebekka raised both of her hands over her head and waved them for a moment. "You're chasing a fantasy that he planted in your head. You're jumping at shadows. She came here to kill you. That's all. She's no more invincible than you are." She pointed at the black patch covering his missing eye as proof of her point.

"Then why did she bring the others with her? Why does she need the girl and that nut archaeologist? What were they looking for in that library while she was keeping me busy? See, I don't believe she really wanted to kill me. It was a diversion from what she was doing elsewhere. She doesn't want me to know what she's looking for."

"Or that was a diversion to keep you guessing. What could she possibly be looking for? You really believe there's some talisman out there that can control dragons? Why would it matter anyway? She can't stop you now." She stepped to his human form and ran a hand across the fabric of his suit from his shoulder to the buttons in front. He felt desire tugging at his trousers. "Have Adrian find her. Let me kill her and all of the others when we find them. That is all below the king of the world. You need to tell your new subjects what you command. If there is a talisman, you can have the whole world search for it once we rule them. We're too close to let this stop us."

Her change in attitude stopped him. She had been fighting him and now she was trying to convince him. He hated the weak approach and turned away from her. Meliastrid was never weak, and she never backed down.

"No. You're not listening. She's protected. I want to know how. I want to know what they're doing. I will never truly control dragons until I know what she is after. I'll send the message to the humans because there's no reason to stop the plan, but I'll decide when. Now, be careful when you entice me to kill. I may decide to kill you, and don't doubt that I can. Your formulaic magic came from somewhere, child. Humans have never been more powerful than the naturally magical."

He turned to face her. He wanted to see how she reacted to his point, but the information was a new realization to him as well. Humans had never been able to master magic like dragons and other magical creatures. That was why he had saved the president. That was why she was locked in a safe place, waiting for the right time. He wanted to know how she had manifested the magic she had without a formula. If he could turn her to his side, he could replace this witch with an innate human. Even through the pain in his head, he knew they had not existed before. They would be a powerful tool in his forces if he could turn them to his will.

His short thought about the other woman had distracted him from savoring his attack on Rebekka's magical ability. He had expected fear from her, but, when he looked into her eyes, he saw defiance. A flicker of desire rekindled. He wrapped his hand around her chin and held her face close to his.

"Understand me. I will not be manipulated by a simple human woman. I've dealt with female dragons. Your charms and wiles, magical or otherwise, are nothing compared to the least experienced dragon. I can kill you whenever I please and never miss you." He lied. He found her fascinating, intriguing, and desirable; and she was right that he needed her power— right now.

"You need me for more than the powers I can command. We'll see who ends up in control. When all of your dragon kin desert you, you'll realize how much you really need me. When the partials find out what dragons did to them in the past, you'll come crawling to me for help. Remember this moment, Nethliast. Your fascination with your mate is going to allow them to become so strong that you can't stop them. It's written in the stars for you. I'm just trying to help you, and you're not listening to me. As for your threat, I'll never be afraid of you. You're too weak and easy to manipulate, and don't think for a moment that you can train that woman you brought here to stand against me. I'll kill her first."

She turned her back on him and walked through a single doorway into a smaller room they had used as a sleeping chamber. She never looked back.

He straightened his jacket and followed her.

September 9 – 0325 CET – In the Swiss Alps

Mikhala closed her eyes and let the image fade in the crystal. That was a scene she did not want to remember at all, so it was best to abandon her connection. Nethliast was keeping a secret from the partials. A secret other than the human witch everyone except Adrian knew was sharing his bed.

She reached out to Adrian's mind again. *"I found her, we need to tell Nethliast. What are you waiting for?"*

"I'm on my way back to you now. Make sure you have their location."

She sent the location to him.

"I'll send Chip and the others ahead. Nethliast cannot be disturbed at the moment. He's in a council. Keep an eye on them."

She grinned at the pride in her success that he let slip in his response. Then she focused her very tired mind on what Rebekka had been talking about before she reached out to connect with Meliastrid's team again. What secret was Nethliast, and all dragons, hiding from them?

Meliastrid's ultimatum from the day before came back to her. She had tried to command them into a rebellion, just like Rebekka had said she would, but the witch had something more than the threat of death to use. What was that extra power she might wield?

Mikhala would need to find that out. Neither side deserved the loyalty of the partials. If she could discover what secret they were hiding, the partials could stand on their own. Rebekka was right about them being superior. As a force of magical beings, the partials could overwhelm a single dragon. They were powerful in their sheer numbers.

As always, information was power. There was not enough information for her to share with Adrian yet, but there was enough to get her a nap. She would tell Nethliast where Meliastrid was— no reason not to— then she would see what else she could find out.

But first, she was going to lie down and sleep for a few minutes. Nothing was going to happen until Nethliast was free.

She looked into the crystal again. It flared with light. The chambers resolved before her as she verified he would be busy for a while. She quickly released the image. As a last check, she reached out to connect with Meliastrid again and found a void. She was not where she had been, but it was not like she had disappeared. It felt more like where she had been had disappeared.

Mikhala inhaled sharply and tried for Kaliastrid. The same result made her nervous. Where had they gone? This would not be good. She needed to verify that Meliastrid was still in the house in Colmar.

She tried the others who had been in the house with her and found them all absent. She released the crystal for a moment to think. What could have happened? It had something to do with how their absence felt. She decided to try a different approach.

She focused on the crystal again and tried to find the house. The structure returned nothing to her at all, as if it were no longer there. She tried again and focused on the area where the house had been. That was when she understood what had happened. While she had been watching Nethliast, someone had blocked her ability to see into the house. It had not disappeared, but she could no longer see into it. They had created a magical null. She could see the yard around it and the building, but when she tried to see into it she saw nothing.

"We have a problem," she sent to Adrian.

"What?"

"They knew I was scrying them. They've blocked the house. I can't see what's going on inside of it."

"Can you find them away from it?" Adrian asked

"No."

"Then they're still in it."

"Maybe."

"They couldn't hide everyone from you easily."

"I don't think so," Mikhala answered, trying to figure out what had happened. *"I don't know. We didn't get into counter-scrying in training. We were focused on staying in touch, not protecting ourselves from being seen."*

"Do you think they are still there?"

"Yes."

"That's what we will report as soon as Nethliast is free," Adrian said, making a decision. *"That's all we can do. I'll tell Chip what has changed. Until we get some eyes in Colmar, we will not know what they're up to."*

"Yes. She's smart."

"We keep underestimating her."

"We seem to always be reacting to everyone. We need to start being a little unpredictable ourselves."

"We're soldiers. We follow orders," Adrian cautioned.

She felt the rebuke and let the argument fall until she had more evidence to share.

"Get some rest."

She felt relieved at his suggestion. There was nothing more she was going to be able to see if they were hidden. If they left the cover of the building, she could find them again. She really needed to rest. Maybe she would feel different on the other side of a nap.

She sat down on the table edge and laid back along its top. It was not her bunk, but it would do until she could get back to it.

September 9 – 0500 CET – In the Swiss Alps

Mikhala was awake again, much sooner than she had hoped, but Nethliast was not allowing any but his most trusted officers to make decisions. He didn't trust any of them with the mission he had assigned his personal guard. His own physical needs came before that mission however, so he had told his aide that he was in council and could not be disturbed.

Adrian, trusting and faithful, had waited until he was available and let Mikhala sleep. Mikhala was not complaining. She had taken advantage of the time and slept on the table in the ready room. She did not feel better on the other side of her nap. She was still angry at Nethliast for killing her priestess, and she was not going to forget that there was some kind of secret the dragons were keeping from the partials.

Adrian had awakened her with enough time to look fresh when they arrived, and she had used the short walk to the King's chambers to check up on Meliastrid. She did want the latest intelligence when she reported in, but it had not changed. She still could not see into the building and they were still not able to be found outside of it. The idea did occur to her that they were sneaking out through a tunnel that she could not see into, but there was no evidence of that.

"I still can't follow them," she sent urgently to Adrian, who showed no reaction as he stood waiting to report their situation.

"I told Chip. He'll see what it looks like when he gets there, but they're still three hours out."

There was a pause while they listened to Nethliast and the witch shuffle about in the bedchamber. At least now, Adrian could no longer doubt her point about the human relationship Nethliast was carrying on.

"Any theories on why they're hiding like this?"

"Obviously they don't want us seeing what they're up to. Meliastrid knew I was watching. She was handing out notes that I could not read, and then they were gone."

"I'm glad Chip and the guys are already on their way. The humans can't communicate with Meliastrid magically. That's where Jay's going to help us. Maybe the first time his addiction to continuously streaming pornography and the pursuit of maintaining it is going to be an advantage. Never thought I would say that."

Mikhala processed his response without reacting while continuing to stand at attention. She wanted to chuckle at the fact that all he had to do was learn how to scry and his fantasies would be fulfilled, and then she cringed at the thought of releasing him on the world that way.

The aroma of flowers, pleasantly absent from her images, suddenly wafted up from the center of the room where Nethliast transformed into his towering black form. With a simple gesture, he indicated they could approach. As they bowed to the ruler, Mikhala realized that any respect she had for Nethliast had been replaced with simple fear. She was following

Adrian's lead out of self-preservation, but she felt no reverence in her demonstration of fealty.

"Report."

"We have succeeded in your charge. We know where Meliastrid and her forces are."

The female witch appeared at his right side. She was controlling her face to avoid giving away something. Mikhala was not sure what it was, but she wanted to know. Her other body language told her she was hiding something. Mikhala watched her carefully but could only read the desire pulsing from her. She thought it was focused on Nethliast, then she realized that it was completely focused on murder. She wanted to kill her lover's previous mate. The blood lust seeped into the room nearly as strongly as the recently refreshed, ubiquitous rose water.

"Where?" the king asked before the woman could supplant him in his own chambers.

Mikhala stepped forward to align herself with Adrian and delivered her report. "Sire, they are in a house in Colmar, France." She felt the need to point it out on a map she had brought with them, but the dragon didn't seem to need or desire the actual location.

"Take your team out there and follow them. Report back to me exactly what they're doing," Nethliast barked at Adrian. Mikhala forced herself not to react to the strange order. Even she expected him to give the order to strike them and be done with it.

"My lord," the witch interrupted, "if I may."

Mikhala felt the irritation pulse from the cuckolded king. No one else reacted to the chilling blast of emotion. The towering figure managed his reaction but failed to hold it back completely from someone sensitive to it.

"What is it?"

"I only wanted to suggest that we send more partials with him. We don't want things to get out of hand. We're not close enough to react from here. We could lose them. If Sergeant Fieldman's team discovers their plot, don't you think we should have troops in place? What are they doing in this house?" she asked Mikhala directly, not waiting for the King's response.

Mikhala waited for a sign that she should continue since the consort was not in the chain of command and had not been identified as their new queen.

Nethliast nodded slightly while Rebekka fumed impatiently for her report.

"Although we have tried to ascertain their plan, they have started using techniques to cover their communications from our scrying. Now they have hidden themselves entirely."

Rebekka could not hide her response as her hand rubbed the cell phone in her pocket. She wanted to call someone. Who was she talking to outside of the command? That would be good leverage if she could prove it.

"What? When did this happen?"

Mikhala started to answer, but Adrian interrupted her.

"It happened while you were in council, my lord. We're reporting all of this as soon as we are able. We've already sent a vanguard out to determine what they're doing."

It did not reduce the dragon's anger, but it kept him from lashing out.

Rebekka rubbed her phone again. That was an important tell. Mikhala remembered that Rebekka had been on the phone before, but she had not focused on her conversation because her target had been Nethliast.

"Let me go out there and stop her, my lord," the witch said.

Nethliast seemed to actually chew on her suggestion while looking for a way to override it. Having found no valid argument, he finally responded.

"I have a better idea."

Mikhala suppressed a grin as she braced for the King's suggestion.

"I want to know what she's after. I want to be close to this. Get to Colmar and make sure we don't lose them. I will join you out there. Take a platoon of partials with you."

Rebekka shook her head and vanished behind Nethliast's bulk. Mikhala knew this was the rift between them. It was broadening. If only she could find a way to leverage it to get more information. Whoever she was talking to might be her way in. Nethliast turned away, giving them a clear indication that they were dismissed.

Mikhala and Adrian bowed and backed away from Nethliast to exit the room. They had their orders. There was no reason to stay in that uncomfortable space.

As they walked through the doors into the hallway, Adrian was now fully focused on the mission. Mikhala scanned who else was waiting for their turn in the new king's court. She had been reviewing her mirror as they had walked in, but she did remember there had been someone waiting to see the King. This time she stopped to look.

One of the dragons who had been in the command center five hours earlier was waiting. He looked as if he had been there a while. His gray scales had an interesting opalescent quality to them as he sat in the prerequisite dragon form. It was obvious from his eyes that he was an older dragon. The shape of his eyes and face told her what the human form would look like, and she could see a resemblance to Nethliast. She remembered him as the dragon Adrian had identified as Gerlias:, Nethliast's father. His expression told her that he had been waiting longer than he was used to. He was controlling his irritation with ancient decorum the younger partials and even the new King could benefit from.

"Is he available now?" The waiting male's question was designed with the correct amount of regal indignation to make the clerk at the desk flinch. Mikhala suddenly wanted to see the outcome of this meeting.

"There's no reason for me to go with you," she said to Adrian. "I can set up communications here to support you in the field and that will allow me to maintain a connection with them. It will take me longer to relocate." She avoided touching his elbow even though she wanted to. It was inappropriate to distract him.

"We're already behind and reacting. I do need you monitoring what's going on even though they're hidden. We have to stay ahead of this, especially considering this new development."

She nodded and then mentally added, *"I need to follow up on what's going on back there. I think it is important to stay on top of everything here."*

"You mean the dragon waiting for an audience? That's Gerliast, the Aide-de-Camp to the old king. The King is sending him back to Berlin. Why would you want to... It's not safe. If they catch you..."

"Things are not safe for us here. I told you I needed to prove it. Let me prove it to you."

"Okay, but be careful. I would rather have you in the field with me."

"I can do more here."

He nodded. They started to part when Rebekka appeared behind them.

"Fieldman, I want you in touch with Salenko while you're out there. I expect there's information you will need coming in. I'm going to make sure we're in touch. Is that clear?"

"Yes, ma'am. She was on her way to get everything set up in the command center."

"This woman is a danger to your King. If you see the opportunity, you will kill her. Is that clear?"

"Ma'am. Those are not my orders."

The witch's eyes flared at the resistance, but she controlled her anger.

"You follow your orders, but you are responsible for the King's life. If your lack of action leads to another attempt on his life, it will be on your head. Think about that while you're on your way."

"Yes, Ma'am," he said with appropriate respect.

Mikhala avoided direct eye contact. Rebekka pulled her phone from her pocket and turned back toward the King's chambers. Mikhala needed to catch that call as well.

Adrian gave her a look of curiosity.

"I told you everything was not what you thought. I told you we were not safe."

He raised an eyebrow.

"Leave that to me. I'll keep you informed."

He nodded and turned away. She wanted to kiss him, but she knew it could not happen. Mikhala turned to enter the command center.

The clerk that had been outside of the King's chamber followed her in and spoke for a moment with a new pair of partials that had not been in the command center earlier. For some reason, they looked over at her as she took her place at the central console where the priestess normally directed communications. Perhaps it was her own paranoia, but she was not taking any chances. She would need to keep an eye on that clerk.

She didn't have time for distractions. She forced the clerk from her mind and focused on the scrying crystal. Pain from the memory of her leader's death rushed over her, but she pushed it aside. It was just another console. It was just another crystal.

She reached into the crystal to settle her mind. It pulsed and shimmered, but instead of going where she wanted to focus it filled her mind with Ariela's mind.

"Mikhala," the disembodied mind spoke directly to her, "I knew you would be the next to use my crystal. I'm telling you this because it has to be known. We've made the wrong choice. I know now that we've followed the wrong dragon. The robe told me as soon as I saw her that I was bound to her. I could not refuse following her. Neither should any other dragon. If we continue to follow Nethliast it will be to our destruction. Do not let that happen, Mikhala. I now see that Nethliast's goals are not right for dragons, humans, or partials. Be careful. Be strong."

The message vanished as quickly as it had filled her mind. Somehow Ariela had stored the message in the crystal for her. She shivered from the invasion. She accepted that there was no other way to get the message to her, but she was getting tired of people playing around in her mind. She was going to have to find a way to block her mind from others. This could not keep happening.

She shook off the agitation and thought about the message. It was short and direct. She must have meant Meliastrid. There was no other being she could mean. It would take time to think through her whole message, and she didn't have the time at the moment. She would process it fully the next time she had a few minutes.

She focused the crystal onto the room that she wanted to watch. As she had expected the meeting had very little formality. The male who had been waiting was already making his case when she joined the conversation.

"...is no need to continue holding their families."

"I think there is. You forget your place."

"I am fully aware of my place. You've made it quite clear where you expect me to be. But I have a duty to my kind, not just to a single ruler. You may choose to ignore my guidance as a father and a wise counselor, but I will not stop trying to offer it."

"Go on, make your argument."

"You have played a dangerous game, taking hatchlings and mates of dragons as leverage. You are safe now because they fear you, but soon they will remember what they are. The rage at your actions will win. You do not want the rage of dragons to turn against you. Let me visit the families. Let me tell their mates that they are being treated well and they are safe. Give me tools to help you. You do not want to let this rift grow."

"You will go back to your post. You will enforce my commands. You will not question me," Nethliast growled down at his father.

The other male shifted in a flash from his humanoid dragon form to an equally large white and gray dragon. When he completed his transformation, they were standing face to face in the large chamber with their wings raised. There was no room left for the witch to stand among them. She retreated to the door to the sleeping chambers. She still had her phone in her hand.

It was clear to Mikhala that they were still arguing, but like Meliastrid's and Kaliastrid's earlier conversation, it was no longer verbal. They circled each other in the center of the room. Nethliast kept his good eye facing the older dragon. Neither of them twitched a single muscle that might be seen as an attack. The standoff continued, and Mikhala focused on the witch as she dialed and put the phone to her ear. Mikhala could not hear the other party, but it soon became clear that this was a batch conversation.

"They have blocked the scrying. I need for you to watch for anything that looks like they're trying to get away. The others are not there yet, so you will have to make decisions on what to do. Call me with any changes that make sense. I need to know what they're doing. Nothing is unimportant."

She hung up the phone and dialed again. This time she got an answer.

"How far out are you?"

"That's unacceptable. Get there. Things are changing quickly. I want her dead now."

"Just do it."

The witch hung up and shoved the phone into her pocket.

Mikhala let her focus slip back out to the entire room. Both males were transforming back into their semi-human form. The older man turned his back on his son and walked out of the chamber, shaking his head.

Nethliast turned to his witch as she walked out to join him. He shook his own head. "Why does everyone want to question me? Just do as I say. That's how a king works. He tells everyone what to do, and they do it."

"There is a bit more to it than that," the witch said, more than a little agitated by the display. "We need to prepare to relocate if we are going to keep up with Meliastrid. We need to get the troops on the way if you want to see what she's up to."

Mikhala again felt the room charge with anger but watched as the king of the dragons backed down.

"You go ahead. I will follow shortly. Make sure they don't kill her. I want to know what she's up to."

There were more subplots in this fortress than Mikhala would have ever considered. Unraveling them might be fun if her life was not in the balance. She sighed and let the crystal fade to white swirling quartz silence.

"Adrian, be careful. Everything is not as it seems. There's another group out there with you, and they are allied with Rebekka. I do not know who they are, but she is speaking with them secretly." She hoped her message would be understood. He did not reply, but she knew he had received it.

CHAPTER 8 - A FIGHT FOR THE CASTLE

September 9 – 0600 CET – Colmar, France

Charles stepped quietly out the back door of the safe house. He had made sure that the lights were out as he slipped through the single screen door off of the kitchen. The arm of the door closer was disconnected so that it would not make any noise. He reached back to close the door gently. His combat boots made no noise on the concrete and stone steps as he descended them. There were dogs in the neighborhood. Many of them were already barking at other noises, but he wanted to avoid becoming a new attraction. His OD green tactical shirt and black pants were selected to make him look more like a tourist than a soldier and for the advantages they provided in keeping him hidden in either an urban environment or the woods around Colmar. He was beyond the yard and heading toward the nearby woods in under five minutes. His hope was that his quiet departure would go completely unnoticed by anyone watching the house. He slipped into the dark obscurity of the woods.

From what Kaliastrid had told him while she tapped the tattoos out around his neck and chest with the needle, they were being watched. Someone was watching them magically the way they had observed Valdiest in his prison back at the estate and in Füssen. Elaine had protected the house so no one could see inside. But since whoever was looking for them could not find them anywhere else, they would probably assume they were still in the house. That was why she had focused so intently on the tattoo around his neck.

He reached up to touch the inflamed flesh but stopped before the fingers could irritate it more. The raw circle felt like it surrounded his neck for a foot all the way around, but he knew it was much more like a two-inch wide band. She had let him watch in a mirror as she etched the protective web onto his shoulders, back, and chest. It was an intricate weaving of interlaced lines that, according to her, would make him undetectable by direct divination, specifically scrying. It would only last a few hours before the magic that powered it would dissipate. He had that small amount of time to complete the mission Melissa had given him via the magical note in his pocket. When the spell had run its course, only the tiny holes would remain. They would heal normally without scarring. He would still suffer the pain until it healed.

She had referred to the magic as the art of *the painted warrior*. While she had worked steadily with the needle and the paint, which was a combination of her blood and a vegetable based oil, she had told him about their history. He was surprised that she could suddenly remember the art she had used so long ago, but he didn't ask her why her memory had suddenly improved. It was a new development. He did wonder if that was the reason their tactics were changing, but he kept that to himself. With each rapid tap of the needle, she told him how many different rulers had used painted warriors in their front lines. Her storytelling may have been a way to keep him from feeling the pain. It had not worked.

Painted Warriors had submitted to days, sometimes months, of intricate tattooing that imbued them with amazing power. The artists who created the tattoos were shamans who had trained in the art and built magical power into each nuance of their creations. In the time she had, she could only give him a rudimentary chain of spells that could be used individually or released together in a single powerful but basic strike.

As the tapping became monotonous, she had delved deeper and told him how the art of imbuing tattoos with power had come from Asia. Oriental dragons had shared their magic with humans this way, in direct opposition to the majority of dragon races who didn't want humans to have magical ability. She had piqued his interest with that tale, and he had started to ask more of that history when she began to chant through a section and then returned to her history lesson. She explained that the ritual she was so poorly demonstrating was where Yakuza ritual tattooing in Japan came from, and why it survived the disappearance of magic. In a rare break, she had wondered aloud if there had been any practitioners who had retained the magical rituals taught to them. He extrapolated from her question that there may be some Yakuza who suddenly realized their tattoos were powerful spells. She didn't pause long enough for him to ask. She abandoned that line of conversation to restart the chanting power transfer of the new chain of spells on his chest. He learned that this procedure included the description of each spell as she was adding it to the chain and a lesson in how to call the power out of the tattoos individually or in sequence.

The entire process was very trance-like and intimate with her hands always touching his skin just ahead of a painful burning that grew with each new stab just deep enough into the skin to inject the ink. The trance, the chant, the ritual, in retrospect, had moved him and Kaliastrid to another place while she was etching him. As he thought back over it as he walked, it didn't seem like it had taken that long. There apparently had been a mercy in the ritual. Considering what he did remember, he was glad for whatever relief there had been.

He could feel his shirt rubbing against the raw circle of flesh near his heart. That second tattoo was a chain of small images that she had strewn together across his chest with interwoven lines that connected each spell across his sternum. The whole chain of symbols were related. Each charm, as she had called them, on the chain contained a specific power. He could choose to release each charm as he needed, in power pairs, or he could release the entire chain. Each charm had a trigger that she had magically embedded in the image. All he had to do was touch the charm or the chain and think of the trigger to release the magic. She had explained that the resolution of her chain was very low compared to some she had seen. Some artists would hide a chain such as this in a space smaller than a fingernail and still imbue the wielder with unimaginable power.

"The power you will release will be equal to me casting the spell. The magic itself will not hurt, but when the spell is released from your skin, it will hurt as much as it did to apply it, only instantly instead of spread out over time."

He had nodded, not thinking much about the future pain as she was intricately stabbing his chest with the needle. He shifted his shirt around and tried to reposition the pack strap that was laying over the very center of the tattoo ring.

All of his gear was either hidden in his pockets or packed into a medium-sized military style day-pack. Its single crossover strap was turning out to be a bad decision, considering the tenderness of the skin on his chest. He had asked Kaliastrid why it had to be on his chest.

"You have not been trained to use these tools of the *painted warrior*, so it is important that I connect these spells directly with your essence. Someone who has trained can have them placed anywhere on their body because they can summon the power to cast them from their essence and focus it through their body. I don't have time to train you how to do that, so I'm putting them as close to your essence as I can."

It had sounded logical at the time.

He shrugged the pack around a little and ignored the unending irritation. It did him no good to focus on it. He had a long walk to the train station and a long day before the mission was complete. Go find the castle Elaine and Aldrich say is on the top of the Schlossberg in Kruth. See if there is any indication that the Heart of the Dragon is there. If he found anything, they would join him and continue their search. If not, it was back to the drawing board with nothing to show from this except Nethliast knowing they are searching for something.

At first he had wondered why Aldrich or Elaine were not going instead of him. Then he realized neither of them stood any chance of making it to the target without drawing attention to themselves. Not to mention that Aldrich was in the middle of healing Silas. If they did attract attention, they couldn't fight their way out of the situation. He could at least try. And the one unspoken reason was that he was expendable.

Charles could see the sense in making a quiet move while reinforcing and recovering. They couldn't move until Silas was better. Moving as a group would attract attention. It would take too long to mask everyone from scrying. So, he was force recon. He could deal with that.

To remain concealed as long as possible, he stuck to the trees. The closer he got to the city proper and the train station, the less cover he was going to have. If he had made it away from the house without a tail there was a chance he would not need as much cover once he was closer. Charles stopped for the first time since he left the house to check his tail. He slipped up against a tree and just listened for any sound that suddenly stopped or started.

When he stopped and slid back against a tree, his clothes helped him vanish into the dark outline. A quiet padding in the distance caught his attention, and his heart jumped. The sound did not start or stop when he did, but it could still be someone following him. He took a chance and looked toward the noise. A large dog was slipping along the edge of the woods. Charles convinced himself that it had to be a dog in this settled area, as wolves did not come this close to large towns. It was a very large dog, though. It didn't look at him, but Charles knew enough about animals to know that whatever it was, it could probably smell him. It was alone. He waited to see if it would come toward him or if it was being followed by someone who was using it to track him. When it continued toward town past his stopping point without much interest and he had seen no indication that it was the vanguard of a tracking party, he decided it was not interested in him and continued toward the train station.

September 9 – 0700 CET – On the road from Füssen to Colmar

"The big one is on the move. He left the house about an hour ago and is at the train station. He's bought a commuter pass, so I don't know where he's stopping. I'm following him. Next transfer point is Mulhouse Ville. The train leaves in about twenty minutes. I could lose him there. Where's my help? I have a phone. Here's the number, call me directly if you need me..."

Rebekka stopped listening to the report from the Loup Garou she had sent to follow Kaliastrid and the sniper the night before. He had been watching the house and calling in all morning, but she had not been able to contact him. He had apparently received her last message to watch for activity and done so.

That particularly arcane ritual had turned out to be quite useful for her. If she had enough time she could build her own army of magical wolves. She was disappointed to find out that they were not protected from harm against anything but silver, but she would figure out where that legend had come from and resolve that problem too. First, she had to keep Nethliast on target and secure her place at the top. What was it about men and losing focus in the last lap? All Nethliast had to do was stand up and take what he had secured. She squelched that dissatisfaction before it drove her to do something drastic.

She hung up the phone. There was no reason to call him back. He was on the trail. She could use the new information to get others out to help him. She didn't really care about the big one, which had to be Charles. He was just another useless human man. She could send the others after him while she focused, with all of the partials she was traveling with, on Meliastrid. However, she could not ignore that Charles was never too far away from the dragon bitch. Following him did make sense.

She dialed the next number in her favorites. A young voice she recognized as the king's aide answered. She had not wasted time on remembering his name.

"Hello."

"I have news. Charles is not in the house anymore. He's getting on a train in Colmar. I don't know where he's going. Are they aware of this change or not?"

"No, they've not been able to find any of Meliastrid's followers outside of the house. What do you want me to do with this information?"

She paused to think about it and decided to take a chance. "Take your phone to the command center and hand it to the Guardian Angel at the center console."

"Yes, Ma'am. Stand by."

She heard the noise of the aide standing up and then silence as he walked down the hall. She heard the ragged edges of the conversation where he got her attention and handed her the phone.

"This is Salenko."

"Sergeant, this is, the king's consort." She paused to consider her options and decided that it was fine to make it official. If it made Nethliast uncomfortable, that would help her as well.

"Yes, Ma'am," the soldier answered without a reaction. "What can I do for you?"

"What's happening at the house?"

"Nothing. I still can't see into it, and I can't find anyone we've been tracking."

"What do you mean by that?"

"There are six members of her team I've been tracking. I cannot find any of them."

"Are there others who we should be looking for?"

"There was a pilot that Kaliastrid rescued. He was in the house before the protection was erected. I don't know where he is now."

"Can you find him?"

"No. I don't have enough of a signature on him."

"Has anyone else left? Have you missed one of the six?"

There was a pause as Rebekka could imagine the young woman checking each of the beings who were supposed to be in the building. She waited for the surprised exclamation when the girl realized he had gotten out while she was watching them. When she found him, it would save Rebekka from having to tell her how she knew.

"Not that I can tell. I cannot find any of them outside of the house."

"Are you sure?"

"Yes. But, that doesn't mean they're still in the house. That just means they're protected from scrying."

"What? I've been informed that Charles left an hour ago and is at the train station in Colmar."

Again there was silence as the young woman found the station and searched individual people. It took a few minutes.

"He's there," was the only response.

"Tell your team he is on the move and seems to be heading to Mulhouse Ville. He'll be leaving in about fifteen minutes."

"I can't track him. I had to find him visually."

Rebekka felt her disappointment rise and threaten her patience. She managed it and only delivered her response with a terse retort of, "Let them know."

"If you don't mind me asking, how did you know?"

"You don't have time for the explanation. Tell them this new information. They may have to adjust their plan now."

Rebekka disconnected before she had to deal with any followup questions.

September 9 – 0715 CET – Colmar train station, Colmar, France.

"Adrian, Charles has left the house. He's protected somehow from scrying. I can't track him. He's at the train station in Colmar and is about to leave on the commuter. He'll be in Mullhouse Ville in about thirty minutes."

Mikhala waited for a reply and almost started to send the message again when he touched her mind.

"Okay. I sent your message to Chip. I need to work though the plan with him. How did you find out if you can't find him?"

"I missed him. I was searching recent places they had all been to see if I could find them backtracking. He must have slipped out while I was somewhere else. Rebekka told me. Her other team must have already been up there and saw him leave."

She believed in admitting her mistakes. She used it to reduce the likelihood of repeating the same mistake.

"Got it. I have to stay with this. Any idea who she's working with?"

"No."

Mikhala did not expect another contact, but she was glad that he did not dwell on her error. If she had help she could have someone watch the house while others expanded her coverage area.

She refocused on her crystal and watched the train station. She could see Charles clearly, but she wanted to find any sign of Rebekka's trackers since Adrian had asked. If she found them or him, she could relax and rely on their tracking, which would be much better than continually shifting to track something that was protected from divination. As soon as she lost sight of him, she would probably never see him again until someone she was scrying directly saw him.

She scanned the crowd repeatedly over the next few minutes, looking for any sign. She knew the tail would be there, but she had only recently become aware that Rebekka had another team working for her. She had no idea who they were.

Scrying was never about sight, although it was used sometimes. Vision was weaker through the magical pipeline. Scrying and divination were more about the signature of the being, and she did not have any of the required emotional and spiritual clues. To avoid losing Charles she jumped back quickly to his location. Luckily he was a big man and was taller than most people around him.

She was glad that she returned to him when she did. He was actively trying to hide in the crowd. He was very good at staying out of sight for such a large man. She would not want to be the man assigned to follow him, but maybe she would find the tail now that Charles was actively trying to lose him. In a series of abrupt direction changes she found the follower and wondered if Charles had found him as well.

She zoomed her view out so she could watch both men to make sure she was right. Charles had stopped in a place where he could remain mostly unseen, and anyone following him would have to expose themselves. The follower stepped out, obviously worried he had lost his charge, and found himself exposed. He pretended to have lost something and turned back. In his reaction, the follower had exposed more than just his role. His emotions filled the area around him. Mikhala recognized him as a partial, but he was more somehow. She attached gently to the man, trying not to spook him. He was not expecting her help.

After a few minutes of stillness, Charles stepped away from his shadowed hiding place. Mikhala wondered what had made him move, and then she realized that almost all of the crowd reacted in unison with Charles. They were boarding the trains. Only one man moved in reaction to Charles and not the trains. His reaction verified that he was the tracker and that she had chosen correctly, if not well. Charles had really shaken his confidence, and she could suddenly sense his agitation. He was worried about losing Charles and having to report his failure. His aura felt chaotic. She wanted to release him and find someone else, but he was her best way to keep up with Charles.

"Mikhala, I'm routing Chip to the station in Mulhouse Ville. He will pick up the tail there if he can. Help him with any information you can. Jay, Walt, and Garrett will go on to Colmar. I'll follow Chip. Keep us in the game."

"Got it," she said.

She remembered the troubling image of the tracker and accessed her memory of Chip. In her personal focus, she reached out to him.

"How's it going, Chip?"

"Racing across Germany in the dark. Kinda boring, but I know that's not going to last. I'll catch them this time, and no dragon's going to stop me."

She felt the surge of excitement when he talked about the hunt. They had come close in Füssen, but Kaliastrid had stopped them dead in their tracks. Luckily she had not had time to just stop them dead. This time it looked like it was just Charles. They should have a good chance of taking him if they needed to.

"I'm tracking him as best I can. He's warded against scrying somehow. I've attached to the man tracking him and will follow them as long as I can. The train's loading and will be leaving soon."

"It's going to be tight. This van's not the fastest vehicle we could have taken, but Jay says it will help us if we need it."

The tracker boarded the train late, just as they were issuing a final boarding call. He was too nervous and trying too hard to look disinterested. He looked like he was coming down off of some kind of drug, and as he walked onto the train it became clear he was not a businessman no matter how he was dressed. It hung on him like a cheap mannequin. He might as well be wearing a sign that said "I'm not what I'm pretending to be."

"You're going to have to get there. The tracker's going to set Charles off. You'll be lucky if he doesn't abort when they get to the next station. Do you plan to take him there?"

"Negative, we need the target to stay on mission. We need to know where he's going. Is there anything you can do about that?"

"I can try, but he's not stable. Rebekka's done something to him." Irritation flared in the back of her mind at how they were treating partials.

"Do your best."

She sighed aloud and drew the attention of the other partials in the command center. One of them looked at her as if she was interrupting him.

"With respect, I could use some help. Would you send someone to the barracks and get the rest of my platoon up here?"

He considered the request, and she could see that he wanted to tell her to do it herself. He could, since he outranked her, but something clicked in his head and he snapped a quick order to another partial sitting nearby who was shuffling maps and papers around a briefing table.

Her focus on the nervous tracker spiked as his agitation filled her mind. She checked the train to see what was worrying him.

Charles was staring at him. He knew the nervous male was tracking him. Charles had shifted from prey to hunter.

"Calm down!" She sent the instruction urgently across the connection, hoping the tracker would listen.

The nervous male jumped and looked around him as if her words came from the person sitting next to him.

"What?" the man said in German to the woman near him.

She looked at him, stood up, and moved a few seats away.

"Stop. You're going to give yourself away."

His reaction was too obvious. Mikhala looked at him closely, and it started to make sense. He was untrained. He was not part of the PLA. He was a partial Rebekka had recruited on her own. She was going to make this worse if she continued to try direct contact with him.

Mikhala focused on his mind and instead of sending a message she pushed a feeling of calm to him as if she was trying to soothe a child. She sent a collection of tranquil and confident thoughts to the agitated tracker before he irritated the entire train.

Mikhala was starting to get nervous. If she messed up this tail, Rebekka would blame her even though it was her own tracker's fault. She looked up from the crystal again, maintaining the connection with a part of her mind. The King's aide was nowhere to be found.

She looked at the partial she had interrupted a few moments before. She didn't want to agitate him, but if he could contact Rebekka, he could help her.

"Excuse me, Staff Sergeant."

The partial looked up at her again.

"Do you know how to contact Rebekka, the king's consort?"

He considered her question and noted the not-so-subtle way she referred to the woman who was never far from Nethliast's side.

"Yes, what do you need?"

"I need to talk to her. She's the only one who can talk to someone I need a message sent to."

He picked up a cell phone from the table, dialed the number, and walked over to her side.

"What should I tell her?"

"Just tell her Sergeant Salenko needs to talk to her."

The ranking NCO in the command center walked away from her to make the connection. As he did, she returned to the train car. She could feel the irritation starting to spread out around the tracker. She touched each person near him and sent a calming thought. She needed to stop the wave of panic that was emanating from the man. With a quick circuit of the closest riders, she had each of them more relaxed, but she could not keep this up for twenty minutes without help.

The staff sergeant handed her the phone.

"Ma'am, this is Sergeant Salenko."

"Yes, I understood that. What is it?"

"Can you contact the man you have tracking Charles?"

"What man?"

"Ma'am, no disrespect, but please stop trying to lie to me. He's about to excite Charles and that will end badly for all of us. He needs to back off, and I can't get him to listen to me. If you can call him, he needs to either calm down or move to another car on the train."

Rebekka didn't respond immediately.

"Can you track Charles?"

"Not directly, but I can track anyone around him."

"Give me a moment. I'll call you back."

The connection broke, and Mikhala set the phone down. The staff sergeant looked at the phone, and she answered his unasked question.

"She's going to call me back. We really should have a way to stay in touch with her directly, don't you think?"

"I thought you did that."

"With partials, I can. We never included anyone other than partials and dragons. We can talk to them directly."

306

"Sounds like we found a problem in our communications system, then."

He was right, but she didn't have time to fix the problem.

She focused on the train for a moment and watched as the tracker nervously answered the phone. While he tried to take the call without letting anyone on the train know it was about them, she urged the people around him to relax. His discomfiture seemed to drop off some as Rebekka delivered her message.

The tracker stood up and quietly walked to the door at the back of the train car. He opened it and stepped through to the car behind them. Mikhala felt a sense of peace settle over everyone in the car. One woman sighed openly, and at least one other person nodded.

Charles continued to stare at the door through which the man had disappeared as if he could still see him. Mikhala could not even sense his emotions through the ward that was on him. He shifted uncomfortably in his seat and looked up at the roof of the train. She suddenly felt conscientious of her own spying. However he was protected, he also seemed to have a warning when she was just watching him. How had they warded him? She looked closely, but she could not see anything obvious.

The phone on her console rang. She reached down to retrieve it and pressed the button to answer the call.

"Salenko," she answered.

"He said you tried to calm him down, but he couldn't tell where you were."

"I did. He's not trained like our partials are."

"I told him to let you follow Charles until he gets where he's going. As soon as you know, I want to know."

"The king's guard will be joining the chase in Mulhouse."

"Good. You can use them as a focus then?"

"Yes."

"Fine. Either way, call me when you know where's he's going."

"Yes, Ma'am," Mikhala answered. The phone disconnected.

She was now on the hook to keep track of Charles, somehow. She sighed and handed the phone to the staff sergeant.

"Can you get me a phone? I'm going to need to call her again when I know more."

"Why don't you let me do my job? You route whatever this command center needs, and we'll keep the players informed through the rest of your team. They're on their way."

She relaxed a little as military order settled around her.

"That would be great."

The staff sergeant grinned and patted her hand. "Work smarter, Sergeant."

He turned and walked over to a set of movable white boards and started writing notes onto them. He looked back over his shoulder at her as if he was waiting for her to fill in what he didn't know. She organized her thoughts and started sharing the specifics of the mission and their status. He wrote as she recited names, locations, and goals.

Charles was sitting quietly staring at the door. He was as calm as she could make him. She didn't dare try to reach out to him. She had no idea how his wards would react to that.

September 9 – 0750 CET – Mulhouse Ville train station, Colmar, France.

Chip crossed the platform cautiously. He felt like he stood out anywhere he was in Europe, primarily because of his age and his Korean ancestry. To at least fit in better, he affected the look of a traveling student using what he had learned in Washington, D.C. He tossed a hand through his hair to make it look like he had just rolled out of the bed in the Youth Hostel in time to catch the commuter to his next tour stop. He didn't look at anyone directly. Instead he looked at signs as if he was trying to find his train. He was glad that his Guardian Angel was guiding him so he could focus on his role camouflage instead of his target.

"That's the train you want. He's two cars ahead of where you are," the comforting voice in his mind told him as he jiggled through the crowd. He reached the commuter and stepped up as the voice overhead was warning that the train was about to leave. As the door was closing, he slipped into the car and grabbed a seat. Most of the passengers had been getting off at this hub for business travel, but they were heading away from major towns. He had to be careful now, since the crowd had thinned.

"Where is he now?"

"He's still on the car he was on. Two ahead of you."

"He may recognize me if I go up there."

"No need. He can't get off the train without jumping unless he's at a station. I can see him because I'm tracking you, and he's on the train with you. I'm visually maintaining a connection to him because I know he's on the train. This will be impossible once he gets off. You will have to track him from there. Anything he does to hide from you will make him invisible to me. I nearly lost him at the station when he slipped into the bathroom. I was focused on the location, and he was using all sorts of shadows and corners to throw me off. I don't know if he still thinks he's being followed or not, but he's being very careful. I've had to refocus on strangers several times to keep him in sight."

"It seems that wherever he's going might be important, but I don't trust them. We're still tracking the others, right?"

"Yes, I agree. This could be a diversion. Now that my team is with me, we are watching the house as well."

"Good," Chip replied.

Chip was worried that they might be leading them on a merry chase while Meliastrid escaped. Could she be that callous about this human? Or, was she planning on trapping them one at a time? Chip remembered the encounter at the abbey. The shock of losing control of his own mind to a dragon and having her take over his actions both terrified and aggravated him.

"Is he alone?"

"I'm not sensing any other dragons with him."

Chip relaxed and rode the train, waiting for his stop. Mikhala's presence felt comforting as she looked out for him. Together they held a relaxed vigil, unsure of what would happen next when Charles did decide to exit the train.

September 9 – 0855 CET – Kruth train station, Kruth, Haut-Rhin Department, France

Charles stepped out of the train car onto a station platform not unlike stations that had covered the southern United States when train travel had been more common. This station was the terminus of the line, and several people waited to take this train back toward larger towns. Some of the passengers were walking toward cars that had been left in the parking lot, but others were walking north toward Kruth. An urgency to rush out of sight passed over him, and he realized there was nowhere to run.

To the east and across the tracks, an open field led to the Grand Rue, the main road that passed up the valley and through Kruth. Beyond it was the safety of woods and the rising walls of the mountains that made up the boundary of the Saint Amarin Valley. Beyond the station to the west he faced a similar open country with a greater distance to any real cover. Then there was the Thur River to cross. The only place he could hide right now was out in the open, and this valley had a lot of open. He turned with the crowd and started walking along the path away from the station and toward Kruth.

Kruth was one of several small villages in the valley and was part of the larger Haut-Rhin Department in the region of Alsace. Although there were nearly three quarters of a million people in the Department, only about seven thousand lived in Kruth. The crowd, which was thin enough already, would naturally thin more as he continued to walk into the village. Soon he would find out for sure if he was still being followed.

He was convinced that the nervous man in the ill-fitting suit on the first train out of Colmar was following him. Then he took the phone call and disappeared from the train entirely, which made Charles very nervous. It was like the watcher was being watched. The tracker had not returned after that. There was no doubt something far stranger was up with him, but even after he left, Charles had not been able to shake the feeling that he was being followed. It seemed that the pain and irritation in his tattoo had intensified to almost a burning for the duration of the trip from Mulhouse Ville. While he was on the train he thought it had been the close proximity of other people, plus the fact that he was sitting still and had time to pay attention to it. But, now that he was clear of the train and somewhat hidden among the passengers, the burning had subsided. He made a conscious effort to compare the pain now to the burning before, and he had no doubt that it was different.

About a quarter of a mile away from the train station, buildings clustered on either side of the road on the fringe of the village. He remembered from his research that he would have to walk through the town to get to his target. If anyone was following him, they still would not know why he was here or which town was his destination. He could still be going to any of the spur communities that surrounded Kruth, or he could be heading toward Wildenstein at the narrower head of the valley. In truth, he was not really going to Kruth.

The ward Kaliastrid had tattooed into his neck and shoulders burned and then cooled, and he noted the change. When it happened, he looked around. He was beginning to think the burning was a warning that someone was trying to find him by indirect divination. Kaliastrid had not told him that would happen. Maybe she didn't know, but as he made his way north he became more convinced that the burning indicated when someone scrying the area was looking at him. So, not only did the tattoo protect him from direct divination, it also warned him when someone was using indirect means of divination to find him.

He had crossed to the left side of Grand Rue and walked along the road among mostly white two-story buildings. He had passed what he recognized as a hotel. He couldn't be sure, but he was guessing based on context since he had never learned French. He was starting to lose the cover of the other passengers, but he still had a long way to go. He glanced at himself in the reflection in a window, but he could not see the tattoo. He had no idea how much longer the ward would work. She had told him that he would know that the protection was over when the ink vanished and left only the raw skin.

On his left, the river Thur rushed beside the road for a while, creating a tight space where the village nestled between the valley walls and the river. It was a claustrophobic section, and he immediately started scanning the surroundings for an ambush. Any other day the walk by the river would have been pleasant. His imagination tormented him as he crossed the tenth of a mile with visions of an army of partials descending on him. He tried to quicken his pace. The trees fell away from the road exposing the river, and creating the illusion of more openness. It was over a quarter of a mile before he felt the hackles lay down, and then only after the river turned off to his left and the wall of rock on his right fell away.

Suddenly realizing that anyone following him would be in the same situation, Charles decided to use it to his advantage. He stopped to look at the sign of what might be another hotel across the street. When he did, he let his peripheral vision scan the ambush zone behind him. Anyone following him would have nowhere to go. If they were well trained they would not let his change in pace or attention stop them; they would keep walking. A young man who looked as much out of place in Kruth as Charles did paused only a moment as he stopped, but it was all Charles needed. He had spotted a potential tail.

Charles turned to face him, and the young man stopped walking. He turned to look at the river as if he had seen something interesting in the rushing waters. That action removed any doubt that the Korean tourist was a tail. Now Charles had to decide what to do about it. Until he was through Kruth there was nowhere to engage him without threatening innocent lives, and Charles didn't know if he was hostile or just following him. Someone could have paid a kid who was hiking through Europe to follow him. He needed more proof before he would consider the kid a threat, but he had plenty of time to find out.

Charles turned back toward the north, shifted his pack around, and started walking again. The movement of the single strap across the center of his chest reminded him of the other surprises Kaliastrid had tattooed on his chest. They were all focused and would only affect whatever he targeted. That might be an option in this urban conflict.

Kaliastrid had warned him that the chain was simple because she only had a little time to put it together. Individually, each spell would be relatively weak, but a weak spell against a single target should be enough to give Charles a little advantage, assuming the tail turned out to be hostile. Charles was still not sure. As he walked up the sidewalk he tried to remember the chant she had used to tell him the sequence. Adrenaline was a great physical motivator, but it didn't always help with memory. That was why the Marine Corps drilled important sequences of action until they happened without thought. Recall required calm, and conflict never came with relaxation.

Charles wiped his palms on his pants legs, inhaled a deep breath, and then carefully released it through his teeth. The stress-relieving exercise should help slow his pulse and reduce the flood of adrenaline churning in his brain. He had been here before. All he had to do was breathe, count, and think.

He slipped his hand under the strap of the pack and unbuttoned his shirt over his sternum. He placed his finger on the top center charm and focused on the memory as he walked. The salt from his sweat and the pressure on the raw skin flared in his memory, taking him back to the repetitive torturous pricks of the needle.

There was only one offensive spell in the entire bundle, and it was the last one in the chain around his heart. The first was a spell to dazzle his opponent, the second would enhance his own dexterity and speed, the next would hold his opponent in place, and the last would call down lightning on his opponent. If he released them all at once, they would chain together and give him an advantage in a fight or an opportunity to escape. If he used them one at a time he could extend their usefulness, but each individual spell would have one quarter of the power available if he cast it as part of the entire spell chain. He had no idea how to measure that difference since he had never seen the whole chain executed. He didn't like the idea of unleashing lightning in the middle of Kruth.

Now he still had to determine if the young man behind him was a threat or just a patsy. The village was starting to close in more as he reached the center on the main road. There was a cafe and what looked like a general store at an intersection. A church graced the next turn. He could try to disappear among the increased foot traffic and shelves of the general store, but there was no guarantee since it seemed his followers had some type of surveillance support.

Charles mindlessly perused the outdoor shelves of the convenience style grocer. A children's insect collection set with its magnifying lens reminded him of the lens Elaine had handed him with the note. It was supposed to help him see magic, but no one had actually proved that it worked. That was part of his mission. He was supposed to use it to search for anything that might lead to the talisman when he reached his destination. He refused to think about where he was going. It was a technique he had used before to protect himself from interrogation.

He reached into his cargo pocket and pulled out the lens. It was the size of his hand and difficult to hold between his thumb and middle finger. It was awkward to use without getting fingerprints all over it. He wanted to polish it clean, but instead, he focused on figuring out how best to use it without dropping it. At the window of the general store, he paused as if looking at something. Out of the corner of his eye the young Asian man stopped to look at a particularly interesting section of wooden fence. Charles turned and raised his right hand much like he would to take a picture, except instead of a camera, he had the lens. As soon as he could see the young man through it, his situation was very clear. The soft recon had just become a hard probe. The young Asian man staring at the wall was not what he appeared to be. The lens showed him to be a slightly taller, fully armored partial dragon.

Charles pocketed the lens, forgetting about the smudges, and turned toward the north. He could now report to Kaliastrid that it did exactly what she thought it did. He tried to keep his realization that his pursuer was a partial from changing his pace and triggering the release of another batch of adrenaline, but failed. His flight instinct had kicked in, and it was not paying any attention to his attempts to remain calm as he walked north away from the shop. He had to get his reaction under control or he could spook the partial into attacking. He didn't know what his instructions were, but, because he had not attacked when Charles had blown his cover, he must still be curious about where he was going. That was exactly what Charles didn't need. He would have to try to ditch him somehow, but there were still too many innocents around for a firefight of any sort. Between the village and his goal there might be an opening where he could turn and fight. Charles finally surrendered to his pace increase as he walked past a hotel, a tavern, and the church.

For the next ten minutes he let the bulk of the village pass by without notice. He knew he was being pursued. He knew there was at least one partial. He knew there was no way he could stand against him in a hand to hand fight. As the village started to fall away and he could see more of the valley ahead of him, his target became obvious and his ability to see it as just an objective vanished. Now he had to consider specifically how he was going to get to it. He could not see the man-made dam that bound up the Thur River and created the lake at Kruth-Wildenstein, but he could see the glacial deposit that formed an elliptical hump in the middle of the valley ahead of him. Back at the church he could only see the nondescript buildings that made up Kruth, but now the Schlossberg was a prominence standing in line with the road, filling a large portion of what he saw ahead of him. He could sense why it had been selected as an appropriate point in the valley to build a castle. The Schlossberg, so named because of the castle that had once sat atop the moraine, was a lone outpost between the enclosing mountain ridges. It would have commanded the valley.

It was that castle, or its ruins, that Charles had come to find. Once he reached them, he had no idea what he was supposed to be looking for, but the lens was supposed to help. His first goal was to reach the ruins. He would deal with the second objective once he had accomplished the first.

The village was mostly behind him. The target was getting closer, and he could not lead his tracker to the goal. A fight was inevitable unless they wanted him to abort. He still had time to make this look like a diversion into the wilds of France. In preparation for the fight, Charles slid the pack around in front of him to retrieve the piece of equipment he had asked the armorer to locate back in Oak Ridge. Inside the long zippered front pocket of his pack was a faithful piece of equipment that had earned fame in the Vietnam War. He had used its cousin slung under his rifle in the gulf. The single shot M-79 grenade launcher was the right size to disappear into his backpack, gave him explosive and high damage munitions he could carry in his hand, and would wound a dragon. He was not sure about killing yet, but he expected he would find out. Most of the rest of the pack was loaded with round canister grenades for it.

His ubiquitous pistol and extra ammo was packed in his gear in the car. He had retired it after he had emptied it twice into the face and chest of the half-dragon back at the abbey and hadn't even really delayed him. It felt odd not to be wearing it, but this new world required new habits. He was not convinced this was the best weapon combination for the fight ahead of them, but it was a start. He had brought a few other hard-hitting surprises Silas had thought to pack for their trip as well, but they had a specific use.

Charles didn't feel prepared for the fight to come. This was supposed to be a recon, so he had left a lot of firepower back at the house. He was not as convinced about the magic tools Kaliastrid had given him, but he would give anything a chance. He had seen what Elaine and Aldrich had been able to do, so he would at least give the chain of spells tattooed on his chest a chance. He had not yet decided which one he was going to use as his opening salvo.

According to her note, Melissa thought they would be able to keep Nethliast's attention focused on them. They needed time for Silas to heal. As long as Nethliast was not sure what she was doing, he would not attack. Charles was not sure her assumptions were correct.

The thought of the injured agent made him wonder how Aldrich was doing. When he had left, he was still wrestling with some invisible force to heal Silas' injuries and had a lot further to go. They had taxed Aldrich over the past twenty-four hours. The fact that Charles just accepted the priest's ability to heal them spoke volumes about how far down the rabbit hole he had come.

Charles compartmentalized the random thoughts by reminding himself that he was still being followed. He put those he loved into the box in the back of his heart where he would pull them out when his mission was over. He focused on the game he was playing until he was in a position to lose his tail or take the offensive. This particular type of cat and mouse mission was the reason he had never been a recon scout. He didn't have the patience for sneaking around. He had always preferred the strong offensive actions, and he was about to prove why.

In another hundred meters he would be out of the village and into a clear area of fields at the base of the Schlossberg. In that open area he would have no choice but take the offensive or change directions. It would be pretty clear where he was going, if it wasn't already. As he continued walking he keyed the mic for his radio and started talking. They should have been listening for his call.

"I'm being followed. He's been with me since I left Mulhouse. I'm not sure if he knows where I'm going, but somehow, we've been made. I think they followed me from the house somehow." He spoke quickly into the throat mike hidden by his shirt.

"Did you use the first package we gave you?" Kaliastrid responded.

"Yes."

"And, what did it do?"

"There's no doubt. He's a partial."

"Exactly what I thought. Don't lose it. You'll need it when you get there."

"Roger that. So you want me to continue?"

"We had hoped for a little more time," was her only response.

Nothing new. He was used to being out in front. Charles inhaled and shifted his pack as he kept walking.

"I think he's one of the five that came after us at the library in Füssen. If that's the case he's probably not alone."

"We're on our way to back you up. I'll tell the others we have to move up the timetable. We held them as long as we could. Maybe it will be enough."

"How's Silas doing?"

"He's up and eating. He swears he's ready, but Aldrich's not convinced. They both look weak."

"The farther I go up this valley, the more cut off I get. I may have to turn and fight. I don't want to get cut off from an escape route. I have no more intel than when I left."

"I'd say you're already cut off," Kaliastrid called back. "That's why we're on our way. They can't track me as easily in the air."

"We?"

"Yes, tell me when you hear the helicopter."

"Really? Then, I'm done sneaking around. No better time to put some distance between me and my tail," Charles responded, not waiting for her answer. It was not a question.

He looked back over his shoulder at the young man. He was just stepping out beyond the last two buildings on either side of Grand Rue. On Charles' right, he was passing a nicely manicured garden that lead along the left side of a driveway to what looked like a single residence on the very edge of town. It would have to do. Charles stopped and turned to face him. The youth didn't turn away this time. Instead, he stopped and smiled at Charles. They both knew what was up. The prey and the hunter had met, but Charles was not sure the youth understood which one he was. With one last quick glance, Charles scanned for any sign of innocent bystanders. They were alone. He slipped his hand into his shirt and touched the center point of the tattoo. In his mind he found the command word she had taught him with pain and repetition. He released the stock of the M-79, pointed his left hand out at the young man, and spoke the command.

The searing pain in his chest was nothing at all like he expected. Apparently she had never actually experienced this form of using magic. It felt like someone ripping barbed wired out of his chest in a counter-clockwise circle as each spell triggered in sequence.

The release was silent. The first spell had struck. The young man seemed to lose focus. His defense mechanism triggered a transition into his full partial form, which verified the lens' accuracy. Charles felt a rush of energy infuse his body as the second spell silently ripped from his chest. His muscles felt relieved, and all fatigue from the stressful morning operation vanished. It helped since the pain was threatening to double him over. If he had ever done this before, he might have thought twice about doing it again. He could not imagine some of the examples she had described of the longer, more intricate, spells crafted into tattoos. The dazed partial was not moving anymore, which indicated the third spell was cast as silently as the first two. Charles felt a sudden pang of guilt as he knew what was coming and his opponent had no way to defend. Any hope of defense had been lost after the first and third spell had triggered.

Lightning flashed from Charles' hand and struck the stationary partial in the chest. The bolt was not silent, but it was nothing like the explosive noise of war. It slammed into his scales and burned away the shirt he had been wearing. His arms twitched in response to the electrical overload that was surging through his body and into the ground. His fists were clenching and releasing in a spastic pattern. Finally, he crumpled to the ground under the thunder that exploded from where he was standing. The menacing sound rolled down either side of the valley.

Charles didn't pause to check his results. There was no reason. His strength and dexterity were enhanced. It was time to put some distance between him and any other partials who might be backing up his tail. The fire in his neck told him someone else was watching him closely again. He had to see if he could get away from them.

He pulled the M-79 out of his pack as he ran, in case there were others moving up behind him. He could not face a partial toe to toe and win. He had seen that on the first day of the emergence when Nethliast had fought him in his semi-human form. He had not even been full strength at the time. Charles didn't want to repeat that type of fight even with increased strength and dexterity. His best option was to put some distance between himself and any followers. His feet pounded on the road, trying to clear the five hundred meters to the edge of the cover ahead of him. He would have to run to the far end of the Schlossberg to climb up to the castle. Most of the other approaches were too challenging, which is probably why they built the castle there in the first place. His first goal was to disappear. Once he was in the tree cover he could slow down. He just hoped the enhanced strength would hold out long enough for him to get the distance he needed.

He pushed himself harder to make the tree line. Once he was there he paused to look behind him and try to get his breathing under control. The fire in his neck was gone again, and he was not sure if it was because they could not see him anymore or because his protection had run out.

September 9 – 0945 CET – In the Swiss Alps

"Chip, look out!"

Mikhala's alarmed warning was out loud and too late. The entire command center looked up to see what was happening. There was no way for her to see the magic as it flowed between the two of them, but she knew it had dazed Chip before she could warn him. He was not responding or moving. He needed to run, now.

"Adrian. It's a trap. Charles has attacked Chip. With magic."

"Charles is not a partial. He's not a dragon. How?"

"It looks like he used something. A magical item of some sort. He's wearing it under his shirt. Oh, Sweet Bridgid, he's killed Chip."

She was watching the lightning rip into Chip even as her connection to him shifted to the valley. She could not attach to Charles, and there was no one else around. Her target and her answer was running north out of her view. She trembled as she watched another friend die, unable to help or follow his killer.

Adrian did not react. She didn't dare shift to him because she would lose track of Charles, whom she was chasing as well as she could.

"He's running for the woods to the north of Kruth. He's on foot. You need to get there."

"Can you track him?"

"No. He's fast and knows how to use cover to his advantage. I almost lost him in the train station, but now he has the advantage of natural cover. There's no one else there for me to use to track him. As soon as he's out of sight, he's gone."

"He's outside now? Where do you think he's heading? If he decided to strike now, there's a reason. He's walking. His target must be close. He's trying to get clear."

"What if it was just a trap? What if he's a diversion?" she asked.

She was taking long breaths to get her emotions under control.

"Kaliastrid's on the move. So is Meliastrid. Where are they going?"

Mikhala looked up from her sphere. Her platoon should have told her that already.

"Track Meliastrid and Kaliastrid. They've left the house. Why didn't I know?"

Her team looked to her. Kara looked suddenly overwhelmed, but recovered immediately.

"It just occurred as you were dealing with Chip. You were busy."

"Not that busy. I need to know what's happening before they do in the field, or soldiers die."

Mikhala refocused on Charles and the valley just as he entered the trees. She lost him.

"He's lost in the trees."

"Mikhala, think. Why are they coming here? Why is he here at all?"

319

She looked around for any indication of what they might be looking for in the pastoral valley in France.

"Kaliastrid is heading southwest from the house. She's heading toward the valley," one of the top tier Angels called up to her and passed an image to verify the contact.

"Meliastrid is heading southeast," another Angel added with her own image. Her platoon was over their malaise.

"Kaliastrid seems to be coming to help Charles. Meliastrid is heading back toward Germany."

"Jay reported that they are using radios. They're encrypted. He's trying to break it. They agree with your assessment. Let me know if either changes direction."

"There's a helicopter at the house. The others are loading boxes and getting in," a voice from the pod of spheres called.

"Let me know which way they depart," Mikhala said.

"Adrian, they're loading a helicopter at the house. Something is definitely up."

"Walt and Garrett are checking on it."

Mikhala watched the trees again, scanning the road that continued north. It passed between a hump of rock and the mountain wall that formed the valley. There was a lake on the other side of the solitary rise. The waters of the Thur had been dammed up by an earthen dam to create the lake. It appeared that it was a sporting location in the summer. There was no reason for Charles to be walking up this valley. Meliastrid was heading east, and Kasliastrid was going west to support Charles. Mikhala thought through what she knew about their last attacks.

She scanned the edge of the water close to the sloping wall formed by the oval of rock covered by trees. She zoomed out to see more of the valley. There had to be some reason Charles was on his way there and the others waited behind. The dragons could fly to support him if he needed help, but the other humans had to drive. They knew they were being watched and had limited time. They needed the helicopter, but that would not take all night. They were healing the other man, the agent who had shot Nethliast. It just made sense that they were going to join Charles.

There was a reason in the valley, and Charles was close to it. She zoomed back in using his last known position as a corner for her search. To his northwest was the hill and lake. To his northeast was a higher valley wall and forest. She focused on the lake. As she zoomed her view into the valley, a cleared area on top of the mound in the middle of the valley caught her attention. There were ruins near the top.

In her head she shouted, but she controlled her contact with Adrian. They had spent a while in the Abbey of Saint Mang in Füssen while Meliastrid was trying to kill Nethliast.

"What if they're looking for ruins?"
There was no immediate response.
"Where?"

September 9 – 0957 CET – Kruth, Haut-Rhin Departmemt, France

Adrian jumped out of the front seat of the Humvee as it rolled to a stop at the edge of town. He had left the base in Füssen in his dragon form and had never shifted back. If Mikhala was right that they were heading for the ruins on the Schlossberg, he had time to check on his friend. He dreaded what he was going to find and felt the tendrils of panic eating at his focus as he rushed across the short distance. He marshaled his parents back from their edge as he stepped up next to the body. There was little doubt of his condition. There had been massive power directed into his torso where his shirt had been incinerated and burns covered his entire chest. His fists were alternately clasped in a tight fist and extended fully with fingers reaching out in a wide fan. Adrian knew immediately that the young boy he had first met after becoming a partial dragon, whom had become his friend and watched his back through the training and beyond, was dead. His dragon eyes, damaged by the physical reaction to the energy that passed through his body, stared blankly into the morning sky. Adrian ran his fingers across the lids and closed them for the last time. His parents fought in the depths of his mind, each struggling to run away or just stop and wait for someone else to deal with this. Adrian shook them both off and allowed his anger to flare.

He sniffed at the air. The smells were all strong, but he picked up the human odor of the man who had led his friend into the trap that killed him. That smell he cataloged. He would remember it until he found it, then he would repay the man who had done this, in kind.

Resolute that he was not leaving anyone behind, Adrian reached down and pulled Chip up and over his shoulder in a fireman's carry they had taught him in training. In his partial form, it was not a heavy load at all. He was back at the Humvee in a couple of steps. He rolled the body into the back and walked on around the vehicle to get back into the driver's seat. He sat down hard, releasing only a little of his anger into the inanimate springs. He wanted a chance to give some of it back to the man who had killed his friend, but he couldn't go into this emotionally. He had to stay focused or they would draw him in like they had Chip.

"Do you still think this is a diversion? Is it a trap?"

"No, there's something to this location. The helicopter is the proof. It's on the way to meet him. The only one heading east is Meliastrid. She's the diversion."

Adrian put the Humvee in drive and accelerated toward the site Mikhala had described to him. Charles was on foot but well ahead of him now. Adrian could catch him still, but following his orders might be tougher now.

The road was mostly deserted. It was too early in late summer for much activity at the lake. There might be other hikers, but it was also late in the season. He didn't spare the speed, and he rushed down the tight gap between the moraine and the mountain. He teased the breaks and roared into the parking lot near the road trail that led up the mountain to the ruins. Again, he was out of the Humvee before it was completely stopped.

"Do you see him?"

"No," she replied. *"He's using the cover well. Since I can't scry him, I can't find him unless you're near where he is."*

"Well, then. Let's go find him. Get everyone else here. I expect this is what Nethliast is looking for. Tell them where we are and that I need orders. It looks like they are looking for something up here."

"They're already on their way. Rebekka is coming with the reinforcements. Nethliast has been directed there from his original path to Colmar. They timed this well. We were all headed to Colmar until they broke for the valley. We're out of pocket."

"Get me orders. I need to know what to do now that they are moving."

Adrian pushed his transformation to a final step he had been practicing since Washington. He had known some partials who could take their already threatening appearance and make it even more severe. From what he could tell, it was like the capabilities of several species of birds where the male used plumage to attract a mate and to scare off predators. His already aggressive looking partial form shifted slightly by increasing the already existing spines running up his arms into spikes and creating a pronounced ridge up his back that joined his flaring armor at his shoulders. He let his tail swish out behind him. He was not about to face this dangerous man unprepared. He opened his mouth and inhaled sharply as he looked up the side of the ancient glacial deposit. The air that danced over his tongue tasted of many things. Once he filtered the natural scents of the woods and the water, what was left was mostly human. One scent in particular was fresh. It was human too, but it smelled slightly of fear and blood.

"Stop Charles. Capture if you can. Kill otherwise."

Adrian knew that the orders probably were not that clear when she had received them. He could tell there was more information behind what she had reported. She was feeling the stress, and it was getting through to the troops. He couldn't blame her.

"You may need this," Mikhala said and sent him a topographical image of the Schlossberg. He now knew that meant "castle hill" and was probably why they were looking here. He focused on his orders and the man he was following.

"I smell you," Adrian shouted. "I know you're up there." He charged down the roadway trail that led down beside the water before it turned up the Schlossberg toward the castle that had been. He wondered as he ran what had attracted them to this place and what they were looking for. It didn't really matter. They were going to die for it. Well, he was, anyway. Nethliast had told him to kill the butler.

September 9 – 1020 CET – Chateau de Wildenstein, Haut-Rhin, France

Charles looked at his watch as he hunkered in the deep growth that covered most of the moraine. He had abandoned the old trail in hope of slowing down pursuit and was resting on a rise looking down on the trail he had left one hundred yards before. If Kaliastrid and the others were on their way to him, he needed to buy them some time. Traveling through the brush and trees slowed him down too, but it was a way to even out the odds a little. The shouting of the partial had given him all the clue he needed that the hunt was on again, but he planned on keeping them defensive as long as he could. Kaliastrid's comment about the helicopter told him that there had been a second mission underway while he was on this recon. Melissa had used him as a decoy, but it made sense. She needed to have someone here to secure the site while they kept the rest of the force in reserve until the last minute. He hoped the ploy was working, but he needed to check in. A nagging irritation at being left out of the planning made him nervous.

"Blackjack, this is Boy Scout. Are you out there?" He decided to keep Silas' assigned call sign.

"I read you, and I'm on my way to your location. I'm keeping low to mask my approach. I'm blind without a longbow helping me out. What's the landscape like down there?"

He didn't mean what the hills looked like.

"Assuming direct from base, check the north ridge of the mountain next to the lake in the middle of the valley as you enter the area. You have one tango in the weeds. I'm above him on the same ridge. I have no view of any other tangos. Do I need to pop smoke?"

"Negative, Boy Scout. Your tango is below my LZ. I'm only a slick today. I'm in and out."

"Roger that. Who's with you?"

"Spook told me to tell you we have Spook, Doc, and Alex on board. Killer's on overwatch. Puff has a different mission. We're a few minutes out."

"Boy Scout, I read your contact with Blackjack," Kaliastrid replied, letting him know she was listening. "We're watching for other dragons. We know they have ground reinforcements on the way, but we hope we can get this done before they all get here. If not, we need to hold the high ground."

Charles understood the plan, if that was what one could call this. If he could get rid of his last pursuer, he could start the search. If that worked they could use the chopper to get out. From his hiding place he could still see the old cart trail that led up the slope from the valley floor on the north side of the moraine. He shifted the launcher around so that it was pointed toward the trail. From his pack he laid out a backup round. He checked the color coded striping and smiled. This was no pistol. Soon he would test how partials stood up to high explosive rounds.

Movement down the trail drew his attention. He lifted the tube of the launcher up and snugged the wooden stock against his body. The partial was sniffing at the air to find which way he had gone. The elevation sight was set for the approximate distance to the trail. The partial was starting to zero in on the direction. Charles' breathing would not affect his aim on this type of shot, but he still waited for the low ebb before he squeezed the trigger. The hollow, metallic thump of the metal tube as the round left it filled the air and sent birds into the sky.

In the instant that the shell traveled toward him, the target's aggressive smile turned to anger. He flung himself downhill away from the attack. The high explosive grenade shattered a tree that was just behind the fleeing partial and sent leaves, rock, dirt, and shards of wood chasing after him. The explosive wave caught the partial and added force to his leap. The accelerated body slammed into the downhill slope covered with rocks and trees. A tree stopped his flight, and he crumpled to the ground. With conscious effort his pursuer rolled behind the cover of a rock. Charles sent the second round into the area of the tree where the partial had hit and abandoned his firing position. He didn't wait to see if the lone partial was getting up. If he survived the explosion, he would think twice about coming after him alone. Charles had scattered his pursuing force. Now he had to find another defensive position until reinforcements caught up. He jumped a few downed trees and continued to climb the spine toward the ruins.

At the top of the ridge the first line of defense for the old Wildenstein castle appeared. There had been a double drawbridge system that crossed a dry moat. The towers above would have provided cover to the closest bridge. The guard house or barbican that sat in the middle of the two bridges provided the first obstacle to entering the castle. If they made it through the central guard house, any attackers would have to get through a cave cut into the rock to get into the courtyard. Steep walls of rock stretched to the left and right of the entrance.

All that remained of the old defenses were a few low walls that had been recovered in recent attempts to revitalize the site's long forgotten stone constructions. Anyone who wanted in now could just drop into the ditches that surround the old foundations and follow more recent dirt paths to the entrance to the cave. They weren't trying to keep people out anymore; they had to make it easier for tourists to get into the castle. Even with the somewhat improved paths, the walk through the moat and back out the other side was not an easy approach.

"What's happening down there?" Kaliastrid asked. "I see smoke coming up from the north side of the hill."

"I had to put his head down. Tried to take it off. I'm not positive that he's dead, but I tried. I've moved farther up looking for a safe hiding place that I can defend." He continued his report even though there was a chance they were tracking his transmissions. They had more than one partial following him, but it seemed reactive so it was not likely that they had enough gear in the field to narrow his location down to this mountain. He had already done that by attacking. The radios were encrypted, but that didn't mean much if they had the right gear.

"Just get inside and see what you can find. I'll see where he's at. Maybe I can keep him off your back," Kaliastrid called back.

As Charles scrambled down into the ditches that circled the old drawbridge foundations and led to the entrance, he pulled a pair of surprises out of the bottom of his pack. Given the chance, he was going to give as good as he got.

Ten feet from where he entered the ditch, he drove the thin metal spikes of the first claymore into the dirt in front of the old support for the bridge. It faced the path that led into the ditch and would shower anyone approaching from that direction with a lethal combination of explosive force and ball bearings.

Following the path to the left he climbed up toward the cave that still forced everyone to walk through a funnel to get into the castle. At the base of the stairs and facing out across the last ditch, he placed and armed the last claymore. They served two purposes. Anyone caught in the blast should be killed, and the explosion when they were set off would act as an alarm and tell them when someone was coming through this entrance.

"Boy Scout, your target is down and not moving. He's not dead, and I can't get to him. I'm coming up to join you. Get into the castle, and I'll help you defend until everyone gets there."

"Puff reports more partials on the way," Blackjack broke in. "Two APCs and a radio truck. It's a platoon-sized force. No sign of dragons yet. We're running out of time."

"Roger," Charles responded.

Leaving his last charge behind, he walked up the stairs and into the rounded out cave. It was wide enough to allow small donkey carts into the castle, so he had no problem walking up through the incline. As he stepped out into the light at the top of the cave, Kaliastrid stepped into view. She was covered in beautiful emerald scales that looked like elegant plate armor. Her face was clearly visible, surrounded by plates of black and green. Five thumb-sized horns created a widow's peak that dropped down to where her eyebrows would have been. She grinned at him.

"You look better than I expected. Are you having fun yet?" she asked.

He smiled and answered, "You don't look so bad yourself. Maybe we like this part more than we should. Blackjack, the top is clear. Bring them in before we lose the window."

"Roger," the pilot responded. The familiar noise of the helicopter climbed over the northeastern ridge. The echo of the rotors spread through the valley, making it hard to tell where they were.

"So, what's really on the way here?"

"Melissa seems to think Nethliast is coming. She's picking up his emotions like she did back home. The amulet warned her again, but she's not sure so she's not reporting that."

He looked down at the grenade launcher and slid it back over his shoulder. "This is not going to hold off a platoon of partials with dragon air support."

He pulled out the lens and pointed at the expanse of grass and stone that spread out around and above them. "You still think we're going to find something up here?"

"Go find out while I close this back door."

"Stay out of the trenches and away from the bottom of the stairs."

Kaliastrid nodded and turned to head down into the cave, leaving him with his doubts as he looked around the ruins. A waist-high wall stretched along the entire eastern side of the ridge. He knew from his approach that the eastern side dropped precariously down to a parking lot and road. There was no approaching the castle from that side, but that left three approaches to defend. The cave behind them created a natural barrier, so that left the southern and western approaches.

The southern approach was not a cliff like the eastern side. It was rounded, steep, and heavily wooded. It would be difficult to climb that side, but it was the most direct route to assault the moraine. It would expose their forces to the least time in the open before they could engage. The western side was an easier approach, but there was no way to reach it without being seen. None of the approaches were easy, but Charles expected they would come at them from the south while flanking to come up the north and western approach. They could only assault the eastern side from the air. The western side was the least risky of the remaining options. Air assault could take advantage of it, but it was mostly the high ground at their backs and a place to fall back to. The southern end was also higher than the north, so they would need to hold it as long as they could. If their force came at them from the lake and village side they could overwhelm them. Charles reviewed his tactical analysis again and considered the forces they had to work with. He would not have enough people to defend the openings. They would need to stop their attackers in the valley and keep them away from the north and western sides.

With his tactical plan forming in his mind, he reviewed any weaknesses. There was a break in the eastern wall where a tower had once stood. It created a slit in the wall that fell down toward the road. It would take a lot of effort to get a force up to that opening, and they would be exposed once they were in it. It was still a weakness, so he cataloged it in his mind and continued his analysis. The total absence of walls above knee high anywhere around the top of the moraine meant that they could not allow them to get a foothold on the top. They would be protected from attacks from the valley floor if they used the walls to their advantage.

On his right, the hill continued to rise and form the second level of the old castle. If he continued to the south, he was sure he would find some way to get up to that second level and to the tower foundations that looked over the old barbican. They wanted to hold the high ground. If they wanted to escape by air, though, the middle courtyard was the only approach for the helicopter.

As if to emphasize his analysis, the increased down blast of air from the helicopter drew Charles' attention as Blackjack expertly flew over the bulge in the ground at tree level. He had come over them from northwest to southeast and hovered over the drop-off on the eastern side. He spun the Blackhawk around until he was parallel with the wall facing south and then skidded the bird to his right. He couldn't see directly below him as he slid the bird delicately over the wall until the left wheel was just above it. He settled it gently until the rubber of his left wheel was sitting on top of the stone. He was facing south, which was his fastest and most direct exit path even though it was uphill. He could drop to his left and continue south down the valley without anything getting in his way.

The only feature in the ruins that was man-made and taller than waist high was an old room or foundation that had been cut into the hillside. It opened out into the middle courtyard where he was standing. While the passengers on the helicopter moved gear and each other around to exit, Charles held the lens up and looked at the back wall that was the stone of the actual hillside and would have been here as long as the castle had. He inhaled as the first magical sign jumped out at him like white graffiti spray painted onto the gray stone. He dropped his hand, blinked, and brought the lens back up to see if it appeared again. It neither disappeared nor changed. The script was a foreign collection of runes. It reminded him of a combination of Kilroy signs left all over Europe during World War II and the unreadable Abjad scrawled on walls throughout combat zones in Iraq. As he continued to look at the wall he could see other symbols. What had at first looked like solid letters now shimmered in the lens. The door in the helicopter slid open to disgorge its passengers and drew his attention away from the new discovery.

The right wheel was not on the ground at all, but the step down was not more than four feet. Elaine, who looked entirely too excited for the danger that was on the way, jumped out and landed on both feet. She stepped one step forward, dropped into a crouch, and walked away from the helicopter toward Charles with her head down. Her red hair danced around in the chaotic currents of air stirred by the hillside that rose away from their landing area. She was again attired in her preferred peasant blouse, a red and green corset, and blue jeans. She looked very natural in the outfit for all of its intentional anachronism. She even paused to smile and waved at him as if she was at an amusement park. Her smile broadened as she took in what were probably the first ruins she had ever seen. Already large eyes grew larger to drink it all in. She didn't belong in this combat zone. This was not a good idea.

Silas jumped down in a similar fashion with a light tactical backpack slung over both arms. Aldrich rolled his legs over the edge to let them dangle before he dropped half his height to the ground. Silas turned back to reach up into the bay and grab a pair of matching Pelican cases. Charles was glad to see them. They contained the upgraded revolver versions of the M-79, the Hawk Engineering MM1. The two portable artillery pieces would be the base of their defense against any dragons. As he looked at how small their arsenal was, he wished they had thought to bring the Mark 19 or anything else to augment what they had. An organized platoon could overrun them if they were not careful.

He forced himself to stow the negative thoughts and focus on what they had instead of what they needed. Silas returned one last time to the bay to grab a wooden crate of ammunition.

The agent/major looked a little gray as he carried the crate a few steps past the helicopter blades. His cocky grin was subdued a little. Aldrich also looked a little solemn. They would not be at full capacity in this fight.

Elaine reached him first with a youthful jump.

"Isn't this amazing?"

Charles nodded and looked at Blackjack, who was visually clearing his departure before throttling up.

Silas and Aldrich slumped over toward Charles. The pitch of the Blackhawk's whine increased, and the rotor wash became heavier for a moment before it climbed from the edge. Blackjack kept the tail and nose straight but dipped the rotors to the left to clear the area as fast as he could without bringing the tail around toward the troops he had just dropped off. When he was clear of trees, rocks, and people he dipped the nose and departed down the valley to the south. As soon as he had broad valley beneath him, he turned to the west and started a climbing turn back to the north.

"Boy Scout, I'm heading back to a staging point to wait your call I just heard a report that someone picked up a slow-moving, low-altitude air target. AA units are on alert but none of them can track it. It's skimming the valleys headed north. I can't stand against a dragon in this. No firepower. Call me if you need me. I'll see if I can't slip back in here and pull you out when you're ready."

"Could you do a recon pass south and tell us what you see?"

"Affirmative."

As the response came back to them the Blackhawk was completing his turn. He cut across the top of the moraine and accelerated to the south just above the trees hugging the eastern wall of the valley.

Charles nodded as the tail of the chopper passed over their heads. He waved a departing salute at the helicopter and felt the same feeling he had felt every time he had walked off the back ramp of the Ospreys in the Gulf. War was coming.

Silas was opening the crate and pulling out bandoleers of 40 mm grenades. From the color coding he could see that they were heavy on the high explosive versions. There were a few other surprises thrown in. Charles let him deal with that while he returned to his current task.

Kaliastrid walked back out of the cave as Melissa was landing in the upper courtyard of the castle. She transformed into her human-dragon form gracefully and walked through what had been the inner curtain wall that divided the middle courtyard from the upper level. There would have been a defensive door of some sort there in the past. Charles wished it was still in place to help hold back what was coming.

She was agitated. The look on her face showed that she had been in battle before, but the young woman she had been a few months before was showing through the cracks in her face of stone. She knew what was coming.

"Found anything?" she asked, hopeful but not expecting.

"Several runes you can't see without this." He held up the lens. "I expect they're magical, but how am I to know?"

"Really? Show me."

She looked toward the rectangular foundation cut out of the hillside where he was pointing. Aldrich and Elaine moved immediately to join him.

He held the lens out and pointed to the place on the wall where he had seen the writing.

She took the lens and stared at the glyph he had indicated.

"You see it?"

"Yeah, it looks like Norse and something else. Where are the others?"

He pointed at the others on the side walls.

"The entrance is blocked," Kaliastrid said as she walked up to join them. "If they come, they'll have a hard time getting in here that way."

"You warded it?" Melissa asked.

"As best I could. It will not hold, but I also put up a barrier over the entrance."

"Our biggest threat is that they can come at us from all sides except one," Charles started his brief. "If they have any military sense at all, they'll know better than come up through the funnel. The back side is the easiest approach, but it leads to that cave. If they come at us from the south, which seems likely, they can't get to the north approach without flanking us. If they can get to the north side, they can get troops to the western side and above us. I expect they will send some forces straight at us up the south face while others flank toward the northern climb. They won't have time to take the western side unless they choose to delay. If they do, we will be able to get what we came for and get out of here. All of that is assuming they don't drop airborne troops in carried here by dragons."

Both Melissa and Kaliastrid blanched, and Melissa answered for both of them, "Dragons are not horses. We don't carry soldiers into combat. We are the airborne assault."

"Then, from what we can tell, we only have to worry about one airborne unit."

They both shrugged. Neither would commit to how many dragons would be involved.

"Let's focus on figuring out what we've found. You and Silas, set up our defenses," Melissa suggested.

Charles nodded with actual relief and handed the lens to Melissa.

"Before you go, show me the others. Elaine, Aldrich, come take a look at these."

He walked across the opening and pointed to the place on the wall he remembered. "Somewhere in here."

She focused on the wall a few steps out, and then leaned in closer when she could see the glyph. "This one's different. I think its elven."

"Elven. Where?" Aldrich asked as he walked around Charles. Elaine was beside him but focused on the wall.

Charles felt a tremor of worry for her. There was a good chance that they would have to fight their way off of the moraine. Innocence was always the first casualty of any battle, and hers would certainly not survive this one. Battle would change her; it changed everyone. If she survived, and there was a possibility that she might not, he hoped that her experience would change her for the better. There was no way to predict until the battle was over, and even then it had more to do with her. The conditions of the fight would set up her reaction. It was all based on how she witnessed the action.

Again Charles forced negative thoughts down and reminded himself that, for the moment, her innocence was still safe. He hoped— for a brief instant—that she would be spared, but he could not see how they would get out of this without a fight. She could read the concern on his face as she looked over at him and winked to put him at ease. It didn't work.

"Boy Scout, Ghost, this is Blackjack. I have verification of the original report. You have two, I say again, two troop carriers loaded with partials coming your way. They are not 10 minutes out. No air support that I see, or at least I can't spot him where they're reporting him. The radio van's there too. Looks like all German equipment."

Melissa and Kaliastrid looked up from the wall and at him. He raised an eyebrow and angled his head toward Silas. Melissa nodded, and Kaliastrid broke off from the search.

"I'm useless here as well. I'm going to get into the air to keep an eye on things."

Charles backed away from the trio, watching how Elaine and Melissa were intent on the wall. Elaine and Aldrich were in their element. Melissa was focused on finding her grandmother's clues. Charles felt a thrill as he watched both of them. That changed into worry as he realized he was about to engage in combat with two women he cared for at risk. There was a finality to what was coming at them and he suddenly realized that one or both of them, or even he, could fall today.

Charles watched them point and describe with hand motions what he knew was there but couldn't see. He suddenly realized how analogous that was to their relationship. If they survived this day, he would not let another day pass between them without admitting how he felt. He and Melissa had closed out any possibility of their ever being anything between them back in the plane, but that didn't change the fact that he still felt an ache whenever he looked at her. Elaine was in love with him, but he had pushed her away. Each day was precious, and he had forgotten how true that was in the peaceful walls of Helena's estate. If they survived, he would not let the feelings he had go without a voice, if he could just figure out which voice needed to speak.

"This may be exactly what we're looking for," Aldrich answered as he took the lens from Melissa to look closer. His positive attitude was tinged with a layer of fatigue, but he tried to hide it. They were all tired, but this man had struggled with magical forces all night to save another man's life. Charles was impressed and wondered where his energy was coming from.

"My, what an amazing lens. Where did we find this?" Aldrich mumbled as he looked at the glyph before he handed it to Elaine. "Good eyes, my lady. It is indeed elven, but it is strange. Not because it's here, but what it says."

"What?" Elaine crowded in. "What does it say?"

"Basically, *Go away*," Aldrich answered.

Charles turned to follow Kaliastrid away from them and walked up to Silas. The spy looked tired but resolute. At the top of the hill, Kaliastrid transformed and lifted into the air gracefully before she dropped over the edge and skimmed the treetops into the valley.

"You up to this?" Charles asked.

"We do what we have to," Silas responded and handed him an MM1 and two bandoleers. "How much ammo do you have left?"

"Everything I brought. I only fired two rounds."

Silas nodded.

Charles looked back over his shoulder at Elaine. Silas watched him for a minute, then spoke his mind.

"She'll be on the other side of the wall in a few minutes, and she'll need someone who's been there before to help her deal with it."

Charles watched her a few more seconds before the soldier took over again. He nodded to Silas' confirmation of what he thought, but the agent was already on to the next task. It was a good reminder. She would need support after this, and he might be the best person to help her.

"If that whole platoon gets up here, this is over. You know that," Charles told the agent, who was doing the same check he had done as soon as he arrived.

"Yes."

"We need to stop them before that."

"Yes."

"If there are a lot of dragons coming, we're also in trouble."

"Yes."

"This is not a good tactical spot for us."

"No," Silas shook his head. "Listen. I planned that last strike down to the finest detail. They hit us hard. They tore into us like we had no plan at all. I'm not going to be caught by surprise again. If it moves, I want to kill it before it gets close enough to kill me, but this is all we have."

"Effective range for indirect fire is 400 meters. Roughly to the bottom of the moraine. We can count on some downhill advantage. Using our best Kentucky windage we can extend it, but it's not going to be easy. Flight time to target will give them time to adjust, so we will have to lead them."

"Then we fight until we're empty, and then we fight some more."

In response to that, Charles shifted his bag around, took out the combat knife, and strapped it to his belt.

Silas grinned and slapped him on the back.

"I've always liked you Marines. Always with that never-give-up attitude and a bloody sharp knife."

"I've always thought of it as plan B."

Silas grinned and nodded. Behind the strong front he still looked tired.

"I'm going to check the perimeter," Charles reported. "See what's up and maybe find a place where we can turn this castle to our advantage."

"Good idea. Keep alert. They'll get bogged down in the research and get us snuck up on."

Silas had been in the mix. Charles immediately recognized the command voice that came from assuming control when things started falling apart. The ease with which it came told him that Silas had done it enough that it came without thinking. Charles was Marine enough to accept that it was not an insult; it was meant to keep them all alive. In situations like this, you didn't have to agree with the one giving orders. He tossed a quick salute to the agent, who was getting his own gear prepared for war. His fight with the partials had actually impressed Charles from what little he had heard about it from Blackjack. He wasn't all bad. At least he was on the front line with the boys he had gotten killed and almost went with them.

Charles turned away and walked to the edge of the castle courtyard on the southeastern side of the precipice where he could see down into the valley. From his perch he could see part of the parking lot below them and the peaceful layout of the valley rolling away from him. The arrow shape and reflection of green off of Kaliastrid's hide caught his attention. From the bottom of his pack he pulled out a pair of Steiner 10x50 binoculars and found her again. He followed her as she plunged toward the long stretch of road that ran from the village toward them. She was skimming over it at less that twenty feet. He could tell her altitude based on her wingspan across the road. Three trucks, German Dingo 2 troop carriers, were racing toward her. The first two looked like the longer troop carriers and the last one bristled with antenna. The weapon stations on top of the first two were not manned, which indicated they were not expecting an ambush.

He touched the throat mic and spoke. "What's happening, Kali? Those trucks are armored. There's nothing you can do to stop them."

A cloud of mist blossomed around and in front of her in a stream that poured out over both trucks. The last vehicle, understanding what she was doing, swerved to avoid the stream and broke through the brush on the side of the road. It bounced across the flat field for about a hundred yards before it turned back toward the road, throwing grass and mud up as it chewed through the soft earth. Kaliastrid pivoted on her wing and came back around on the running target. She hovered over the field, flapping to hold her position, and released a bolt of fire energy at the vehicle racing to rejoin the other trucks.

The bolt was not aimed at the truck. It was aimed ahead of it, and it slammed into the land less than a truck's length ahead of it. The bolt exploded up from within the earth, showering the Dingo with mud and rock as its nose dipped into the crater it created. Its nose dug into the ground at the bottom of the crater and plowed into the opposite wall. Charles nodded as Kaliastrid turned and flapped over the road to regain altitude and advantage. Smoke was rising from the body of both trucks that were still slowly rolling toward them.

"They may be armored, but acid is not something most modern military units are ready for."

Both vehicles continued for another fifty yards at their reduced pace before stopping. The windshields were fogged by the acid, and their tires were coming apart. Once they stopped, they remained motionless in the middle of the road. Charles knew the partials were not dead in the still smoking shells, and it would take a while for the acid to eat through the metal armor. Estimating their position at close to fifteen-hundred meters, he sighted down the tube to check the sight picture and felt sure he called it right. There was no way he could reach them where they were sitting.

Kaliastrid had stopped them for the moment, but that would not keep them out of the fight. They would have to approach on foot. She had taken away their armored advantage. As he was thinking through their options, fifteen partials and one blond female exited the Dingos from the six available exits. Two additional partials climbed out of the bogged down Dingo but stayed near it. They were obviously communicating mentally like dragons did because they were operating too smoothly in the separated vehicles to be uncoordinated, and none of them carried radios. That meant the radio truck was there to listen in on any communications in the valley.

The light infantry platoon coalesced and then divided into squads of five and raced for cover, looking up for the next attack from the air. From this distance they looked like human soldiers moving across the fields parallel to the road, but Charles' experience with troop movements told him they were moving faster than human soldiers in the same type of terrain. Each squad was collected into a group of five with one man on either side of the central three. The two flankers had their hands projecting out ahead and at angles to the other three. The motions reminded him of shields, and he decided that was their role. They were shield men, protecting the others from projectiles and missiles. He wondered how much the shields could take.

Two of the remaining three soldiers were doing something else with their hands. Charles could not tell what, but he didn't see a weapon. The middle soldier was scanning for threats and repositioning the others based on what he saw. They were moving forward as a steady front. If they were worried about modern weapons, it wasn't obvious. They were bunched up in a way that he would never group soldiers, but they didn't have to worry about rifles. He wondered if their shield men could protect them from explosives and artillery. It probably gave them an advantage, so he would need to lay his rounds behind the shield man's protection. Their approach was an impressive display of coordinated drill.

On the perimeter of the field, five large canines broke out of the cover of the woods and surrounded the witch as she walked through the grass in her business suit. Charles had not faced her in combat, but something about the way she was walking across the field told him she was not worried. She was not a woman to be trifled with.

Silas joined him at the edge of the cliff with his own field glasses.

"You see how they're working as a squad. We faced that. No way to get through the shields with anything we carry."

"Artillery would still work if we can land it in behind them or if we have any airburst rounds."

"True. We just happen to have some. Not many, though. I wish we had a mortar. They would be easy targets with a mortar."

"With this elevation we might be able to stretch our range to 750 meters. I think the M-79 can reach that far, fired correctly. We can use it like a 40 mm mortar. It'll be a stretch."

"We should find out. What's your estimate?"

"1300 mike and closing on the first group. They're spreading out. Someone's guiding them in. Probably the one I knocked out before. You have to get them in the kill zone if you plan to do any damage at all."

Charles unlimbered the M-79 and raised the sight. He adjusted it to max and popped open the breech. Silas handed him a color-coded round. Charles remembered the striping so he could find them easily. Silas was laying the rest out on the wall in front of him.

"That's all we have," Silas told him as he rearranged bandoleers. There were about 10 airburst rounds total that he set out with two high explosive rounds.

Charles sighted down on them and adjusted for windage. As he scanned the approaching soldiers through the sight, he struck a line across the road at what he felt was the maximum effective range. With everything set, he laid the launcher on the stone and recovered his binoculars.

When he returned to the field, the green arrow of Kaliastrid sliced through the air toward the witch and razed the grass around her. A bubble of protection surrounded the woman and her escorts. One of the covering squads released blue bolts at the dragon as she flew past, but none came close.

"Looks like the witch is surrounded by some kind of shield. We can't drop anything in on her, and airburst will do no good," Charles reported.

"Check the horizon over Kruth," Silas said. "What do you see?"

Melissa stepped out of the ruins and shouted up at them.

"Nethliast's here."

Charles raised his glasses to where Silas was indicating and found the black shape flapping just above the roofs of the buildings.

"Kali," he called over the radio. "You have company. Nethliast directly south."

She was gaining altitude already. Melissa must have reported his presence to her.

A coppery blur passed below their perch, drawing Charles' attention away from Kaliastrid's climb.

"Things just got real," Silas said as he tracked Nethliast's climb.

Charles turned his glasses back to the approaching partials. The first group was one kilometer out now, based on his imaginary line. He quickly scanned across the field and counted five squads, plus the witch. A new group was bringing up the rear, the last three from the radio van. When things really started hopping, it would be hard to keep track of all of them.

"We need to get out of here. I'm going to check on the others, see what they've found. We have a minute."

"Negative," Silas responded. "You're better with that than I am. You hold here. I'll check with them." Silas turned and walked back to check on the archaeologist and team.

September 9 – 1100 CET – Chateau de Wildenstein, Haut-Rhin, France

Silas walked into the cutout square foundation and into the middle of an argument. It was clear that they had found something they did not agree on.

"That doesn't make sense," Aldrich said and waved his hands at Elaine in frustration.

"Doesn't matter because that's what it says." She was pointing at something she had drawn onto her large sketch pad.

"What doesn't make sense? We don't have a lot of minutes left up here. We're either finding something or leaving, and probably not by the comfortable helicopter we came here in."

Elaine's eyes suddenly shifted to him, and she raised her hands in frustration. She handed him the crystal lens and pointed to the wall. "There are glyphs engraved magically on the walls at different intervals. They are all either warnings in draconic not to enter, or they're in elvish or dwarvish with similar meanings. The elves warn that what they seek is not here, and the dwarvish indicate that the searcher must dig harder for their prize. They seem to be disconnected even though they are connected parts of the same message."

"They were carved at the same time, by the same hand," Aldrich added.

Silas took the lens and looked around the wall. He moved a few steps and scanned again. Then he crouched down close to the ground and looked at all of the glyphs again.

"They're nearly at the line," Charles called back.

Silas nodded. The Marine could not see the response, and Silas was not really aware he had given one.

"I think there's a message here besides what's written on the walls. They're aligned." He pointed to a place on the ground inside the foundation. The stone floor was blank to the human eye, but when he looked at it through the lens it was a different story.

"Holy...Elaine, Aldrich, I need your help."

"Kali, Mel. We're about to drop some fire in around you. Stay clear of the partials," Charles reported. "Mel, I may need you to fall back to hold them off if they get through."

Elaine reached Silas' side and looked at the ground where he was pointing. An intricate diagram spread out around them for nearly ten feet. He scanned the entire glyph with the lens, but he could not put it all together. It was like looking at a puzzle through a straw.

Silas gestured at the stone floor of the old building. He was pointing the lens at the complex diagram that reminded him of a very difficult puzzle on the wall shelf back in his office. "What do you see?"

Elaine focused on the ground through a triangle formed by her hands. When she was satisfied with the image, she enlarged the space between her thumbs and fingers. Once the motion was complete she continued to stare at the ground. Aldrich grabbed Silas' hand and pulled the lens over a little to see what they were looking at.

"I see it, but I don't know what it is," Elaine answered. "It's very complex."

She pulled her pad out and started drawing. Silas watched over her shoulder and tried to see what she saw on the stones. She was getting a very accurate drawing. It was the whole picture, unlike the view he could get through the lens. A thump rang from the top of the castle wall. Silas jumped as adrenaline surged to prepare him for combat. Elaine and Aldrich both looked up toward the southern end of the castle. Several seconds passed without any sound. Then, an explosion, distant and small, indicated Charles' shot had reached the ground. Another thump. He was firing again. Charles was engaged.

"He has that for now. Let's stay focused here," Silas suggested, "We're running out of time."

September 9 – 1105 CET – Chateau de Wildenstein, Haut-Rhin, France

Charles watched the imaginary line he had drawn across the road and field that approached the base of the Schlossberg. The first group was approaching the line, and he had to allow time for the flight of the grenade to reach the long range target. They would not hear the light thump of the launcher from this far away, so the rounds would drop in on them without warning unless they had supernatural help from whomever was scrying them. He had to give that over to the fog of war.

Kaliastrid's green form flashed across the field again. This time she was skimming over the grass itself. Her claws were out and extended to rake the line of soldiers who had attacked her when she strafed the witch. She was striking across their flank to do the most damage to the entire file. At maximum speed for the attack, she was fully committed. There was no option for defending. Charles' gut constricted as he watched the black blur that was coming at her from above. She might not be able to see his approach as she held her attack line. A third blur of airborne motion above and to the left of Nethliast drew his attention and explained Kaliastrid's absolute commitment to her attack, independent of Nethliast's counter. They were drawing him in to a trap.

Charles swallowed the warning he was preparing and released the pressure on the transmit button. She knew she was bait.

The green arrow unwaveringly tracked toward the partials on the ground. The black shape was on target to strike Kaliastrid before she reached them. An instant before Nethliast reached her, Meliastrid struck his back and shoulder. It all happened too fast to see the actual strike, but they pounded into the soft turf in a confusing tumbling mass of red and black. Grass and dirt sprayed out around their impact, obscuring the outcome.

Charles tore his eyes away from the melee and tracked Kaliastrid's more critical attack as she struck the squad at the left rear of the approaching platoon. The leftmost shield man took the brunt of the attack as her foreclaws sunk into his side. Her speed threw him into the others and disrupted their advance in a tumbling jumble. Her rear claws raked the four partials that were now rolling underneath her. Charles could see her clutching as each claw touched something until she instinctively grabbed two partials. Talons drove into scaled flesh and drug them into the sky as she climbed away from the field.

Charles had never witnessed dragons in battle, so he was a little distracted as his first target crossed his line. He had to scramble to get on target. He adjusted his aim and let the thumper release its first airburst toward its target. As the round was arching over the battlefield he was working the breech, yanking out the spent round and slamming in the next.

Kaliastrid dropped her baggage at the apex of her climb, allowing them to fall to the ground with little hope of surviving their plummet. The distant tumult of black and red scales broke up. Grass and mud exploded away from the two dragons that were grappling for altitude. Neither wanted to stay locked in a melee on the ground.

With the next round in, Charles brought the tube up and placed his sight onto his next target. The first round exploded above and behind the first squad, showering the advancing force with shrapnel and explosive concussion. The second round thumped away, and he repeated the load as the forces on the ground reacted to the invisible assault coming at them in addition to the air assault. He was reloaded and back on target, searching for his next group, when their reaction surprised him.

Each squad broke into a pair and a triplet and then jumped together. Each group covered fifteen meters in a single bound. A quick scan told him that there were five dead partials. He had lost sight of the witch's group. The remaining partials were now formed into a V made up of the remaining five sub-groups. Now there were six teams, One was no longer on the field, as far as he could see. Each group was now moving much faster.

The last round he had fired exploded over unoccupied ground. A new round was in the tube as their movements settled into a pattern. He waited, adjusted the sight for the reduced range, and then targeted where a triplet of partials was jumping. He pulled the trigger and started to reload without looking. He watched the flanking maneuvers start to form. Some of them were going to their right to take the pass toward the north. An equal number were rushing the left side and planning to leap up the front face of the moraine. His last round exploded exactly in front of the triplet as they were landing. The force slammed into the shield man's shield directing all of the force directly into his arms. Although the shield deflected all of the shrapnel uselessly away, the force of the explosion destroyed his arms and sent him sprawling behind the approaching pair.

The advancing groups to Charles' left had reached the cover of the precipice. He could not fire on them without leaning out over the wall and exposing himself. As he was considering putting a round down there to keep their heads down, a magical blast of explosive fire engulfed the wall next to him. The heat from the blast surrounded him in an uncomfortable hug, but the bulk of the fireball was deflected away from him. Pieces of rock from the wall fell down the precipice or showered down on him. He ducked, losing sight of the field for a moment. As he repositioned away from the exposed edge he calculated what was left. There were about twelve partials still fighting, and some of those were wounded. They were evenly split between the southern approach and their flank. The flankers were protected by the squad that had Charles pinned down. He would have to reposition north to keep them from reaching the northern approach to the castle, but that left six approaching from the front. Then there was Nethliast.

"Kali, Mel, we're going to be overrun. I can't hold the front and the flank. I'm repositioning to the north. The south face is vulnerable. I need support."

As he started to retreat toward the wall where he could see the northern approaches, he aimed his M-79 over the wall to the south and pulled the trigger. It was a guess at where they might try to come over the edge. It might keep their heads down, but it probably would not stop their approach.

He slung the single shot launcher over his shoulder, grabbed the loaded MM1, and twisted his left hand through the two bandoleers. He threw them over his chest as he backed away from the wall. They had nearly a kilometer to climb to get to the top. It was a calculated risk, but he had to take it. The larger force was moving to his unprotected rear.

He turned his back on the southern front and rushed down the hill to the overlook that would let him see the road as it approached the lake and the slope that led up to the castle. When he reached the edge, he could see a pair moving quickly under cover of trees along the ridge opposite the moraine. He aimed the MM-1 ahead of them and fired three rounds in an advancing pattern. Then he dropped below the wall.

Someone had been watching for him to pop up. Blue bolts of lightning exploded into the rock at the top of the wall where he had been only moments before. Another fireball slammed into the wall as static energy ran over his body, reminding him that lightning could arc. He didn't have a clear shot at anyone, and they had him bracketed where he was.

He looked to the south as movement drew his attention. Melissa was landing and releasing a massive cloud of fire into the trees beyond the southern wall. She remained in her dragon form and stood sentinel on the southern rampart. Charles rolled onto his knees and risked a look over the wall at the group that had been moving forward.

They had avoided his attack, at least most of them had. Two partials were under cover of a fallen tree. A third was crushed beneath it. One of the survivors pointed at him, and he instantly felt the push of an invisible force brush his shoulder and throw him back onto the ground. If the force had hit him square, it probably would have crushed his ribs or his skull. As it was, the glancing blow had bruised his shoulder. Expecting that he had a moment for them to prepare their magic, Charles pushed himself up to the wall and sent five rounds down onto them in a reactive circle. It was a Hail Mary play to force their heads down. If he was lucky, maybe it would kill one of them.

A blur of movement over his head as he rolled back behind the wall drew his attention to the air battle. At least she was keeping him busy. If Nethliast ever broke through, they were unprotected from air attacks. There was nothing he could do about it. Charles looked back at the tunnel entrance. It was obvious they wanted to keep his head down so someone could flank then. They wanted to get something through the tunnel, but what? It had to be the witch and her wolves. She was the only group unaccounted for.

He had not seen her since he had started firing on the partials. He had no idea how fast she could move, but the partial squads had given her time to cover the distance and get to the trail. It was still a climb to get up here, but she had those wolves with her. He had no idea how long it would take for her to take down Kaliastrid's barrier, but with it unprotected except by passive defenses it was a weakness they could leverage. Charles rolled over and onto his feet while keeping his head below the waist-high wall. In a crouch, he ran for the black hole in the grass-covered stone. As he ran through the black maw of the cave, his vision took too long to adjust. He had to slow down. He couldn't fire the launcher in the cave. It would not have room to arm. He didn't have the closer-range flechette rounds loaded. He wasn't sure they would even work against armored partials.

As he reached the end of the tunnel his vision was having to adjust to the bright light beyond again, but he saw movement that proved his instinct was sound. Something had made it up the trail faster than he would have expected. Four large wolves were rushing over the edge of the ditches leading up to the stairs and the central pillar of stone that had been the barbican. The first two wolves scrabbled down over the edge and triggered the first claymore.

The blast erupted from the base of the pillar and filled the space in the ditch with lethal ball bearings, concussive force, and pieces of wolves. Both of them died in the ditch. A third and a fourth reacted to the attack and changed directions. They leapt over the ditch to land on the center of the gate house foundation. Their next jump would put them on the stairs and in front of him, but their movement broke the laser of the last claymore. It had the same effect on them as they were jumping. The two riddled corpses fell into the the ditch in front of the stairs. A fifth wolf bounded over each ditch now that the traps had been sprung and bounded up the stairs at him. Charles' nerves almost failed him. He wanted to stroke the trigger, but in the last instant he waited until the wolf slammed into the invisible barrier. It was hard to trust the invisible. The face of the wolf smashed into the barrier, and then the whole wolf tumbled down the stairs. It was still alive and would be coming back at him soon. It stood slowly and shook off the impact.

An order in German from the trees called the lone wolf back into the woods. It joined a blond woman in a brilliant yellow business suit at the top of the hill. She pointed at the barrier and shouted a long string of words Charles could not understand. After her initial stream of commands, she shouted one at him while pointing at the entrance to the cave. Each command struck the barrier like a hammer. Cracks crazed the previously invisible surface. Charles watched as magic slammed into magic.

As the barrier succumbed to her magical battering ram, it shattered into a shower of magical sparks that fell harmlessly around Charles. The loup garou rushed from her side with foam dripping from his jowls. Charles hesitated a moment until, almost waiting too long, he saw death in the animal's eyes. The witch by the trees was chanting at him with a murderous grin on her face.

Charles leaned into the launcher and pulled the trigger. He didn't know if he had the range. It was close. The first round thumped into the side of the wolf but didn't explode. The range was too close, and it had not armed. The wolf yelped in surprise and shook his head, causing the shiver to travel down his whole body before he prepared to jump again. Charles backed away from the entrance, extending the range enough to let the rounds arm. Then he fired all that he had remaining down the cave. All of them exploded, filling the air beyond the cave entrance with fire, smoke, dirt, and blood. The battle was truly joined.

September 9 - About the same time - Inside the castle.

Elaine inhaled deeply, erased the place on her drawing where her hand had jumped and dug deeper into the complex image.

"Fix this." Aldrich pointed to a particularly difficult to see section. The two mumbled together as she looked closer. He raised the lens for a closer look.

Silas took a moment to look around and sighed at the delay. He hoped he was right that the Marine could hold off the partials a little longer. He felt a glimmer of pride fill his gut about the butler, but he still reached into a nearby bag to grab a string of hand grenades. More rounds from the grenade launcher tore into the air beyond the cave entrance. If Silas' count was accurate, that would be the last of the MM-1 load. He would need to reload, and that was a long process when you were alone. He was still able to use the single shot tube, but it was slow.

Silas grabbed his launcher and walked over to the edge where he could see the cave entrance. Charles' controlled retreat from the cave told him he was right. He dropped the empty MM-1 and pulled the single shot off his shoulder, breaking it down as he did to shove a grenade into the breech. As Charles backed up to the protection of their dug out building, Silas motioned to let him know about his backup launcher. The Marine looked appreciative and then fired a round into the cave entrance before taking the backup from Silas. As he lifted it onto target he looked over as if to say, *don't you have something to do?*

Silas nodded and rushed back to the others. Aldrich harrumphed next to him and pointed back to the glyph. "Wodin protect me, I never believed it possible. Is this what I think it is?"

Silas looked at the man. His eyes were wide, and he stroked the long beard at his chin as he looked at the ground again.

"It's Gnomish," Silas answered. The very intricate glyph was a thief's sign. It was a challenge thrown down to any who would come here. Silas had read books about them when he had downtime to spend on his fascination with ancient secret societies and the thieves who started them.

Aldrich looked up at him over his shoulder and shook his head as if he was a child who still believed in Santa Claus, which was basically what Silas had just said. It was interesting that a man who believed so much in elves and dwarves would limit his scope and ignore the possibility of gnomes.

"It's a thief's signature. There's a lock here that is nearly impossible to open. Or, that's what the signature says."

"Note the alignment of that," Silas murmured as Elaine drew. She looked at her tablet and compared it to the ground, then quickly erased her mistake and drew it again. The signature was becoming clear, but there was always a trick. One author had described solving these puzzles as defusing a medieval bomb, in theory. The traps hidden by these signatures were as famous in secret society circles as the reported treasures they protected, but Silas had always cared more about the traps than the treasures.

The sound of magical explosions to the south were getting closer. Melissa was being pressed. They were going to need help.

"Show me that again, quickly." He looked over her shoulder, tapped Aldrich on the arm, and held out his hand for the lens. He would need it to disarm the lock.

He knelt, looking at the keystone as the image drew him deeper into the game. The ancient author was already mocking him. The image she was drawing was older than the local history indicated there had been a castle here. It warned of serious danger if this glyph was decoded. It actually said, what was sealed behind this glyph should be left sealed forever. It was signed with the signature of a member of the *Folkvardr*. Nothing good would be found beyond. He smiled. In thieves' tongue that meant whatever was beyond this trapped lock was worth the effort and possible death. His grandfather had said the *folkvardr* hid things that needed to stay hidden. Silas had spent his life looking for those things, and now he was standing over one of their greatest troves.

Another thump followed by an explosion told him there was no choice. They weren't going to get out the way they had come. With all of the remaining partials converging on this peak there was no way Blackjack was going to land here long enough for them to get away. He glanced over toward Charles holding off any breach in the tunnel. If they made it through, he would not have the range for the weapon to arm and he would be down to plan B.

He was reporting that the barrier on the cave entrance had fallen and that they were forcing him back. Melissa reported that they were using cover and speed to make it up the rise of the moraine. They were surrounded, but the attacking force was down to six partials and the witch. Kaliastrid reported breathlessly that she was keeping Nethliast busy, but it sounded more like bravado than fact.

Silas made his decision quickly. The only way out of this was through. If this was as important as it seemed, Nethliast would close off any retreat they had. They couldn't let this fall to him.

"Here." She ripped the page out and handed it to him. "I think it's right."

"I hope it's right." He sighed as he took the paper and laid it down in front of him. She had marked some basic scale so he would know how it spread out. She was impressive for her age, and he understood but had not seen that she was as magically powerful as she was smart.

He looked over his shoulder at her. Her legs were spread out and bracing into the ground. Her hands were raised in the air and sparkling with power.

"What's all this?"

"You're going to need time to solve it. If they break through, you'll be defenseless. I'm here to keep them off of you."

He could see where many ancient sculptors had found their muse. She looked like any number of classic paintings he remembered from his grandfather's collection. The semi-tight jeans and the corset highlighted by the sunlight and eminent danger, gave her the heroic lines of a comic book cover, a romance novel, or a Wagnerian heroine. A sudden trickle of excitement ran through his body. He grinned and looked back through the lens at the ground. All challenges came with dangers. She had a collection.

A horrible crackling sound came from the entrance.

"Here they come," Melissa yelled into the air.

Charles was reloading the second launcher as he waited. They had twenty-four rounds, but he would be unable to load again. If he was even able to use the launchers in the confines of the castle without endangering his allies, that is.

"See if you can help them. I've got this," Silas said to Elaine and Aldrich.

They nodded and moved out to support Melissa and Charles. Aldrich was mumbling grave warnings in Norse, and Elaine was covered in a crackling blue aura.

Silas shrugged appreciatively and re-focused on his task. The Boy Scout had bought him all the time he was going to get. He would have to deal with what was in front of him, but to get started he needed a stick.

Silas reached into his pack and pulled out the leather kit he never traveled without. At the very top of the tool roll was the only item he had ever needed to add: an expandable metal baton. He picked it up and slung it out with a flick of his wrist to extend it to full length. It locked open with a *shtick*, and he stuck the point onto the first mark that indicated there was a stone button beneath it. With only a slight pause to steady his nerves and to prepare for what came next, he pressed, releasing a breath as it slid in with some resistance. There was a final click but nothing else. So far, so good, but he was committed now. Solve it or run, because the timer to the ultimate killing strike designed by a maniac thief and apparently an army of gnomes started with the first move.

From this point forward it was like speed chess to the death with a demonic Bobby Fisher, and he had just pressed the timer.

Based on the sounds behind him, Charles was holding the entrance with Elaine's help. Sizzling magical bolts flashed behind him, and Elaine squealed with excitement. He could not focus on what she was doing, but whatever she had done it gave her a moment to back up to stand next to him. His battle sense said nothing had made it through the entrance yet.

The hairs on the back of his neck and arms stood up as a shimmering glow descended around him and the puzzle in a box. Elaine was finishing the last corner as he looked up at her. He was not sure if she was protecting him or them. He shook his head and plowed on. He had to focus; no time for distraction. Whatever it was, it wasn't hurting him. Looking at the diagram and exhaling, he pressed in the next trigger stone.

Dust, mud, and air sprayed out of an invisible joint that he had exposed when he pressed in the invisible stone button. It sank and scraped into its position, and Silas jumped back to sit down roughly. He looked down to make sure he wasn't stabbed, cut, or injured from some invisible trap. This was taking too long, but with each step he knew he could die. That would kill them all. Either the warning on the trap would be true, or the partials would break through. Either way, the stakes had never been higher.

Movement above him and a shadow on the ground distracted him for a moment to look away from the puzzle. A black dragon seemed to hover above him. He felt a fear he had never known and sat, stunned until his mind fought its way back from the edge. The dragon was not hovering; it was descending very fast toward him. The huge body was getting larger with the wings folded behind it. A green-black streak that had to be Kaliastrid flashed past Nethliast, but failed to strike him with her extended claws. He actually grinned at timing his drop correctly to avoid her as he remained intent on his target. His mouth was open. Silas' mind cycled agonizingly slowly through what might be happening. The giant black dragon was falling toward him to bite off his head, which made sense to him for a moment before he realized the truth.

"Incoming! Fire!" Silas screamed to warn the fighters rushing around the central courtyard while trying to hold off the invading partials. None of them could see what he could. It was a master stroke if it worked. Either way it would buy the invaders valuable time as the defenders had to brace.

Kaliastrid was circling back, but she would not make it in time. As Silas watched doom descend upon them, he couldn't focus on the puzzle. He knew he had no way to stop what was coming.

Elaine dove for Charles and held her hands above them both as if to shield them. Melissa and Aldrich were out of sight and probably out of range. But Silas suddenly realized he was exposed and too far away from anyone. Well, this was not how he thought he would die.

About roof height above the foundation, the huge black spear flared His wings expanded into an enormous canopy blocking out the sky and daylight. The snap of wing material sounded like an evil parachute opening, and it was like a malevolent night descending on him. In slow motion, the single angry eye devoured him. He could see the sharp white teeth in the broad black jaws. They were set in greenish gums. White pulsing glands hung from the back of his throat. The detail was amazing before it was all obliterated in an expanding cloud of fire. All Silas could do was close his eyes and brace for the searing pain as the cloud engulfed him. He hoped death would be quick.

He clenched his jaw and tightened his body as if the dragon were going to punch him.

When neither occurred, he expelled the breath he was holding and opened his eyes.

A crystallized dome had formed around him. The noise of battle he had heard an instant before had become silence. Fire was swirling around the dome, and the heat of the inferno that was charring grass across the top of the moraine was only a minor sensation through the now-solid wall. Cracks started to appear around the compressed, egg-shaped bubble he was in.

As the fire dissipated, the crystal dome exploded outward as the compressed energy rushed away from him. The menacing black form was already flying away, convinced he had fried them all. He could not linger because Kaliastrid had circled around and was now the screeching green vengeance nipping at his wing tips.

It still took Silas a moment to shake off the amazement of being alive and not crispy. When he could finally think again he realized that whether they were dead or not, he had been right. Partials were rushing both edges to break through on either side of the moraine. His time limit to solve the puzzle had been reduced not by the puzzle but by the situation. He grabbed the lens he had dropped as Nethliast descended upon them.

It was hard to tell what was next. There were several ways the lock could go. In this situation, knowledge of the person who built it would help, but he didn't have that. He would have to trust his instincts and years of study. He looked at the paper and realized why he had known to have Elaine adjust the drawing. He had seen that particular combination of runes before. It was something his grandfather had drawn and shared with him many times. This trap had that rune at its heart. Silas suddenly knew what to do.

He closed his eyes in an attempt to pick the right path from the many laid before him.

The sound of battle intensified.

He looked back at the stones and faltered.

It couldn't be that simple.

He heard Elaine expel a breath as something hit her. She groaned behind him, but she was still alive.

He hesitated again.

It could kill them all if he was wrong.

No one would believe this was anything but a trap, and that was exactly why his grandfather had shared it with him.

The sounds of battle were closing on him. They were falling back. Charles discarded the heavy launcher and drew his knife and pistol. They were within the minimum range. Silas had to act.

Mind made up, he drove the steel rod into the three stones one after the other, thinking of his grandfather, the tattoo on his own shoulder, and the amulet the old man had always worn around his neck.

As soon as the last stone reached the bottom he jumped back, just in case he was wrong.

The central stones in the invisible design fell into the ground and moved around until a broad circle nearly four feet in diameter opened in the foundation stone. In the center of the circle a metal door that resembled an airtight door on a submarine appeared. A handle appeared in the middle of the metal dome.

He moved to the other side of the hole and looked at this new twist. When he reached the far side, he glimpsed a young boy rushing at them across the courtyard. Charles was firing uselessly at another partial that had come through the entrance from the tunnel.

Melissa had retreated from the south and had caught two partials in a web that spread from two trees farther up the hill. Elaine and Aldrich were focused on the witch and a small squad of three half-dragons protecting her. This lone remaining partial soldier's armored shoulder drove into Charles' chest with a loud crack. The impact sent the Marine sprawling. The knife that had been expertly positioned to kill the charging opponent bounced away after it had failed to find a place between the plates of his pectoral armor.

Instinctively, Silas drew his own Desert Eagle from his shoulder holster and fired in a snap shot that surprised the running attacker His face, for some reason, was still in human form. Silas watched the scales start to close over to protect him from the bullet that had already closed the gap. The transition was too late to beat the 470 meter per second muzzle velocity. Because the shot had been instinctive and not aimed, it was off just enough to save the boy's life. The half-inch slug of copper and lead ripped the boy's ear off the side of his head and spun him around to Silas' right, where he crashed into the ground. He stayed down, screaming in pain and holding his head, now covered by thick armor scales and transformed into a long snouted dragon's head. Silas pumped five of the remaining six shots into the armored chest of the partial dragon where he lay. They did not penetrate, but he knew what it was like to get shot at close range in a bullet-proof vest. He'd have some broken ribs to go along with the missing ear.

"Should have changed into something meaner," Silas taunted and fired the last shot into his head.

The massive round deflected off the armor and bone, slamming his head into the stone foundation and knocking him out. Silas reloaded, holstered the weapon, and turned back to his job.

The handle turned one way. Doubt filled his mind. Maybe he had missed something. Was this the end of it?

He looked around at the others. They were running out of options as the last of the partials and the witch were in the castle wall. He saw no other choice in the solid stone at his feet either. He grabbed the handle and turned it until it stopped with a loud clang. The door was suddenly heavy in his hand and nearly pulled him toward it. He braced his legs against the weight and released it slowly. The ground around the door gave way as the weight of the door pulled the rest of the mud and dust with it. When he could no longer control it, he let go of the door and let it drop. After a few inches of drop, it turned under, exposing an opening in the ground. There was a cave beneath the door. The daylight showed that it descended away into darkness, but it was at least another position to fall back to.

"Let's go!" he shouted as he leaned over the edge to look for what was below him. There were stairs just below the opening. He quickly recovered his kit and the lens, threw them into his pack, and tossed it over his shoulder. He levered himself over the edge. His feet reached the landing, and he stood up. As he walked down the stairs into the ground, he noticed Aldrich heading toward him, helping Charles. A bloody hole in the side of his shirt showed where the partial had slammed into him with his spiked shoulder. There were other signs of singeing and cuts, but that seemed to be the worst of it.

Elaine was behind them, throwing balls of blue fire at the very attractive woman in a now tattered yellow business suit. He wanted to shoot the witch for sending her dogs after him on the mountain, but he had to focus on the exit. One side of her suit was badly burned, and some of her blond hair was missing. Amazingly, it seemed that everyone's magical potency was dropping off. She was leaning against a tree and pointing her hands at Charles' back. The blue balls hit her before whatever she was conjuring left her fingertips. Each one threw her back a step and engulfed her body with blue fire. When she hit the ground, she didn't get up.

Silas whooped as Aldrich guided Charles to the hole. The image of the four foot tall man acting like a crutch for the football player was comical enough without the insanity of the battle raging around them. The teenage half-dragon with the missing ear was rising from where Silas had left him unconscious. He sat up and glared at Silas as Aldrich reached him. The small cleric grabbed the boy's shoulder as if he was going to use him for support, and terror filled the partial's scaled face. His mouth opened to release a scream of intense pain. The entire battlefield seemed to pause to listen as Aldrich released all of the pain and injury he had consumed over the past forty-eight hours into the young boy. It included the entirety of Silas' injuries from the night before.

As the transfer progressed, Charles stood up straighter and walked on his own for the last few steps, leaving the cleric behind to release it all into the attacker. Aldrich held onto the boy's shoulder until every weight lifted from the short man. He seemed spry compared to how he had started the battle.

When his face cleared, Aldrich grinned, released the partial's shoulder, and walked on toward the hole in the ground. The boy's leg appeared to blossom burns and cuts. Cuts formed on his chest along with scratches that reminded Silas of the claws of the brutal beasts who had attacked him. The young half-dragon continued to scream as the many tattoo points from Charles chest appeared on his armor clearly. Then he suffered the wide gash he had caused when he slammed into Charles. The boy twitched several times as more of his ribs splintered, and then he fell back to the ground where Silas had left him. Tears streamed from his eyes as he fought to breathe.

"Thank Wodin," The little man said as he flicked his hand like he was throwing something distasteful off of his fingers. With a satisfied and relieved grin he dropped into the hole behind Charles.

"Thank Wodin, you're on our side," Silas said as he passed by.

"And you."

Elaine and Melissa folded in toward the hole watching the two fronts. Movement at the top of the southern crest caught Silas' attention. He drew and aimed his pistol between Melissa and Elaine. Melissa continued toward the hole, but Elaine paused. He compensated as he squeezed the trigger. The first round thudded into the armored chest of another partial that was racing toward them, leading two others. The solid impact made him pause, but it did not penetrate. The red and yellow partial with what looked like first sergeant stripes and rockers on his arm and "Rodriguez" on his chest in the same scale pattern quickly decided he was not dead and would not be killed by the man's pistol. The three males charged, and Elaine raised her hands above her head.

Silas continued to unload the heavy gun into the protected chest of the male, but he was not stopping. Each round made him flinch but nothing more. He was fully covered in scales, so Silas knew there was no hope of stopping him. He had to slow him down so Elaine could get away, but she had not moved.

"Get in here," he screamed at her, but she still didn't move.

As the last round left the chamber, the partial soldier was still rushing at her with murder in his eyes; Silas had no choice but hope she could take him and the two others, who were now shoulder to shoulder with their leader. While Silas had been distracting them, Elaine had taken time to focus herself. She was standing straight up with her hands raised above her head. Each hand was bent at the wrist and pointed at the leading partial. Blue bolts of energy rushed up and down her body and pulsed up her arms toward her hands. With each breath and footstep of the approaching attack, she drew in more energy.

Silas was sure she was going to wait too long.

The angry partial opened his mouth to release his flaming breath just as she released the energy in her hands. The blue energy arced from her finger tips in a brilliant bolt like she was a human Tesla coil. It crossed the meager distance instantaneously. The superheated air around her exploded in thunder. The bolt struck him in the chest and raced through his body to the ground. Arcs leapt from him into the other two partials who had followed him. Thunderous reports threw them back and away from the worst of the powerful discharge, but not without damage.

The stunned partial's arms trembled from the power she released. The last vestigial hair of his human form running like a mohawk along the center of his dragon head burst into flames and vaporized. His convulsions from the power racing through his body snapped his neck. The energy he had gathered to generate his breath attack sunk into his chest, where it burned what remained of his internals. His last glance at Elaine as realization struck him that he was dead was a terrified and pitiful surprise, as if he was asking her to stop. There was nothing she could do until the energy she had called up was dissipated. Silas could tell by the look on her face that she had tried to stop it, but there was no way to call it back. The already dead body stumbled forward and dropped next to her, twitching the last of the energy into the ground. The internal fire engulfed what remained in bursting explosions of superheated gases that ripped out of the body. By the time the twitching form had completely come to rest, it was a charred, disfigured, and unidentifiable human-shaped mass.

All of the partials remaining on the peak of the moraine stopped when the thunder of her release had struck them. They watched the bolt that slammed into their comrade and the aftermath of the massive release of power. Elaine stared at the body next to her and didn't move.

"Damn it!" Silas shouted. "Elaine! Move! Now!"

She looked back at him with terror in her eyes. She could not reconcile what she had just done. Up until that moment she had not witnessed herself killing anyone, even though she had probably killed several while trying hard to defend her friends. She had certainly never watched someone's life vanish from his eyes as she poured magical death into him. She suddenly realized what she was capable of.

"No time for it. You have to run. Now," Silas said strongly as she looked between him and the corpse that smoked next to her.

Something in his final words broke her from her stunned state, and she turned her back on the partials who were watching her. None of them were in any state to attack her, but they were recovering.

"Can you close it?" Melissa asked, looking at the door and the remaining attackers who could still reach them. The attacking force was no longer a platoon, but what remained would overwhelm them if they made it to the hole.

"Close it? Yeah. Lock it? I don't know."

"Close it."

Silas looked up and watched as a green body, cut across the chest, singed, and smoking, plummeted for the hole in the ground. A black form chased her.

He was sure she was going to hover.

Her form grew larger as her speed maintained.

She would need to slow down a little.

"Close it," Melissa's voice grated in his ear as he hesitated.

She was not changing direction.

She was not stopping.

"Incoming," he cried and backed out of the way of her hurtling form. Behind her he saw the black mass of Nethliast catching up. It was going to be a very close one.

He grabbed the door handle and waited.

"Close it," Melissa shouted.

Silas hesitated.

Five feet above the hole Kaliastrid transformed into human form and her flight changed to a dive. She straightened out and stretched her hands out in front of her. Fire blossomed behind her as Nethliast took advantage of her change. It closed on her and was going to take them all with her if Silas was too slow.

She cleared the hole, and Silas slammed the door closed as her heels passed his head.

He could feel the heat from the blast rush into the metal.

He spun the wheel on the bottom of the door and released it as it became red hot.

The smell of searing metal filled the air.

It worked exactly like a modern pressurized door in a submarine. He jumped back from the door in case it didn't seal, but nothing came around the edges.

Unseen magic slammed the locking hooks up into the base. They vanished into the metal, forming a solid plate where the door had been. He assumed something similar had happened above them when the magical lock reset.

Darkness consumed them all until Silas groped for a flashlight in his pack and switched it on.

"There's nothing more I can do," he said. "I don't know if that reset the lock or not. It seems that it did on this side, so we're in here now. Either the last blast destroyed the lock, or it re-engaged."

"Wherever here is," Elaine said in the darkness. Her shaken nerves were showing signs of breaking. Someone would need to pull her back. Her hand trembled, and she was wobbling like a drunk.

Heavy thumps struck the ground above them, and dust filtered down on their heads. Silas shined his flashlight down the stairs and motioned forward. At the foot of the stairs, Charles was laying against a wall with a naked Kaliastrid draped across him. That was where they had landed when her flight had ended in a plunge into the hole. She was not moving. The Boy Scout was stroking her hair while removing his own shirt to cover her up. He raised a blood-soaked hand up to block out the bright light.

Aldrich was by his side as soon as he could get down the stairs.

Kaliastrid's leg was bent at a bad angle underneath her. Three deep gashes were laid open across her back. Red blood was pouring from them into Charles' lap. Another unseen gash across her chest was contributing to the growing pool.

Elaine stood with her hand over her mouth as the last few moments continued to flow through her and the image of Kaliastrid's broken body sunk in. Silas felt a knot form in his throat. The dragon who had saved his life was lying at the foot of the steps, smashed and unmoving. He wanted to race to her, but he had no idea what he would do if he did.

Melissa grabbed Elaine's shoulder and ushered her down the stairs to get them out of the shower of dust. Silas followed them down, looking all around for more signs from the braggart architect of the lock above. Charles and Kaliastrid had cleared any tripwires down to the bottom of the stairs in their fall.

"If she could transform, she could heal better. But there's not enough room, and she's unconscious. We really need to move, Aldrich." Melissa looked back over her shoulder as more thumping indicated Nethliast was trying to get through the ground. "Can you stabilize her? We kept them unsure of our plan so they didn't bring more, but they may be able to get through to us."

"What do you mean, more? I think it was almost enough," Silas blurted, letting the emotions of the moment overcome even him. He quickly reigned in the sudden release of suppressed panic.

"I've nothing to fight them off with," Charles said as if to support Melissa's question. "Everything I had except this is up there." Charles raised the M-79 he had somehow kept over his shoulder and a half-filled bandoleer that was wrapped around one arm. He shifted to lay his shirt across Kaliastrid. He looked down at the unconscious woman in his arms, and the pain he felt for her crossed his face. Silas noted that he had recovered his knife and grinned at how Marines always seemed to keep their heads even when being overrun.

Aldrich turned to look at Melissa and then at the metal panel behind them. He nodded and straightened the leg. Bones audibly cracked and popped as he moved it, and Silas felt his breakfast surge toward the top of his stomach as he shivered with empathic pain. He turned away for a moment so no one would see how it affected him. He had seen injuries like it before, but the sound made it worse.

When he looked back, Aldrich had his hands on her leg and was mumbling something that sounded like *Wodin Healan*, but his tone sounded commanding instead of pleading like he would have expected. He released the leg, which looked straight now, and ran his palms across the deep bloody wound. His face turned gray in the light. When he closed his eyes, his forehead lined sharply.

The pounding above increased.

The bleeding seemed to stem, and Aldrich stopped his chant. The wounds still looked open and red. The vitki stood up and looked at Melissa. "That's all I can do. I'm spent. She can be moved, but for some reason Wodin is refusing my power to heal her. I must deal with that wound soon. I will try again, but arguments with Wodin are not often successful. There are internal injuries as well. We're all tired, and I'm afraid Wodin's will is where my powers come from. I will entreat him again, but he seems to think her healing is for another."

Melissa blanched but nodded "You did what you could. She's stable and moveable?"

"Movable," the healer replied.

Charles started to stand. Silas pushed around everyone to reach under Kaliastrid and support her as Charles stood up.

"Charles, wait. There's no reason to get up."

Silas looked over his shoulder at Melissa, but she was resolute that they needed to move.

Once Charles was up, Silas helped him adjust to carry Kaliastrid. Everyone looked beaten and battered, but still standing. Melissa looked as lost as Elaine. The shock of the battle was settling into them. Silas knew the next few moments would decide their fate.

Charles shifted his burden, cleared his throat, and drew everyone's attention to him. He was standing taller than the rest of them and carrying

Kaliastrid's weight like he didn't feel it. "Silas was nice enough to open this corridor up for us. Let's see where it goes, then."

He turned to head toward the stairs that led deeper into the earth.

His commanding voice lifted Silas and the others like it was designed to. No one questioned that there might be safety down the stairwell now, even though none of them had any idea what was down there. Silas smiled at the big man as Charles marshaled his own fear and fatigue to reassure the others and make the decision that needed to be made. They had no choice but to go forward, and Silas suddenly felt that they might find a way through.

Acknowledgements

There are always so many people who are involved in making a book actually happen, and as an author I never want to forget anyone who has helped me through the challenging writing process. For this book and the series as a whole there continue to be many people who have helped me. I must always start by acknowledging the unending support I get from my wife who listens patiently as I talk through some challenging plot point even though she is working on her own writing across from me. I am beyond thankful that I have her support and understanding in this process.

I also want to thank Mike Dunn for his always useful perspective on my writing and Becky Bumgardner for her critical edits at the last minute. I also want to thank Chris, Lisa, Christopher, and Courtney for always being an inspiration and refuge and Rose for her smile and opinions on anything from characters to covers. I can't forget the conversations on plot, characterization, and numerous other technical points of good story writing that I have with Jeff Smith. I'm sure there are others who have slipped my recall, and if I missed you, it was not an intentional slight, so forgive me and remind me.

In October of 2012, at a local fan convention called HallowCon (Thanks, Dutch and Mickey), I ran into an artist who I remembered from my childhood. His art work in Conan comics was part of my coming of age and was responsible for my perception of fantasy fiction. I had always said that I would love to have "someone like that" do my cover art, so when I had the opportunity I asked if he was interested. We talked about this project and, to my surprise, he was actually interested. This cover was an absolute joy to produce with Rob E. Brown, and I look forward to working with him on many projects in the future.

For this book and the next in the series, I have to highlight and thank a special group of people. As I was completing the first draft of this novel, I selected a little known ruin in the Alsace region of France as the setting for the final scene of this book. As I worked through the story, the castle and the valley where it is located became an important setting for my novel. Early in 2015, I reached out to the Wealth and Employment Association for Kruth-Wildenstein who managed a web site that described the history and current state of the ruins I had selected in the Saint Amarin Valley north of the town of Kruth. I asked them what I am sure was a very odd question. I told them I was writing a fiction book about dragons and I wanted to use their town and the castle ruins as a setting in my book, and I asked if they could send me any documents, maps, and images of the area so that I could better describe it. There was no way that I could visit in time for the release of this book, but I wanted to make sure I at least described the location right. I am sure that I have missed some important details, but that is entirely my fault, because everyone involved with the Wealth and Employment Association were helpful and accommodating to my requests. It is because of their help that my description of the Chateau de Wildenstein is anywhere close to accurate. I want to specifically thank Dominique Tomasini for his interpretation of my very English request for help and spending time answering my questions and providing images and maps to help me orient the scenes to reality. I would also like to thank Denise Arnold, Francois Tacquard, Claude Walgenwitz, Robert Hetsch, and Virgine Hetsch for their support of this effort. I recommend anyone who is looking for an interesting location in France to visit that the Saint Amarin Valley and particularly the Schlossberg of Wildenstein is a beautiful place to consider with lots to offer. If you go in the summer, watch out for their dragon.

Other Books By T.D. Raufson

Legacy of Magic Series
Legacy of Dragons: Emergence

Reviews for Legacy of Dragons Emergence

"A visionary masterpiece of sheer brilliance..." - Lucinda - Published on Amazon.com

"It is a book that will make the reader imagine the wonders of a world where magic is real." - Maria Beltran - Readers' Favorite

"A complex dragon story, with modern and arhcaic elements" - Georgina Parafitt - towerbabel.com

The Queen's Yeoman Midgrade Series
The Queen's Yeoman

Reviews for The Queen's Yeoman

"Delightful little story about the power of imagination." - Georgina Parafitt - towerbabel.com